ACCLAIM FOR TRACY L. HIGLEY

So Shines the Night

"I love Tracy Higley's novels. Meticulously-researched, spell-bindingly written with luscious prose and compelling and complex characters, each one is a treasure. Higley knows her history, but more importantly, she knows just how to capture the struggles and questions of the human heart—yesterday and today."

—TOSCA LEE, *NEW YORK TIMES*
BEST-SELLING AUTHOR OF
HAVAH: THE STORY OF EVE

"*So Shines the Night* is a mesmerizing novel that completely immersed me in the culture of early Ephesus. Higley's writing is gorgeous, and I loved the romantic plot. Highly recommended!"

—COLLEEN COBLE, AUTHOR
OF *SAFE IN HIS ARMS* AND THE
MERCY FALLS SERIES

"[A] rich and beautiful story of redemption, *So Shines the Night* will sweep you away into first-century Ephesus. It will stir your imagination and touch your soul. Highly recommended!"

—MARLO SCHALESKY, AUTHOR
OF CHRISTY-AWARD WINNING
BEYOND THE NIGHT

Garden of Madness

"Readers will find much to enjoy here: fine writing, suspense, mystery, faith, love, and a new look at an old story."

—*Publishers Weekly*

"The author's insights into a woman's inner strengths . . . will leave readers rejoicing."

—*Romantic Times* Book
Reviews, 4½ Stars TOP PICK!

"Mystical as the Seven Wonders, exotic as the Hanging Gardens. Higley has outdone herself with this exquisite story of intrigue, elegantly told and rich with all the flavors of ancient Babylon. Simply magnificent."

—Tosca Lee, *New York Times* best-
selling author of *Havah: The Story of
Eve* and the Books of Mortals series

"Even more riveting than the historical background is the mystery that Higley creates as the backdrop to her exploration of the ancient world. . . . Readers will not be satisfied until they have discovered the truth along with Tiamat."

—Dr. Shannon Rogers Flynt,
assistant professor, Department of
Classics, Samford University

"Each of Tracy Higley's historical novels is more powerful than its predecessor, and *Garden of Madness* continues the trend. I was drawn into the ancient Babylonian world from the very first page and held spellbound until the last, savoring every moment of Tia's journey from despair to redemption. Whether you've read Higley's previous works, or are just discovering her amazing stories, you must not miss this one!"

—Janelle Clare Schneider,
author and spiritual director

Isle of Shadows, previously released as Shadow of Colossus

"One of the most beautifully written books I've ever encountered. The prose is amazing, the story is riveting, and the characters are complex. I was absolutely and completely satisfied with every aspect of this story, which is rare for me. I am now a HUGE Tracy Higley fan."

—RONIE KENDIG, AUTHOR OF
THE DISCARDED HEROES SERIES

"Fast-paced adventure, fascinating characters and insights into the culture, politics and people of this ancient world make this book a unique and unmissable read."

—REL MOLLET, RELzREVIEWZ.COM

"Higley's talent as a storyteller is obvious as she weaves the threads of Tessa's salvation into a story that both inspires and entertains."

—CURLEDUPWITHAGOODBOOK.COM

"This is such a unique historical novel that it really sets itself apart from all others. Higley's portrait of day-to-day life in the ancient world drew me in and her strong heroine kept me reading."

—JILL HART,
THESUSPENSEZONE.COM

"Blending suspense, romance, political intrigue, and a healthy dose of drama, Higley brings the struggles, class differences, and pagan culture of ancient Greece to vivid life. . . . Strong characterization combined with rich historical detail have won this book a home on my shelves of keepers."

—JENNIFER BOGART,
TITLETRAKK.COM

ALSO BY TRACY L. HIGLEY

Garden of Madness
Isle of Shadows

So Shines
the Night

TRACY L. HIGLEY

THOMAS NELSON
Since 1798

NASHVILLE DALLAS MEXICO CITY RIO DE JANEIRO

Published in Nashville, Tennessee, by Thomas Nelson. Thomas
Nelson is a registered trademark of Thomas Nelson, Inc.

Thomas Nelson, Inc., titles may be purchased in bulk for educational,
business, fund-raising, or sales promotional use. For information,
please e-mail SpecialMarkets@ThomasNelson.com.

Publisher's Note: This novel is a work of fiction. Names, characters,
places, and incidents are either products of the author's imagination
or used fictitiously. All characters are fictional, and any similarity to
people living or dead is purely coincidental.

Scriptures taken from the Holy Bible, New International Version®,
NIV®. Copyright © 1973, 1978, 1984, 2011 by Biblica, Inc.™ Used
by permission of Zondervan. All rights reserved worldwide.
www.zondervan.com.

Library of Congress Cataloging-in-Publication Data

Higley, T. L.
 So Shines the Night / Tracy L. Higley.
    pages cm
 ISBN 978-1-4016-8682-6 (trade paper)
 1. Civilization, Ancient--Fiction. 2. Christian fiction. 3. Historical
fiction. I. Title.
 PS3608.I375S6 2013
 813'.6--dc23

                          2012044195

Printed in the United States of America
13 14 15 16 17 QG 6 5 4 3 2 1

To my Readers
More than any of my other books,
this one is a reflection of your thoughts,
questions, input, and encouragement.
Through e-mail, my website, and social media,
you have continued to encourage my
heart and stir my imagination.
Thank you for allowing me to write stories for you,
and for joining me in the adventure.

Those who are wise will shine like the brightness of
  the heavens,
and those who lead many to righteousness, like the
  stars for ever and ever.

Daniel 12:3

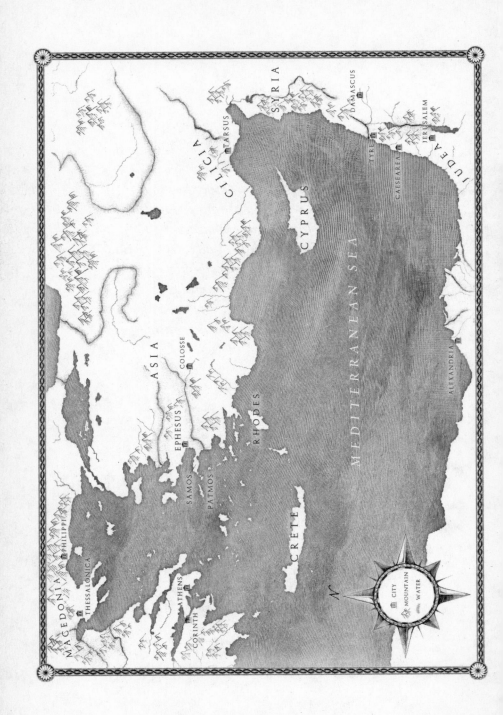

PROLOGUE

I AM AN OLD MAN, AND I HAVE SEEN TOO MUCH.

Too much of this world to endure any more. Too much of the next to want to linger.

And though I have nearly drowned in the glorious visions of those last days, yet I know not *when* it shall come, nor how many years I must tread this barren earth before all is made new.

There is a Story, you see. And we are still in the midst of it, ever striving to play our roles, battling on for the freedom of hearts and souls and minds yet enslaved by darkness.

But I have seen a great light. Oh yes, I have seen it. Even now it is breaking through, as it did on that grassy hillside so many cool spring mornings ago, when Moses and Elijah walked among us and my Brother shone with the glory He had

1

been given from the beginning and will rise up to claim again at the end.

You will wonder, perhaps, at my calling Him *brother*. And yet that is what He was to me. Brother and friend, before Savior, before Lord. In those days when we wandered the land, going up and down from the Holy City, we shared our hearts, our lives, our laughter. Oh, how we laughed, He and I! He had the irrepressible joy of one who sees beyond the brokenness, to the restoration of all.

I loved Him. And He loved me.

But I speak of beginnings and of endings, and these are words that have no meaning, for the day of His birth was both the beginning of the Kingdom and the end of tyranny, and that magnificent Day yet to come—it is the end-which-is-a-beginning, and my eyes have seen such glory in that New Jerusalem, my very heart breaks to tell of it.

And yet they come, young and old, to this tiny home in Ephesus that is to be my last dwelling outside that New City, and they beg me to tell the Story again and again.

And I do.

I tell of seals and scrolls, of a dragon and a beast and a Lamb. Of music that makes you weep to hear it and streets that blind the mortal eye. Of a Rider on a White Horse with eyes of blazing fire whose name is Faithful and True. It is a great Story, and greater still to hear the final consummation of it, for how often we forget that we are living it still.

But I have another tale to tell. A smaller story within the One True Story that began before the creation of this world and is echoed at its end, as all our stories are. It happens here, in this port city of Ephesus, but many years ago, when the darkness lay even heavier than it now does upon the people, and their souls cried out for relief from anyone who could give it.

This smaller story does not begin here in Ephesus, however. It begins a day's sail away, on the sun-kissed shores of the Isle of Rhodes, where the light first began to break upon one woman and one man, even as they walked in darkness . . .

1

Rhodes, AD 57

IN THE GLARE OF THE ISLAND MORNING SUN, THE sea blazed diamond-bright and hard as crystal, erratic flashes spattering light across Daria's swift departure from the house of her angry employer.

She carried all she owned in one oversized leather pouch, slung over her shoulder. The pouch was not heavy. A few worn tunics and robes, her precious copy of Thucydides. She clutched it to her side and put her other hand to the gold comb pinning the dark waves of her hair, her one remaining luxury.

The bitter and familiar taste of regret chased her from the whitewashed hillside estate, down into the squalid harbor district. Why had she not kept silent?

Along the docks hungry gulls shrieked over fishy finds and work-worn sailors traded shrill insults. The restless slap of the sea against the hulls of boats kept time with the anxious rhythm of her steps against the cracked gray stones of the quay.

She had run once, haunted and guilty, to a fresh start in Rhodes. Could she do it again? Find a way to take care of herself, to survive?

"Mistress Daria!"

The voice at her back was young and demanding, the tenor of a girl accustomed to a world arranged to her liking. And yet still precious, still malleable.

"Mistress! Where are you going?"

Daria slowed, eyes closed against the pain, and inhaled. She turned on the sun-warmed dock with a heaviness that pulled at her limbs like a retreating tide.

Corinna's breath came quick with exertion and the white linen of her morning robe clung to her body. The sweet girl must have run all the way.

"To the School of Adelphos, Corinna. I will seek a position there."

Corinna closed the distance between them and caught Daria's hand in her own. Her wide eyes and full lips bespoke innocence. "But you cannot! Surely Father did not mean what he said—"

Daria squeezed the girl's eager fingers. "It is time. Besides"— she tipped Corinna's chin back—"you have learned your lessons so well, perhaps you no longer need the services of a tutor."

Corinna pulled away, dark eyes flashing and voice raised. "You do not believe that, mistress. It is you who says there is always more to learn."

They drew the attention of several young dockworkers hauling cargo from ship to shore. Daria stared them down until they turned away, then circled the girl's shoulders, pulled her close, and put her lips to Corinna's ear. "Yes, you must never stop learning, dear girl. But it must be someone else who teaches you—"

"But why? What did you say to anger Father so greatly?"

Only what she thought was right. What must be said. A few strong phrases meant to rescue Corinna from a future under the thumb of a husband who would surely abuse her.

Daria smiled, fighting the sadness welling in her chest, and continued her trudge along the dock toward the school. "I am afraid discretion is one of the things I have not yet learned, Corinna. Your father is a proud man. He will not brook a mere servant giving him direction in the running of his household."

Corinna stopped abruptly at the water's edge, her pretty face turned to a scowl. "You are no mere servant! You are the most learned tutor I have ever had!"

Daria laughed and looked over the sea as she walked, at the skiffs and sails tied to iron cleats along the stone, easy transportation to the massive barges that floated in the blue harbor, awaiting trade. Papyrus and wool from Egypt, green jade and aromatic spices from far eastern shores, nuts and fruits and oils from Arabia. Her eyes strayed beyond the ships, followed northward along the rocky Anatolian coast to cities unknown, riddles to be unraveled, secrets and knowledge to be unlocked. More to learn, always. And somewhere, perhaps, the key to redeeming the past.

They approached and skirted the strange symbol of the Isle of Rhodes, the toppled Helios that once stood so proud and aloof along the harbor and now lay humbled, its bronze shell speckled to an aged green, reflecting the impenetrable turquoise sky. The massive statue had lain at the quay for gulls to peck and children to climb for nearly three hundred years since the quake brought it down. Daria found it disturbing.

"May I still visit you at the school, Mistress Daria?"

She smiled. "One challenge at a time. First I must convince Adelphos that he should hire me."

Corinna's tiny sandals scurried to keep pace. "Why would he not?"

"It is not easy to be an educated woman in a man's world of philosophy and rhetoric. There are few men who appreciate such a woman."

"How could anyone not appreciate someone as good, as brave, as you?"

The child gave her too much credit. She was neither good nor brave. She would not be here in Rhodes if she were. Though she was trying. The gods knew, she had been trying.

Corinna lifted her chin with a frown in the direction of the school. "I shall simply explain to Adelphos how very valuable you are."

And how outspoken? Interfering? But perhaps the girl *could* help in some way.

"Will you demonstrate some of what I have taught you, Corinna?"

The girl's eyes lit up. "Just wait, mistress. I shall amaze and delight that crusty old Adelphos."

Daria studied the impetuous girl and bit her lip. But it was a chance she must take.

The School of Adelphos lay at the end of the docks, its modest door deceptive. Daria paused outside, her hand skimming the rough wood, and inhaled determination in the sharp tang of salt and fish on the breeze. Who would believe that such distinguished men as the poet Apollonius and Attalus the astronomer had studied and written and debated behind this door? Sea trade had kept Rhodes prosperous for centuries, but in the two hundred years under Roman control, the Greek island had grown only more beautiful, a stronghold of learning, of arts and sciences and philosophy.

Inside its most famous school, she blinked twice and waited for her sun-blind eyes to adjust.

"Daria!" Adelphos emerged from the shadows of the antechamber with a cool smile and tilt of his head. Tall and broad-shouldered, he was several years her senior, with the confident ease of an athlete, a man aware of his own attractiveness.

She returned the smile and straightened her back. "Adelphos. Looking well, I am pleased to see."

He ran a gaze down the length of her, taking in her thin white tunic and the pale blue mantle that was the best of her lot. "As are you."

"I have come to make you an offer."

At this, his eyebrows and the corner of his mouth lifted in amusement and he gave a glance to Corinna, still at the door. "Shouldn't we send your young charge home first?"

She ignored the innuendo. "My employ as Corinna's tutor will soon come to an end, and I desire to find a place here, in your school. As a teacher." She swallowed against the nervous clutch of her throat.

Again the lifted eyebrows, but Adelphos said nothing, only strolled into the lofty main hall of the school, a cavernous marble room already scattered with scholars and philosophers, hushed with the echoes of great minds.

She gritted her teeth against the condescension and beckoned Corinna to follow, with a warning glance to keep the girl quiet, but the child's sudden intake of breath at the fluted columns and curvilinear architraves snapped unwanted attention in their direction, the frowns of men annoyed by disruptive women.

Adelphos disappeared into the alcove that housed the school's precious stock of scrolls—scrolls Daria had often perused at her leisure and his generosity.

Daria spoke to his back. "Do you doubt my abilities—"

"What I doubt, my lady, is a rich man's willingness to pay a *woman* to teach his sons."

Daria waved a hand. "Bah! What difference does it make? I can do a man's work just as well. And if they learn, they learn!" But a cold fear knotted in her belly.

Adelphos traced his fingertips over the countless nooks of scrolls, as if he could find the one he sought simply by touching its ragged edge. "And you, Daria? Do you want to live a man's *life* as well as do a man's *work*? What woman does not long for love and family and hearth?"

Her throat tightened at his words, too close to the secrets of her heart. Yes, she longed for those comforts. For a love that would accept her abilities, complement rather than suppress. But for now, for now she had no one and she must assure her own welfare.

She coughed to clear the dryness of her throat and stepped beside him, examined the great works of philosophy and literature, their tan Egyptian papyri wrapped in brown twine, sealed in waxy red.

Adelphos reached past her to a nook above her head, and his muscled arm brushed her shoulder.

The touch was intentional, clearly. Manipulative. Even so, his nearness left her breathless and her usual sharp-tongued wit failed. When she spoke, it was a harsh whisper, too raw with emotion, though the words emerged falsely casual. "And why should I not have both?"

At this, Adelphos huffed, a derisive little laugh, and turned to lean his back against the shelves and unroll the scroll he had retrieved.

"A woman of ambition. Does such a breed truly exist?" His

gaze darted to hers. "But what am I saying? You have already wedded a husband, have you not?"

Daria pulled a scroll from its recess and pretended to study it.

"You are interested in the work of Pythagoras? That one is newly arrived from Samos."

Daria shrugged. "I find his work repetitive. What new has he added to Euclid's previous efforts?"

"Indeed." Adelphos pulled the scroll from her hands and replaced it in its nook. "But you have not answered my question."

"I am a widow, yes."

"A widow with no sons. No dowry." He glanced at Corinna, clutching the doorway. "And no employment. Is there anything more desperate?"

Daria lifted her chin and met his gaze. "It seems you are in an enviable position, then, Adelphos. You have found a skilled teacher, available for a bargain."

Adelphos circled to Corinna, an appreciative gaze lingering on her youth and beauty. "And this is your prize specimen? The pupil of whom I have heard such wonders?"

The girl straightened and faced Adelphos with a confidence borne of knowledge. "Shall I demonstrate the superior skill Mistress Daria has given me with languages?"

Daria silently cheered and blessed the girl. "Corinna has been working hard to master the tongues of Rome's far-flung empire."

Adelphos's brow creased and he opened his lips as if to speak, then sealed them and nodded once. No doubt he wanted to ask what use there might be for a girl who could speak anything but common Greek. As Daria herself was such a girl, the implicit question struck a nerve. She turned a shoulder to Adelphos and nodded encouragement to Corinna. "Let us hear Herodotus in the Classical first, then."

The girl grinned, then gushed a passage of Herodotus in the proud language of her Greek forebears, the language of literature and poetry, before Alexander had rampaged the world and equalized them all with his common *koine*.

"And now in Latin, Corinna."

The girl repeated the passage, this time in the tongue of the Romans, the new conquerors.

Adelphos tilted his head to study the girl, then spoke to her in Latin. "Anyone can memorize a famous passage in a foreign tongue. Few can converse in it."

Corinna's eyelashes fluttered and she glanced at her hands, twisted at her waist. When she answered, it was not in Latin, but in Persian. "Fewer still can converse in multiple languages at once, my lord."

Adelphos chuckled, then glanced at Daria. "She does you proud, lady."

A glow of pride, almost motherly, warmed Daria's chest. "Indeed."

Corinna reached out and gripped Adelphos's arm, bare beneath his gleaming white tunic. "Oh, it is all Mistress Daria's fine teaching, I assure you, my lord. I wish to be an independent woman such as she someday. There is nothing she cannot do."

"Corinna." Daria smiled at the girl but gave a tiny shake of her head.

Corinna withdrew her hand and lowered her eyes once more. "I have told my father this, but he does not understand—"

"Her father has been most pleased with her progress." Daria tried to draw Adelphos's attention. "He saw a superior mind there from an early age and was eager to see it developed."

But he waved a hand in the air. "I have seen enough. You may go."

2

CORINNA REACHED TOWARD DARIA, BUT ADELPHOS stepped between, his expression on Daria unreadable. "Not you, my lady. You shall stay."

A flutter of excitement chased down Daria's spine.

Corinna embraced her and clung tight, too tight. "Good-bye, then, Mistress Daria." The words were muffled against Daria's neck, tear-filled and final, with all the drama to which young girls are prone.

Daria patted the girl's back and whispered, "You go on, then, Corinna. We shall see each other everywhere. In the theater, in the market. You have my promise."

Corinna flitted from the hall, and her departure felt like an ending when something new had not yet begun. A place-between-places that was most uncomfortable.

Daria turned to Adelphos, who leaned his shoulder against the shelf of scrolls beside her, his body close enough that she could smell the cook spices of his morning meal.

"If we strike this bargain, you and I, we must understand each other." His voice was hard and clear, his eyes calculating. "You will give yourself to art and science and letters, and in this you will become a curiosity, and therefore an asset to this school. But you will not give yourself to a man. You shall not marry."

It was a quick twist in her chest—like the wringing of a tiny bird's neck—not particularly violent or painful. But irrevocable.

"You shall have me undivided, Adelphos. I will make you wealthier, I promise."

He shrugged and lifted his body away from the shelf. "Not that I expect your celibacy to be a problem. I have never met a man who would want a wife as clever as you."

She dropped her gaze to the marble floor and held her tongue. For once.

He jabbed a thumb toward the back of the hall. "You may take the small room here as your own, if you wish." He led her to the tiny space that held only a sleeping mat and indicated a small, unlit lamp in a wall niche.

If she had sought for a place to belong, she had been disappointed. Adelphos's grudging tolerance had all the icy detachment of a slave purchase. But it was enough that she would survive. It was enough.

At the entry, he turned, one hand on the door frame. "The school is rented in the off-hours to a private group. Take care not to disturb them."

"What kind of group?"

"I believe you cannot help but question everything, can you, woman? I am still unconvinced that you are not more trouble than you are worth."

With that he left, and it was his mysterious patrons who disturbed *her* late that evening when she raised her head from where she sat against the wall of the alcove, poring over her cherished scroll of Thucydides. She had lit a lamp against the fading day, but the hall beyond lay in half-darkness, filled with whispers.

She let the scroll furl upon itself, then slipped the loop of twine over and held it lightly in her hand. She crept to the door, peered around the frame to survey those who paid Adelphos for a private meeting place.

A tight circle of men in the center of the vast hall allowed only glimpses of a light burning between pressed bodies. The secretive slant of their shoulders and the raspy murmurs slid a chill across her skin.

They all whispered at once, the same words, over and over, in a language even she did not recognize. Some sort of chant, a religious ritual. Priests?

She craned her neck to see into their midst. What did priests do when they gathered in private? Why did they not serve the gods in the temple, where rituals belonged? Would not strange deviations from the rules invite the gods' wrath?

But they wore ordinary tunics and outer robes, the dress of prosperous businessmen, not the elaborate robes of priests. Even so, their hands reached into the circle and they swayed along with their chants, lost in religious ecstasy.

A mewling cry, like that of a young lamb, squeaked from within their circle and froze Daria's blood. A sacrifice? Here in the School of Adelphos, in the center of the marble floor? Were there not temples and altars for such rites?

It came again, that pitiful cry, and for an instant their bodies parted and Daria glimpsed the whiteness, not of a lamb, but of a tunic covering pale skin.

She straightened, stepped into the doorway, reached a hand toward the group.

She must get closer.

Her sense of danger roared a warning, but she slipped along the edge of the hall, kept to the shadows, circled to a gap where a small table had been set with dark-colored amphorae, strange amulets, and yellowed scrolls.

Through the breach she saw their captive and at the sight sucked in a ragged gasp, too loud, too sudden.

The girl was no older than Corinna. Young, and pretty once, but now with stringy hair that hung about her eyes and scratches gouged into the pale flesh of her arms and face. Where was her family? Her mother? Two men held her arms, heedless of her injuries, and a third forced her lips open to receive the contents of a tiny amphora.

But at Daria's gasp the group stilled as one, then turned a cold gaze along the marble floor to where she stood. She fought to breathe against the constriction in her chest, a tightness borne half of ordinary fear and half of something far darker.

She found her voice and raised it above them. "What are you doing? Free this girl at once!"

One of the men, tall and gangly with mottled skin like a snake and bulbous, watery eyes, sneered at her. "Has Adelphos taken a wife at last? Or simply a pretty washing woman?"

She tucked her valued scroll into the roomy sleeve of her robe and crossed her arms. "I am a teacher here in the School of Adelphos, and whatever ill you plan to inflict upon this child will not be tolerated."

The girl's wide eyes were focused on her, as though she clung with her soul to a rope that had been tossed when Daria appeared.

The snake-skinned man pointed a bony finger. "A teacher, you say? Then leave us to our learning."

"You are sorcerers, then?" The word felt thick and lifeless on her lips, a leaden reminder of the past, of the evil she had seen once. Barely survived. "And this girl?"

Another spoke, unshaven, with missing teeth. "A fortune-teller, my lady. She is possessed of spirits who see beyond. She plies her trade at our behest."

"And you pocket the earnings, I assume?"

He shrugged one heavy shoulder. "She has little use for money."

Daria moved toward them, outrage hardening in her chest. She pointed to the table of scrolls and amulets, to the amphora still between the fingers of one. "And this? What do you force on her?"

"Only a little something to . . . aid . . . in her talents. A bit of *pharmakeia,* nothing more."

Daria pushed through into the center of the circle, laid a hand on the girl's sweaty brow. In spite of her captors, the girl managed to grip Daria's wrist, her eyes still locked on Daria's face.

"No." Daria swept a hard glance around the circle. "This is unacceptable. I demand that you release this girl."

At her back, the snake-man hissed, his breath hot and wet on her face. "Take care, my lady. You meddle with power of which you are ignorant. And you shall not long be a friend to Adelphos if you continue."

"A widow with no sons. No dowry. And no employment."

Adelphos's ugly words snagged against her thoughts, caught in a dark web. She shook her head and pulled away. Resisted the snare, let the heat build in her chest and give her courage.

The girl, so like Corinna, still held Daria's gaze, though her eyes held secrets too—secrets of the underworld, perhaps, that whispered into her madness. Poor child.

"If the girl has such talents as you claim, she should have no need of your potions and charms." Daria swept a hand across the air, taking in the littered table. "You are all charlatans who take money for fortunes when you have nothing more than a drugged and desperate child." She circled an arm around the girl's waist and tugged her toward the entryway of the hall, toward the door beyond, her eyes on the circled group. "I shall take this girl back to her parents, where she belongs."

She backed against one of them, a solid wall of resistance. He grabbed her arms above the elbows. She lost her grip on the girl, dropped the Thucydides scroll, and tried to wrench her arms from his grasp.

His voice at her ear was like the distant rumble of a storm. "What shall we do with her, Cronos?"

The snake-man sidled across the floor to face her.

A shiver of fear chased along her veins and she averted her eyes.

She twisted again, loosed herself from her captor, but now Cronos was reaching for her, his bony fingers raking through her hair.

She spun away, several steps backward, until her heel caught the leg of their low table of horrors.

Cronos's eyes flicked to the table, alarm lighting his features.

A surge of power filled Daria, and she hooked an intentional foot around the table leg. "Let the girl go."

Instead, Cronos lunged.

In one smooth motion, Daria swept her foot and raised an arm to protect herself. The table cracked against the tiles, amulets scattered and amphorae smashed, leaking foul-smelling liquid across the scrolls like acid eating flesh.

Cronos screamed, his face a mask of fury at the destruction, and threw himself at Daria, grabbing at her arms, her shoulders, her hair.

She fought back her own scream, revulsion streaming in waves across her limbs, and clawed at him. Dragged desperate fingernails across his cheek and felt the pull of skin and trickle of blood beneath her nails.

He screamed again. Clutched a hand across his damaged cheek.

Daria pushed through the clustered group of sorcerers, fighting over each other to save what they could of their incantation scrolls and treacherous potions.

She snatched up her Thucydides and grabbed the girl's hand. "Come!"

In the entry, the clamor had brought Adelphos. Daria breathed out her relief and pulled the girl toward him.

"Adelphos! These men are—"

"What have you done, woman?" He took in the ruined chaos, then turned his eyes on her. The rancor, the hatred, the absolute fury that shone from his face shut her mouth.

Behind her, Cronos shrieked, "Kill her, Adelphos! Kill her and be done with it!"

3

THE PALE DISC OF THE MOON WAS CLIMBING OVER the lip of the darkening Rhodian sea when Lucas Christopoulos, merchant of Ephesus, clapped the captain of the *Kynthia* on the shoulder and nodded toward a cluster of men bent over tangled rigging.

"I'll be back before those sailors find two loose ends, Melanthos."

Melanthos, a brawny, hairy brute as all ship captains seemed to be, eyed the wafer of moon, his brow creased. "We've naught but a couple of hours, my lord, before we must set sail, or wait—"

Lucas grinned. "I'll be snoring below deck before you cast off. Count on it." He crossed to the rail, gathered his himation high on his legs, swung one leg over, then the other. He paused, balanced precariously over the murky sea. "And there'll be one more shipment—some copper—delivered before we sail. Tell the seller if he wants to get paid, he'll need to wait for my return."

Melanthos shrugged and turned his ponderous frame to his men, slicing the air with a sharp mix of curses and orders.

Lucas hopped to the skiff tied beside the ship and made quick work of a paddle toward the moonlit dock. Alone for the first time since arriving in Rhodes two days ago, he released a heavy sigh and let the exhausting pretense of carefree merchant slip away and the true reason for the port of call fall like a heavy cloak over his soul.

Ahead, the grotesque form of the fallen colossus threw sinister shadows into the night and drove a shudder down his spine. They should have let Egypt's Ptolemy rebuild it as he offered. Its prone form whispered of strange shiftings of the earth and the ruin that eventually came to all men.

Lucas had spent the two days purchasing a boatload of sweet African dates and gleaming ingots of Cyprian copper. Only one more task here, and by tomorrow he would be back in his own Ephesus—a Greek-influenced harbor city like this one, but grand and elegant. No thanks to the current emperor Nero's stranglehold on his empire—it was the generous building program of his predecessor Augustus over forty years ago that made Ephesus the cultural capital of the entire Asian province. That, and its magnificent temple.

Lucas recited the street name and the name of the man he was to meet for the hundredth time, the words like a thunderous chant in his head as he climbed away from the dock into the seedy harbor district. Above the rooftops an angry sunset gashed the horizon with fiery orange wounds and purple-blue bruises.

A world away from his estate. No sweet-scented gardens lined the streets he crossed to find the man Imbrus. Glowing torchlight beckoned from doorways with the seamy hospitality of taverns and brothels. It reached out to him—foul handclasps of temptation and deceitful promises of comfort. All the better. The walk through the darkness strengthened his resolve.

Unsafe and unknown, who would miss him if he never emerged from the underside of Rhodes? The truth of his isolation had driven him here, to this island, to these streets. It would drive him further still, if he were successful, perhaps to his own destruction. Or perhaps to justice, at last. It was too soon to say.

He found the street of Themis with only a few well-placed questions. More back alley than street, the grimy walls pushed inward on a claustrophobic strip of fetid darkness, foul with the washed-up refuse of humans and beasts. The scritch of unseen rats clawing garbage along the base of blank walls turned his stomach. A cat hissed and ran, arch-backed, across his path. Lucas pushed through the maddening shadows, hand hovering at his dagger.

Half-obscured in a doorway, a figure leaned toward him, eyes whitened with moonlight.

"Imbrus?"

Imbrus emerged, shoulders hunched.

Lucas removed the distance between them and took in hooded eyes, twitchy mouth and fingers. "You have it?"

A papyrus emerged, creased and smudged and gripped in an oily hand. "He said no one but you." The tone was nasal, an ingratiating whine.

"Yes, and now I am here." Lucas thrust a hand into the darkness. "Give it."

The crushed scroll disappeared again, hidden in folds of a tattered tunic of unknown color. "How do I know—?"

Lucas growled out the agreed-upon words, "In the name of Artemis, great goddess of the Ephesians, who fell from the sky!"

The sworn allegiance to the goddess felt strange on his lips. Recent events had left him confused about the nature of the gods. He would not have known where, or how, or to whom to pray if prayer had seemed his only recourse. And with the words of the feigned oath, the alley seemed to press in upon him, the darkness thickening. He felt the rank odor of the streets, the sweaty stench of Imbrus, as it sank into his pores.

The crumple of tightly held papyrus was forced into his hand and Lucas unrolled it greedily, consumed its sparse contents in an instant.

He raised stricken eyes to Imbrus, but the man was a messenger, nothing more, and could not know what these few sentences, this short list of names, would mean. How they changed everything.

"Go your way, then." Lucas tossed the words out like hard pebbles, seeing nothing but those names, feeling nothing but the fierce fury of this truth.

"Perhaps not so quickly." The tone changed. There was the hint of impudence, the whisper of threat.

Lucas eyed his informant. "You have made your delivery. We are finished here."

Imbrus's heavy-lidded eyes traveled the length of Lucas. "I should think a man of your *stature* would pay for such information."

"I have paid! And you have been well paid too, I would guess. Now take your greed—"

Moonlight caught the glint of metal in Imbrus's hand. The knife flashed outward, the tip a breath from Lucas's midsection. "Not well-paid enough."

Lucas laughed. "You would rob me, then? Take what little I carry on my person, in exchange for certain flogging—or worse—when Kyros hears of it?"

Imbrus leered, his canine teeth sharp and protruding, one of them turned oddly on its axis. "And how shall he hear of it from a dead Ephesian?"

No, no more killing.

Lucas's mind roared resistance, even as his hand moved toward self-defense.

"Leave it, Imbrus. A little more coin is not worth your life."

"And who is going to take it from me? A soft-handed nobleman who could not even protect his own wife?"

All the anger, all the rage borne in the smoky fires of Ephesus, boiled in Lucas's chest in that moment, and the dagger he'd held, tucked away in the left sleeve of his crimson robe, was the only precious thing he understood. Its obsidian handle slid into his palm like water.

He raised it, let it catch the light, his eyes a warning on Imbrus.

But the man was a fool. He rushed at Lucas, knife upraised, with no thought to strategy, nicked Lucas's upper arm with a glancing scratch, then spun again for another try.

No more killing! The words seared like a hot iron against his heart, even as the thrust of his blade, belly-high and driven deep, was the elemental crash of the tide against a rocky coast.

Imbrus's white eyes bulged, fully visible at last, and the sneering laugh fixed itself in a death-grimace. He went down in silence, into the sticky filth of the street.

Lucas yanked the knife from the man's gut as he fell, but the hole seemed to be left in Lucas's own body. He wiped the blade on his robe. Strange, the colors should match, and yet the swash of dark blood stood out like a grisly, toothless smile.

There was no welcome rush, no relief that someone else had also suffered. The hard knot of grief and pain he bore in his chest tightened. Regret, always regret. And guilt.

Imbrus had given him little choice, and the violence should have released emotions too long trapped. But there was no satisfaction in it. Like screaming into a thunderstorm and not hearing your own voice. Like a bloodletting on an altar already stained with gore.

There had been too much killing and there would be more before it was over, and Lucas was tired. Exhausted in a way more basic than physical fatigue, dragged downward, collapsed inward into the weight he carried in his chest, now with another dead at his feet.

The alarm would soon be raised. Even in an out-of-the-way alley, a dead body would bring officials storming the night, searching for the killer.

He could stay, explain, hope for a witness to confirm his story.

Or he could get back to his boat before it sailed.

With a glance to darkened doorways and the brighter light at the alley's end, Lucas sheathed his dagger, shoved the folded papyrus into his money belt, and ran for the docks.

4

THE LIGHT IN ADELPHOS'S EYES, LIKE SPARKS thrown from an iron furnace, sent a quivering fear through Daria's body—a fear and a memory better left suppressed.

He would not kill her, would he? Adelphos was a scholar, an intellectual.

She would not wait to learn.

"Come." She tugged the girl's hand. "We must hurry."

Those wild eyes showed no understanding, so Daria simply ran, yanking the girl. No destination in mind, only to get far away from men who would use a troubled child for their own greed.

Outside, the harbor was no less chaotic in the dark. The scrapes and jangle of masts and rigs accompanied the tuneless singing of dockworkers in their duties, shifting cargo to sail the choppy black sea propelled by night winds. The still, dank air belied their plans, a stench of rotting fish heavy and close and pressing against Daria's nostrils, invading her lungs.

The sorcerers would be on them in an instant. Daria hurried her young charge along the dock's edge, avoided coiled ropes and boats moored to iron cleats, skirted sailors and merchants inspecting new arrivals. Few took heed of a woman and girl dashing past. The stones were slick with seawater and rutted with cracks, and more than once she nearly lost purchase.

The flash of red at the brink of her vision came too late. A figure leaped across her path, from dock toward boat, hit the stones where Daria's fleeing feet landed.

Heat blazed through her body at the impact. She thrust an arm in protection, connected with a solid chest, and shoved. "Watch yourself!"

The man she'd rammed teetered on the dock's edge, feet scuffling and arms wheeling. Moored boats churned the water below into a furious foam.

Daria released the girl and grabbed at the sailor's arm. She missed. The flailing arm smacked her face and she grabbed again, caught, and pulled. "Steady!"

He was laughing. A deep laugh of full amusement, when there was nothing humorous about nearly falling off the dock.

"I thank you for the rescue, my lady." He gave her a slight bow.

Well-dressed, well-groomed, with dark hair kept longish but brushed back from his face. The man was no sailor, though he had the build of one. The red she'd glimpsed in the air belonged to a woolen cloak thrown over his white tunic. He was of average height, with a breadth of chest that looked as though he'd known labor before money brought him ease. A merchant, no doubt. Though the dagger strapped at his waist seemed odd.

"There would have been no need of rescue if you had not taken such a reckless leap through the air."

He glanced at the bobbing skiff, ridiculously far. "Ah yes, you are correct." There was that flash of a smile again, though somehow it seemed to cover sadness. "How fortunate for me, then, that I chose to fly at that precise moment."

She willed away the flush that crept up her chest and throat.

Beside her, the girl rocked back and forth and scratched at her arms, head trembling, lips moving with an incoherent mumbling.

The merchant started forward. "But your daughter—she is hurt!" He reached a hand toward the girl, but she screeched and smacked it, and took a step backward.

"Hush, child." Daria held up her palms. "He will not hurt you."

But the girl seemed incensed by the near collision with the merchant. She screamed again at Daria's approach and thrashed her arms, warding her off.

"Please, I want to help—" Tears filled Daria's eyes and her voice thickened. *She is so alone, so frightened.* "Let me help you find your family."

With an unholy shriek, the girl hurtled at Daria. She crashed against Daria's chest, wrapped arms and legs around her body, and clung like a parasite.

Daria recoiled at a fiery slash of pain at her neck. *She bites!* A hot flood of panic chased the compassion from her veins. She craned her neck away from the girl's teeth and scrabbled at the iron hold of her arms. Somewhere behind her, a gull screeched and dove with a mimicking raucous call. It was all too familiar, too wickedly reminiscent of that last night . . . Her vision darkened with the memory, her head weightless and spinning.

With a sudden wrench, the girl released her, tumbled away, fell to the stones. She screamed obscenities at Daria and at the merchant who had broken her hold, her lips drawn back over blackened teeth, foam flecking the corners of her mouth.

Daria sucked in a salty breath, put a hand to the sticky warmth of her neck.

The merchant jumped to her side and freed her fingers from the wound. "Let me see it."

Daria stepped away to better watch the pitiful girl, then swiveled a glance down the docks. In the darkness she could not see far. Were those some of Adelphos's friends flying toward her from the school?

The wild child skittered backward across the stone, jumped to her feet, and ran.

Daria kept her eye on the approaching figures, tried to still her shaking limbs. "She is not my daughter."

"I am glad to hear it."

"I must take my turn in thanking you for the rescue." She nodded once and tried to continue. Perhaps it was not too late to find the girl again and help her.

"There would have been no need of rescue if you had not been in the company of such evil."

He mocked her earlier rebuke, but Daria ignored the sarcasm. "Do not say such a thing!" Daria positioned herself so the merchant blocked her from view and searched the street for the girl. "She is a child, tormented but not evil. Surely there is hope for even her."

He was silent and she turned her attention back to him. His look was dark, intense. "Surely."

"I must go." There was no question now—Cronos and two of his colleagues stalked the dock, attention jumping to harbor, street, and ships alike.

He followed her gaze, glanced back to her face. "Are you in some danger?"

Daria bit her lip, decided to trust. "Those men." She jutted her chin toward Cronos. "They were . . . abusing the girl. I took her from them. They are displeased."

At once he turned on the approaching men, placing her at his back and sliding a hand out from his side as if to block their access.

Daria peered over his broad shoulder. They had not yet spotted her.

"Get in the boat." His words were low, demanding.

"What?"

"The skiff, there." He waggled his extended fingers to the paint-peeling boat he had been attempting to board when they collided. "I will take you out to my ship until they are gone."

She exhaled in a rush. His hasty suggestion was absurd.

He turned, still shielding her with his body, his words a whisper against her injured neck. "You shall be safe with me."

She knew nothing of this man. But she knew something of Cronos. She had seen that brand of evil once before.

Head down, she slipped into the boat, lowered herself to the splintered bench, and held her robes out of the rolling sheet of seawater. Thankfully, the Thucydides scroll had remained tucked in her belt through the night chase and attack on the dock.

Her rescuer jumped in after her and the boat rocked and pitched.

"Careful!" Daria pushed her hands outward, reaching for absent rails.

He caught her hands in his own. "Did I not tell you that you were safe—?"

"You, sir, are a reckless man." She snatched her hands from his and gripped the bench.

He paddled with long, sure strokes, proving her first impression of a powerful upper body, and the little prow cleaved water, sluicing it into white bubbles that floated above the dark surface.

She risked a glance at his face and took in the square jaw, the stubbled chin, and a smile gleaming white in the moonlight. "You find this amusing?"

He shrugged. "A bit. It's not every day that I chance to rescue a beautiful woman."

She turned away, to the smudge of the far Anatolian coastline, an ink stain across the nighttime horizon. Above the hills, the bloodless moon stared with hollow eyes. Daria shivered, then found she could not stop. No doubt a blend of shock over the confrontation with the sorcerers, the girl's wild bite, and the dash across the sea with an impulsive stranger.

He helped her up the ladder to his ship a moment later with firm and steady pressure on her arm. The *Kynthia* was all glossy wood and polished rails, its name hull-painted in dark blue slanting letters, as though already leaning into the wind, eager to be off. Daria boarded the deck and felt the rock and sway like a mother's arms, then the heavy red mantle on her own shoulders, still holding the warmth of his body. A weathered wooden swan topped the bow, its curved neck dipping toward the water, coquettish eyes facing out to sea.

"Now let me see your neck."

She tilted her head, exposed the raw skin. "How bad?"

He held her chin with gentle fingers and narrowed his eyes. "I'm afraid I can see clear through to the other side."

Daria pushed his hand away. "Do not speak foolishness."

He grinned. "Your pretty neck will be fine. But it should be cleaned. Come."

He left her at the prow, strolled past a crew of six or seven, and returned with a clean rag dipped in cool water.

"Those men"—he swabbed at her scratched neck and murmured an apology when she winced—"what did they do to that girl? She was clearly possessed of a spirit of the underworld."

Daria eyed the docks. Could she yet find the child? "I believe they found her that way. But they were using her—fortune-telling and the like."

His hand stopped its ministrations and his eyes focused on hers. "Sorcerers?"

Something in the way he said the word, searched her eyes, forged a link between them. Had he too known the evil that could be wrought by such men?

She swallowed, took the rag from his hand, and pressed it to her neck. "Yes."

"Then you will stay here until I am certain they are gone."

Daria huffed. "Unfortunately, they know where to find me."

Two sailors approached and drew his attention. Darker-skinned than her protector, from lands farther east. The older suffered a puckered eye, some long-healed injury that kept him ever-winking, an expression more false than friendly.

"Master Lucas, you wished to purchase?"

He bartered with the sailors for another cargo of copper ingots, apparently to add to his growing supply. *Lucas*. A strong name.

Was it safe to return to the quay? The light of a dozen torches ringed the pedestal of the fallen Helios, erupting skyward like the flaming sentries round an arena before a battle of men and beasts. She could see little beyond the light.

Her failure to help the girl chafed. Her actions had been meaningless, foolish. How long until they grabbed the child again?

Daria moved toward the rail, but Lucas stayed her with a

possessive hand on her arm, his attention still on haggling with the sailors, but his message clear. His hand was warm where it lingered on her skin.

She waited, pulse jumping, and wrapped the mantle closer. Her hand found a sticky wetness and she drew it away. Blood? Was it her own? Surely her neck had not bled so much. She eyed Lucas again. What kind of man was this?

Lucas brought the price down considerably, and the sailors fidgeted and exchanged glances.

"You will certainly rob us." The younger spoke to Lucas in Persian.

He shook his head. "Greek or Latin, please."

At this, the two took to squabbling with each other in their native tongue. Daria stifled amusement at their argument. The older of the two seemed a mentor to the younger, who insisted on his ability to broker the deal successfully. Lucas watched their exchange, clearly understanding none of it.

"There will not be enough profit—"

"You see how he is taken with this lady? We'll line the bottom of the crates with stone while he is distracted."

The older sailor lifted his furrowed eyebrow. "You learn quickly." He nodded and the younger turned to Lucas.

In Greek again, he said, "We accept your price." He extended a hand, indicating Daria. "Please, master, take your ease with your delightful lady while we load the copper."

Daria lifted her chin and stared at the two, then spoke in Persian, her tone cold. "Be assured that Master Lucas will be quite attentive to your cargo. To ensure there is no *extra* merchandise lining his crates."

The younger sailor seared her with a hateful look and the older flung his hands upward, as if he'd expected such a failure from his protégé.

The two turned to the crates and Daria glanced at Lucas, who watched her again, that smile of amusement back in place, this time mingled with a bit of awe.

She suppressed her own smile. "Watch them carefully. They planned to add false weight to your cargo while you weren't looking to improve their profits."

He flicked his gaze toward the sailors. "A woman who speaks Persian. How much more money I should have made by now, if—" He broke off and shrugged. "You have discerned my name, but not given yours."

"Daria."

He looked as though he would push for more, but only said, "Tell me of the girl. Where did you find her?"

"In the School of Adelphos along the docks. I am a teacher there." She eyed the harbor, searched for Adelphos's fury. "At least I was."

"And you tried to rescue her?"

"You saw. I did her little good, I'm afraid."

"There are few who could."

"Anyone can be saved—if one is brave enough and strong enough to fight for those in danger." The words spilled out more passionately than she'd intended, as though the ruling tenet of her life.

"So. You are a teacher. Of languages?"

"Language. Rhetoric. Sums and sciences."

He was silent, so she glanced at him again and found him watching, his usual amusement gone.

She tilted her head to the sailors, finished with their loading and descending over the side. The disfigured one winked unpleasantly at her, followed by a rude gesture Lucas did not see. "Are they always so dishonest?"

"I have much need of honesty in my life."

The words were spoken from a hidden place in him, from a place of hurt and suspicion, perhaps. Though he seemed rarely serious, the shape of his mouth was naturally sad. But this was a deeper melancholy, sadness of the soul. The words left her chilled.

The captain approached, round and solid with legs like posts. "Ready to sail, my lord." He glanced at Daria. "Not good to tarry."

She straightened. "I thank you for your help. I will be fine."

"Shall I take you to your husband? Your family?"

She half smiled. "There is no one."

Those eyes were on her again, dark and deep. "Indeed."

He was an attractive man. She had not seen that at first, somehow. When they had collided on the dock, she thought him quite ordinary. But now, now she saw something else . . .

"I sail home to Ephesus."

Daria nodded and stepped closer to the rail. Why did he tell her of his plans? She turned her eyes to the rugged coastline of Anatolia. How far north along its mountains would she need to travel to reach the magnificent capital of the province? *Lumen Asiae*, one of the Roman writers had called the city. "Light of Asia." Ephesus trailed behind only Rome and Alexandria in wealth and glory and beauty. What excitement would it bring to belong there?

He followed her gaze. "There are schools in Ephesus."

Her heart stuttered along an uneven road, then righted itself. "I am sure such a fine city has many opportunities for learning."

"I should like a private tutor, though."

She raised her eyebrows. "You seek a tutor for your children?"

"No children. It is my own education I would like to further."

She nodded. "You should learn to speak the Persian language if you wish to trade for eastern goods."

"Perhaps you would care to teach me."

If the moon had struck a path across the water at that moment from Rhodes to Ephesus and invited her to walk upon it, Daria could not have been more surprised. She tightened her robe about her body with shaky fingers and would not meet his look, would not acknowledge the offer he made. The moon across the three square masts flicked shadows across the deck that lapped at her feet, and she fought against the tremor in her chest. When had she become so weak?

"I know nothing of Ephesus. Nothing of you. Why would I make such a rash decision?"

He did not answer at once, but when he spoke, his tone seemed almost angry. "I misjudged you, then. I thought I saw a bit of the adventurer in you. Someone willing to take a chance."

She turned on him. "A chance for what? What does Ephesus offer me that I cannot create for myself, here in Rhodes?"

"Yes, you are quite able to handle everything *alone*, I see that."

That sudden pang in the chest, the twist she had felt when Adelphos said she could not marry, gripped again.

She swung a leg over the rail and found footing on the top rung of the ladder. She removed Lucas's mantle and tossed it to him. "Then you have not misjudged me after all."

———

Lucas caught his robe in one hand, flung like a blood-red challenge across the ship's deck by this fascinating woman. Brilliant mind and beauty to match. Dangerous combination. As he well knew.

But he studied her gray eyes, clear and hard with nothing but frankness and refreshing honesty. And he wondered . . .

He stood above her at the rail, breathed in the soapy purity of her skin. Let it wash over him, futile as it was. Innocence was not so easily transferred.

She was halfway down the ladder now, her dark hair disappearing. Lucas leaned over. "I believe you'd take the skiff back to the dock yourself, wouldn't you?"

She jerked her head upward. "Would you prefer that I swim?"

He grinned and bit back his first answer. "I will take you."

He watched the little war between heart and mind rage behind her eyes and could read it as though she spoke her thoughts aloud. She was independent, intensely so. But she was also cautious. Guarded. With a curt nod, the war ended. Caution prevailed.

"Very well." She continued her descent. "And I thank you for your kindness."

He could be more than kind, but this girl seemed immune to his wit. He paddled them back to the dock, his attention on Daria's straight-backed figure more than the water. Her robe was threadbare but impeccable. He traced the curve of her neck with his gaze, beneath the upswept dark hair and gold comb. Even the line of her jaw, the set of her shoulders, was clarity. No ambiguity, no doubt. She was like the sky and the sea—perhaps a bit stormy at times, but open, no secrets. And her compassion for the demon-tortured girl . . .

At the dock he looped a rope over the cleat and secured it well, held the little boat as steady as possible for her, then took her hand as she stepped to the platform. Her sideways glance revealed surprise at his caution. But she was a woman to be kept protected.

He cast a gaze over the dark street and the city beyond, stretching upward from the sea. A thousand lamps had burst to life on the hillside, their gilded eyes blinking from rooftops, through windows, along streets. "Where shall I take you? That is, if you will not go with me?" He smiled, his eyes holding her glance.

But she turned away, without the girlish giggle he had come to expect from that particular effort. Instead she inhaled, as though searching for courage. Did he frighten her?

He tried again. "I would love to hear more of your fine city as we walk. Point out its best features. Other than yourself, of course."

Again, nothing. She wore sadness like an unseen layer of silk—nearly transparent, yet one could not see her without looking through its mysterious sheen.

But she gave him a slight, forced smile. "Thank you for the escort. And for helping earlier—with the girl."

He bowed. "And I thank you for saving me from being taken, both by the water and by unscrupulous sailors."

She smiled in earnest and held out a hand. "Then we are evenly balanced."

Indeed we are. He took her fingers and kissed them lightly. Ah, there was the first flush of womanliness in her cheeks.

"I go alone from here."

Lucas frowned and skimmed the length of the docks with a glance. "I should not like to think of your meeting those men before you reached home. How far must you walk?"

Something flickered across her features—perhaps an attempt at deceit—but she hadn't the ability.

"I—I have no home. I was to stay at the school, but the schoolmaster, he is one of them—" She broke off, her eyes focused over his shoulder in alarm.

"What is it?" He whirled to the threat, saw two figures running, one pointing and yelling, the other brandishing a torch as though they would lash her to a stake and set her ablaze.

He turned back, grabbed her hand, and beyond saw two more

loitering, watching—the old sailor with the ruined eye, snarling, and his young cohort, approaching as though he would be the first to seize the girl.

She sensed the menace behind and took a step toward him, her eyes wide with the look of a trapped bird.

The skiff was still tied, but it took only a moment to loose its mooring. Lucas leaped across, steadied the craft. Behind him, Melanthos was calling out orders to push off.

"Jump, Daria." He pierced her with a look, as serious and dependable as he could muster, and held a firm hand across the water. "You are coming with me."

5

TRULY, THIS WAS MADNESS.

Caught between murderous sorcerers, outsmarted merchants, and the proffered yet untrusted hand of a stranger, Daria's body reacted with paralysis.

She knew nothing of this man. Nothing of his integrity. She had no one but herself to arrange for her happiness, and she must be careful with her choices.

His hand remained outstretched, his eyes—intense and perhaps desperate—as though he would take her for reasons of his own.

They drew close on all sides. She had only a moment.

Breath caught, teeth clenched, the sounds of ships and water, sailors and gulls in her ears, she must decide.

She reached for that strong hand, felt it grip her own. Met his eyes.

And leaped.

He whirled and grabbed the paddle, shot the little craft out to the *Kynthia*, then urged her onto the aft deck and pointed to a coil of ropes. "Sit."

Her face flamed at the curt command, but she obeyed.

Lucas stood at the rail, staring back at the docks.

"Do they follow?" Her heart struck against her chest and cut short her breath.

He did not answer at once. Then shook his head. "The merchants have slunk away. The others—they seemed to debate, then give up. But . . ."

"What?" She rose to her knees and peered between rail and hull. "What is it?"

"They have the girl."

She huffed and slumped to the ropes.

"I am sorry, Daria."

Pointless, all of it. She had lost her chance at security by defying Adelphos, and the sacrifice had done nothing for the girl. She had told Lucas that anyone could be saved. But only if the champion had the strength needed. Clearly, she did not.

"I will get off at your first port." She looked up at him. "Halicarnassus, I assume?"

Lucas still watched the Rhodian harbor. "Everything I need is on this boat."

A flare of fear triggered in her chest. "You don't plan to put in anywhere? Surely Samos?"

He turned at last, the wind tangling at his hair. "What would you do in Halicarnassus? On Samos?" He pointed to her clothes, to the scroll tucked into her belt. "You appear to have nothing but that scroll. No money, no employment."

"A widow with no dowry. No sons."

"So why not come to Ephesus with me? Be my tutor. The city makes Rhodes look like a barbarian province."

Daria rubbed at the back of her neck. "Are you always so . . . so impulsive?"

"Are you always so pragmatic?"

She exhaled her frustration, her confusion. "This is madness. I do not even know you. Besides, if I returned to Rhodes, there might still be a chance to help that girl—"

"I will get you a position in the School of Tyrannus."

A sudden sensation of falling, of hitting bottom, jolted her senses. She struggled to her feet to stand beside him at the rail. "You know Tyrannus?" The school was legendary, and its master more so. To teach in his hall . . .

"Yes. He is an acquaintance of mine. I have some influence there." He pressed close to her. "Go with me to Ephesus as my personal tutor and I promise I will have you installed in his school within a few months." He grabbed her hand, squeezed her cold fingers, sending warmth into them, and studied her eyes. "Perhaps the child is not the only one who needs rescuing."

She breathed heavily at this confession. What to make of this strange man? He was all cheerful, reckless abandon one moment and deep misery the next. She pulled her hand from his and gripped the rail. "You must think me pathetic—to have nothing and no one to return to."

"I think you are deserving of much more than you have received. And I still believe what I saw in you at the first, Teacher. You long for adventure. And you were meant for more than this." He waved a hand at the retreating coastline of Rhodes.

Oh, he was charming.

She glanced behind, at the small cabin in the stern, at the

steersman on its roof, regulating the tiller. "Tell me about your family. You said you had no children. A wife, certainly?"

"No."

In his simple answer there was both pain and anger. She would press no further in that direction.

"And you spend most of your time at sea, on the trade routes?"

"No. I rarely travel. I have trusted workers whom I send on most trips. And I do much of my business in the Ephesus port."

"What, then, occupies your time in Ephesus?"

He turned his attention to sea. "You will be well compensated, Daria. I—I am a wealthy man." This he said with as much modesty as she could have expected. "And when you are employed in Tyrannus's school, you will also have the respect you deserve. Ephesus will be good to you, you shall see."

He spoke as if she'd given her answer. She should have been annoyed. But he already knew her too well.

Yes, something about Lucas drew her. And frightened her. Perhaps he understood what her life had become, but did such understanding mean he had the power to change it? Did she even want a change?

His question, when it came, was low and deep. "You will come?"

She could not answer. Feet rooted to the past but heart already sailing for Ephesus, she could not bring herself to say the words. She hung suspended from a precipice, her heart clenched like a fist around all she had known, around the rigid rules she had carefully put in place for her own safety.

At last the memory of his outstretched hand at the dock, the whispered words, *you shall be safe with me,* won over caution and prudence.

"You will be a difficult pupil, I fear."

He laughed, that sonorous, carefree laugh that was the first thing she'd heard when she smacked against him on the dock. "Oh, have no doubt about that, Teacher."

It took surprisingly little time for Rhodes to appear as an illusion on Daria's horizon. All she had known disappeared into the frothy wake of the ship. Lucas left her to her thoughts, which played out like a rope trailing the ship, ever reaching back toward Rhodes.

What had she done?

The wind tugged at her hair. She yanked the gold comb that pinned her dark waves and slipped it into her pouch. She would not lose the one thing she still had of him. Without the comb, her hair blew against her face, as if it, too, were reaching back toward home. The churn of the water beneath her feet was like a long sigh, mournful with nostalgia.

Teacher, he had called her. Yet a position as a private tutor in a wealthy estate was often occupied by a slave, educated in his home country before Rome conquered a new province and scraped the finest minds from its schools and temples. True, he would not own her, but she would be little more than a servant in his household.

The voices of the sailors, barking instructions and replies, dwindled as they slid along the rocky brown coast of Anatolia toward Ephesus. Still she watched, as Rhodes became a dove-gray silhouette against the watery midnight sky and sea.

"Second thoughts?" Lucas stepped beside her, gripped the rail. He smelled of cinnamon and salt.

"And third, and fourth."

"Precisely why we shall not put into port! I'll not have you jumping ship on me."

"How long until we reach Ephesus?"

"By nightfall tomorrow. I am sorry the city will not greet you in the daylight. She is . . . friendlier . . . in the day."

A flicker of foreboding chased along Daria's veins. "I have heard it is beautiful. The Temple of Artemis, surely, is a wonder to behold."

He turned away. "Yes, the pride of the city." The words were spoken with bitterness, with sarcasm. His shoulders hunched as though she'd wounded him with her commendation.

"You are not a devotee of the goddess?" How could that be, in a city made famous by her temple? The Temple of Artemis, rebuilt three times after being destroyed first by flood and then by fire, was one of Herodotus's famed Seven Wonders of the World. It had created the wealthy city of Ephesus, bringing visitors from all over the province to worship and deposit funds in its central treasury. How could Lucas not be loyal to the patron goddess of his city?

"I do not know *what* I am."

The simple statement struck her with some concern. The gods must be served, their rituals performed within the structure laid out by priests who taught them how the gods were to be pleased. Without such order, all would move toward chaos, toward the evil of the demonic that seemed to hover at the ready call of men like the Rhodian sorcerers. Did Lucas not follow the prescribed rites?

Sometime later Lucas prepared a comfortable place for her with blankets among the heavy woven ropes, and as the hour grew late, she dozed, head propped against her arms.

She awoke with a start. Sailors shouted fore and aft and the sky had pinked with sunrise. She rubbed her chilled arms and sat upright, then climbed to her feet and reached for the rail.

They hugged the coastline, a gentle south wind filling the mainsail. Ahead, in a crescent harbor, a lofty square building of shining white marble jutted above the surrounding buildings. Each of the four corners boasted a prancing marble horse with a warrior rider, but it was too far to see the intricate details of the massive carved frieze along the top.

"It is the tomb of old King Mausolos." Lucas joined her, shoulder pressed companionably against hers, warm in the morning breeze.

"Halicarnassus. I have never been to the city."

True to his word, they sailed past the harbor without the chance for her to escape. It took until late afternoon to pass the tip of the island of Samos, made famous by its mathematician Pythagoras. They shared a midday meal of olives and cheese and barley bread drizzled with olive oil from a small jug. She asked a hundred questions about his travels—from Ephesus to Cyprus and Crete, even the grand Alexandria in the Nile Delta. He had seen so much of the world, and she would absorb it through him if she could.

When she asked about the famed Temple of the Muses in Alexandria and its adjoining library, Lucas laughed and held up a hand. "If your persistence in teaching is matched by your appetite for knowledge, I shall be speaking like a Persian by the time we reach Ephesus."

Through the afternoon that impulsive smile flashed often, but just as often there was the far-off look of pain, usually directed northward, and seeming to settle heavier on him as they drew closer to Ephesus.

At last, when the sun had dropped, a sizzling scarlet ball falling into a cobalt sea and bathing the sky in filmy pastels, the coastline speckled with outlying villages, Lucas declared they would soon arrive.

She watched from the bow, one hand resting against the

swan, until ahead the city of Ephesus shimmered with the light of a blanket of torches spread from its vast harbor. Above the streets, hovering as though the goddess herself watched over the city, the massive columns of the Temple of Artemis thrust to the heavens. The yellow torchlight at each pillar base cast an unearthly glow upward along the white marble.

Daria sucked in a tremulous breath. Rhodes had nothing like this monstrous temple on the hill. The sight was enough to humble anyone before the gods. Surely, if the gods dwelled anywhere among men, it would be in splendor such as this. She would bring offerings soon. She must do her part to appease and honor, if she was to expect blessing in this place.

It was another hour before the ship was safely moored. The harbor here was deep enough to bring the boat to a pier. Daria disembarked and took her first steps into the great Roman province of Asia and its capital city on legs made jittery by the sea and with a heart to match. The dock was deserted, with dark hulls of ships lingering for the next day's business and water surging against the moorings with a cold slap.

She was eager to explore, but not much of Ephesus could be seen at this hour. A street wide enough for six chariots and bordered by columned porticoes on either side ran straight from the harbor into the city. A series of arches drew the visitor inward, and the elegant marble walkways under the colonnades opened to shops and galleries. The end of the business day had come and gone, but a few torches still lit this magnificent entrance into the city. A chill mist arose from the sea, a gray fog that snaked along the harbor and reached into the streets. Like Rhodes, the familiar harbor smells turned rotten in the dank humidity, pressing against her skin like bluish fingers.

Lucas joined her a few minutes later, barely looked at her, and strode past. "It is a short walk to my estate. I apologize that no one will meet us. I was unsure of the timing of my arrival."

Daria hurried to catch up, fog swirling away from her legs. "I do not mind the walk."

She snatched glances at his profile as they rushed along the harbor street. Stone-faced. Grim, even. "Is all well with your acquisitions?"

"Fine."

Does that include me?

They reached the end of the street, and in the moonlight a huge, bowl-shaped amphitheater would have scooped them into itself, but Lucas turned right and marched through another street, this one taking them past an agora, desolate at this dark hour. Farther into the city the architecture degenerated, and the plaintive music of taverns and sultry glow of brothel doors introduced her to the seamier side of Ephesus. All of it shrouded in filmy white and ashy gray under the dark blue sky. From places unseen came strange screams and catcalls that raised the hair on her arms, but Lucas did not seem to hear.

In truth he seemed insensible to everything in their hasty advance through the city, and Daria struggled to remain at his side, searching for something to say, a question to ask, and in the end remained silent, apprehension constricting her chest with a tightening band.

At the end of this main artery was a hillside dotted with homes, and Lucas led her upward, along stone steps that twisted at right angles as they ascended.

Without warning he abandoned the steps and cut across the hillside on a narrow street. Several minutes later he slowed, then stopped and faced a large home that sat slightly above.

Daria studied his face, hardened into an impervious mask of stone.

He is angry. Angry to be home at last?

"Come."

She followed him upward, to the portico that fronted the house, and couldn't help a glance backward over the city. His home was not on a level with the temple above, nor the lip of the amphitheater, but it still afforded a view of the city that should have been lovely. Instead, the gray mist that had pursued them from the harbor drifted through the streets like the rivers of the underworld.

"Daria."

She turned away from the unpleasant comparison to the open door of Lucas's home.

"Master!" A bent servant loped toward them, head thrust forward on a wrinkled neck and eyes wide. "You have returned."

"Yes, Clovis." Lucas stepped into the entryway, a narrow chamber but decorative with floral reliefs carved high in the wall. "Do not fret. I require little this evening."

Daria stepped close to Lucas, but he shifted away, left her isolated in the entryway. At the slight movement her heart thudded an uneasy rhythm.

Clovis's eyes went to her, a slow glance that took in the plain tunic, the worn robe. She put a hand to her loosened hair. She should have secured it when she left the ship.

"Clovis, I have brought an addition to our household staff. Please show Daria to a room in the rear of the house and give her anything she needs."

With that Lucas crossed into the atrium and disappeared beyond the darkened courtyard.

That was all. No mention that she was to be his tutor rather than a mere house slave. A room in the servants' section of the house.

Clovis gave her a shaky nod and turned. "Follow me, girl."

He walked with a plodding step and a slight lean, favoring his left. The pace gave her time to ascertain that Lucas's claim of wealth was not unfounded. The courtyard boasted the deep green of a lush garden with a central fountain, now silent. Large rooms gave hints of elegant frescoes in their dark interiors and statuary guarded each doorway.

Clovis deposited her in a small room near the north side of the house with mumbled promises that he would soon bring bedding and a lamp. She found a rickety chair in the half-light and sat, removed the scroll from her sash, feeling the shame of having nothing.

In the rear of the darkened house, at the back of this dark city, she had been swallowed, as though she had plunged underwater and could not take air. The chill of the room seeped into her bones, weighted her limbs, pressed against her chest, and made breathing painful.

Yesterday a new life in the School of Adelphos had awaited her.

She had discarded that life and taken hold of the unknown because of one man who seemed trustworthy in the sunlight of Rhodes, but now had become a hostile stranger.

There was little doubt. She had made a grave mistake.

6

LUCAS HAD THOUGHT, EVEN DARED TO HOPE, THAT a return to Ephesus from the sun-washed shore of Rhodes with Daria at his side might push back the icy shadows that crowded his soul when he walked its streets.

But the city's oppression proved too strong for even Daria's goodness, and the galling wound within his chest, the gritty ache that drove him, raised its sickly head and hissed at him the moment Lucas's feet struck the Ephesus dock. The peaceful day spent with her on the boat melted away like mist, and regret at having brought her to this place washed over his heart.

He stalked toward home, uncaring that he forced her nearly to run. She would face worse in the days to come. He had brought her for nothing.

Worse than nothing—he had brought her to a city of ruin.

51

He escaped to his bedchamber, left her in Clovis's able care. He waited out the watches of the night, slept little, and rose only once to slip outside and study the moon.

And when a colorless dawn broke over Ephesus, he lay abed a long time and watched the pale grid of light slide across his chamber floor.

Clovis served bread and cheese in the central courtyard, under an overcast sky. Lucas spread an olive paste over the crusty bread, then chewed and waited.

She appeared within minutes in the same tunic and robe she'd worn since they met.

He would need to rectify that problem.

But first there was the matter of the names scribbled on the papyrus he'd wrenched from the greedy Imbrus.

"I am going into the city, to see to the purchases brought from Rhodes. I will bring back some clothes for you."

Her eyes narrowed. Those clear, gray eyes that had first convinced him she might do some good here. Eyes that saw through him.

"I should like to see Ephesus by daylight."

"I shall be busy through the day. Another time."

She shrugged. "Then I shall go alone."

Lucas huffed. "You are in my employ—"

"I assumed our arrangement was for tutoring alone. Am I also to tend your house while you are otherwise occupied?" Her gaze swept the courtyard garden and he saw it through her eyes—an overgrown and tangled confusion.

"Of course not. I only meant that a woman alone in the city—"

"I can take care of myself."

He stood, brushed crumbs from his fingers, and waved a

hand toward the remains of his meal. "Eat. I will come for you when I am ready."

She nodded once, all deference. "Yes, my lord."

Lucas winced at the title, appropriate as it was. Their shared adventure in Rhodes and the day aboard the *Kynthia* had drawn them closer than master and servant, but it was best now to remember their true situation. Nevertheless, he did not need to be unkind. "Is there anything I can get you?"

Something flashed in her eyes—anger?

"I require nothing."

———

The chilly morning trek back to the harbor took them under the great arched gate, past the agora, filling now with merchants and shoppers, but Lucas did not slow. Neither did he speak to Daria, who followed, her gaze darting from shop opening to brothel, and ever back to the temple that dominated the hill above the city, its roofline visible even from the street level. Did she catalogue and arrange all she witnessed, locking it away in that knowledge-hungry mind? Did she sense the mood of conflict in the city? The wave about to crest?

"Such a city Augustus has rebuilt for you! It is like a smaller version of Rome, I would imagine."

"Do not let the city's noblemen hear such a thing. They cling to their Greek heritage—in both tongue and aesthetics—as though Rome would snatch it from their fingers, no matter how Roman they have become in political outlook. But your tribute is well placed. You would never know that two decades of civil war nearly destroyed the cities of Anatolia."

"And Imperial Rome since the days of Augustus? What have the rest of the Julio-Claudians done for Ephesus?"

Lucas waved a hand. "Ha! A string of madmen, if you ask me. Tiberius running paranoid to Capri, his lunatic nephew Caligula, and the stuttering fool Claudius. And now the young Nero, who promises to be as mad as the rest of them."

Daria laughed. "And I see you are as much a Greek as any Ephesian nobleman."

"You asked a painful question. But I suppose when one asks as many questions as you, a few are bound to provoke a heated response."

Lucas hurried ahead to avoid more questions. As much as he had once loved this city, his feelings now did not match the fervor of his attack on Rome. He would banish thoughts of Rhodes and the crumpled papyrus in the hands of a greedy informant— there was nothing but evil for him there, in pursuing what he had learned—and leave this city to consume itself while he disappeared into his estate and learned Persian from a tutor both beautiful and brilliant.

But that was not to be. It could not be, now that Imbrus had given him the key he needed to infiltrate the closed group. The city tax collector, Numa.

He would speak to as few as possible this morning. Arrange for his purchases of copper, Athenian wool, and dates from the dark lands of Africa to be traded at the docks or sold in the market.

They entered the wide basin of the harbor area through a lofty arch, hurried past the scattered marble sculptures and lines of merchant tables selling items of interest to sailors, dockworkers, and visitors alike—from baskets of pomegranates and quince to silver shrines of the lofty temple and figurines of the many-breasted Artemis.

The *Kynthia* still floated in the harbor, sails lowered and hull a bleached russet against the washed-out gray of the horizon. The city fought a battle with the River Cayster, the waterway that carried silt from the higher elevations down to the sea and ever tried to block their harbor with the impassable sludge. How many times had the harbor been cleared of the muck? One day, perhaps, Ephesus would lose the battle and what was now the harbor would be a grassy plain. Without the port, would the city die?

But for today the docks still buzzed with sailors and merchants, dockworkers and opportunists, and Lucas focused on shouts of commerce and swishes of the sea.

His crates had been unloaded in the night and one of his men guarded the heap of purchases. Lucas nodded to the middle-aged man, Ocealus.

"Any trouble?"

Ocealus flicked a wary glance left and right. He was a lean, bony sort of man, but he would be more than a match for any would-be thieves in the night. "None, sir. You want I should fetch carts?"

"Not yet. Let's see what we have first."

Daria stepped beside him.

Lucas startled. He'd nearly forgotten her presence.

"What will you do with all of it?" Her voice held more curiosity than awe.

Ocealus handed him an iron claw and he pried the splintered lid off the first wooden crate. "Trade some. Sell the rest."

"And this is how you have gotten rich?"

He eyed Daria's face, but the question was innocent, without rancor. "Yes. Seems like something any fool could accomplish, I imagine."

She shrugged one shoulder and turned her head to take in the harbor.

Very well. Lucas plunged a hand into a woolen sack of dates and pulled out a fistful. He took a bite of one, ripe and sweet.

Daria watched again, those eyes unreadable.

Lucas removed the pit from the date, then held the remainder to her mouth. "Taste. Tell me what you think."

She glanced at the date, so near her lips, then back to his face. Wary. Untrusting.

"Come now, it's not as if I asked you to take a swim in the harbor!" He nearly pulled away, but then she stayed his outstretched hand with her fingertips, opened her mouth, and bit the date. The cool touch of her fingers was smooth as glass against his skin.

"Delicious."

He finished the fruit. "And thanks to your intervention, I am not instead the owner of a half crate of stone along with my copper."

"Which brings more money—to trade or to sell here in Ephesus?"

Lucas glanced at Ocealus and waved a hand at the crate. The servant tied shut the sack of dates and worked to replace the lid.

"It depends on many factors. If the goods are perishable, I cannot wait for the right buyer to land in port, so if there is no one eager to buy, I must trade with someone local, if he has need. Often that means a lower price."

"But if the local demand is high and supply low, you might fetch a better price in the agora than on the docks?"

Lucas appraised her with a sideways glance. "Exactly."

She scanned the water, as though assessing who might be in port to purchase his Rhodian goods. "And the nonperishable goods, how long can you afford to warehouse them while waiting for a buyer? I assume you have a warehouse?"

"Indeed. And that answer again depends on the expense of the goods. But generally I look for a buyer within the same month as a purchase." He looked to Ocealus. "Remain with the crates. We will return shortly." To Daria, he extended a hand. "Come. We will see who is anxious today for copper and dates."

Within the hour, he had an offer from Cassius, an occasional buyer of his from Napoli, where the grapes grown on the black-soil slopes of Mount Vesuvius created unrivaled wines.

Cassius named his price, twenty-five *aurei* for each of the twelve crates of copper.

Lucas counteroffered with twenty-seven. "And fifty bottles of that excellent wine."

"That wine is worth twenty *denarii* a bottle!"

"Making your total price 370 aurei, still a bargain."

Daria leaned toward him. "It's 364."

Lucas glanced at her.

She kept her eyes on Cassius but spoke quietly to Lucas. "The total price including the wines is 364 aurei, not 370." To Cassius she smiled and said, "An even better bargain."

Within the hour, Lucas wondered how he had ever traded without her. She could figure sums faster than Archimedes and possessed a steely charm that at once disarmed and dominated. Merchants were wet clay in her hands, and with her, he disposed of nearly all his new purchases at a greater profit than he would have imagined possible.

Perhaps she had brought him luck after all.

They returned to Ocealus and his post beside the crates. Lucas directed their transport to the appropriate buyers and arranged for the remainder to be taken to market. When all was arranged, he led Daria along Harbor Street toward the central part of the city.

Ahead, a clamor in the street drew his attention.

Beggars and shop owners often clashed in the colonnaded length of Harbor Street, the former harassing customers and the latter chasing them off with sticks. But this was no simple scuffle between the classes. A swirl of dark robes and smoking incense glided through the street center, with townspeople rippling outward.

Lucas's heart seized, not with the frozen indifference he had cultivated since returning, but a heated rush from his chest to his limbs. He grabbed Daria's arm and yanked her toward a shop door.

"My lord!"

"Come, Daria." He pulled her into the shadowed doorway, turned to conceal his face from the knot of figures traveling the street, forced his heart to slow.

"What is it?" Daria peered over his shoulder. "Who are they?"

Inside, the shopkeeper—a tiny woman selling papyri and wool—clucked her tongue. "You'd do well to keep questions to yourself, girl."

Lucas still faced inward, blocking Daria's body but not her eyes from the street. He glanced at the shopwoman, but no recognition crossed her expression. The shop smelled of the urine and dye used for the wool.

"Sorcerers." Daria's harsh whisper edged across his shoulder like a knife stroke.

They passed behind him now. He needn't turn to know it, for the wintry blast of their presence burned against his soul.

Following along behind the group came the ill-fated demon-victims, who slavered and screeched and tore at their hair while they rained curses down upon the heads of all.

It was a rare display of power. What had happened in his absence to warrant such a scene?

The shopwoman answered his unspoken question.

"It's because of the killing, you know." Her tinny voice rasped over the words as though she delivered a weighty secret.

Daria turned to the woman. He should have prevented her from inquiring, from searching out truths better left buried.

"What killing?"

The little woman rubbed bony hands together and chewed against her bottom lip. "They found another body last night, they did. Just like the others. All torn up."

The news was bitterness in his mouth, his nose. It ran along his skin like a spark along dry grasses, until it burst into flames somewhere in his chest.

Daria grabbed his arm with a slight gasp, and her touch was like a needle prick.

They passed and continued on.

Gone was his desire to hide himself in the midst of studies. The procession had been like an omen. He needed to find Numa. There was a chance now, a chance for justice.

"Can you find your way home, Daria?"

She watched him, studied his eyes as if divining his secret thoughts.

He blinked, looked away from her concern.

"Yes, my lord. I can take care of myself."

7

DARIA GRIPPED THE DOORWAY OF THE WOOL SHOP and watched the black cloud of men and half humans spin toward the harbor. Was Ephesus no different? Did men with strange powers, who whispered into darkness and could bring to pass all manner of spells, wield power here as they did in Rhodes? A flush of perspiration warmed her skin and she inhaled against a tightness in her chest.

And Lucas? Why his fierce reaction to the appearance of the sorcerers? Did he fear them, or did he only wish to avoid them, to remain unseen? The news of a brutal killing seemed to shock his senses. Clearly he desired to protect her, but why here?

Waking in his sprawling estate on the hill and the morning spent in the harbor had shown her that Lucas was both wealthy and respected. But he was also deeply troubled by something, and she had been a fool to tie herself to him without enough information. Now she was stranded in this city with nothing.

Very well, she would make the best of it. Starting with finding the School of Tyrannus and making herself known there. She had come to find security, and she would find it. Lucas would not need a Persian tutor forever. When he had learned enough, she would need other employment. His promised introduction to the city's largest school would be all-important, but she could not rely overmuch on anyone else. It fell to her to arrange for her happiness for her life.

And there was an unknown city to discover, a muddled maze of streets and temples and shops to unravel—this is what life and learning were all about.

She released her clammy hold on the door frame and lurched into the colonnade, oddly off balance.

Harbor Street bore a path into the city, past shops and baths and even what looked to be the city's prison. At its entrance, a toothless man grinned at her. Jailer or escaped prisoner, it was difficult to say. She hurried along the street toward the end, past a gymnasium. To her right, the sprawling agora awakened with merchants and shoppers churning about its columned square, and far ahead, the gray-stone bowl of the amphitheater faced her, rising up the hillside like a crescent-shaped stairway to the gods. What sort of entertainment did the theater offer? She could almost hear the imagined roar of crowds, shouting over a fight between man and beast or even man and man.

The city was busy and crowded, but strangely quiet. As though its people glided its streets hoping to remain secret in their tasks, eyes always watching, flicking from pedestrian to wagon, from shop entrance to the wares displayed along storefronts. Daria moved toward the street's end, where it culminated at the theater, and those wary eyes seemed to light on her too often, to take her measure and find her wanting.

At the theater entrance another street intersected, wide and paved with white marble, jutting to the right toward Lucas's house and past the agora. They had rushed down this street last night, its fantastic marble paving obscured by darkness. It should have gleamed in sunlight this morning, but even here, the city cast a pall and the marble swallowed the light and gave nothing in return.

Should she turn left, away from Lucas's house, and up toward the Temple of Artemis? There had still been much to see between the theater and his house, and even beyond, in the streets leading up and away from the sea.

And there was something comfortable in the familiar. Much as Daria enjoyed discovery, Ephesus had an undercurrent that instilled unease.

She pushed through the crowd that seemed to be traveling against her and hardened herself against the brush of arms and even hands that skittered against her skin like the feather-touch of insects.

Ahead, a massive three-arched gate marked the end of the agora. Or was it the entrance? Somehow it felt as though she wandered the city backward. Perhaps the harbor pooled at the rear of the city, and Ephesus was accustomed to greeting visitors from a loftier height. Would she have felt well received if she had entered above?

Only if he had welcomed her himself.

She detoured off Marble Street, into the agora itself, and soon passed under the arched gate and turned to survey it from this far side. Indeed, the carved inscription above proved that it marked the entrance to the agora. Built in honor of Caesar

Augustus, the block letters proclaimed, by two freed slaves, some fifteen years ago.

A few citizens sat about the gate—two tattered beggars and three long-bearded men with sharp eyes, muttering amongst themselves.

Daria approached the bearded men, who ceased their dialogue and stared with parted lips at her advance.

"I am new to Ephesus." She smiled, a demure smile meant to look self-conscious. "Can you direct me to the School of Tyrannus?"

One of the three, whose hooked nose nearly touched his upper lip, scowled. "What do you need with Tyrannus?"

She was not ready to divulge such information, not to strangers nor anyone else. The falsehood came easily.

"I believe my husband may be . . . studying . . . there this morning." The hesitation would show uncertainty, and perhaps provoke pity.

Beside the hook-nosed elder, another of them growled under his breath. "Better than studying there in the afternoon."

The comment soured Daria's stomach. Too like Rhodes, once again.

The first man pointed a knotty finger up the street beyond Lucas's hillside home. "Up the Embolos, between the Prytaneion and the Augusteum." This last he spit with contempt. Temples built to honor Rome and her past rulers-turned-gods were a constant irritation to any non-Roman.

Daria followed the extension of his finger, up the sloping street whose name meant "wedge"—assumedly for its diagonal cut across the grid of streets, following the natural curve of the valley. Fountains, monuments, and statues lined the streets, and here as on Harbor Street, the colonnaded sidewalks along two-storied shops enclosed pedestrians. Daria nodded her thanks.

It took the better part of an hour to pass along the wedge-shaped Embolos to the upper part of the city. Even at this higher elevation, the gloom did not lift, and more than once she eyed the sky, half-expecting to be drenched by the ominous clouds.

The Prytaneion, where the sacred flame symbolizing the heart of Ephesus was kept ever burning, presented only a four-columned portico to the street. Here the goddess Hestia, patron of the hearth and all that represented security and happiness, was worshipped with an eternal fire. Despite Hestia's promised blessing, Daria shivered as she passed. A flame of any kind would be appreciated this morning, to dispel the chill she could not shake.

And it was Artemis to whom she owed a sacrifice. Would the goddess understand the delay caused by her lack of resources? Daria was anxious to prove that in spite of her previous alliance with Athena, goddess of wisdom, in Rhodes, she could worship a new patron here. At least it was another strong female to whom she could pledge and not some warlike, dominating god that held sway in Ephesus.

She needn't have feared difficulty in finding the school. Adelphos's modest door in Rhodes was like a poor cousin to Tyrannus's entrance, which boasted marble columns and a carved quote on the lintel from the philosopher Aristotle. *Education is an ornament in prosperity and a refuge in adversity.*

She had no reason to enter. What would the scholars within think of a woman entering their school without introduction?

And so she stood in the street and stared at the wide, polished door behind which lay her future. Hopefully.

"A woman in search of something."

She jumped aside at the words spoken behind her shoulder. The speaker was a short, slightly bent man with an age undeterminable. A balding head and energetic youthfulness seemed at odds. He spoke an accented Greek. Jewish, perhaps? Jews were a wealthy part of many Anatolian cities, working in banking and trade, with separate communities protected by Roman law. They had caused some disturbances in Rome a few years back, with many fleeing Claudius's wrath, but here in the Greek-culture cities of Anatolia many were no doubt prominent members of the city.

He gave her a half smile, the sort of knowing smile that usually came with a wink. But something about his eyes, some strange weakness, seemed to preclude such an expression.

"You have heard good things about this school? You wish to be a part of what goes on behind its doors?"

It was a question, but not a question. As though he knew the answer.

"I—I have heard it is the best in the city."

He tilted his head and examined the door with her. "I suppose that depends on what you are looking for."

What am I looking for?

"Sanctuary." She spoke the word with little thought.

"Ah." His heavy-lidded eyes blinked once, twice, and he asked for no clarification.

He had the bearing of a learned man, a rabbi, perhaps. "You are a teacher here?" But rabbis would teach in the Jewish synagogue, not an unclean Greek school.

He shrugged. "I can be found here at times. With others."

Something in his tone brought a flutter of anxiety to her chest. Sorcerers in Harbor Street. Mysterious men meeting in the school.

"I am new to the city." Would he offer more information?

"It is not a city of sanctuary, I fear." His eyes were still on the columns, the shallow portico, the polished door. "Even the past day has taught us this."

"I have heard there have been killings."

"Aye, vicious and foul. As all death is."

A swell of dizziness rose at his words, then fell away, and she swayed on her feet. Her companion eyed her but said nothing, did nothing. Only peered from out of those weak eyes that seemed to see with uncanny clarity.

"When do you teach?" Perhaps he could introduce her to Tyrannus . . .

"I did not say that I was a teacher." The comment was sharp, acidic. "I meet with others here, in the afternoons. Tyrannus rents his space while the city rests to some of us who can find acceptance nowhere else."

There it was, then, as she suspected. It was the same here—men committed to the dark arts, to controlling the demon forces of the underworld, meeting in secret in the afternoons. As if in response, a thunderclap snapped in the north and reverberated through the city, through her bones.

The man narrowed his eyes at the clouds. "A storm is coming."

Daria shuddered. "I should return home."

He turned his gaze to her face. "I hope you find your sanctuary."

She hurried from him, down the street toward Lucas's home. Townspeople scurried ahead and in her wake, fleeing the coming storm.

The first heavy drops bit into her skin like stinging pebbles. Head down, she barely glanced at the hillside estate as she approached, even though she had yet to see it from a distance in the daylight. Feeling like an intruder in a strange house, she pushed through the front door into the entryway.

"There you are!" Lucas appeared in the atrium, red-faced and stormy himself. "Where have you been?"

Daria wiped the wetness from her bare arms and raised her eyebrows. "Did you wish to start your lessons so soon?"

"I told you to return directly here. It is not safe to walk about the city alone!"

She lifted her chin, then pushed past him. "I apologize for concerning you."

He grabbed her arm as she passed. "You have no idea—"

"Perhaps if you had cared to show me the city yourself."

He released her arm and spun toward the courtyard, where the rain fell through the open roof to the snarl of greenery that was Lucas's poor excuse for a courtyard garden.

"For someone in my employ, you speak with unnatural boldness."

She laughed, hollow and frosty. "Bolder than you in the face of those—"

"Stop." His face was ashen now, the color of the sodden clouds above the Embolos. He turned away. "I should not have brought you here."

She should apologize for her lack of respect. But the words did not come. Uncertainty, insecurity left her shaky but silent. Lucas was a different man in Ephesus than he had been in Rhodes. She had been deceived. Or was it only this city that tortured and smothered the carefree heart she'd encountered on the Rhodian docks? He had a tendency to withdraw when threatened. What kind of pain lurked in his past?

Lucas was leaving, pushing deeper into the house. "We will begin instruction tomorrow. Until then, stay within my estate. The weather is bad."

"We could start today." She tossed the suggestion at his back, disappearing in the shadows along the covered walkway astride the courtyard.

"I have business this afternoon." He turned, and she could barely make out his face in the gloom. "At the school where you are so anxious to teach. I shall inquire for you if they are in need of scholars."

And then he was gone, leaving her reaching for the wall, steadying herself against a painted fresco vase overflowing with vines, breathing against the constriction in her chest.

Business in the school during the afternoon? Was he one of them?

Had he avoided the sorcerers so she would not discern his associations?

The morning's chill hardened to ice in her veins and she stumbled along the wall, looked for a place to drop, for her legs rebelled against her own weight.

Like a rope around her ankle, dragging her down to the underworld, evil had tethered itself to her and followed here from Rhodes.

There was no escape.

8

A DEEP MELANCHOLY, A WEIGHTY FATIGUE, STOLE through Daria's limbs. She should seek her bedchamber, sleep away the shivery shadows of the afternoon.

But she would not hide, not from the unknown, or from nameless fears. If her impulsive decision to come to Ephesus had been a fool's choice, she must know the truth. Could she make a place for herself in this household? Only if she better understood the mystery of Lucas Christopolous and what it was that haunted his steps.

She had seen little of the house since arriving last night, and even less of the staff that the estate must require. Clovis had brought her bedding and oil in the darkness of her arrival, then trudged off. Silence claimed the courtyard now, save for the violent splatter of rain against courtyard stones and the wreckage of the garden.

Rain chased along limbs of a scraggly orange tree, then fell in heavy, bulbous drops from insect-chewed leaves to cracked stones. Other plants, so overgrown they were indistinguishable from each other, bowed under the weight of water and disease like feeble old men with bent spines. The few blooms that survived poked dirty faces through the labyrinth of shrubbery, colors muted and dingy in the half-light. The disorder nearly caused Daria physical pain. How could it have been allowed to happen?

She slipped along the peristyle in Lucas's wake, but when she reached the narrow hall where he had turned deeper into the house, she pushed instead toward the rear of the estate, toward kitchens and latrine and the cramped halls of servants. Did she dare to explore the house without his permission?

In the gloom of last night she had seen only the wealth of the estate. But daylight revealed a forlorn shabbiness, borne of inattention and neglect.

Here the frescoed walls of the front of the house gave way to muddied plaster in mottled gray. Marble statuary became plain earthen pots, stacked and scattered, and claustrophobic walls crowded close. Unexpected passages detoured into darkness, and more than one narrow flight of stairs beckoned her into the bowels of the house with a draft of musty air. A warren of rooms she had no right to enter, with more above. One could get lost in this maze of a house.

She resisted the insidious draw of subterranean depths and burrowed deeper until she found at last the kitchen, where surely light and heat would banish the estate's stormy pallor.

She breeched the kitchen's door but stopped inside. There was a corner cook fire, but its blackened embers glowed with only a dying orange, sputtering and gasping for life. Brittle herbs hung like cobwebs from pegs in the beamed roof and more littered the oil-stained table along the wall. Coriander, from the sharp scent. And dill, perhaps. Across the room, two figures turned as one, regarded Daria with suspicion, and spoke not at all.

"Clovis." Daria nodded to the old servant, then to the equally aged woman at his side.

They stood suspended, she with an ochre terra-cotta bowl wedged between bony arm and narrow waist and a wooden spoon in hand, and he with a frayed rope coiled round his forearm. Wide eyes, parted lips, pale and shallow-breathed, it seemed as though she'd shocked them into immobility by her appearance at the door.

Clovis recovered first. "Do you need something?"

No "mistress" or "my lady." She was neither slave nor servant, yet as one who served the master of the house, she could hardly expect deference from his other staff.

"I—I am only getting to know the house better." She pulled her lips into a bland smile for the old woman. "This is your wife?"

He bent his head. "Frona."

Clovis spoke only her name, nothing more, and the woman gave a slight nod of haughty acknowledgment. She seemed taller than her husband, perhaps because he was so bent, but her skeletal frame belied her position as cook. She wore a heavy woolen tunic that could not hide her gauntness and stood with bare, bony feet on the tiled floor. Her downturned mouth held no welcome for Daria.

A tiled floor. Even at the back of Corinna's house, the kitchen floor was a packed earth. "I should like to meet the rest of the staff. Sometime. When it is convenient." Inwardly, Daria cursed her timidity. It would only strengthen their condescension.

Frona's lips tugged into a deeper frown and the wooden spoon stirred measured circles in the porridge-filled bowl. "There is no one else."

Daria blinked. "The two of you keep this entire estate?"

Frona ceased her stirring, peered at Daria through half-squinted eyes. "The master requires little. There are never any guests."

Clovis nodded. "Not since—"

But a glare from Frona silenced him. Frona resumed her churn of the bowl's contents, eyes still trained on Daria.

The woman was unreadable, and in the smoky air her eyes seemed to waver.

Daria cleared her throat against the smoke and leaned against the door frame, as oily and rough as the table. "You have been in service with him long?"

"Aye." Clovis shifted slightly and looked to Frona as if for permission. "Many years."

"Then you knew his wife."

Frona's glance shot upward at Daria's boldness, locked onto her face, pinned her there with an expression of dislike mixed with outrage. "Beautiful, she was. With a quick mind. You do not favor her as much as he says."

Daria sucked in a breath, glanced at Clovis.

He leaned to his left, braced a wrinkled hand against the table, then gave a forced shrug of one bony shoulder. "I told Frona that you . . . bear some similarity . . . to her."

At this, an unwelcome premonition, furtive and stealthy, wormed into Daria's heart. She pressed a hand to the back of her neck, rubbed at the tension.

"She was a fine lady. Like a queen. Or a goddess." Frona's sulky interjection came from behind her husband.

Daria fingered the frayed gold ribbon stitched to the waistline of her dress. "He was most distraught at her death, then?"

"He has fallen to ruin, much as the house."

Clovis's words had a finality about them, a declaration that invited no further discussion, a verdict pronounced. But in them there was something of the same wistful longing, a longing for the reclamation of a precious loss, that also struck her heart when she looked at Lucas.

Daria backed from the doorway, escaped into the passage that snaked along the rear of the building, and found herself soon in her own chamber, the air thick and damp, with an insipid light leaking through the square-cut window. It was the room of a servant, certainly, though she was thankful for the raised bed, to keep clear of any rodents. Besides the bed, only a small table in the corner with a bowl and jug for bathing.

But what was this? On the bed, folded in neat squares? She ran her hands against the soft fabric, linen and cotton, of four new tunics and the light wool of three mantles in the soft colors of a rose garden.

She stripped her dirty clothes at once, scrubbed thoroughly, and donned the first new tunic she'd had in many months.

Within the hour Frona appeared at her door. "The master wishes to see you in his sitting room."

Daria rose at once, smoothed her tunic, and reached for an ankle-length robe in light pink. "The sitting room?"

Frona curled a lip. "I will show you."

Daria trotted behind the older woman like an obedient pet, across the courtyard to its opposite corner. Beyond a narrow door pale light flickered.

Frona jutted her chin toward the door and continued along the colonnade toward the kitchen.

Daria hesitated in the entrance, awkward and nervous. The sitting room was tiny, smaller than her own bedchamber, and windowless, though the ceiling was high. Lucas sat at a cluttered desk along the back wall, hunched over a papyrus and scribbling.

A small oil lamp beside his right hand cast a warm but uncertain glow over the dark walls.

Should she announce herself? Knock?

She glanced over the frescoes, elaborate in spite of the small and private nature of the room. No laughing nymphs here. A lion, crouched for the hunt, crept on massive paws toward an azure-feathered bird that preened itself unaware in the grasses.

She slipped into the warm room and lowered herself into the only other piece of furniture—a polished wooden chair along the wall opposite Lucas's desk. The wood was smooth and cool under her palms.

The chair scraped when she sat, and Lucas jerked upright and spun.

"Oh, it's you." He tossed his quill to the jumbled collection of scrolls and ink, quills and string, even scattered coins and a few small leather pouches that littered his desk. "I forgot you were coming."

"Frona only now called for me—"

He waved a hand. "Your punctuality is intact, never fear. My mind does not hold anything very long these days."

"Did you change your mind about beginning language study?" She half rose from her chair. "I will need to retrieve—"

"Sit down, Daria." He turned his chair to face her, then sat with it tipped backward until its frame touched the desk.

Daria eyed the two front legs lifted from the floor and the back legs balanced precariously. If they slid forward and dropped their foolish master to the ground, justice would be served.

Lucas flexed his wide shoulders, as if his work at the desk had tightened them. "You are so far away, there against the wall. Pull yourself closer."

"The room is the size of a storage closet. I hardly think you'll lose me."

His forehead creased at this. "Do not be so sure. Come closer."

Daria dragged her chair forward, following the continued beckoning of his fingers, until they would have touched knees if she were to sit.

His eyebrows waggled and a slight smile pulled at his lips.

She huffed, backed away a few steps, and settled herself. "Are you certain you do not want me to fetch my materials?"

"I wish to know more of my tutor before our lessons begin. Tell me how you came to be so learned at such a young age, and as a woman, no less."

This near to him, she noticed that more than his desk was in disarray. His hair was still ruffled from the sea breezes of the morning, and the hard line of his jaw had not been recently shaved. A small rip pulled at the collar of his tunic.

"I have needed to take care of myself for some years. Much as I did in the street this morning."

His full lips drew downward into a frown. "Ah, the tutor is hurt by my inhospitable nature."

She gripped her hands in her lap and met his hard gaze. "It is not my place to be hurt, my lord. I only stated a fact, as you asked the reason for my accomplishments."

"And what is the reason you have been so long on your own?" His voice was low, as though he begged her to share secrets.

"My husband—"

At this, his chair legs dropped to the floor with a thud and his face darkened. "You are married!"

"My husband died. My father was a scholar. He had taught me much as a child. When I became a widow, I fell back on the gift he had given me and furthered my studies while offering my services as a tutor."

"You loved him very much?"

"Yes, my father was a great man and never held it against me that I had been born a girl."

"I meant your husband." His eyes bore deep into hers, penetrating, interrogating.

Daria unclasped her hands and rubbed them across the roughened texture of her robe. The room had grown smoky from the oil lamp, and the haze cocooned them in the small space, seeming to draw them together.

She lowered her eyes to hold herself back from that gaze. "Marriage is complicated."

"I need no tutoring on that subject." His voice had taken on a low growl, like the lion stalking the blue bird on the wall, glinting in warm golds and browns in the lamplight.

Daria leaned forward, pulled into his secrets now. "How long—how long has it been since your wife—?"

"Ten months."

Could he have named the days if she had asked? The undercurrent of pain in his voice matched the deep melancholy in his eyes.

"Ten months since I failed her."

This secret was given quietly, so Daria bent her head to his lips to catch the words, to absorb them. She reached a hand toward his, fisted on his thigh, then pulled away. "I am certain it was not your fault."

"Are you?" He stood, shoved his chair back against the desk, paced the floor around her. "No, but you are right. Others are at fault and she was a victim. Others who must be held accountable."

Daria turned in her seat to follow his movement. "I know this pain, my lord. I have felt it too. But believe me when I tell you that when evil rises up to take those we love from us, our best choice, our only choice, is to learn to avoid its curse."

If he would stop his pacing, sit again, she could better express herself. "I see it in your eyes, the way you are falling prey to this evil yourself. You must resist. It is not safe—"

"Safe? Bah! I care nothing for safety."

"You must care!" Daria stood now, came as close as she dared. "You must take care for yourself. Or your fate will be the same."

He brought his gaze to her face, fiery and yet sad. "And such a fate I deserve."

"Come. Sit." She turned his chair back to the desk. "We will begin your new studies. Focus your mind on something beneficial, helpful."

Lucas fell into the chair with a sigh that signaled an exhaustion deeper than the physical. "You think I can be saved, then, Tutor? Rescued, like the little girl on the docks of Rhodes?"

Daria studied those pain-filled eyes. "I am unsure if you desire rescue."

He exhaled again, a sharp breath, as though she had knocked it from him, and closed his eyes.

Daria gathered the loose scrolls on the messy desk and stacked them evenly, then lined the quills and inkpots along the wall. He needed order in his life, this unhappy man, and it would begin here. She lifted a pouch and began to fold it into sharp creases, but Lucas reached a hand across the desk and flicked a finger against the stack of scrolls, scattering them.

She paused, did not look at him, then laid the pouch aside and restacked the scrolls. Before she finished, he knocked aside her straight line of quills.

In spite of the dark tone of their conversation, or perhaps because of it, she laughed.

She laughed and met his eyes and he was laughing too.

"There is the smile. I had begun to despair that you had lost the ability. You should laugh more, Daria. It becomes you."

"I have had little to amuse me, I fear."

"Hmm."

She returned to folding the leather pouches, then weighted them with the coins. She reached for the loose string that perhaps had once tied a scroll, but Lucas caught her wrist and held.

Did he still tease? But no, his look had grown serious. She pulled in a ragged breath at his touch and studied his fingers tightening on her arm, that grip that seemed almost desperate, then searched his eyes, equally so.

"You would put all things right, wouldn't you, Daria? Bring beauty where there is only ugliness?"

"If I could, my lord."

"Do not call me that. I do not deserve such respect."

"You *do* deserve it, and you have it."

He released her wrist but slowly, sliding his fingers up her forearm to the inside of her elbow, his breathing shallow.

A flush of warmth spread across her skin. Daria reached for the collar of his tunic, somewhat breathless, and ran a finger under the torn edge. "I could mend this for you."

He held her gaze and a draft of air pulled the lamp's flame toward her hand, as if to warm. Or perhaps to burn. His hand drifted to hers on his collar and the silence between them lengthened, speech and movement suspended.

From the doorway, a cold voice slapped against the walls. "Is my lord ready for the evening meal?"

Daria raised her eyes to Frona's emaciated frame outlined by the patch of light from the courtyard behind. The woman's eyes were like dagger points trained on Daria.

Lucas pushed away from the desk. "Yes, Frona. Thank you."

He turned on Daria. "You may go." His voice had grown as cold as Frona's. "I have no further need of you today."

9

DARIA CLUTCHED THE BEDCOVERING TO HER CHEST in strangled fists, sat half upright in bed, heart thudding.

What had woken her? Had it been a dream? She blinked against the moon-slashed darkness of her bedchamber, a feathery, unseen touch on her neck.

No lingering trail of lamplight betrayed another presence. And yet, and yet . . .

It must have been a dream—those haunted eyes hovering at her head, a lamp waved high—a dream brought by the day's confused emotions and the unfamiliarity of a new home.

Daria lowered herself to the narrow cot once more, but sleep had fled. The bedchamber's chill darkness oppressed. An oppression that spawned nightmares. She needed air.

She rose and covered her under tunic with a robe, grabbed her volume of Thucydides, and escaped the room. Her door scraped a protest along the floor and she cringed and hesitated.

A half-moon washed the courtyard greenery in a sickly light, turning thick vines into twisted arms that reached out in death throes and the orange tree's pendulous branches to a giant's head and shoulders. Daria hurried along the colonnade to the narrow stairs at the corner.

She had not been to the second level, had not been invited, and why should she have been? Lucas's bedchamber and undoubtedly others resided there. But from the street below the estate, she had seen something else on the second level, and it was this terrace, jutting out from the house to overlook the city, that drew her upward tonight, to escape the stifling gloom below.

Three sides of the second-floor balcony that ran around the open courtyard held a series of doors, but the north side lay open to the city. Built into the hillside as the estate was, the roof of the dining rooms below formed the terrace above, with a half wall of stone protection surrounding. Daria crossed to the wall, past several couches for reclining. A breeze lifted the unbound hair from her clammy neck.

What hour was it? Had half the night passed already? The eastern sky held no promise of daylight and the city below had gone dark, with only a few scattered lamps flickering at windows. The dark blot of the deserted agora lay beyond the hulking Gate of Mazaeus and Mithridates, and along the long marble street that led down to the theater a torch bobbed in an unseen hand, traveling the street like the single yellow eye of a cyclops.

She ran her hand along the rough stone of the wall, but the solidity did little to reassure. The day's events had battered and confused, and more than the night wind left her feeling blown about tonight. Was she haunted, chased by the demons of her past? Had Lucas aligned himself with some sort of evil?

Her earlier certainty slipped away with the memory of their hour in the sitting room. Surely he was tortured by past memories, as she was, but was he looking to assuage the pain with something darker? It did not appear he had yet succumbed. There was still time, time to pull him back, though the desperate state of his house seemed to foreshadow his downfall. Even here on the terrace only the remains of plants poked gnarled fingers from cracked pottery and brittle leaves sloped against corners.

Their lessons would be the key. She could both distract and persuade with education. Knowledge had been her answer in the dark time, and it could be his answer as well. She must be careful, careful not to let him pull her into his morose and hopeless mood nor any inclination toward darkness. She would not let it happen again. And in the process of helping him, she would make a secure place for herself.

She ran a finger along the rutted wax of the scroll's broken seal. Too dark to read its comfort here. She should return to her chamber, light a lamp if she could not sleep.

She turned from the wall, but an unnatural noise arrested her step.

From within the house, a deep and mournful moaning drifted through the darkness. Daria pulled her robe tighter, clasped the scroll to her chest. What had made such a desolate sound? The tone seemed neither human nor animal. She slipped across the terrace on silent feet to the balcony that overlooked the courtyard.

There, along the colonnade. Just as she had felt in her dream, the afterglow of a flame just passed, the faint smell of burning oil. And a figure—tall and wispy, dressed in white—vanished before her eyes had fully taken it in.

The moaning had ceased but in its place came a faint murmur

like wind troubling the leaves of a great tree, like fingers sweeping along a wall.

Daria's limbs held suspended, breath paralyzed. She huddled against the balcony wall, watching the empty courtyard. The sound, the strange sight, had filled her with dread, like an empty jug filled with icy water. The thing seemed an apparition, a spirit also tortured by its past, wandering the earth. Had it been another dream? Did she lay sleeping in her bed even now?

And then another form followed it, this one darker and more solid, speeding along the colonnade. She saw little but a tiny lamp held in a white palm.

Daria.

Her name, whispered along the stones. She shuddered, throat tight.

"Daria, where are you?"

Lucas?

She pressed her body to the balcony wall, leaned as far as she dared. "I am here. Up here."

He appeared below, the lamp in his hand rising toward her but too weak to illuminate.

"Here, on the balcony."

He was gone again, but she heard his footfall on the stairs, and then he was at her side, his face gray in the lamplight, reflecting the gray wool thrown over his shoulders.

"Come, come away from there." He pulled her to the terrace, away, all the way to the wall.

"What is it, my lord? I heard the strangest noise—"

"It is nothing. Only Frona walking in her sleep. Clovis has retrieved her." He propped his elbows on the wall, looked over the city.

It was the first untruth she had seen in him. The night

wanderings of a servant would not have roused him from his bed, sent him running through the house in search of his tutor.

"Why did you seek me?"

He did not answer at once. Daria joined him at the wall, resuming her earlier post, and put a self-conscious hand to her loosed hair.

"I was concerned that her strange habit might frighten you."

"You were correct."

"Did you come upstairs to find me?"

A blush warmed her throat and face at the thought. The darkness hid it, thankfully. "No. No, I was already here on the terrace. I could not sleep."

He pointed to the scroll in her hand. "Do you ever stop learning?"

She smiled. "These words are as familiar to me as my own name."

"Let me guess." He tapped a forefinger against his bottom lip. "The love poetry of Archilochos."

She narrowed her eyes at his jest. "The history of Thucydides."

"Hmm. Yes, that should have been my guess."

Daria lifted her face to the breeze coming off the sea, tasted the salt of it on her lips. "It was a gift from my father. My first teacher."

"Clearly your father saw *your* special gift. I've met very few women who can even read, let alone one who reads such depth."

She caressed the scroll again, felt the wax seal, smiled. "He loved all of me, I think. He never treated me as a son—I was a princess in his eyes—and yet he knew I could learn as well as any son, and he cultivated that part of me also."

"He saw both a great mind and great beauty. He sounds like a very wise man."

"He promised that when I mastered Thucydides, he would secure the second volume for me."

"And you achieved this immense success, I am certain."

She studied the faint flicker of a torch in the distance. "He died before he was able to locate a copy. And by that time I was married."

"And your husband did not share your love of philosophy?"

"My husband felt that philosophy in the hands and mind of a woman was a dangerous thing." Daria bit her lip. Why had she said so much?

"How did he die? Your husband. Not your father."

A tiny spider crawled across the stone wall. Daria lifted her hand to let it pass. "I prefer not to speak of it. Besides, in the end he was right. All my learning did nothing to save him. Perhaps the gods punished me for reaching too far."

Lucas flicked a finger at the spider, sending it shooting into the night. "You are quite religious, aren't you?"

She seized the opportunity. "You should take more care yourself, my lord, about pleasing the gods. Success in life requires their help. And a failure to honor them will bring punishment." She nodded toward the inside of the house. "Your estate is built in the Roman style, and yet I have seen no *lararium*. Where do you honor your household gods?"

He snorted, leaned his forearms on the wall, and clasped his hands. "I admire your devotion, Daria. But life has taught me otherwise. The gods care nothing for us, and our behavior sways them not at all. If their eyes are on us, it is only to laugh and mock as we destroy ourselves and fail to save others from destruction."

The pain in his voice went deep and struck against Daria's heart like a flint against stone, sparking both fear and pity.

He pointed to the Temple of Artemis, a pale glow in the distance even at this hour. "Her temple is supposed to provide asylum for any who claim sanctuary within its walls. Did your father teach you of her most famous refugee?"

Daria inhaled the cool air. "Cleopatra had her fifteen-year-old sister Arsinöe murdered by a priest to remove her as a threat to the throne of Egypt."

"Exactly. A perfect illustration of the protection of your gods."

"You cannot—"

"But I must take you to see other parts of the city." He pointed into the darkness, to the amphitheater and beyond. "The stadium lies beyond the theater. And the Roman barracks nearby. Rome would not want us to forget that although we govern ourselves, she is always standing ready to intervene." He nodded toward the great arch. "The harbor agora is there, of course, but up the Embolos"—he pointed north—"there is the state agora, with administrative and political buildings surrounding it."

Daria tried to stifle a yawn, unsuccessfully. She pulled away from the wall. "I should return to my bed—"

"What? You would leave me so soon?" He grasped her hand where it still lay on the stone. "I am just beginning to learn your secrets."

She swallowed against the pressure in her throat. "It grows cold."

Lucas pulled the woolen blanket from his shoulders and held it aloft with raised eyebrows. She nodded her permission and he wrapped it around her shoulders.

She clasped its corners at her chest, bent her cheek to the scratchy warmth.

Lucas eyed her hair, trapped beneath the blanket, then stepped behind. His fingers brushed her skin and Daria's muscles seemed to turn to water. He lifted and freed her hair, then stood beside her again, shoulder touching hers as he had done at the rail of the *Kynthia*.

"Are you hungry? There may still be some mussels in *garum* sauce left from the *deipnon* meal."

She shook her head. Her eyelids felt heavy, and she sighed and resisted the desire to drop her head onto his shoulder.

Here, on the terrace, with the strange sounds of Frona or the spirits of the dead now silent, she could almost believe that she was safe. That Lucas would keep her here in his home, protected from the past and from the future.

But hiding was not life. And she wanted to be a teacher more than she wanted to be hidden away in the home of a man, especially one whose inclinations seemed to stray toward shadows. She had been down that path before. Never again.

She would not reopen herself to hurt, no matter how charming he might seem in his better moments.

But Lucas stood again with forearms braced along the wall.

"It seems we both must deal with the pain of the past."

The feelings of warmth and groggy contentment were fleeing. She fought to hold them for only a little longer. "Not all that happens is just. We must learn to accept—"

"I do not accept."

"But we must. We can only show compassion for those who have felt the sting of injustice—"

He turned on her, the glint in his dark eyes hard and cold. "There is room for compassion. And there is vengeance."

The blanket slipped from her shoulder and Daria tried to catch it but it fell to her side, and the night air chafed her skin.

It was there again, the fear that hounded her steps since the final night of her marriage. Whatever flame of virtue still resided in Lucas was quickly being extinguished by the smothering presence of something other.

And it was something Daria had learned long ago had the power to destroy.

10

DARIA FOUND THE DARKENED DOORWAY OF AN unused dining chamber, hid herself in it, and waited. Lucas had refused to begin their lessons this morning, claiming he had business in town.

He had not gone to visit the school yesterday, as he said he would. Was it trickery, his claim to know Tyrannus? Or would he go this afternoon, where a strange sect met in its vacant hall in the lull of the day?

Her legs cramped, her stomach complained for lack of a midday meal, but still she waited. She had to know. Her need to create security for herself was in jeopardy. Or was it only her need for answers that drove her?

At last Lucas appeared. Outer tunic draped over his shoulders, head down, he strode along the opposite side of the wet courtyard.

She let him go, let him pass through the lofty entryway, out into the still-foul weather. Listened for the latch of the door. And then followed.

Outside she ducked her head at the stinging rain and cut across the graveled street that ran to the stone steps. Lucas had reached the street below already, and she eyed the back of his head.

He turned north as expected, toward the school she'd so recently visited, tramped up the center of the street in spite of the weather, wrapped in his tunic and his secrets. Daria hurried behind, kept to the edge of the right-hand covered colonnade. The slap of her sandals in time with his footfalls seemed too loud, like a betrayal. Would he hear and turn and find her following?

Halfway to the upper portion of the city, where the school's entrance invited scholars and pupils, Lucas deviated from his rush up the Embolos and wrenched left to pass into the narrow entrance of a darkened shop.

Daria slowed, then stopped, her back against a wall opposite. The sidewalk, empty of products, gave no clue to the shop's contents. No painted or carved letters above the strange door, which glared like a single black eye in the white face of the wall.

Again she waited, shifted on her feet, avoided the glances of those who came and went from the bakery door beside her post. Finally he exited, a brown-wrapped package clutched in his grip and head down, and made for the school again.

She hesitated. Curiosity about the enigmatic shop, the contents of the package, tempted her to cross the street. But she would lose him to the city if she tarried. She chewed her lip and tapped a heel against the stones. Which way?

Eyes still on Lucas's upward-advancing figure, she sped across the street to the opposite sidewalk, waited until he was a smudge against the sky, and ducked into the shop.

At the door the pervasive odor of eastern spices assaulted her senses. Teeming shelves lined the walls, their wares crammed like glittery-scaled fish bulging at nets, sagging the aged wood and spilling onto the floor where they crowded and jostled for a share of the choked space.

Was it a bookshop? But no, the scattered scrolls were only a fraction of the shelves' clutter. A mismatched collection of objects attached themselves to the jumbled scrolls—dusty, miniature amphorae with unknown contents, black Persian amulets, and blue scarab stones from Egypt, reflective gems of red, and dull-gray stones that somehow seemed malevolent in their ordinariness. Within these overcrowded walls, the swish of rain and clatter of commerce ceased, swallowed into a macabre hush.

All this she perceived in an instant, and in the next, the smoky eyes of the shop owner watching from where he leaned, arms folded, against the shop's back wall.

He said nothing, which seemed a greater menace than if he had shouted her misbelonging. Only watched, waited. He was older than she, old enough to be her father. Or was it only the white hair, long and tied at the back of his neck, that aged his otherwise unlined features?

"Good afternoon." She nodded in his general direction, then glanced around as if she shopped for a bolt of fabric or a reed basket to carry market purchases. The curious bits and pieces vied for attention, and a sense of dizzy unbalance swept her, as if she herself might be gathered up, stashed away at the back of a shelf. Irretrievable.

The shop owner lifted himself away from the wall.

She felt his eyes on her, looking through her. Should she escape? Catch up with Lucas before he entered the school?

She drifted to a shelf, fingered a bound scroll, then resisted a questioning glance at the owner and unrolled the deck-led edge with shaky hands. The papyrus was stiff with disuse and browned with age and crackled at her violation of its long seclusion.

It was lettered in the Persian script, ancient and heavy-inked, as if the words it bore were too ponderous for mere Greek. She read it aloud, softly, as she often did when translating.

> *Barrier that none can pass,*
> *Barrier of the gods, that none may break,*
> *Which no god may annul,*
> *Nor god nor man can loose.*

A tickle of apprehension ran insidious fingers up her spine. The unnamed terror of ageless curses and wicked intentions.

"You can read Persian?"

He had spoken at last, edging forward into the half-light falling through the narrow door and watching her in shock. His voice was smooth and low, tinged with a cold pleasure, and in the light his near-perfect features seemed chiseled from marble, though alive with curiosity.

"Y-Yes. I can."

His gaze roamed her features, as though she were a fascinating book herself. "A woman who reads, and in Persian!" He whispered the words, as if only speaking to himself. To her, he said, "And you are in need of a spell?"

She let the scroll roll inward upon itself, enclosing its secrets once more. "No. I—I mean, I am not sure what I am looking for." She wedged the scroll back onto the shelf. "A friend of mine—Lucas Christopoulos—comes here . . ."

"Hmm. Then you have just missed him."

"Have I?" She slid a quick look toward the door, then back to the owner. "You have quite a collection. I can see why he frequents your shop."

His movement toward her was deliberate and slow, the sensual tread of a wild cat. "We have all you might require for the practice."

The practice of sorcery? Her breath came shallow and quick.

She eyed the tiny amphorae, remembered the men in Rhodes and the jug they forced to the young girl's lips. What potions settled inside that fired clay? What unnatural horrors would they call forth?

She ran light fingers along a string of black stones. They were cold, like they had been unearthed from the underworld only moments ago. "My needs are simple."

"These are uncertain times. It is wise to be prepared."

She stalled, searched for a response. "Disturbing news recently of more killings."

"There was no avoiding it, as your friend well knows. Vengeance must have its day."

She crossed the shop to the opposite wall, still searching the shelves as if her intended purchase eluded her. "You approve of this vengeance, then?"

Behind her, he did not answer at once and she did not turn to catch his expression. When he spoke, his tone carried suspicion.

"Those who have suffered as Lucas has cannot be expected to remain indifferent."

The damp chill of the street seeped under Daria's skin and she flexed her fingers against their numb tingle. She took a chance, tried to further the cryptic conversation. "You knew his wife?"

A longer pause this time, until Daria turned, thinking he had not heard.

His face was a mask. "Aye. She was a woman impossible to ignore."

What else was there to ask? She had nothing further. How to escape?

"You did not tell me your name." He moved to her side, looked over his wares.

She floundered. If Lucas returned here, it would not do for him to hear of her visit, of her questions. "Eleni. Of Crete. Newly arrived to Ephesus."

"You are of a curious nature, Eleni. A woman who seeks knowledge, to control the will of the gods."

"Control? You believe such a thing is possible?"

He shrugged one shoulder, his gaze steady on her. "Why should they have all the power? Why should we be at their mercy?"

His confidence was fascinating, if not startling.

"What can I show you today, Eleni?"

"Oh, I am simply out exploring the city, I'm afraid. Stopping in at the favorite haunts of friends, meeting new people."

"Hmm."

That little murmur again—of dissent or suspicion? The predatory light in his eyes was frightening.

"Then I hope you will remember Hektor's shop when you are in need."

She forced a tight smile. "To be sure. You will be the first that comes to mind."

He extended a hand toward his merchandise. "Be at your ease in looking over the shelves."

"Oh, I must go. Much more to see of your fine city."

He inclined his head toward the door and sniffed. "Take care, then. The air smells of Zeus's anger."

She escaped from his watchful eyes into the wet street,

deserted now in the rain and the customary midafternoon seclusion of its citizens.

She gathered all the words she had exchanged with the shop owner and layered them into her memory. She would draw them out later, to ponder and dissect. But between the layers of memory ran a cold thread of apprehension mixed with denial, black thoughts like shadows drifting across the moon.

Lucas would have reached the school by now, but she would repeat her earlier watch—from across the street she would catalogue those who entered and exited the school, try to determine their associations, their intent.

She hurried upward, past the Temple to Augustus and the Prytaneion. How did the flame of Hestia and her altar compare to that of Artemis? When would she see the famed temple, inside and out?

The rain pelted the street now. It trickled in the mossy crevices of stones, gushed along deep ruts worn by years of passing chariot wheels, and poured off the colonnade, a liquid wall. She faced the School of Tyrannus from under the roof, peered through the sheet of water to where the rain slashed at the schoolmaster's silent door.

The door opened.

Daria sucked in a breath, retreated to the wall at her back.

A dark head thrust from the door, looked left and right, then vanished again into the school's depths.

Daria released her pent-up breath and let her shoulders drop.

Stiff fingers dug into her upper arm and yanked her backward.

Terror shot through her limbs. She gasped, clutched at the hand, took in the arm, shoulder, face—

"My lord!"

His eyes were chips of black ice under drawn-together brows and his tight lips whitened with fury. He retained his unyielding grip on her arm, dragged her three doors down and into a dark and empty shop, in a bizarre repeat of yesterday's incident on Harbor Street.

"Let go of me, my lord!"

He released her and spun, and the rage behind his eyes scorched the reproof from her lips. He took a threatening step toward her and she pressed against the shop's inner wall, hands braced against dusty stone.

"I told you to remain in the house."

Scalding hot words, delivered through clenched teeth. Like Zeus's eagle swooping down to peck at Prometheus chained to his rock.

Perhaps he was not well. Perhaps not even sane. She hunched her shoulders, stilled her trembling arms. "I wanted to see—"

"You followed me."

Daria lifted her chin, tried to inhale courage. "I have a right to know—"

"You know nothing!"

"Exactly!" She leaned forward, closing the distance between them, and risked confronting him with the harsh truth. "I came here without thought, without wisdom, on the word of a charming merchant with lofty promises. Yet all I have seen since has taught me that you are not the man you seemed to be—"

"Aagghh!" He whirled away as if to retreat, then returned, the narrow space between them too aggressive, too intimate. His breath drummed against her neck, his gaze roved her face.

"You are afraid of me."

Not a question. Not even a statement. A realization, a dawning of wretched understanding.

Daria blinked away the strange stab of tears behind her eyes. "Why do we hide in here? Whom do *you* fear?"

Would that she had the courage to ask her true questions. What connection did he have to the city's strange killings? Did the killings avenge the deaths of others—others like his wife? What part in sorcery did Lucas play?

She glanced to his waist, to the small pouch fastened there, but it was empty. What had happened to the package he had taken from the appalling little shop?

He was breathing harder now, as though his past chased him into the present. He braced a hand against the wall above her head and leaned against his arm, trapping her in a strange half embrace.

She studied his profile, so near. The heavy lashes, the fine lines around his eyes, the enigmatic expression. Could she unravel its riddle?

Anger. Torment. Sorrow.

But anger held sway. A wrath that would not be denied.

"If you wish to keep your position, Daria, you will *remember* your position. You are a tutor, not my keeper, and you will focus on the task for which I brought you, or I will send you back!" His eyes bore into hers. "I value my privacy above all else. Make no mistake."

She felt no anger herself. Not any longer. There was too much pain. And she had asked of fear, but he gave no answer. Instead, he studied her a moment longer, then pushed away from the wall, drifted into the dark interior of the chamber.

"You tell me to focus on my duty, but you refuse your lessons. Come, my lord, return home and focus your mind on something productive, something purer than—than the evil magic of that foul shop."

"Ha! Is that what you believe, Tutor?" His voice came from the shadows, flat and soulless.

She pressed against the cold stone at her back. She should never have followed him. Presumptuous and foolish.

Still unseen, he spoke out of the darkness, his voice resigned. "Very well, I suppose you deserve the truth."

Daria held her breath. Would his truth mean that she could not build a safe life here in Ephesus?

"I received some information while in Rhodes."

She squinted. Strange beginning.

"It was information that afforded me a way to become part of a secret sect here in Ephesus. Hektor—whose shop you *followed* me to—is the leader of that sect."

"Step into the light, my lord. I want to see your face while you tell me why you should desire such a thing."

"Because I believe they killed my wife."

He obeyed her command, then, and when the murky light from the street fell upon his features, they were twisted in an anguish that pierced her heart.

"And now you seek—?"

"Justice. I want to see those responsible held accountable for their actions. Hektor, and all the rest. But I have no proof. Not yet."

"Last night you spoke of vengeance."

He waved a hand. "Vengeance. Justice. What difference—?"

"There is a very great difference and you know it."

"Then perhaps I shall have them both, if that is what I want!" He drew close again, as though challenging her to defy his intent.

She lifted her chin, stared him down. "And how will you accomplish such a thing?"

He lifted a strand of her hair that had escaped her comb and twirled it around his finger. "What is it *you* want, Daria? I promised to find you a place in the school here and I will keep my promise. Why do you care what I do?"

She turned her face, pulling away slightly. "I do not know."

But she did know.

It was the same as always. She could not help but try to put things right when they were out of place. Including people. She had failed the last time she saw a man heading toward self-destruction and had been strangled by guilt ever since.

She had not come to Ephesus to be a teacher. Nor to escape the sorcerers on the docks. Even on the *Kynthia* she had known the truth. Somewhere under Lucas's easy charm in Rhodes, she had sensed the beginnings of this same descent.

Lucas shoved away and strode to the entry. "I will take you home."

"I can go alone. You have business, you said—"

"Daria." He inclined his head toward the door.

Yes, they were to be master and servant. Nothing more. What had she expected?

But it mattered little what he thought of her. She was here for a reason. She acknowledged it to herself as she followed him into the street, and even welcomed the clarity that such knowledge brought.

She had sailed to Ephesus to redeem the past. She had come for a second chance.

11

DARIA STRAIGHTENED THE LINE OF SCROLLS FOR the fifth time and placed the two quills exactly parallel to scroll number four, beside a bowl of mildewed oranges on the low table. She glanced once more out of the *triclinium* toward the hall.

Had he forgotten?

She shoved the bowl of oranges. They'd come from that foul tree in the courtyard, no doubt. Probably mildewed before they were picked.

The smaller of the estate's two dining rooms, the room held the requisite couches along three walls, with tables placed at each for banquet spreads. But the room was musty with disuse, and the lamp she'd placed on a grimy corner table sputtered and struggled to fulfill its mission. The room bore only artificial windows—painted frescoes of tangled garden scenes beyond false-framed openings that would deceive no one. Romping between the mock window scenes was a series of frescoed maidens, skin taking on a dingy cast, giggling and frolicking as though the weight of the house had no bearing on their greedy consumption of life.

Daria turned away from the young girls to the strange choice of statuary—no gods and goddesses here, only an open-mouthed fish on its tail with a half-swallowed smaller fish in its mouth. The eyes of the fresco girls seemed to follow and glint at her from behind, watching to see if the new tutor was capable of placating the master's anger. She took a deep breath to quell the fluttery annoyance in her chest and rubbed the tension from her neck. The room was cold. Clovis must have forgotten to feed the furnace that heated the hypocaust under the floor.

Did she have everything she needed for their first session? Scrolls of Zarathustra's writings, a Persian primer on script—

"There you are, Daria." Lucas sailed into the room, barefoot and disheveled. "I couldn't remember where we agreed to meet."

"If you prefer, we could relocate, perhaps the larger triclinium—"

"No!" He sighed and seemed to force a softening to his voice. "I—that room is never used anymore. Not since—not since I gave up entertaining."

He sprawled along the length of the couch nearest the door and propped his feet, crossed at the ankles. "Well? Are you going to stand over me like an angry scholar with his errant pupil?" He pointed to a second couch, perpendicular to his own. "Sit."

Daria forced curled fingers to relax and lowered herself to the couch. A bit of the Lucas she had met in Rhodes flickered behind his eyes. Had his anger of the previous day abated?

She had spent the night fighting sleeplessness, replaying his fury, his threat to return her like an unwanted market purchase.

Should she run herself, before he had the chance to fling her back? Did a better life still await her in Rhodes? But in the tremulous light of early dawn, memories of the past mingled with the present, and the call of second chances fixed her once again to this city, this house. This man. She would bring order and structure.

She retrieved the primer from the table, tried to grip its elusive, unruly edge to pull it open. "I thought we would begin with some familiarization with the logograms and script of Imperial Aramaic, which form the basis of the Persian's spoken language."

Lucas grabbed an orange from the bowl and ripped at its skin. "Very well." He tore a section from the fruit and tossed it whole into his mouth. "Enlighten me."

Her stomach rebelled at the thought of oranges, but she sat at the edge of the couch, her back straight to counteract the soft pull of the cushions, and reached for a quill. Her fingers twitched, fumbled at the table edge, and bumped the pen. It shot from the table and secreted itself under Lucas's couch.

Daria jumped to her feet, took a step.

"Leave it." Lucas extended a sticky hand toward her line of scrolls. "You have another."

She sat but could see the tip of the quill lying there, abandoned. "No, I should retrieve it." Before he could argue, she kneeled beside his couch, rescued the pen from the shadows, and returned to her place.

Lucas was watching, but not with the amusement she might have expected. "So, do you think an old man can still learn? Or is education only profitable for the young?"

"First, you are far from old. But second, I'm surprised you should ask. We Greeks have a long tradition of education and learning at any age."

He snorted and chewed the last of his orange, wiping juice

from his lips with the back of his hand. "A long tradition of spouting opinions, waxing eloquent about nothing, and getting pulled into dangerous philosophies, if you ask me."

"You believe philosophy to be dangerous?"

"Some of them. Very dangerous." His eyes went cold and he looked away, to the sadly cheerful girls whispering endless secrets to each other on the wall. "I have seen what dangerous philosophies can do."

"As have I."

His gaze came back to her, hungry and searching, rabid in its intensity. "Then you know we must do whatever we can—what we must—to destroy—"

But he broke off, sank back into the cushions. Studied the window that was not a window.

"Sometimes it is better to avoid what brings danger. To pursue other, safer—"

"No." His gaze did not return from the sham window. "No, it is too late for that."

Daria shifted on her couch. Her ankle-length tunic had twisted and was binding her legs. She reached for a pitcher, poured wine-tinged water into a cup, and sipped the tepid mixture. "Shall we begin?"

But an hour later she had nearly given up. Lucas was distracted. And if she could not teach him, how could she save him? But it was more than distraction. He was plagued. Tormented, even. Was it too late, as he had said, to pull him back?

She shuddered, an involuntary chill snaking its way up her spine.

"Are you cold?" He jumped from the couch, as if roused from the dead. "It *is* cold in here. Clovis!"

The servant appeared in an instant, as though he had been

hovering outside the room. "My lord?" He was calm and deferential in Lucas's presence. No fumbling fingers or nervous twitches like hers.

"Feed the furnace, would you, old man?" He clapped Clovis on the shoulder. "The lady is chilled."

Clovis looked into the room, taking in Daria's stiff position on the couch. "I apologize, my lord. I did not realize you would be . . . entertaining . . . in here today."

Daria flushed. Did Lucas see the scorn in the servant's eyes, hear the derision in his voice? If so, it bothered him little. His eyes crinkled with a good-natured grin and he did that casual, impatient raking of hair from his face.

"No apology necessary, Clovis. You know me—keeping you informed always seems to slip my mind."

The old servant gave a slow smile and bowed out of the room.

They were like a family, once. The thought came unbidden, along with aching flashes of imagination—Lucas and his wife entertaining here in this room, Clovis serving guests. Frona bustling about the kitchen, filling platters and bowls with fragrant fruits and yeasty breads while laughter and music spilled out into the courtyard.

He has fallen to ruin, much as the house.

But he was not entirely ruinous. Not yet.

Clovis returned a moment later, before either of them had turned from the doorway. "My lord, you have a visitor."

A figure appeared at Clovis's shoulder, towering a head taller but narrowly built like the older man. He wore a robe in a shade of orange Daria had never witnessed—something between salmon flesh and hammered bronze.

"Demetrius." Lucas's tone was cool and smooth as marble.

The visitor slid past the servant into the room, arms extended in greeting. "Lucas, I heard you had returned. Tell me of Rhodes." His gaze alighted on Daria. "Ho, what have we here? I thought you went to acquire information and copper!" He skirted Lucas to enter the seating enclosure, took in Daria from eyes to sandals, and let a low whistle escape through closed teeth. "This is far, far better than either one."

Daria leaned backward, away from the silken voice and the many-ringed hand that reached for her, its silver glinting like the eyes of those painted girls. He had the long, thin fingers of an artist, and there was something sickly-sweet about him, like the cloying scent of burial myrrh. "My lord, we should return to our studies—"

"Demetrius, this is my tutor." Lucas's words were dagger-sharp.

Demetrius dropped his hand. "So you did bring back information after all." He smoothed his eyebrows with one long finger, then traced a line down her arm. "But all of it stored like precious perfume in this *magnificent* container."

"She is a brilliant scholar. I brought her back to teach me—"

But Demetrius wasn't listening. "Hmm, perhaps she could teach me some things."

Did the room's already close walls tighten? It was too soon for Clovis's furnace stoking to have pushed heated air into the spaces underfoot, but a clammy perspiration sheened the skin under her tunic. She lifted her chin to the visitor, kept her voice controlled. "Perhaps I should begin with Aristotle's debate over whether man has any advantages over animal."

"Begin anywhere you like, my dear."

The barb had done little to deter him. Perhaps he did not even understand. "I believe I will retain the pupil I already have." She turned to Lucas. "Shall we—"

"Ooh, Lucas, she is splendid. I want one. Are there more like you in Rhodes, girl?"

"What do you want, Demetrius?" Lucas pushed between the couches.

"I told you, I came to hear what you discovered in Rhodes. But as you seem to be still *studying* . . ."

The leering innuendo was clearly not lost on Lucas. He scowled and pushed a hand against the taller man's chest, shoving him away from Daria.

Demetrius whirled and settled onto a couch, his bright robe floating around tapered ankles. He straightened the fabric, then smiled serenely.

"We will speak of Rhodes later, Demetrius."

"Simply tell me. Did you get the information you need to exterminate—"

"Later, Demetrius!" Lucas's face darkened, then whitened, and his sleeveless tunic revealed bunched muscles in arms and shoulders.

Demetrius held up a palm. "Tsk, Lucas. Such temper. You'll frighten your tutor."

Lucas shot a glance at her and she bit her lip to keep from speaking. She feared only for Lucas. This man was no good for him. And such anger, like churning water rising in a cistern, brought memories of another day. Another triclinium. That same devouring rage.

And the rage had apparently been contained long enough. Lucas grabbed two handfuls of the man's tunic, lifted him, and shoved. He kept shoving while Demetrius two-stepped backward, out of the room.

12

LUCAS LOWERED HIS JAW TO DEMETRIUS'S EAR AND growled. "You don't deserve to even look at her."

The man's attention was gained at last and he thrust Lucas's hands away from his chest and yanked at his rumpled tunic. "Be easy, my friend. I was only inspecting the new purchases—"

"I told you, we will speak later of my time in Rhodes."

Demetrius crossed the hall, strolled toward the open courtyard and its defunct fountain. "I think we had best speak now. Every day that passes is a day wasted. You heard about the latest body?"

Lucas scowled, glanced over his shoulder to where Daria stared from the doorway. No good thing could last.

He jutted his chin toward her. "Return inside the chamber, Daria. I will only be a moment."

He didn't wait to see if she would comply. He pushed past Demetrius into the courtyard, where scraggly green vines seemed to twist around his feet to suck the life from him, and a hazy sun glared through scudding clouds and did nothing to warm. He had tried for a while to keep the garden going, but none of the three who now lived in the house had a knack for it.

"I have told you, Demetrius, the killings are unrelated—"

"Don't pretend with me, Lucas. You cannot be so naive. Have the memories so quickly faded?"

No, he could not forget. Not even when he tried. The morning with Daria and her scrolls, if not exciting, had been pleasant. Like better days the house had seen. And he had made her smile once. A small smile at a small joke, but he had seen it. Had hoped again that his plan might work. Perhaps he could simply be a man of business and trade, focused on his new studies and leadership in the city. Let the goodness of one woman bloom inside his house, transform it.

"But they are not involved. I have told you that."

Demetrius cocked an eyebrow. "You have become one of their strange sect, perhaps? Latched on to their foul philosophies?"

"No! No, I am only saying that if you are looking to blame them, you will not find any guilt regarding the murders in the city."

"Then if that is so, all the more reason for you to help. We have to show the people what they truly are. And this is no time for useless studies—"

"She is teaching me Persian."

A flicker of understanding crossed Demetrius's face. He tapped a finger against his full lips and nodded once. "I see. And perhaps that will help you in your private quest with Hektor. But my interest lies elsewhere. I need you for other tasks."

"You do not own me, Demetrius. I'll thank you to stop

treating me like your slave." Lucas inhaled, expanding his chest. The man might have a hand's breadth of height on him, but Lucas still spent frequent mornings at the gymnasium, wrestling younger men, throwing the discus. A vision of tossing Demetrius down the hillside in front of the house amused him.

But Demetrius was chest to chest with him now, hostility breathing down his neck. "We've come this far, my friend—"

Lucas shoved him once again and stepped to the side. "We are not friends."

Something flared behind Demetrius's eyes and he moved sideways as well, mirroring Lucas's movements. "That's right. But we could be partners, could we not? You are the only one positioned to protect the city from this threat. You must do your duty, to Ephesus and to the Lady Artemis. And if you will not . . ." Demetrius let the threat hang, then shrugged. "Do not forget that I know your secret. A few well-placed words to Hektor would certainly end your efforts there."

"You would force me to help or expose me to Hektor?"

"The time is growing short. Why should you not be forced to do the right thing?"

Lucas risked a look toward the triclinium again, but it cost him.

Demetrius laughed, a laugh like cold silver, and wore that knowing expression that came with his extraordinary ability to dissect another's private thoughts. "I take it *she* doesn't know? Does she know about the killings? That Zagreus follows you like a dog digging up bones?" His voice was rising now, carrying past the algae-infested fountain and chipped statuary, lifting above the mocking scent of dying flowers.

"Shut your mouth, Demetrius. Or I swear by Artemis I will do it for you."

Demetrius's amusement vanished and he bared even white

teeth between red lips. "Do what I need you to do, Lucas Christopoulos. Quit this pretense of being a scholar and agree to my plan. Jews and priests, sorcerers and citizens—the city is about to erupt and we need to throw fuel on the fire. The Great Festival will soon be upon us."

"Fine." Lucas waved a hand, trying to appear disinterested. "Whatever you say. I will connect with them again at the temple on the feast day this week, make contact at the *stoa*. Begin to gain their trust again." He would agree to anything to get Demetrius out of the house, away from Daria. Whether he meant the words or not.

"Good." Demetrius stalked toward the front entry, his sandals slapping on the cold mosaic floor, and stopped at the square *impluvium* that caught rainwater and diverted it beneath the house. He toed a loose stone at the lip of the pool, knocked it inward, then turned, his blood-red lips against pale skin visible across the atrium. "Have some self-respect, Lucas, and fix this place up. It offends the eyes."

He ran a hand through his hair—the vain gesture of a man aware of his looks. "I'll expect to hear from you very soon. With news of how our plan progresses." Another glance at the empty doorway where Daria had stood, then back at Lucas, his threat clear. And then he was gone.

Lucas spun back to the courtyard, kicked against a sculpture of Hermes, watched it totter, fall, and crack into two pieces. Dissatisfied, he snatched the broken plaster, thrust it above his head, then hurled it to the courtyard paving. The statue smashed into a thousand fragments, and he ground them under his bare heel, uncaring if he drew blood.

He was too cunning, Demetrius was. Able to see into a man's mind.

Lucas had been selfish to bring her here. Had thought she could help. But he must give up this connection he felt, must pull away before Demetrius sniffed out any more than he already had. Before Daria asked any more questions from that exceedingly inquisitive mind of hers.

But even if he pulled away, this thing he was becoming—had become—would hurt her still. People were already dying. He feared they haunted his halls in the night. Had he truly thought she could save him?

Lucas reached a hand to another sculpture, rocked it once, but had no more strength for useless damage. A soul-deep fatigue had stolen over him and he was too tired to fight anything anymore. To fight Hektor, Demetrius. Even to fight against the wreck of the house, which was going down like a ship with all its cargo lost.

Daria would be in danger, yes. But weren't they all? Did life have any meaning, anyway, or did one merely pass through it, like so much dirty water running under the house? Perhaps the best anyone could do was strike a blow on his way out.

He was so tired.

He turned back toward the dining chamber. He would lie down, have Clovis bring them some olives and cheese, a bit of wine.

She stood in the doorway again, watching. Had she seen him rage against the statuary? He lifted gritty eyes to her stricken face. Saw himself reflected there—the reckless anger that was all he had left.

She was like a wilted plant now, life draining away. Like a flame extinguished.

Already the dying had begun.

13

THE ERRANT VINES OF CLIMBING ROSES IN THE malformed courtyard garden eventually yielded to Daria's corrective touch. The pebbled paving stones puckered her knees, but she trained the last smooth tendril around the latticed frame found half-buried in dirt, then rested on her heels to examine her work.

With the estate built into the hillside, an herb garden behind the kitchen was impossible, and so this courtyard garden had apparently been used as such at one time. She had found sticky remnants of yarrow for treating inflammation, feathered stalks of hyssop whose oil could soothe a cough, and wilted chamomile for headaches, along with the cook's requirements of garlic, thyme, and parsley. A riotous mix of sharp and spicy scents and unruly textures crowding each other to survive in the weed-choked soil.

The mulberry and cyclamen were beyond hope—blighted with insects and half-starved—and would need to be dug out. Hardy sage had well survived neglect, as it always did. She would need to do some research to save the rest. But it would take more than skill with plants to bring the garden back from wreckage. The fountain, the paving . . .

A hint of white fluttered at the edge of her vision, near the door of an unused chamber. Daria turned away from it, bent to the crumbly soil.

He was watching her again.

In the two days since she witnessed Lucas's argument in this very courtyard with the mysterious Demetrius, he'd asked for only a few hours of discourse and instruction. She filled her time with an attempt to liberate the garden from decay, and each time she worked the plants, she felt his eyes on her.

She dug a weedy bit of something from the soft dirt, carefully set it on the increasing pile.

For as long as she could remember, men had looked at her, watched her. From the lecherous calls and whistles of Rhodian dockworkers to Demetrius's smirking grin when they met, she'd grown accustomed to men seeing nothing but her body. Her husband had been little different.

But Lucas's eyes on her—was this not something unusual? When she turned and caught his gaze yesterday, his expression was that of a man staring at a distant horizon. Across the sea, perhaps, to a land unknown. Since then she pretended not to see him.

But she thought of him. Thought of his grim preoccupations with justice and Demetrius's ominous charge. And, truth be told, she watched him. Watched for the chance to convince him he must take a safer path. She had failed at that task once, to disastrous effect. She wanted that second chance. She would not believe that he was beyond hope, any more than his garden.

There was nothing more to be done here today. She gathered weeds in grimy hands, stood under the diseased orange tree, and turned. Could not resist a glance toward that empty chamber and its darkened doorway.

He did not look away.

She dropped her hands to her waist and they watched each other for a long moment, as though the answers to life's riddles lay in the other's eyes.

When he spoke, his voice was thick, muffled. "There is not much good in it, I am afraid." He jutted his chin toward the garden. "It will only return to its wild state."

His deeper meaning was not lost on her. Daria looked down, cast a glance at the newly ordered plantings. "I am hopeful." She lifted the handful of weeds. "Let me throw these in the furnace and wash, and we can begin our afternoon lessons."

Lucas stepped from the shadows. His eyes were smudged with sleeplessness. "Not today. I must go out."

She waited. When he was in one of these moods, it took time for details to seep from him.

"It's a festival day in the city. I have some business to attend near the temple. I will return by nightfall."

Daria leaned forward. "Then I will come with you. I am eager to see the temple and make my sacrifices—"

"No." His lips seemed to whiten around the word. "Another time. Festival days are madness. The city will be clogged with twice the tourists and half the restraint. It is not safe."

"Then perhaps *you* should remain."

"I cannot."

"Why? What is it you are going to do there, my lord?"

He stalked forward, halfway across the courtyard, then stopped, fists balled at his sides. "Why must you always be questioning, woman? Is there *nothing* you can leave unknown?"

Daria swallowed, the hot bitterness of indignation burning her chest. His anger sometimes sparked at the least provocation, ready to devour. "Go, then. Take care of your business in the city. You'll have no more questions from me."

She left the garden with his angry stare burning holes in her back. Not surprising. What tutor ever spoke thus to a master? But he provoked her.

She reached the kitchen, empty of Frona and Clovis, and tossed the pile of weeds into the fire. Moisture bubbled and hissed and a white smoke sent her stepping backward, eyes burning, waving a hand to clear the haze.

Lucas had told the man Demetrius that he would meet with this strange "sect" at the temple, gain their trust before betraying them as Demetrius wished. Was it the sorcerers again? But they seemed to speak of others. What additional trouble was Lucas finding for himself?

She would find out.

A whisper of restraint over her insatiable curiosity floated across her thoughts and she quickly dismissed the chiding. It was part of her plan. To help him, she must understand him.

Within the hour she had washed at the jug and bowl in her bedchamber, changed into a simple white tunic and white chitôn that would not draw attention, and was straightening her few belongings when she heard him leave. She gave him time to reach the Embolos, then headed for the door.

It was past time to pay the Lady of the Ephesians her respects, to ensure good fortune during her stay in the city by offering proper worship. Why should she not go on her own? She did not need his permission.

He had been right, the streets were in turmoil. The city's importance as the province of Asia's largest banking center brought enough visitors for any given day, but add a religious festival and the streets overflowed with carts and wagons, horses and their leavings, and with men, women, and babes on their way upward to the temple. Would she even be able to find him at the temple? With no room to walk beneath the colonnades, Daria tip-toed through the ripe-smelling, horse-littered street itself, in the wake of a matched pair of sables drawing a wheeled black chariot.

The temple drew them, one and all, like the Great Sea pulling the tide to itself, and Daria joined the upward flow.

Ahead, the crowd slowed, then stopped. She stood on her toes to see above people and a flutter of dread tickled. Was this part of whatever Lucas had become entangled in?

An unholy shriek went up from the street and the crowd rippled backward with the sound. Daria held her ground, let people retreat past her.

She saw nothing in the street to warrant flight. Neither did she see Lucas. She took a few hesitant steps forward. The attention of those who remained in the barren section of street seemed trained on a particular shabby door—part of a section of tenement housing, it appeared. The sun did not reach this section of wall, and the door lay in eerie midday shadow.

Daria approached a young woman dressed in gray and bare-foot. Her arms were wrapped tight at her waist and hollow eyes fixed on the door across the street.

"What is it?" Daria glanced between the girl and the door. "What is happening in there?"

The girl did not raise her eyes and her lips trembled when she spoke. "They are trying to cast it out." Tears chased each other in tracks on her cheeks, ran into her mouth, dripped from her chin.

Daria circled the girl's shoulders with her arm. "What do you need? What can I do for you?"

At this, the girl turned fierce eyes on her. "What do I *need*? I need my husband healed!"

As if in answer, another terrifying shriek screeched from within the house. Pottery crashed, the sound of breaking wood and tumbled bodies streamed over the barking shouts of numerous men.

A figure appeared in the doorway, tottering like a drunk, tunic hanging in a long shred from one shoulder, leaving him shamefully exposed. The girl within Daria's grasp started forward, then fell back.

Daria took her hand. "Your husband?"

She shook her head, swiped at her face with a callused hand. "That is one of the healers."

The man released his grip on the door frame and stumbled into the street. Blood coursed from a cut above his eye, and he raised his ragged tunic to staunch the flow, as if unaware of his increased shame. Daria averted her eyes, but the girl at her side still stared.

"What ails your husband?"

"He has the demons." The girl's voice was barely audible above the tumult within the house.

Daria dropped her arm from the girl's shoulders. A cold breeze lifted the hair on her neck.

I should go. Lucas needed her, perhaps even now. What help could she be here?

Another man ran from the house, this one completely naked.

Gasps erupted from those who watched from a distance and the girl covered her face with her hands.

Daria watched the door. Some kind of fighting still went on within. "How many have gone into the house?"

"Seven." She dug her hands through her hair, pulling it away from her head until she looked half-mad herself. "The seven sons of Sceva."

"Sceva?"

The girl's eyes turned on her as though Daria were the lunatic. "You are not a Jew, then? You do not know the chief priest?"

"I am new to Ephesus."

Another scream, more breaking of furniture, perhaps the breaking of men.

The girl's chest heaved. "The priest's sons are said to be able to drive the spirits out."

"How long has he been like this?"

"Five weeks. Since the day the killings began again."

Daria's stomach knotted. What was happening in this city?

Another clot of men burst from the doorway. A quick count revealed that the remaining five sons had been expelled, bleeding and torn.

And then he was there, in the doorway. The husband-turned-monster. And the poor girl at her side cried out, then covered her lips with stiff fingers and closed her eyes.

The crowd in the street moved back once more with a collective moan. Daria did not move, did not breathe. She could not take her eyes from the sight.

The "healers" collected themselves in the center of the street and faced him. He staggered forward, eyes bulging and fingers curled like tentacles. He was tall but bent, and wore only a loincloth, with a bloated belly hanging over the grimy rag.

"Aaagggghhhhh!"

The sound, issuing forth from cracked lips, froze the blood and thrust visions of the underworld into the imagination, but still Daria stood fixed in place. A deep and stunning connection reached from within her, across the empty street to the tortured man, and a violent nausea twisted her body.

He slithered into the street, toward the failed exorcists, toward Daria and his wife. Daria watched his movements, as if unnaturally slowed. Watched those fingers reaching, reaching.

The huddle of men shivered in the street. The monster circled them and laughed.

"You come at me with names you do not know!"

His wife gasped and her head shook violently. She searched out Daria's eyes, gripped her arm with stony fingers. "Not his voice." Her hand trembled against Daria's skin. "He speaks with a voice not his own."

Still circling, still laughing, he shouted again, "Jesus I acknowledge, and I know of this Paul." He raised a wicked hand and jabbed a pointed finger at the men. "But who are *you*?"

With a leap he jumped at them, grabbed the hair of the closest man, and clubbed at him with an arm that seemed to have foreign strength to match the voice.

They fled, all of them, and he stood cackling in the center of the street.

Then he whirled and fixed his attention on his wife who still gripped Daria's arm.

Run. I should run. And yet she did not. Wrapped in an unnamed horror Daria felt herself step toward him, pulled in the way the crowd had been pulled toward the temple.

What was happening to her? The air around him was foul with the unwashed smell of him, and she was close enough to see

117

yellowish fluid drain from a boil on his neck. Her nausea surged and she clamped her lips against her teeth.

And then there was a shadow, something that passed between them and broke the connection. Daria sucked lungs full of air and put out a steadying hand.

It was a man, another man had come between them and faced her now. She looked into concerned brown eyes, the clean-shaven jaw of youth, full lips pulled into a frown. He had turned his back on the demon, this young man, which did not seem like a good idea.

But his attention was on her. "You must step back."

A fuzzy confusion fogged her mind and she did not answer.

He put his hands on her arms—where was the young wife?— and walked forward, nudging her backward as he walked, until her heels tapped the stone walkway at the edge of the street.

"Step up." The command was given kindly, and all the while he did not take his gaze from her eyes. She stepped, and they were on the sidewalk, in the shade of the colonnade. A pressure she had not realized was present suddenly lifted. Her shoulders dropped, her limbs felt like water. She moved to stand beside her rescuer and watch the scene she'd left in the street. Beside her a crippled woman hunched against a stone column and stared at the two men.

The wife was gone, and another man, this one older, had approached the madman. The two faced off like wrestlers in a gymnasium. The second man was shorter, stockier than his opponent, and as he circled, the light played against his face.

There was something familiar . . . Yes, he was the man she'd met in the street, not far from this spot, when she had been watching the School of Tyrannus. The man who was neither young nor old, who spoke so strangely about sanctuaries. She had thought him a teacher, but he wore the apron of a tradesman over his tunic today, its strings flapping loose at his sides.

She started forward. "I should find the girl—"

Her companion grabbed her shoulders and pulled her back against his chest. A head taller than she, he growled into her ear. "This is not your fight."

"And that one man is going to do what seven others could not?"

"These are things you do not understand."

She jerked her head upward to study his face. "Do not assume me ignorant!"

At this he gave a little smile, then lifted his eyes to the street. "Watch."

The demon-bound man lunged at the shorter one, swiped at the ties of his apron, and missed. The tradesman yanked the cloth from his body, balled it up, and threw it from himself.

Strangely, the crippled woman at Daria's side stumbled forward. Daria reached to catch her, but the woman was not falling—she was running, as best she could, into the street. Daria's rescuer held her back, preventing her from stopping the woman, who hobbled across the stones, snatched up the fallen apron, and clutched it to her chest. She then shuffled toward the crowd.

Did she walk straighter? Did her shoulders lift and her spine straighten, and did she walk erect and smooth by the time she disappeared into the crowd, still clutching the cast-off apron? A chill ran through Daria, prickling her skin and stealing her breath. She looked to the young man who still held her arm, but his eyes were on the two still circling in the street. It had happened so quickly. Had she imagined it?

The beastly man was mocking the newcomer. He called out curses and heaped insults on him, from his balding head to his worn sandals. "Another fool come to try to best me?"

The older man stepped closer, held out a palm. "And I thought I heard that you knew me."

At this, the fiend straightened a bit, eyes wary, and his guttural voice hissed through the street. "Speak your name, little man."

"My name is Paul of Tarsus. But I come in the name of One much greater. And it is He who comes to set you free."

14

DANK ODORS OF EARTH AND SLIME AND BRACKISH water wrapped themselves around Lucas and constricted his breath in the narrow stairwell that plunged below Hektor's shop. An incessant dripping from unknown corners irritated, and the closeness of the walls as he slid downward nearly scraped his shoulders.

His feigned task for Demetrius at the temple would wait. He had agreed, only to stall the man's blackmail. He had no intention of following his orders. The sect Demetrius would have him betray seemed harmless. And even if their beliefs were strange, they were good people. Unlike those he would find down here. He'd meet with them, perhaps warn them of Demetrius's ire.

But first he needed to weave the next strand in his tapestry of deceit and take advantage of the entry Numa had gained him to the enclave that met below the shop. Only there would he find the proof he needed to exact justice. The need for it was like pain in his gut, tempting him to rash behavior, taunting him with accusation.

The stairs opened to a shockingly vast underground hall. Oily torches, thrust into blackened sockets and coating the skin and tongue with residue, burned at erratic lengths along two walls, illuminating rat-chewed mats on the floor.

Around the edges of the hall, in corners too dark to see and at tables littered with strange accoutrements and piled with scrolls, a dozen or more men worked in silence or muted conversation. The information he'd gained in Rhodes earned him access, but he would not yet be welcome.

Lucas slowed his rush at the bottom of the stairs, breathed out the stench, and kept his lungs empty as long as bearable before closing his eyes and sucking in required air. How could anyone grow accustomed to such a smell?

"Lucas." Hektor spoke from the shadows, the unnatural white of his long hair and glow of his eyes all that was visible. He drifted toward Lucas but did not extend his hands in greeting. Did not look pleased. "Numa said you might be coming."

"I wanted to see how your work progresses." Lucas's voice sounded too loud, filled up too much of the room.

Hektor bent to a dingy mat where a young woman lolled in seeming leisure, eyes half-closed and features placid. He ran light fingers over her brow, smoothed the hair from her face. "There is much to do, much to learn, Lucas. We keep very busy."

"You know I seek only to help."

"Yes. Well." Hektor flicked a glance again around the room. "You understand our need for privacy. Some of the others are unhappy that I have allowed you here at all, opened our secrets to you. It is critical that our . . . *work* remain unknown."

"I have as much cause as any to pursue understanding."

"Your friend also seems a pursuer of knowledge."

Lucas narrowed his eyes. "Friend?"

"The woman in my shop a few days ago. New to the city, she said. Very meticulous in speech and dress. She said she was a friend of yours."

Lucas's jaw tightened and he resisted the urge to strike a fist against the wall. "Idle curiosity on her part, nothing more. She is harmless." Though she was likely to come to harm with her cursed need to uncover secrets.

Hektor laughed, cool and musical. "Oh, I would guess she is far from harmless. Any woman with that much intelligence . . . Lucas, you must understand that the others are not quite . . . trusting."

Lucas rolled his shoulders. Hektor was his social inferior and his smugness deserved to be struck from his face. "So make them understand that our goals are the same."

Hektor smiled and looked away. "I very much doubt that."

"You think I do not need answers? Would not do anything—?"

"Yes, it was a terrible tragedy what they did to your wife. The others understand. But vengeance makes a man careless, and we must have nothing but prudence and discretion here."

The woman at Lucas's feet moaned in pain or pleasure—he could not tell—and he forced his attention elsewhere, to that infernal dripping that could drive a man insane.

The place weighted a man with unnamed dread, and no amount of physical strength, of rash bravery, could fight against the power resident here under Hektor's shop. A power Hektor claimed to understand, to harness for his own purposes.

"I understand discretion, Hektor." He kept a tight rein on his anger and pushed toward the back of the hall.

"Numa." Lucas nodded to the city tax collector who held a flattened scroll against the table beside a tiny clay lamp.

"Lucas." Numa straightened and let the scroll furl. "I hear you brought back something of interest from Rhodes. Decided you're not too old to learn something new, eh?"

Lucas forced a tight smile and waved a hand at the piles of scrolls. "I thought it might be helpful to learn the language of the spells."

Numa pursed his lips, and beside Lucas, Hektor appeared and examined Numa's work.

The tax collector lifted his chin, studied Lucas through half-slit eyes. "It is a great gift, what we've received from the East. Many centuries of understanding, of experimenting."

"Indeed."

"And you have been given a gift." Numa's glance went to Hektor. "To be allowed to see some of the work we do."

The condescension scraped at his raw nerves. "I would join you in your work."

"Yes. Yes, I know. Your wife."

At this second reference, Lucas's gut twisted. The claustrophobic pressure of the slimy cavern bore down on his rage. He must rein in the anger. Never let them know that he held *them* responsible and no one else. He eyed the instruments on the table—metal objects that could jab and slash and eviscerate—and his fingers twitched in response.

Numa followed his glance. "You wish to begin now?"

"What would you have me do?"

Numa took a thin blade from the table and flicked across it with his thumb as if to determine its abilities. He indicated one of the women on the floor with a tilt of his head. "She is feverish. She needs to be bled."

Lucas took the knife in his right hand, turned it over twice, feeling the cold beauty of it. Without a word he bent to the woman, studied her tear-swollen face, ran firm fingers down the length of one arm, then the other.

Hektor and Numa returned to their former pursuits, leaving him alone with the woman. Pity overtook him. Even though she had done this to herself, coming here to this place for answers and finding only questions. The room full of sorcerers offered spiritual ecstasy for a price, spells to bring on love and destruction, health and disease, wealth and poverty. Everyone wanted what they could give, and those who could pay found their way here. Sometimes the cost was greater than they had meant to pay. But still, they came. As he had.

As she had.

That monotonous sound of water—it trickled against his ears and into his mind—*drip, drip, drip.*

His grip on the knife tightened, and the girl on the tattered mat beneath him stared with vacant, puffy eyes that slid back and forth, unseeing.

The pain and bitterness were like a venom inside, like the fever in this girl. He wanted to cut it out, to slash it into the open.

He jammed the knife into the worn mat and dragged it downward. The fabric ripped open, bled straw and bits of feathers. The damage gratified, but only for a moment. He eyed her arm, the pulsing spot where it bent inside the elbow.

"How much?"

"Eh?" Numa half turned, lips parted as though he had forgotten Lucas, surprised by the question.

"How much blood?"

Numa thrust a small dish at him. "Fill this. And be careful. We don't need another one—"

Hektor's throat clearing stopped Numa's instruction. He shrugged and returned to his work.

If the girl felt the pain of the incision, she bore it well. Lucas held the clay dish under her elbow, let the blood run in tiny rivers and drip into the bowl.

She was about Daria's age, perhaps. Daria, whom Numa had mentioned. Why had Lucas not kept her better hidden? His selfish act would ruin her. He was not to be trusted, and this he had known since the alley in Rhodes. He had brought her anyway, like a balm purchased in a market to soothe an angry wound.

But a soothing balm would not draw out venom. Venom must be pulled out, cut out, bled out, or it would kill.

The bowl was full. Lucas set it aside, found a rag, and tied the girl's arm to staunch the flow. But he did not rise.

The knife was back in his hand, cool and comforting. Perhaps he needed to bleed. To suffer in his body the way he suffered in his mind. If he hurt physically, perhaps it would relieve the other, deeper pain.

He slid the blade along the inside of his own arm, watched the line of bright-red blood chase the tip. It dripped from his arm like the water dripped everywhere in this cursed place.

And it did no good.

He returned the knife and bowl to Numa's table, found another rag to tie around his own arm, and left the crypt without speaking.

The temple area would be getting crowded. It was time to play the other side of the game. Perhaps he would fail. Perhaps he would be destroyed. But he owed a debt and it must be paid.

15

DARIA WATCHED HIS EYES, ALWAYS HIS EYES. THE eyes were the place where the evil shone out most plainly, like dirty water leaking from chinks in a clay pot.

The man possessed by spirits of evil stumbled backward at the words of the man who called himself Paul. He thrust hands rigid with tension between them and fixed his eyes on the smaller man.

Daria glanced up the street, to the crowd pushing toward the temple. How long before Lucas completed whatever he had set out to do? To see this tortured man, on her way to spy on Lucas, was like a prophecy, an omen. Writing itself on the face of the man, in the air, in her heart. This was what could happen when you got too close.

But he was not avoiding evil, this man Paul. He was nudging

ever closer, his face creased with a smile that spoke compassion without fear. How was such a thing possible?

Paul reached his own hands toward the man, stepped closer. "I come to bring you peace."

Half-stooped and wild-eyed, yet there was something else—a longing shining out of those eyes, from behind the bitterness, deeper, but not stronger than it.

He wanted to be free.

Paul grasped the outstretched claws in his own hands, pulled the man toward his own chest, until they were face-to-face.

The nausea rose again in Daria's throat. Too close. She was too close.

Paul was whispering. What words, at such a time?

And then, as though the sky had opened and poured crystal-clear water down upon him, washing him from tangled hair to dirty feet, the man's appearance began to transform.

Like the crippled woman walking upright into the crowd.

It was not imagination, not trickery. Daria's breath caught in her throat.

His body lengthened, straightened. Muscles relaxed, shoulders drooped. Chest—filling with clean air. Chin lifted. His eyes fluttered closed, and when they opened again, the wildness had gone out from them, like a deep thirst finally quenched.

His smile was slow in coming, as though he had forgotten those muscles, had to call the memory back from the dark, but it shone full upon Paul at last. And then the man fell on Paul's neck in an embrace shuddered by weeping.

Daria put a hand to the nearby column, released the hold on her breath, a desire to weep surging through her body.

Was he a sorcerer, this Paul? Who else could produce such magic? Yet when did sorcerers ever draw the evil *out* of a man?

Whatever secret he held—she wanted to know it, had to know it.

To be able to defeat evil rather than avoid. To draw close and not be destroyed. If it were possible, it could change everything.

The nausea had fled. In its place, a deep and settled calm.

From the crowd, the young wife ran forward, stopped, ran again.

Paul pulled away, invited the woman into her husband's embrace, then glanced around until his gaze fell on the young man beside Daria who had dragged her from the street.

The restored one caught his wife in his arms, cupped her face with his palms, kissed her eyes and cheeks and lips within full view of all who witnessed.

Paul approached the sidewalk quickly, peered at Daria through narrowed eyes. "A second meeting is not of chance, I do not believe. No, there is more in this." He glanced at her companion. "Timothy, is she an acquaintance of yours?"

"No, Teacher. I only brought her out of the street a moment ago."

Teacher. But tradesman also?

"How did you heal him?" Her voice shook a bit with the overwhelming desire for answers and she inhaled against the tremor. "You have great power—"

Paul held up a palm and made a little sound of rebuke with his tongue behind his teeth. "There is power at work, my dear, but it does not reside in me. Only acts through me."

The street crowd was surging once again, past the couple in the street who still embraced in tears and laughter, toward the temple and its festival activities.

She watched the flow, watched the jumbled confusion of multicolored tunics and heads and bare arms pressing forward.

Her gaze darted left and right, searching for a familiar figure. She hated to leave her new acquaintance, but if she waited longer, she might never find Lucas, never discern his motives. "I must go. There is someone I must find."

Beside her the young man, Timothy, chuckled, "You will have a time of it, I fear."

Paul patted her arm. "Walk with us, child. We are going that way."

She bit her lip but then nodded. Her limbs had grown stiff again with the thought that Lucas might have already passed out of the reach of her help.

Paul walked a little ahead, but Timothy seemed content to be at her side. People rushed in and out of Paul's presence, some begging for blessing, others muttering curses.

"Who is he?" Daria half turned to Timothy. "He is both loved and hated."

"Are not all teachers both?" He gave a shy smile, his gaze trained toward his feet.

"I have never seen a teacher who could do what he did."

Timothy did not answer, and she glanced again at his profile as they walked. He was about her age and exceedingly attractive. Skin a bit sun-darkened and brown hair lit by yellowish lights. And something more, something joyous about him, as though he carried the peace his mentor Paul had spoken of.

She wished she had some of it. Instead, the swelling of the crowd as they drew closer to the temple matched her increased concern, and the jumpy, anxious tenor of the people tightened her chest.

She pointed ahead, to Paul's back, with another question. "He is not Greek?"

"Jewish. Once a former teacher of the law in Jerusalem."

"And you? Are you Jewish as well?"

"My mother is a Jewess. My father was Greek."

Ah, an explanation for his beauty—the best of both cultures had found their way into his features.

"We have been in Ephesus nearly three years. Paul teaches the way of the One True God."

"Yes, I am familiar with the Jews' strange insistence on only one."

"He also teaches that the One God has made Himself known in His Messiah—Jesus of Nazareth." The words were delivered hesitantly, with a sideways glance as if to watch her reaction.

She kept her gaze flitting across the heads of the crowd, still searching for the one face she needed to find, but creased her brow. "The Jews seem to claim a new Messiah as often as the tide rolls in." Too late, she closed her eyes, regretting the insulting comment.

Timothy smiled. "Yet only One releases men from all that keeps them in bondage."

She studied him, the way he spoke so confidently, with that wonderful stillness. A stillness that rippled outward from him and might include her if she allowed it. Would that she could wrap up this moment, shut everything else out, and believe his beautiful words.

"Such teaching must make enemies here among pious Greeks."

His face grew grim. "It is only a matter of time, I fear. The powers of the evil one are gathering like storm clouds on the horizon." His gaze went to Paul, still walking ahead. "He so much desires to keep safe those who follow the Way. But I fear it is not to be."

Ahead, the Temple of Artemis could no longer be ignored. Rising on the plain, even the long grasses outside the sacred precinct bowed their feathery heads toward the goddess, and the air seemed hushed of birdsong. A far-off singing, perhaps of priestesses, drifted down to them in their ascent. The road they traveled to reach the temple was joined by other paths from the city and surrounding plain, and the crowds pouring upward seemed endless.

She pulled in a shaky breath. So many. More worshippers than stars in the zodiac. How was she ever to find Lucas in this chaos?

"I must go faster." She muttered it under her breath, looked for a gap to push through.

Timothy touched her arm. "This crowd can get unruly. I would not have you aggravating the situation with undue haste."

"You don't understand. There is someone I must find."

Timothy scanned the people swarming toward the massive temple above them. "Where is this person?"

"I don't know." She searched her memory. "Near the stoa, perhaps. I do not know the temple area. Perhaps there is more than one."

He nodded once, in that unruffled way of his. "Come."

And then the gap she had wished for opened in his wake. They weaved past Paul, whose only response was a slight twitch of the eyebrows, and moved toward the temple.

They passed under the massive double-arched gateway announcing one's passage out of the profane and walked the Sacred Way, the paved route that marked the processional path toward the huge open-air altar at the base of the temple's steps.

A small grove of trees lay just inside the gateway, the low-hanging branches of each tree hung with small terra-cotta figurines, an offering to the goddess that now drifted and clinked together in the morning breeze. A cacophony of praise.

The temple was oriented east so the rising sun shafted into the temple's interior, lit the larger-than-life statue of the goddess at the back of the first chamber. Positioned this way, Artemis would have full view of the offerings and sacrifices dedicated on the main altar outside. Gold plating covered the wall behind that statue, and Daria turned her eyes from the blinding glint to the cluster of smaller buildings that lay along the south side of the temple— both the treasury and more practical structures like kitchens and dining areas.

It was like a small city unto itself, the temple and its out-buildings, the citizens and priests milling about, farmers selling sacrifices at long tables and merchants offering replicas of the shrine and figurines of Artemis made from clay, wood, or silver. Artemis in all sizes, but always with her legs and feet of a solid piece and her upper body covered with those ghastly bulbous protrusions.

"Antipater was right."

Timothy glanced back over his shoulder. "Who?"

"Antipater, one of Alexander's Macedonian generals. He wrote, 'I have gazed on the walls of impregnable Babylon along which chariots may race, and on the Zeus by the banks of the Alpheus, I have seen the hanging gardens, and the Colossus of the Helios, the great man-made mountains of the lofty pyramids, and the gigantic tomb of Mausolus. But when I saw the sacred house of Artemis that towers to the clouds, the others were placed in the shade, for the sun himself has never looked upon its equal outside Olympus.'"

Timothy had slowed and turned, listening to her speech with parted lips. "You are better educated about the temple than most."

She scanned the plateau. "Nothing like this magnificent structure exists in Rhodes. It takes one's breath away."

And yet they could only offer a passing glance to the hundred gleaming columns supporting the massive architraves. The crowd dragged at them, pulled them backward from their mission. She kept her arms wide, creating her own passage behind Timothy.

Ahead, a little girl lost her grip on her mother's hand and the crowd separated them in a moment. The mother's wide eyes appeared above a beaked nose, then vanished, appeared again between the heads and shoulders of others.

To her left, the little girl cried out. Daria slowed, glanced back at the girl.

She had been knocked to the ground. No one seemed to care, or even notice. The crowd teemed past the child like a river rushing past a pebble, and the girl drew her knees to her chin and bent her head to protect herself.

Timothy was disappearing ahead, unaware she had stopped.

Daria exhaled and moved against the current, using sharp elbows and stiff arms to reach the girl, who lifted her head to reveal hair cut crookedly across her forehead and missing front teeth. "Do you want me to take you to your mother?"

The girl's face was already dirtied with tears and her lip quivered.

Daria sighed and picked her up, searching the crowd now for a different face.

There. The mother's gaze found Daria's, and Daria held the daughter's arm aloft. The two were reunited with a hug and then a scolding and no thanks for Daria.

She pushed onward.

Timothy's concerned expression, appearing ahead, stilled her shaking limbs.

"What happened?"

"It is not important. Are we nearly there?"

"The Northern Stoa is just ahead. I know it well. Paul comes here often to teach whatever small groups will gather to hear."

A niggling suspicion entered her mind, but she pushed it away. She needed to find Lucas. Figure out how to set things right before it was too late.

Timothy pulled her to the left, toward the stoa that ran along the north side of the temple, beyond its steps. The covered portico, lined with columns, was less crowded than the plain surrounding the temple. More came for sacrifices and festivities than for philosophy today.

"Here." Timothy pulled her into the stoa's shade to stand beside a thick column.

They watched the tide of man flow past and Daria tried to slow her breathing, increased by the hasty climb and by a sudden nervous thought that Lucas might be furious to find her here.

"If he was to meet you in the Northern Stoa, this is where he would come."

There was no point in a better explanation. "Thank you, Timothy. You do not need to stay—"

But he was smiling at her, head tilted, in a way that bespoke amusement and concern. "I will wait."

There was nothing more frustrating than waiting after rushing to arrive. Was this even the place? Would he come? Her hands twisted at her waist and she pressed a thumb against her palm. The day grew warmer, but still a damp chill teased the back of her neck.

Angry shouts erupted at the base of the temple steps, near one of the smaller altars. Daria stood on her toes, rocked left and right for a better look. She could see nothing.

"No." Timothy's hand was on her arm again, holding her back. She had barely realized she was moving toward the fray.

"Stay here."

"But it might be him!"

Timothy's eyes betrayed suspicion that the one she sought to meet might be in the midst of whatever tumult was happening out there.

She turned her gaze back to the glut of people on the steps.

But then he was there. Striding toward them, toward the stoa, head bent in concentration. As if he sensed her presence, his head jerked upward and he halted, still swaying in his charge. "Daria!" His glance went to her companion and his eyes shot sparks. "What are you doing with *him*?"

Daria looked between the two men. Obvious recognition. Timothy's smile was less sure, placating even. Lucas's scowl could have incinerated dry leaves.

But she did not care. The unbearable tension of the past hours released in a rush, leaving her drained, fatigued. Relieved.

Timothy held out a palm, as if to pacify. "Your friend was searching for you. I merely helped her find the place—"

"I told you I wanted to see the temple today, my lord."

He marched the remaining distance to the stoa, crossed under its roof, and thrust himself between Timothy and her. "And I told you it was unsafe."

She lifted her chin. "You do not own me."

"Yes, well, perhaps someone should. Clearly you cannot take adequate care of yourself!"

"Listen, Lucas—" Timothy's voice seemed so youthful, eager to please.

But Lucas shoved a hand against his chest. "You will have nothing more to do with her. Do you understand?"

Timothy's lips compressed, but in resignation more than anger. "Very well."

Lucas took her elbow in his tight grip. "We are leaving."

She should have protested. Should have insisted on seeing the temple. But to leave would mean that whatever deed he had come to carry out would go unfulfilled.

Unless he had already done it. But no, he would not be only now approaching the stoa. She had come in time.

"Thank you, Timothy." She smiled at the young man. "You have been most kind."

At this, Lucas jerked her forward, off the stoa's platform. She glanced back at Timothy, who wore a frown of concern but said nothing.

"You are being rude, my lord."

He barreled into the crowd, still pulling her. "I do not need you to instruct me in social niceties."

She planted her feet and yanked her arm from his grasp. "It appears that you do!"

He turned fiery eyes on her, stepped close, and spoke through clenched teeth. "I believe that since you arrived, you have not once followed my instructions."

"I am only trying to help—"

He grabbed her arms, pulled her even closer, and for a moment it seemed he would embrace her there on the Sacred Way with the sweaty crowds pressing against them. She held her breath, watched his eyes, tried to still her voice.

"Why did you come here, my lord?"

The moment broke. He released her, turned away, and continued down the hill. "It is not your concern."

She followed. "You have met Timothy? Do you also know his teacher, the man called Paul?"

Lucas whirled, his face a storm of emotion. "What do you know of Paul?"

Daria walked past him, continuing on. "Only that he has great power."

"Do not get involved with him, Daria. It could be dangerous."

"Dangerous? They seem quite the opposite. Have they hurt someone you know?"

The muscles in his jaw bulged and he did not answer.

"Your wife?"

They had reached the road back into the city now, and here the press of people thinned, most of them already passed. Lucas strode along the crumbled edge of the road, and Daria hurried to keep pace.

"Did she get involved—?"

"Enough!"

Daria chewed her lip. She was getting nowhere. What would he do if she asked again why he had gone to the temple? He spoke of danger. Might it extend to her?

"Shouldn't you just go to the magistrates with what you know? What if there is another killing? Wouldn't you feel responsible—?"

At the look he turned on her she decided perhaps silence was her best choice. For now.

He moved so quickly down the Embolos, she could barely stay with him. But each time she lagged, he seemed to sense it and turned, waiting with crossed arms or an angry frown, as if she were a recalcitrant child.

At the hillside leading up to his estate, he took the steps two at a time, as if only the morbid sanctuary of his home would relieve his anxiety.

She followed him into the dark interior, and he disappeared into the gloomy hall without a word, to the brooding withdrawal that seemed a frequent response.

She watched him go and sighed. The morning had been exhausting. But had it been successful? Hungry, she made her way to the kitchen. Frona stood over the fire, stirring a pot full of something. The old woman half turned at Daria's entrance, her eyes vacant.

"You have been out."

"Yes. I went to the temple. I hadn't seen it since arriving."

"What did the master think of that?"

"The master seems little inclined to be pleased with anything I do."

"Aye." She lifted her spoon, tapped it against the lip of the pot, and crossed to a worktable. "He'll take no pleasure in the likes of you, I daresay. Or much else."

"Since his wife's death?"

Again there was that look of resentment mixed with condescension. Frona rubbed at a place on her chest, just below her throat. "It was a horror. The . . . brutality—"

Daria found a loaf of bread and pulled a hunk from its end. She must be casual. Too many questions would stop Frona's mouth. "Yes, I'm sure it was very hard to hear."

"Hear? Harder to see. The way they tore up her body. Still dying when he found her."

Daria's hand stopped midway to her mouth. "She was murdered, then? And Lucas was there?"

But the woman's cold and empty look cut her off. "I will not speak of it further. You should see about your duties."

Daria drifted from the kitchen, chewing slowly. So Lucas's wife did not die a natural death. His reaction to another killing the morning after her arrival became clear. But who had murdered his wife?

Frona had sent her to "her duties," but Lucas would not call for her today, not in his present mood. She had only one obligation, and that was to herself.

It was time to learn more about Lucas's dead wife.

16

"WE SHOULD SPEND THE MORNING ON LESSONS, NOT escaping the city." Daria shifted her position in the horse-drawn cart, pulling away from Lucas.

"What is this? The tutor is not curious to see everything for a hundred miles around?" He flicked the reins over the back of the mare as the massive Aqueduct of Pollio came into view, with the entire Marnas River spanned by a single arch and two more arches alongside incorporating the road and filling the gorge.

Daria bit her lip and studied the top of the aqueduct, its second tier of six smaller arches impossibly high above the road. "You should not tease." Her voice drifted at the thought of what Lucas had proposed. "It is my curiosity that taught me five languages and brought me to Ephesus."

He laughed and directed the horse to a pull off near the river's edge. "Very well. I shall give you your curiosity. But you must admit that you would love to see the city from that height." He pointed to the top level, the smaller arches nearly dainty from this distance.

"I would rather live to see you learn Persian."

Lucas dismounted from the cart first, then took her hand.

She stepped to the muddy ground. The tree-covered hill to their right shaded the road here, leaving the ground sloshy with runoff from the river.

Lucas's continued dodging of their planned lessons was becoming habit. He seemed more eager to escape his house, and even the city, than he did to learn. When he had suggested this outing after the morning meal, Daria had sighed with frustration.

"Ah, the impatient sigh of the thwarted tutor." Lucas had laughed.

And it had been good to see him laugh. Good enough that she had agreed to this mad plan. They would climb the forested hill for the view from the aqueduct that supplied Ephesus with water.

Daria was still staring at that line of arches.

Lucas poked her arm. "Well? Do you intend to climb the hill, or shall I carry you on my back?"

"You wouldn't dare!"

He grinned. "No, of course not. I fear you would be much too heavy."

Daria narrowed her eyes but smiled. Yes, it was good to see him laugh.

She took a deep breath for courage. The air here was different. Removed from the city and the sea, with a freshness that filled the lungs with something pure.

And purity was in rare supply in Ephesus. After her journey to the temple and Lucas's angry reaction, Daria had wondered if her plan was hopeless. Perhaps Lucas's preoccupation with revenge had already so colored his spirit that she could do nothing for him.

But out here, away from the city, it was as if the Lucas she had met in Rhodes had reemerged. Could she help him cling to this other man, even after they returned?

She followed a worn track upward through the trees. It would seem the aqueduct drew visitors out of the city as faithfully as it delivered water into it.

"I should have brought the primer we started with. We could have had our lesson in the open air today."

From close at her back, Lucas huffed. "Leave off the lessons for today, woman. Enjoy the countryside."

It took half of an hour's time to reach the top, crisscrossing over fallen logs and skirting fern-filled gullies. They cleared the trees at the top of the hill, where only the level of smaller arches spanned, leading down to the next valley where the larger arches would supply the gap below. Daria kept her gaze trained on her feet.

"Right there." Lucas pointed past her to a narrow set of steps built into the stone. "That will take us to the top."

"Can we not simply enjoy the view from the hill here?" She glanced toward the Marnas River below but looked no farther.

Lucas wrapped a hand around her arm and turned her to himself. "You are truly afraid?"

She snorted. "Anyone with sense would be frightened to climb out on that narrow ledge, perched like a bird on a limb."

"Then why did you come?"

She looked away. "Because you asked."

He was silent a moment and she did not look at him.

"Come, Daria. It is not so narrow. You will see. Trust me, and take a little risk."

She had despised looking down from great heights since she was a child. The sight always caused a queasy swaying in her belly and irrational thoughts of jumping, soaring, plunging.

She let him lead her up the steps, then along the man-made ridgeline.

The light gray of the stonework gleamed in the sun, and a channel of water ran alongside a walkway cut slightly higher than the water.

Lucas stood at her side. "We will have to jump the water to the walkway so we can go farther down, over the river."

Daria's stomach flipped in protest, but she said nothing. She had come this far.

Lucas nodded. "I'll jump first."

It looked to be a simple leap. The water channel was no more than two cubits across, perhaps. And not particularly deep. But it was the height of their position that made her heart thud the warning she was about to ignore.

From the other side, Lucas reached out a hand, too far for her to grasp. "You saw how easily it was done. Come."

She studied his eyes, his hand. He would not let her fall. She jumped.

Landing with an expelled breath and a scuffling of sandaled feet, she felt Lucas's arm around her waist, solid and protecting.

"There," he whispered into her ear, "was that so difficult?"

They followed the walkway along the water, Lucas leading over the gorge below until they reached the center.

He turned and pointed to the opposite side of the stone trough, across the water channel, where only a narrow wall separated the water from empty space. "Time to jump back over so we can sit on the edge of the wall, with our legs dangling."

"Wh—you—I will not—"

But he was laughing again. "Perhaps we should stay on this side."

Daria turned to face the city and leaned against the wall at her back, arms folded. "You are going to be the death of me, simply with terror."

"Hmm. We cannot have that." He edged closer, and she felt the slight slant of the edifice, the way it seemed to lean his body toward hers. "So close your eyes a moment. Listen and tell me what you hear."

She did as he asked, letting her fear fall away, focusing on the stillness. "Birdcalls. The water running at our feet. Nothing else."

"Exactly."

She opened her eyes to find him staring over the open air before them, down toward the city that webbed the plain with strands of streets and alleys.

"From here you can only see the beauty. No stench, no grime." His voice was low and thoughtful.

"No memories?"

He inhaled deeply. "No memories." Then he turned to her with a smile. "Or perhaps new ones."

Daria bent to let her fingers trail through the water, let it run its cool passage over her hand. "Strange to think that this very same water will pass into the city, spurt up from fountains." She looked up at him. "Running water is a symbol of life. You should have your fountain repaired."

He sniffed and looked to the city once more. "Indeed."

She stood and dried her fingers on her chitôn, following his gaze. The hillside they had climbed seemed like a vegetable garden, sprouting clusters of greens in all variations, and the cool breeziness of the great height exhilarated, in spite of the fluttery fear in the pit of her stomach. The promised panorama was indeed marvelous, with plain melding into city, city into blue seawater, and water fading to the white horizon.

She lifted her face to the sun, warmed it as the stones at her back were warmed. Lucas toed a rock along the water's edge, then picked it up and tossed it over the side of the wall. They waited, straining to hear it hit the river, and were rewarded with a satisfying *plunk*.

They stayed as the sun lowered and cooled, talking of subjects light and impersonal, with the occasional outrageous comment by Lucas intended to make her angry or to make her laugh, and sometimes both.

When the shadows grew long, Lucas declared the holiday at an end and led her back along the aqueduct, across the water channel, through the forest to the waiting horse contentedly munching weeds at the side of the road.

They rode in silence, and Daria had no desire to clutter the comfortable peace between them with chatter. By the time they reached the edge of the city, crickets were chirping accompaniment to their wheels on gravel and the moon was rising over the sea.

She had begun the day wondering whether it was too late to do any good here.

But tonight, drifting along the Embolos with Lucas at her side and the warmth of the afternoon still banked like a fire in her chest, it occurred to her that perhaps Lucas was not the only one in need of goodness.

17

LUCAS CLOSED HIMSELF WITHIN THE CONFINES OF his sitting room, with only a near-empty lamp for company.

Perhaps it was here he should remain. Alone and apart from the world. Left to his thoughts and memories. He sat at his desk, still orderly in the wake of Daria's ministrations, and pressed the heels of his hands against his burning eyes.

He should not have taken her to the aqueduct. Better to remain distant, to leave things strained as they were after she had found him at the temple.

She had come, heaven help her. She had followed him to the temple, despite his instruction, out of that cursed need to know everything. Why could she not leave it alone?

And he had treated her cruelly. As though she erred, as though *she* were the one with the scarred heart and dark ambitions. When he saw her with the boy Timothy, the realization of the danger she might encounter drove his task from his mind, and he had run along to the estate like a child caught skipping lessons. But then today, overlooking the city from such a distance, it was as if none of it had happened.

Lucas lifted his head from his hands, rocked back against his chair, and watched the dying flame. Outside the sitting room the evening waned, and when the lamp expired he would be left in obscurity.

Should he continue? Avow himself of his path, regardless of the new addition to his household? Or could he absorb her goodness, like one of the sponges sold at the edge of the sea, let it heal him, rescue him from whatever gnawed at his soul?

But what if *she* was the sponge, taking in the bile that leaked from him? She was not safe here. Not with those eyes that questioned everything, that peered inside. Not safe with him. He had proven that once.

And it was more than a fear of corrupting Daria. All he had heard lately—the scandalous teaching that there was only one God and that the time of sacrifices had ended—urged him to release his need for vengeance to this God who supposedly cared. Yet all he learned of Hektor compelled him to do whatever it took to exact justice.

The lamp flickered and died, along with the day, but still he remained holed in his sitting room, examining his two paths, until voices in the courtyard roused him.

Demetrius had come, of course. It had only been a matter of time.

The door swished open and Lucas rose to his feet.

The man's lean figure was silhouetted in the doorway, and the absurd royal purple of his robe glistened with gold threads.

He laughed in the darkness, cool and low. "Are you a rat gone underground now, Lucas?"

Lucas shoved past him, out to the twilight courtyard, its central fountain silent. Even in the gloom, the garden had a friendlier air. Furrowed soil and tidy rows of plants. When had he last seen such order in this place?

He turned on the visitor. "What do you want, Demetrius?"

The metalsmith joined him slowly, gliding as though he were indeed imperial. "I need answers, my friend. The festival was an opportune time—"

"Some business arose that needed attending. I will find another time." Lucas crossed to the fountain, dipped a hand below its murky surface, patted the back of his neck with the chilled droplets.

Demetrius stood framed between two columns at the courtyard's edge. He curled a lip at Lucas's contact with the decaying fountain, took a step back from the taint, and smoothed his robe. "Yes, I've been informed of your *business*. Urgent tutoring, was it?"

Lucas dried his hand on his tunic, fury pounding a rhythm in his chest. "You have people watching me?" The accusation rose and echoed off the far walls.

Demetrius laughed, derisive and arrogant. "Of course."

"Listen to me, you smug toad." Lucas stalked to the man, brought his face a breath from his. "I have agreed to help with this scheme of yours, but I am not your hired hand." His chest expanded, hot and tight. Somewhere in the house Frona was cooking meat, and the smell left a sick and bitter taste in his mouth.

Demetrius leaned backward. "It is *your* hired hand that concerns me, Lucas. This new tutor seems more distraction than advantage." He ran his tongue over his lips. "Though she is a worthy distraction, I am sure."

Lucas shoved a flat hand against Demetrius's chest, fire burning along his veins. "Say no more about her, man."

"Ah, but this reaction is exactly why I must—"

"No more!" Had his voice taken on a feverish pitch? Did Daria lurk in the shadows even now, listening to him rage, understanding at last what sort of man he was?

"You play a dangerous game, Lucas."

He whirled and thrust a fist into the air. "Do you think I do not know this? It has been this way since we began."

"You did not have a beautiful scholar living in your house when we began."

"What difference does it make?"

"You cannot have both."

Lucas closed his eyes and let his head roll back on his shoulders. When had his muscles grown so tight?

Did Demetrius see into his soul as well? See that he was being carried to the juncture of two rivers, that he must choose and choose quickly, or the current would make his choice for him?

Demetrius stepped close behind and spoke in a tone both low and threatening. "I will contact you with a new time and place. See to it that your lessons do not interfere."

Lucas responded with a well-placed elbow thrust backward into Demetrius's middle.

The breath left the man's lungs with a *whoosh,* and he pulled back a fist to retaliate.

Lucas turned and caught his forearm in his larger, stronger grip and squeezed until he felt the fight go out of the man.

Demetrius's eyes smoldered.

"Get out, Demetrius. Before I take actions I may later regret."

The metalsmith crossed the courtyard, heaved a spiteful look over his shoulder, then disappeared into the entryway. The door slammed a moment later.

The chaos still churned inside him. Tossing Demetrius out had done nothing to alleviate the fragmentation of his mind. Black and white, dark and light, he was drawn and repulsed by both. The dissonance was like physical pain.

Pain that sought relief.

———

Lucas descended below Hektor's shop seeking both respite and answers. Never mind that the solace was to be found with those he most despised and the answers might annihilate his sanity.

"Lucas?" Hektor glided out of the shadows, past mats of girls in various states of ecstasy or agony. His white hair lay smooth along his shoulders and torchlight played along the fine-boned angle of his jaw. He reached a hand to Lucas and clasped his arm, warm but firm. His eyes were luminous in their intensity. "We were not expecting you."

"What is it you give them, Hektor?" Lucas pointed to a girl nearby, hair matted and stuck fast to her lips.

"Only what they want, Lucas." He spread his palms, inclined his head with a fatherly smile. "Only what they want."

"And if I wanted it?"

Hektor's eyebrows lifted, his full lips pursed. "Much of this is experimental."

Lucas eyed the girl's arm. Circular marks dotted the pale flesh. "Why the burns?"

Hektor's face looked on the girl with something akin to affection. "They only feel the pain for a moment. Then it sends them soaring—flying with the gods, looking down on this pitiful earth, which is why they come to me. To rise above the gods' control, to unlock their secrets, even gain their respect."

"And the potions? There are things you sell."

Hektor led him away from the girl, into a dark corner where the wall slimed and the invisible dripping echoed. "We offer spiritual experiences for a price, it is true. And there are certain— rituals—that can be counted upon to work effectively when the gods are unresponsive to the usual sacrifices and offerings."

"Spells, you mean? Incantations? For money?"

Hektor gave a slow, almost coy shrug of one narrow shoulder. "We have collected many books, as you know, that contain the wisdom of the ages. Can one put a price on such knowledge?"

"Try."

Hektor touched his arm again and leaned close. "What is it you are looking for, Lucas? Have the gods denied your desires? You wish us to draw favor your way?"

Lucas pointed again to the girl on the mat. "I wish to feel nothing."

"Ah." Hektor's smile was conspiratorial and he used slender fingers to smooth his hair. "That is another matter."

"But you will help?"

Hektor returned through the maze of women, toward the far end of the hall.

Lucas followed.

"These women do not feel nothing, Lucas. They are helping us to experience the true nature of the life of the spirit, see the unseen powers at work all around us." His eyes seemed to light with desire. "To seize forbidden knowledge from the gods them-selves and use it to break free of their tyranny. This knowledge is the very core of power."

"You wish to experience it yourself, do you not?"

Hektor inhaled slowly and his eyelids fluttered. "I have. I have experienced it all." He focused again on Lucas, his expression colder. "But it is sometimes better to be an objective observer. And the women"—he spread a hand to the mat-covered floor like a potter displaying his finest work—"they are often more sensitive, more intuitive than we men. Though of course they lack the intelligence to understand their experiences." He licked his lips and smiled. "Although your visiting friend would make a fine subject." His voice grew soft, velvety. "Oh, what I could do with that mind . . ."

"Show *me* what this knowledge is like."

Hektor raised an eyebrow, grazed Lucas with a look from head to foot. "Very well."

It was only a powder, this secret magic that would show him things he had never seen. Hektor ground it with a mortar and pestle, stirred it into an earthenware cup of tepid wine, and handed it to Lucas with a slight smile that seemed dubious of Lucas's courage.

He took the cup, swirled its dark contents, watched the firelight catch and sparkle. Would it taste like poison? Would it deliver all that Hektor promised?

Inhaling resolve, he put the cup to his lips, cool and rough, then drained it in one swallow and wiped his lips with the back of his hand.

Sometime later—was it weeks, or years, or perhaps he had died and gone to the underworld where time was no longer measured—Lucas studied the sky and its cold silver stars. How had he never noticed that he lived among those very stars in the vast black expanse, floating, floating with them, unnaturally large and cold?

Was he alone in the sky, only himself and the stars? Did no one else live here?

No, there were others. He could see them at the edges of his vision, though they disappeared when he turned his head to face them fully. He reached a hand to one of the yellow-gray shapes, tried to catch it before it passed.

It was rough, scaly even. He brushed its skin and it turned and let him see its face, its dark and snarling maw and yellow-bright eyes and a look of such hatred it turned his blood to ice.

But the vision evaporated as quickly as it appeared, melting into something soft and light, the vaguest outline of a woman's body, beautiful in its curves, inviting and warm.

It was like her, or the memory of her. Before she had been torn and mauled and gashed. Before he stood over her body with her blood on his hands, hearing the last gurgle of life in her throat, the last sigh before death.

And now the vision before him changed to *that* vision, that last memory of her, and he turned from it as he had done that night.

He was floating no longer. Sinking now, down, down into the slime of the earth and below the earth to someplace horrid and unknown, where clumsy, cold fingers snatched at his limbs and thick lips hissed at his ears.

He let the cold blackness cover him, let it extinguish thought and sensibility like a smothering, like a drowning.

Later, when awareness returned, it came sudden and hot, and Lucas jerked upright, swiveled his head left and right, took in surroundings both familiar and strange.

The agora.

He lay on the marble stones of the harbor agora, alone.

Was his mind shattering?

The visions hovered still. They were not hallucinations, not imaginings. He had seen the unseen, as Hektor had promised.

The powers and authorities that ruled the air, that had chosen this path for him.

He could not keep this tenuous hold on reason much longer. What he had done in the past, what he would do in the future, all of it melded into one huddled mass now. All those disparate parts of himself, the divergent and conflicting paths, all collapsed inward upon him. Around the agora, the world seemed hushed and silent, watching as though appalled at who he had become.

He wished to believe that Hektor was right, that man could control the gods. But what good was physical strength against these powers? What good was Daria?

She was not safe with him, true. But he would not give her up. His hands formed into fists, but the fury subsided in an instant.

In its place, a shame washed over him where he sat on the stones. He drew his knees to his chest, wrapped his arms around his legs, and wept.

18

DARIA SLIPPED FROM HER CHAMBER INTO THE darkened colonnade, one hand trailing the cool wall. It had been some minutes since the angry argument had ceased and the door had banged behind Lucas, but the courtyard still seemed to throb with his wrath. She had not heard the words, only the tone, but whatever he had gotten involved with was escalating.

The raised voices had drawn her from her chamber, but she shrank back when she saw that it was Demetrius, come again. Something about him disturbed her. And she did not want Lucas to believe she was prying into his affairs.

Although that was exactly what she was doing. Trying to understand him better, to understand *her* better, the wife he grieved, so she could encourage Lucas to do the right thing. Their time together today had been sweet. And yet his mood had quickly soured.

Was it safe to prowl the house now?

As long as Clovis and Frona kept to the lower floor.

She turned toward the steps that led to the second level, but a knocking at the door froze her steps. Lucas?

No, he would not knock at his own front door, of course. She retreated against the wall, kept to the shadows, waiting for Clovis to greet the arrival.

He shuffled there slowly, too slowly, with that heavy lean to the left. Would the stranger stay until he reached the door? But then she heard muffled voices of Clovis and another man, younger and more energetic. Her name mentioned. She lifted herself from the wall and waited for Clovis's appearance.

He was there in the gloom, plodding toward her chamber. She walked toward him, head down as if unaware.

"Someone to see you." He still would not use her first name, nor anything more formal.

She looked up, eyes wide. "To see me?"

"In the entryway. He says his name is Timothy. That you met yesterday." Condescension, disapproval even, saturated Clovis's voice.

"Thank you, Clovis. I will see him immediately."

"Perhaps you would like to invite him into the courtyard. I will light torches." The obliging words were not matched by his attitude.

"Thank you."

She hurried to the front door and found Timothy pacing.

He straightened when he saw her, his face breaking into a smile.

Daria shook her head. "How—why—?"

"I asked around. It didn't take long to learn that Lucas had brought a tutor back from Rhodes. He is always a topic of conversation somewhere."

This last she ignored and focused on his first comment. "Why did you ask about me?"

He grinned. "You seemed so . . . interested in Paul, in our work here in Ephesus. I thought perhaps you would like to know more." His smile faded and he took a step toward her. "More than that. You also seemed worried about something, fearful. I—I wanted to see if I could somehow help . . ." His voice trailed off and he looked down, a faint flush rising on his cheeks.

"You are kind, Timothy. Thank you for your concern." Daria extended a hand toward the courtyard. "Will you come in and sit for a while?"

His gaze snapped toward the atrium, then back to her. "Oh no. I couldn't. I only wanted to invite you to hear Paul's teaching tomorrow." He rubbed his palms together, as if they had grown damp. "Or any day, mostly, except the Sabbath. He teaches there most days."

"Where?"

"Oh—in the School of Tyrannus. It's not far—on the Embolos—"

"Yes, I know it."

"You do? Then you'll come?"

"I—I don't know. I would like to hear more of how your friend accomplished what he did in the street, with that man possessed by dark spirits."

"Yes, he will tell you all that, and more. He will tell you how the gods of the Greeks are nothing but falsity, or even demons themselves—"

"Timothy!" Daria looked left and right to ensure neither Clovis nor Frona had heard such blasphemy. She would take an offering to the temple herself tomorrow to negate any ill effects his words might have caused.

Timothy took her hands and squeezed her fingers. He smelled of honest labor, the scent of a leather worker. "Come to the school, Daria. Come and hear the truth."

His warm grip, his eyes shining with eagerness in the dark entryway, were like a balm to her friend-starved soul. She smiled and returned his grip. "Perhaps. Perhaps I will."

He nodded, opened his mouth as if to say more, but then shook his head. "I will watch for you."

And then he was gone, leaving her alone in the entryway with the warmth going out of the air too quickly and the task she had set herself still undone. How much longer before Lucas returned? Did she yet have time to explore the upper level?

Time or not, she would do it. She risked her new position, perhaps. But the truth, answers, must always be foremost. She had to know whether she could yet pull him back.

And if she was truthful with herself, she wanted to know more of the woman whose memory still tortured him, whose death had brought him to such grief he sometimes seemed unable to breathe.

With a glance to be certain the courtyard was yet empty, she took a lamp, burning on a column in the garden, and hurried to the stairs. She tried to take them slowly enough that the aged wood would not creak under her feet, despite the anxious pounding of her blood.

She reached the terrace where she and Lucas had looked over the night-covered city and spoken so intimately. Already it seemed long ago.

Keeping watch over the balcony's edge, she quickened her steps along the gallery, around to the west side of the house, and began looking into rooms, waving her lamp hand to reveal the interiors. Which room was theirs? Would she find anything of hers remaining?

A room at the end of the corridor beckoned with its closed door. Daria held the lamp aloft with a shaky hand, chest-high, and slipped to its threshold. She paused only a moment, then pushed the door open, thrust her lamp into the breach, and followed with her body. Then gasped.

The room was a thing of beauty, kept well-ordered and with no trace of a man's presence visible to her brandished lamp. She had expected a simple bedchamber, perhaps the slight touch of a female hand still remaining, but succumbing with each passing month to Lucas's chaotic spirit and jumbled possessions, flung-across furniture, perhaps, or piling against the corners.

She pushed farther into the chamber, eyes wide to accommodate the darkness.

A bed covered in sumptuous creamy-white fabric claimed the center of the room, and Daria ran light fingers along the covering, cool and smooth as silk from the East. Baskets of neatly folded garments lined the far wall, under what must be a large window, though it had been covered with a tapestry.

A flicker of lamplight in the corner startled her. It was only a tall bronze mirror on a wood frame, returning Daria's image and a reflection of her own lamp.

She drifted through the room, her small flame illuminating only tiny patches of the space at a time, the rest of the room a mystery. She waved the light past walls brimming with colored frescoes—nymphs and satyrs with rounded white bodies, grinning and bounding across flowered fields. Even the planked ceiling was painted with such scenes.

A narrow wooden table stood against the side wall, a petite chair set at an angle before it, as though its occupant had just risen only a few moments ago and gone downstairs to a meal.

The table held squat little pots of kohl for lining the eyes and red ochre to brighten the skin and lips, ivory combs and tiny Syrian glass jars of perfume.

In fact, the sharp tang of perfume still scented the air. Perhaps that was why she seemed so—so *present*.

Daria touched an alabaster jug, resisted the desire to unstop it and sniff its expensive contents. She nudged a comb where it lay on the table, felt the weight of it under her hand.

Was that a footfall in the corridor? She sucked in a tight breath, held her lamp aloft, and watched the door. But no movement, no inquiring eyes appeared. The room remained silent as a grave. How long until Lucas returned? She should abandon this forbidden search. But she could not.

It had been her room. It was still her room. Lucas did not reside here. There was nothing personal of his, no clothes strewn about, no telltale washbasin and shaving knives. A very rich woman's room. A woman accustomed to extravagance.

Had Lucas purchased all these fine things for her? Walked alongside her in the agora, laughing and shaking his head as she pointed to luxuries? Did she clutch at his arm and look up at him with a coy, pleading smile until he gave in with an indulgent squeeze of her hand?

Did his enthusiasm for life and his courage to risk, his encouragement to experience new things and his quick laugh make her feel that she was truly *living* for the first time, rather than constraining life into structure and order?

Daria set her lamp on the bed, gathered a robe from one of the baskets against the wall, and tangled greedy fingers into its white silk, heavy and full and warm in her hands. Gold braiding at the shoulders and waist glinted in the light. She held it against her body, tried to catch her blurry reflection in the bronze mirror, turning back and forth to see herself at different angles.

She did not belong inside such finery. She was the daughter of a poor scholar, married with a pittance of a dowry to the first man her father had found who would take her, and all the clothes she had ever owned together did not equal the price of this one piece. She was as different from Lucas's wife as Lucas was from her husband, Xanthos.

But what would it have been like, to be brought up to this? To riches and luxury, to honor and respect? To be married to a man such as Lucas? Could she have made him happy? Would she have kept a separate room such as this, or would she have wanted to be with him always? Her chest ached with such thoughts and she pushed them away.

Unknown corners of the room were still to be examined. Daria relinquished the white silk and took up her lamp.

There in the corner, a black square. What was that? Some sort of chest, for traveling? Would it open to her searching fingers?

There was no latch, only leather bindings not fastened. But the lid stuck fast, resisting her one-handed tugging against it. She kneeled and set the lamp on the floor, perilously close to her thigh, and applied more pressure against the trunk. The lid gave way with a sucking sound, as though she had torn a seal from something sacred, and a fearsome odor like that of the dead wafted about her head.

Daria waved the lamp around the contents of the trunk. What sorts of things would the woman have found precious enough to keep here?

The objects were a muddle, unlike the fresh order of the rest of the room, and did not reveal their uses at once. A cache of leather parchments, stacked, not rolled. Some clay tablets with strange symbols pressed into their crumbling surfaces. Strings with odd-shaped rocks knotted into them at intervals. Little jugs with stoppers that were too common, too rough to be perfumes. And the *smell*. Daria forced breath through her mouth to avoid that terrible odor.

She reached into the trunk's contents, set some items aside to more closely examine others. What did this strange collection signify?

There was something familiar about it. She lifted a parcel, unwrapped it slowly. Where? Where else had she seen items like these? Spread on shelves . . .

The parcel fell open and revealed itself in the same moment she remembered.

A dead frog.

The sorcerer's shop.

Her fingers went cold, numb, unable to rewrap the dried, pressed carcass. She thrust it back into its crypt.

All of it—like the things she had seen crammed on those shelves. Books of spells, stone amulets strung into necklaces. Jugs of questionable potions. And the frog.

She retrieved the parcel, tried to wrap it. Her breath was rapid and shallow now, her fingers stiff.

Such a strange feeling. Like moving along, translating a bit of rhetoric from Latin into Greek, and then suddenly coming upon a language one doesn't know at all. Incomprehensible and strange.

She gave up trying to rewrap the rigid remains and dropped the parcel back into the trunk. Her fingers burned now, and she flexed them to regain feeling.

Was this the woman she had envied? She glanced to the basket of robes, to the white silk she had pressed against her own body, and her stomach churned, queasy and heavy.

She had been relying on her mind, her intellect, to fight the darkness inside Lucas, to bring him back into the light. Her second chance.

She had been a fool. All of this was beyond her, so far beyond her ability to fight.

She snapped the trunk lid closed, sealed off the inquiries and their horrid answers that only led to more questions.

She pulled herself to her feet, then clutched the lamp with tight fingers, its brightness keeping her connected to all things that were light and good and beautiful.

The room repelled her now, as strongly as it had drawn her in. She must leave, must never come back.

She swept the door open, heedless of any noise it might create, and thrust her lamp into the hall.

A pair of white eyes stared back at her.

Daria gasped and nearly dropped the lamp. The blood that had pounded in her temples seemed to drain to her feet.

"Frona!"

"Was there something you needed, girl?" The woman's lips were a white slash against paler skin, stretched taut over prominent cheekbones.

"No. No—I—I was only—"

"This is my lady's room."

"Yes, I see that. I did not disturb anything."

"It is kept the way it was on the day she did not return to us."

Daria swallowed and brushed hair from her eyes. "It is a lovely room."

Frona's face creased into something fierce. "She was a lovely person."

Strange, paradoxical words. "Of course. Well. I will retire for the night, then, I believe."

"Very well."

She could feel the weight of Frona's stare against her back as she fled the strange exchange.

She flew to her own chamber.

Closed the door against both the living and the dead.

19

"WATCH MY MOUTH, LUCAS. WATCH ME FORM THE sounds."

She spoke the Persian phrase slowly, distinctly.

His eyes were on her lips, her tongue, but he shook his head. "Useless, Daria. I will never produce such strange syllables correctly."

They sat in the small triclinium on adjoining couches, Lucas sitting upright for a change and Daria leaning into her instructions with an eagerness he did not share.

Since her discovery of his wife's chamber, no censure came from Lucas for intruding upon his privacy. No side remark, half in jest, about exploring where she did not belong. Whatever reasons Frona had for keeping her secret, the woman kept them to herself.

And Daria did not enter the west side of the upper level again. Better to focus on her duties, on coaxing Lucas to take his morning studies with her and encouraging his halting pursuit of the Persian language.

It was not the morning, now, however. Lucas had come for her after the evening meal, the courtyard torches smoking behind him, his eyes clouded.

"Come and teach me, Daria."

She held a scroll of Epicurus, one she had borrowed from Lucas's collection, at her side. "Now?"

He eyed the scroll. "You are occupied. I should not have—"

"No. No, I will come." She knew that haunted look. He needed distraction.

And so she had joined him in the dining chamber, had returned to the morning's lesson, but his mind was still elsewhere.

She forged ahead with her instruction, a current of anxious thought running behind the words she formed with little concentration.

He had been so changeable in this past week. The occasional smile, a flash of the charm and wit she had seen in Rhodes. He sometimes sought her company, treated her as an equal.

And then there were the dark hours when he retreated within himself, to the solitary place where she could not follow. In these moments he was abrupt and rude, and one would have thought her little more than a kitchen slave in his eyes.

And yet, the offense she had first taken at such treatment had fled, and she saw nothing but the pain that caused it and felt the sting of it in her own chest.

"Bah!" Lucas swept a hand across the low table, knocking scrolls to the floor. "Enough of this."

She eyed him warily, but his expression quickly softened.

He stood and held out his hand. "Come, Daria. We will escape this prison."

She took the offered hand and he pulled her to her feet.

"You have not yet been to the theater since you arrived. There is drama tonight, and music, I believe. I shall show you the best Ephesus has to offer. Go and fetch something warmer, though. The night air may grow chilled."

Minutes later they were stepping down the hillside terraces toward the lowest street level. Perhaps she could find a way to draw him out.

Lucas's sigh was deep and heavy. "I am glad to be out of there."

"Sometimes I think you never want to leave it."

He glanced at her, eyes narrowed. "Do you? I have not been there so much in ten months as I have been these past weeks."

She remained silent, but his words warmed her. The entire evening was warm, in spite of his warning. Warm and stiflingly close with rain in the air. From the height of the hillside, a misty haze like the first night she'd arrived swirled along the street toward the theater and snaked into the empty agora. It wrapped her in its humid embrace and the night seemed dreamlike, unreal.

"What do you fear in the house, Lucas?"

"What have I to fear?"

"I know not. But I see it in your eyes."

He kept his gaze fixed on the end of the street, the theater in the distance, hugging the slope of Mount Pion. "Yes, you see everything, do you not?"

"I wish that were true. You have more secrets than an oracle."

"And you would pry each of them from me, like an oyster cracked open, revealing its weaknesses." His tone was sharp, accusatory.

She had crossed a line, once again jeopardizing the tenuous ease their relationship had acquired. "Yes."

He barked a little laugh. "You are a bold one, are you not? Do you ever fear I shall weary of your questions and decide I do not need a tutor after all?"

"I fear worse things."

"Such as?"

"I fear you will succumb to your torments, that your heart will be irretrievable."

He said nothing at this, only breathed heavily.

The city seemed emptied of life, perhaps all of it had been sucked into the theater tonight. They passed the brothel, one of few establishments open at this hour, and trod along the agora. The night was hushed and silent, as though expectant, with that ethereal mist still slithering along closed shops and between stone columns, insidious and furtive. The warm air smelled of wet earth and spring growth, a smell of promise but also of decay. They walked in silence, shoulders nearly touching, and the theater grew closer.

Daria broke the silence at last. "Have you spoken yet to Tyrannus about me?"

"Ah, so you *do* fear being cast out."

She swallowed. "You will not need a tutor forever. I must ensure that I have employment when you are finished with me."

"Yes, when I am finished with you."

The strange repetition left her without reply.

He rubbed a hand across the back of his neck. "The night is sticky."

"It is menacing, I think."

"You fear being about at night?" He thumped his chest with a fist. "Even with such a strong protector at your side?"

She masked a smile. "Are you strong? I had not noticed."

A dark cat shot across their path. Daria jumped and grabbed his arm. Then released it, heat flooding her face.

Lucas laughed. "I must find that cat and offer it some fresh fish for redeeming my manly pride."

They had nearly reached the theater. Inside, the crowd and coarse jokes of the drama would probably once again create a barrier between them. Daria slowed. Could they not continue as they were?

"I—I have lost my appetite for the theater, Daria."

She exhaled, relief loosening her tight muscles.

He took her elbow, led her to the inner corner of the dark agora, where benches lined a portico. "Let us sit awhile, you and I."

"Gladly."

The sound of laughter from the theater swelled over the *skene*—the two-tiered portico that separated the half circle of stone seats from the street and formed the backdrop of the orchestra and stage. Daria turned her head away from Lucas to the theater, though she could see only the torches that lit the upper lip of the seats.

"It is very large—much bigger than the theater in Rhodes."

"The largest in all the province of Asia. Twenty-five thousand could be seated there tonight."

Nobleman and aristocrat, merchant and laborer, they would all crush into the theater for the entertainment. "The city falls silent with so many occupied with its diversions."

Lucas had draped an arm along the back of their bench, and Daria sat straight-backed on the edge of the stone.

"Yes, it would seem we have the city to ourselves."

She studied the theater, aware of his closeness. "I thought you sought diversion tonight as well."

"I have all the diversion I need."

"I am no actor, nor musician."

"No? My house feels more . . . harmonious with you in it. And I believe you wear a mask nearly always."

She turned a surprised gaze on him. "*You* are the oyster, remember?"

He flashed a slight smile and looked away. "Always with an answer, that is my tutor. So careful, so in control. Do you not ever act on impulse, Daria? To do something dangerous, perhaps? Even a little . . . fiendish?"

"I have not the luxury. A widow without means must be practical above all."

"And if you had been born to wealth, what then? Would you have pursued a life of license?"

He teased, but she considered her answer anyway. "No. No, I think I should have tried to please the gods, to secure their blessing, no matter the circumstances of my birth."

He sighed. "I am not so convinced anymore that it would benefit. Lately I have been questioning such ideas. And hearing others, from those of a different sect. But I believe you are right, you would have been the same pure soul if you had been born a senator's daughter."

"As your wife was?"

His gaze traveled across the agora, to the distant gate and his estate beyond. "You envy her, perhaps?"

"Not her money." Daria bit her lip. The admission had slipped out, too near a confession of her heart.

Lucas brought his attention back to her. "What, then?"

She dropped her head. "I could not envy the dead."

"No. No, that would not do."

They sat in silence, sheltered from the breeze by the shops

behind, listening to the rise and fall of the unseen crowd's laughter and gasps of surprise. They were spectators to the spectators, removed from both the farce and from those who participated in it.

"She was expecting our first child when she died."

The admission, delivered in such low tones she barely heard it, was like a blow against her chest. Heat flooded her limbs, then receded, leaving her chilled. She studied her hands, twined in her lap, and dropped back against the bench.

"I only learned of it a few days before—before—" He inhaled deeply and left off speaking.

"Lucas, I am so sorry."

"Yes. Well. I was ecstatic, as you might imagine. Nothing could have pleased me more."

"You would have made a wonderful father."

His arm tensed behind her shoulders. "Thank you for saying that. You always make me feel like a better man than I am."

"I wish you could see what I see, Lucas. Know that you are a good man. But you must choose to act in accordance. This desire you have for justice—and I understand it much better now—it is pulling you toward a hopeless urge for revenge."

She studied his profile, hard and cold in the darkness. The muscles of his jaw quivered.

"Talk to me of something else, Daria. Tell me more of *your* husband. How did he die?"

"I have no wish to speak of that."

"So it is only I who must be pried open?" He turned to study her.

Could he see much of her expression under the clouded sky?

"Yes, I see you have secrets as well. Your eyes have a sorrow all their own." His gaze traveled to her lips. "Your mouth was made for laughing, but rarely indulges in such, and when your jaw is set in that manner, I believe that your staunch will alone would prevent any more evil from befalling you."

"My will, and the will of the gods, I pray."

"Well, if the gods watch over any soul to keep her from evil, it would be yours, Daria. But I fear they do not have the power to keep you from the corruption that surrounds you. Tell me of your husband."

She inhaled and gazed around the silent agora, its two-storied colonnades empty on all four sides of merchant tables, its few outlying buildings dark. Tomorrow sellers would swarm across the marble paving to claim favorable spots, and buyers would pick over fish and fowl, jewelry and pottery, and every luxury item that could be brought across the sea.

But tonight it was quiet. And with Lucas, safe. A good place to tell a story.

And she began, closing her eyes with the telling of it, allowing the memory to wash over her as she rarely did.

She had prepared a lovely meal that night. His favorite foods, thinking she would soothe the restless anger that seemed to be growing in his heart. Would not a quiet evening of wine and bread, spent in their small but well-appointed triclinium, remind him of all that was good in his life? The young flutist she offered a small sum sat cross-legged in the corner, already piping a pleasant tune as Daria laid the last of the barley bread and goat cheese on the tables and pushed the cushions into place. She smiled at the girl and nodded her approval.

And then he was there in the doorway, with a fierce scowl and tunic torn and dirty.

"What has happened?" She crossed the triclinium, hands out-stretched. "Were you hurt?"

He swatted her hands away and breathed heavily through

clenched teeth, a strange hissing sound like steam escaping a vent hole.

"I—I have prepared—"

"You must be stopped, Daria." Cold words in an odd, strangled voice she did not recognize, growled half human in his throat.

The fits were coming on more often. Growing more violent.

Daria glanced at the girl in the corner. Should she dismiss her? Surely he wouldn't harm his own wife in the presence of another?

But what concern was one poor slave, not even his own, to him?

"You may go," she said to the girl. Pulled a few denarii from a pouch and pressed them into her hand as she passed. "Thank you."

The girl glanced at Daria, at the beast of a man before her, and hesitated. But then she saw sense and fled.

"Come, sit." She tried to draw him forward.

Xanthos yanked his arm from her touch as though burned. "You are a danger."

How could he say such a thing? Was he not the one she feared, every day, every night?

Knowing his own death approached, her father had yearned for her safety. He had married her to this man, much older than she, believing it was her best security. But it was too soon, done too quickly, before his true character was revealed.

That he had longed for a power greater than himself to fill him and satisfy him, she had seen within a week of her father's death. Within a month she had heard of his earlier life as a priest of Zeus on Crete. But the god had not given him all he craved, and he had turned to darker powers, to those that roamed the underworld, and opened himself to them.

Daria had seen the demon-possessed. Had seen how they

thrashed and groveled and threw themselves into the dust, clawing and drooling. This was something different, though no less deadly. It grew in Xanthos, a silent parasite that ate away at any integrity he retained.

Did the darkness obliterate the man that he was, devour him completely? Or only smother him with its foul presence? At times he seemed the man she married.

Tonight there was none of him left. The evil had swallowed all of him, from his eyes to his fingers to his voice.

And it had come for her.

She had run once. Xanthos had found her, dragged her back.

She could see in his eyes that there would be no running tonight.

He grabbed her upper arm and pulled her toward the table, laid with his favorite foods. Would he calm after all, sit with her and take a meal?

He snatched up a knife set there for the cutting of the oranges she had purchased in the market that morning, fragrant and juicy.

And he slashed at Daria's arm.

A cut the length of her smallest finger, on the inside of her arm, bubbled with blood.

She stared at it. Had he truly cut her?

"You must be stopped."

"What—why are you doing this?" She tried to pull away, but he held her fast.

Then, unbelievably, he dragged the knifepoint across the inside of his own arm. A matching cut.

His own pain weakened him for a moment, and Daria slipped his grasp. But he moved fast, leaped to block her flight from the triclinium. Hunkered there, knife scraping the air in front of him.

"It is time." Again, the hissing voice, but now it was threaded with something deeper and harsher, as if two voices issued forth in unison from his throat. "We have let you live long enough. It is time."

Daria could not breathe, could not think. The darkness seemed to fill the room.

She screamed for the staff. She screamed for what seemed hours, as she and her husband performed a deadly and macabre dance of death in the triclinium, and no one heard her screams or his. No one came.

Xanthos had gotten fat and slow as his mind and health had wasted away. He reached her but twice with that knife, one a slight prick against her belly and then a cut along her thigh that sliced her robe and flesh as one.

Each time, each cut, he inflicted a matching injury on himself.

His eyes were fixed on her thigh, on the fabric that stuck fast to the seeping blood.

Another lunge.

She saw the knife penetrate before she felt the pain, but when it came, it seemed to scoop out her inner self and leave her hollow. She gasped, lunged for one of the couches.

"You will not come against us. You will not." That bizarre split voice.

It was the first he had spoken in some time, and she tried to grasp at the words, to find some way to gain access to his befouled mind. "I am your wife. I do not seek to come against—"

"But you will! You will! One day you will join them and fight us. We have seen it! But we will not allow it."

He stood upright, stretched to his full height. "We will take your mind, we will own your mind."

Daria still bent to the couch, her hands buried in its soft cushions, and she felt the truth of the words. A feeling not quite like pain, more like a pulling, like the tide receding from the shoreline, tugged at her mind, at her thoughts.

No. She would not lose the only thing that made her strong.

She pointed to her thigh, then to his. "You have not taken your second cut, as I have."

He seemed to falter, glancing at her leg, at the blood that ran there, and then at his own.

And then he swiped at his thigh with the knife, a smooth cut as she had seen the butchers slice across the shank of cows and goats in the market.

It was not a surface cut, as hers had been. He had not jumped away from the knife as she had.

A deep gash. It spurted blood in an arcing spray, a fountain of red, bursting from leg to table, splashing the bowl of waiting oranges.

Xanthos laughed. In that horrifying moment he laughed to see the blood flow. And it was not the hissing voice, nor the deep voice, but the laugh of the husband she had known, as though he had triumphed at last over the powers that would use his body, had snatched their tool from their hands and rendered it useless.

He sank to his knees, a penitent before her, watched her eyes for a silent moment, then fell forward. His chest hit the floor with a hollow smack.

She had tried to stop the blood. Pressed cushions from the couch against the wound, but it would not stop, and there was too much.

"Later, when the magistrates came and asked me questions, I said it had been an accident. That he was cutting fruit there in the dining room and the knife had slipped. But they saw my bloody tunic, my hastily bandaged arm, and they knew. Everyone knew what he had become."

Somewhere in the telling, Lucas had taken her hand and he squeezed it now, giving her courage to finish.

"I buried Xanthos with what little was left of his estate, then got on the first boat to Rhodes and offered myself as a tutor in exchange for a room and food. Several pupils later, you found me running from the School of Adelphos." She sat back, winded and nearly panting.

A strange breeze arose, warm and scented with that earthy wetness, and loosed strands of her hair from her gold comb, trailing them across her eyes.

Lucas's gaze watched the errant strands and then his fingers followed, tracing their path across her cheek, her eyelids. "You are a good woman."

Daria closed her eyes and breathed in the scent of his hand, felt the cool touch of it against her flushed skin. How long had it been since anyone had touched her face?

His cheek was near hers now, his mouth close to her ear.

"But I am not a good man, Daria."

She opened her eyes to find his eyes a breath away. The fear and the pain and the loneliness and desire were an eddying whirlpool of emotion, pulling her into its center relentlessly. Her grip on order and rationality were the only safe anchors to keep her from being drawn down into the whirlpool, but she released them, released her hold on them and closed her eyes and leaned into his solid warmth.

Somewhere nearby, a grunt and a scraping sound stole the moment. Daria opened her eyes, and Lucas was already searching the darkness beyond for the source.

A man came into view, heavy of body and sweating profusely. He dragged a burden, wrapped in fabric—goatskin or wool, perhaps. At their movement, he raised his eyes, drew in breath, and squinted.

"Lucas? Is that you?"

Lucas jumped to his feet, his arm knocking Daria's shoulder. "Pharnaces! What—what are you doing?"

"Thank the powers you are here. Help me, man. I have not the strength to finish the job."

Lucas glanced back at her, then to the newcomer. He seemed at a loss, and the look that came into his eyes had that desperate, haunted shade she despised.

He stepped between her and the man. "Where are you going?"

"To the harbor. Hektor says he doesn't want this one found. Too soon since the last one. Says to pitch her into the water, like an accident."

Daria stood, slowly, automatically, like a curtain being lifted on a macabre play.

The wrappings had come loose from the stranger's burden. From the goatskin covering, there spilled a mass of lank hair, a white arm with strange markings, a gray face.

He was carrying a body, this man was.

And he had reason to believe Lucas would help.

20

NOT HERE. NOT WITH HER.

Lucas traded glances between Pharnaces and Daria's stricken face, then to the tight roll at Pharnaces's feet. His blood surged and his stomach constricted, burning a bitter trail in his throat. She must not get involved. Not with this. Pharnaces would only bring her danger.

The fat man used the taut edge of his outer tunic to wipe at sweat cutting a narrow channel down his heavy jowl.

At their feet, did the bound fabric move?

By all that was holy, the girl was moaning. She still lived!

Pharnaces took a quick step back, as though the girl had returned from the dead to plague him. "What? Hektor told me—"

"I will handle it, Pharnaces." Lucas circled the girl, wedged himself between her prostrate form and the startled Pharnaces. "You haven't the stomach for this sort of thing, I think. And look at you, your heart is ready to give out, I believe."

Pharnaces swiped at his brow with the back of his arm. "The night is hot." His voice was defensive, suspicious, perhaps.

"Indeed." Lucas glanced down Harbor Street. "Just the sort of night for a dip in the sea. But you go home to your family. I will see to it."

Pharnaces leaned sideways and peered around Lucas, to where Daria stood, silent. "Who is she?"

"Just a hired girl. Part of my staff. Of no consequence."

Pharnaces's eyebrows lifted.

No doubt he had seen or sensed the two of them on the bench as he approached.

"She can be trusted?"

Lucas lowered his voice, leaned in as though confiding. "She is simpleminded. Does only what I tell her." He gave the man a leering half grin.

Pharnaces's gaze on Daria was still too inquisitive, too interested.

"Go on, then, Pharnaces. And tell Hektor when you see him that I have done him a good turn."

Pharnaces took another gulp of the humid air and nodded. "Aye, I will tell him. And you have my gratitude."

Lucas nodded, then bent to the girl, his body blocking her from Pharnaces's view. He sensed the man hesitate, then heard his heavy footfalls scurry across the agora's marble paving.

Lucas lifted the wrappings that had loosened from around the girl's face. She was young, perhaps not even twenty. He had not seen her under Hektor's shop, but then he rarely looked at their faces. Her mouth was bloody and her dark hair against the paleness of her flesh was an awful thing. Her eyelids fluttered and she looked at Lucas without recognition.

"Sshhh." He shook his head slightly. Pharnaces was still too close. "Be still," he whispered.

Pharnaces's footsteps echoed off into nothing, but another set of feet trod closer. Slowly, as though wooden. On the other side of the girl's prone body, Daria's small feet appeared.

He lifted his face to hers but could not meet her eyes. "She is badly hurt. We must get her to a physician."

Daria said nothing, and he risked a glance at her mouth, her lips, bloodless and white when they had been so full of life only moments ago.

"I need your help, Daria. Dare I ask for it?"

She bent to the girl, laid a hand on her cheek. "Where are her injuries? Can she be safely carried?"

His heart surged with gratitude, with admiration for the woman Daria was.

He slid his arms under the girl's shoulders and her thighs and lifted. "Yes. Cover her, though. Yes, that's it, her face even. She won't know it, she's barely sensible. It's safer that way."

He glanced toward the street, then the theater. "Come. We will find a physician."

Daria hurried beside him, matching his long strides across the agora, into the street. "Lucas—"

"Ask no questions, Daria. None."

She huffed in protest but was silent, thankfully.

Behind them, the theater exploded in sudden applause and then a rumble that seemed to shake the paving stones.

Daria cast an anxious glance backward. "What is it?"

"The drama is over. The theater is emptying."

He was slowing, the weight of fear and shame tiring him as much as the weight he carried.

Daria plucked at his sleeve. "Faster, Lucas. It will not do to have the city pressing down on us."

Yes, pressing down on them. Like the humid air and the future he could not avoid. Sweat ran into his mouth and he tasted the salt of it, like tears.

They were flooding the street now, the theatergoers. Released from their evening of sitting in cold stone rows, jumpy and jittery with the inactivity. The first wave would be upon them in moments. Would the praetor Zagreus be among them? How overjoyed he would be to find Lucas with such damning evidence.

Ahead, the yellow light of the brothel doorway near the end of the street was the only sign of life. Lucas closed his eyes briefly against the humiliation of it. Though the brothel was perfectly legal for men to enter without reproach and even received a license from the state, it seemed shameful to enter with Daria or any woman, and those who worked inside were objects of scorn.

"Come, Daria. She will be safe in here." He reached the establishment in a few strides, ducked under the low door frame, and maneuvered his heavy burden through the opening with care.

A middle-aged woman with a painted face and loosed hair appeared at his entrance, all smiles and open arms. The smile turned to puzzlement at the sight of the weight he carried and Daria following behind. He tried to speak, but the flush of shame trapped the words in his tight throat. The odor of the place—a mixture of reeking cosmetics and heavy perfumes to cover their stench—was enough to water the eyes.

Daria circled him and pulled the fabric from the injured girl's face. "We need your help." Her tone was low and urgent, without judgment, without ill will. "A girl's been badly hurt. Do you have a place we can lay her?"

"We've got beds aplenty, I can assure you." The woman's face creased in confusion. "But we've no doctor here."

Lucas found his voice. "I will locate the physician. We only need a place to keep her safe. The streets are filling with people from the theater. She—she would not be safe out there."

The woman nodded and eyed the open door. "Say no more. I've seen my share of girls in trouble. Bring her back here."

Lucas followed her through a narrow hall, turning sideways to keep the girl's head from striking the grimy wall and ducking her under a torch wedged into a wall socket.

"You'll need to pay, mind you." This the woman tossed over her shoulder as she walked. "Tonight's a busy night, with the theater performance, and I can't afford to take up space—"

"You will be well compensated, you have my word."

She stopped and jabbed a thumb toward a darkened alcove, grinning a half-toothed grin. "That's what I like to hear. You can put her in there. I'm not tending her, though."

"No. Thank you."

The woman disappeared, and Lucas laid the girl along the stone outcropping and pulled the fabric from her body. Above the rude bed, mosaics of men and women set his face flaming and he turned from Daria to busy himself with the girl.

The burns were there, as he knew they would be.

What was he doing? Everything about this had been a bad decision. If word got back to Hektor or Pharnaces that he had not gotten rid of the girl in the harbor waters . . . And Daria, what must she be thinking? He still could not meet her eyes.

And yet there had been no choice. Of course there had been no choice.

Daria stepped beside him, clutched his arm, and sucked in a breath at the girl's injuries. "Lucas, she is badly hurt. It may be too late for even the physician—"

"I know." He raked a hand through his hair. "I know."

Curse Pharnaces and his timing. Would that he and Daria could be back in the warmth of the agora, closer than they were even now in this tiny space, close enough to feel her breath on his neck.

"Go, Lucas. I will do all I can while you find the physician."

He rubbed at his eyes, his forehead. He could not think. Did not know what to do.

"Lucas." Daria had his arms, was turning him to herself. "Look at me."

He blinked twice and returned her stare, then matched the grip she had on his arms, clutching her like a man drowning.

Her eyes were steady. "I will stay with her. We will do what we can. You must go."

He nodded, embraced her, crossed to the narrow door. He looked back over his shoulder, but she was already bent over the girl, pressing the loose fabric against her wounds to stop the bleeding.

She must have sensed his hesitation for she looked up, caught his glance. And in that moment, in the meeting of their eyes, some understanding passed between them.

No matter what came, he would always be connected to her somehow, would he not? He had felt the connection from that first moment on the Rhodian dock, when she had run into him with that evil-spirited girl in tow. When he watched her at the prow of his ship, leaving her home in its wake at his request. On the night terrace overlooking the city, whispering of her father.

Between them lay a chasm of age and of social class and of all they held as sacred, and yet under the chasm ran a deep current, a current that connected them like two pools fed from the same spring.

The realization left him short of breath and weak with a sort of sadness that only now had he found her. Now, when it was too late.

"Go, Lucas. Go."

It took him less than an hour to rouse a physician, but it was time enough to realize that this night marked a change in his relationship with Daria. He admired her search for truth, had become dependent on her goodness, needed her if he was to ever become whole and healed.

He dragged the physician along to the brothel and found Daria still bent over the patient. Lucas breathed his relief as they entered, for Daria's pressure of a cloth against the girl's brow meant that she lived still.

He pulled Daria from the room, down the hall, out into the street, still crowded with late-night revelers.

Daria's gaze strayed back to the brothel door. "What about Maia? Can we leave her there?"

Not surprising that in her compassion she had learned the girl's name. He nodded. "I've given money and instructions to the physician and the—the—woman—"

"Leto."

He frowned.

"The prostitute. Her name is Leto. But what of those who harmed her? What of them?"

"They will answer for their actions. I promise you that."

He took her by the elbow and guided her through the crowd. They kept to the edge of the street, weaving between drunken merchants and strolling nobility, until they reached the end of the

185

street where the hillside homes climbed partway up the mountain and they broke free of the oppressive crowd at last.

But the quieter terraced steps leading to his estate afforded too much chance for conversation, and he should have known Daria was only waiting for enough silence to begin.

"I have helped you with your grisly errand, Lucas. But I will not be put off. You must tell me what occurred here tonight. What have I been part of?"

"I cannot answer this, Daria. You must trust that it is for your protection—"

"I care more for the truth than for my safety!"

Lucas glanced at her outrage, and she seemed to have surprised even herself. They had reached the street that ran below his home and turned right to walk along the rutted stone. "All the same—"

"No." She stopped, shaking her head, as though she would not take another step without the truth.

"Daria, come to the house. We cannot talk like this in the street."

She brushed past him, stalked to the front of his house, up the steps, and through the front door, but then whirled on him in the entryway. "Now. Now you will tell me everything."

The night's events, the fear and the shame, and even the denied desire of the agora, churned into something angry. The words spit out without thought. "You are a hired hand in this house, Daria. It is not your place to demand—"

"Yes, hired staff. Of no consequence, wasn't that it? Simpleminded?"

"You know I only said that—"

"I know nothing, Lucas. I know only that you are tortured by your past, driven by others to do things you do not wish to do, and fearful that your own heart has turned black with evil!"

He turned away, pressed a hand against the plaster wall of the entryway. She understood more than he realized. And he would not allow it to damage her. Not after hearing her story tonight.

"But I would know everything. Starting with that girl tonight—"

"Enough!" He spun on her, and the heat in his chest matched what he saw in her eyes. "Enough. This—this—arrangement is not working. I was foolish to think that language lessons would fit into my life." He breathed in courage and determination. "I will arrange another teaching position for you somewhere. But we are finished."

He moved to walk past her, but she caught his arms, stared into his face with those clear gray eyes. "Lucas, do not do this."

He broke her hold on him, grasped her shoulders, and shook her until the light in her eyes turned to fear. "Do you understand nothing, Daria? Do what you know is right! Run from this place, from this evil, and do not look back!"

With that he left her, pale and shaking and alone in the entryway.

It was the only way.

21

THE EARLY MORNING LIGHT, DULL AND GRAY, LEFT the Embolos in murky shadows and did little to illuminate the door of the School of Tyrannus as Daria wandered to it. She shivered in the damp chill, trying to find courage.

The previous night's threat of rain had been realized and the warmth had fled. Daria slipped from the estate before the eastern sky lightened. Before Lucas rose from his bed.

Now she knocked. Waited.

No answering call from within, no door swung wide to welcome an outcast.

She knocked again, then again, punishing her knuckles against the rough wood.

At last the door cracked and a cold eye appeared at the slit. "What is it? The school is not yet open."

"Yes, yes, I am sorry. I wish to inquire about a teaching position within. Do you know if—?"

The door yanked wider, revealing a man too well dressed to be a servant, but not of a class to be Tyrannus himself. He looked left and right.

"Who is inquiring?"

"I am." Her voice was too soft, too timid.

The man sighed, as one would with an ignorant child. "Yes, I know you are *asking* about a position, but who is the *teacher*?"

Daria inhaled, lifted her chin. "I am fluent in several languages, can teach both philosophy and rhetoric—"

"A woman?" Eyebrows raised, a cynical smile creasing his face.

"Yes, I—"

"We have no need for women here."

"I have been a tutor to Lucas Christopoulos."

He shrugged. "Who?"

Daria rubbed at the tension in her neck. "Please, can you tell me if the teacher Paul is here?"

"You are acquainted with Paul?"

"Or his pupil Timothy. Could I speak—?"

"They come only in the afternoons. When lessons are suspended."

"I shall come back, then."

"Not today." He rolled his eyes, as if disbelieving that he even carried on such a foolish conversation. "They do not come on the first day of the week. Or the last, for that matter."

"Do you know where I might find them?"

But the door was closing on her question, and on her hope.

Must she suffer the humiliation of having Lucas arrange her future? It did not appear he was even known at the school. Could she truly expect him to secure her a position?

She turned from the door, hovered there on the sidewalk. The solitary drip of water from the eaves of the portico landed at her feet. Which way? The full weight of last night's events fell upon her afresh.

Her worst fears had been realized. She was cast out, vulnerable and exposed. Without connection or means to survive. Her second chance snatched from her.

Behind her, the door slid open once more and she turned to the sound.

A figure slipped out—a young man, younger than she, his eyes wary. He crossed the portico in halting steps, worrying his bottom lip with his teeth.

"You are looking for Paul? And Timothy?" His voice was low, and he glanced back at the door.

"Yes! Can you tell me—?"

"They live in the shop district, in the Jewish quarter." He jutted his chin in the general direction. "Paul works with a man and wife from Rome. Husband's name is Aquila. Tent makers. If you ask around you will find them."

Daria squeezed his forearm. "Thank you."

He nodded once, then slipped back into the school.

She moved on surer feet now, toward a goal. She would go to Timothy, beg him to use his influence with Paul to secure her a position in the school. She did not need Lucas's help nor his charity. Did not need Lucas.

She came to the lower end of the Embolos, turned right toward the theater, but would not look upward at his estate. She blinked away the tears that pricked behind her eyes, inhaled the sodden air, and hardened her heart.

Why had the man in the agora been certain that Lucas would

help him dispose of a dead girl's body? And why had Lucas tricked the man, then helped the girl?

There were no answers. Only one thing she knew—she had grown tougher in these past weeks. Proven herself with cool-headed thinking and courage.

It was time to return to earlier ambitions. Keep herself safe, work hard to please the gods, get a teaching position in a school.

Yes, Rhodes was repeating itself, even this walk through the city with hopes to secure a guarantee against starvation, against homelessness. The beggars she passed along the agora under-scored her determination.

It took less than an hour to locate the home of Aquila in the Jewish district. She had expected a small dwelling, but the home's impressive front door stood open, revealing a spacious courtyard within.

Spacious and crowded.

There was no sense in knocking. She would not be heard over the buzz of conversation. Instead, she slipped into the house unnoticed and blended into the crowd.

And a strange group it was. Servants in plain tunics who con-versed easily with men in Roman togas with the purple senatorial edge. Men with the squared chin of the Greeks and others with the woven head coverings of the Jews. Women with gold filigree jewelry seated beside slaves with metal collars.

Too early for a dinner party, too diverse for a synagogue, what was this gathering?

The home smelled of baking bread, but surely Aquila could not fill all these mouths? Torches had been lit against the morn-ing gloom, and the multicolored hues of tunics and robes gave the courtyard a festive air.

"Daria?" The voice at her shoulder was happy and light.

She turned to it, grateful. "Timothy."

"You found us."

"Yes." She eyed the crowd. "I came to speak to you, and to Paul. But this is not a good time."

He squeezed her arm with affection. "Stay awhile. It will not be long. We meet on the first day of the week for a bit of teaching, but then everyone will go."

She nodded. What sort of teaching would she hear?

It was Paul who jumped to the lip of the courtyard's impluvium to be heard above their heads. He gave a shout of welcome with an upraised hand. From the warm return given, it was clear he was much loved among this body.

"We must be strong, my friends."

The crowd quieted at once. Smiles faded. Heads turned upward, like a nest of birds with beaks open to their mother.

"The city is in turmoil, as you know. Light is breaking into darkness and the evil one will not be idle. He will fight back." He spoke with passion, sharp gestures punctuating his words. "The powers of the air will come at us with all the evil they possess. But we will be ready."

Daria surveyed the people at these dire words, but Paul's prediction called forth only squared shoulders, raised chins, nods of agreement.

"The worshippers of Artemis would have us believe the gods are only pleased with rituals and rites while hearts remain in darkness. They say that all their work to earn blessings will indebt the gods to them, will earn them security and wealth."

He spoke with such energy, such charisma, he could have been a philosopher or a politician. His words came in a torrent, tumbling over each other to reach his listeners.

"We know the truth, that the One True God desires a relationship with us as His children. That He has redeemed us from our slavery to darkness, made our adoption possible. We are secure in *His* hands alone, not in our own workings."

The group murmured in agreement, and Paul raised a fist.

"Nothing can separate us from His love, friends. Not death, not life, not angels or demons. No power on earth can separate us from the love of God that is in Christ Jesus our Lord!"

The words poured over Daria's heart like water on parched ground. Such strangeness, perhaps even blasphemy, and yet it felt truer than anything she had ever heard.

He spoke only a few more minutes, and then the crowd broke apart. Despite the differences in class and gender, they dispersed with laughter, embraces, and familial kisses. Even standing against the wall, she almost felt part of it. How different it was here, in this home, than in Lucas's sepulchral estate.

What would Lucas think of these people? This teaching? Would his heart reach out to it as hers did? Be healed by it?

A thought nagged at the back of her mind. Something Lucas had said last night . . .

"Daria, this is Aquila." Timothy pulled her to the center of the few who remained. "He generously lends us his home, as do several others in the city."

She nodded to a portly man some years her senior. His humble tunic belied the wealth she saw around them.

"And this is his wife, Prisca."

A woman still beautiful in her middle years reached a warm hand to Daria. "Call me Priscilla, please. Everyone does."

"And some of the others. Gaius. Aristarchus. Tychicus and Trophimus. Onesiphorus. And this is Seneca and his wife, Europa."

The parade of names made her head spin. She smiled and nodded at each.

"And Paul you have met, I believe."

The older Jew clutched her hands and grinned. "Yes, I wondered how long until we saw you again."

"I have come to ask a favor, I fear."

He patted her hand. "You should not fear."

The group drifted off to speak of other matters, and Paul led her to a courtyard bench. Timothy sat nearby in a narrow chair.

She took a deep breath and plunged into her plea. "I have been a private tutor, but that position has recently come to an end."

"So soon? Lucas has learned all he can already?" Paul winked at Timothy. "He must be sharper than he appears."

Daria bit her lip. Was Paul so well acquainted with Lucas? Would news of her coming here get back to him? "You know Lucas?"

"He searches for answers."

Lucas's words last night. *"I have been questioning . . . hearing from others of a different sect."* These were the people he had come to know? The people he agreed to betray for Demetrius? Should she speak her suspicion when she was unsure?

"He has decided that he—has no time—for language lessons."

"No heart for it, you mean." Paul nodded. "He has been under a dark cloud since this thing began."

Daria sat forward. "What is it that has begun?"

Paul frowned. "The killings, of course. The first of which was his wife. Her death seemed to start it all, I think. The whole series of women, with those strange circular burns on their arms and their bodies horribly disfigured."

The courtyard spun around her, torches smoking and blurring. She blinked and gripped the edge of the bench. "I fear he is only going to hurt himself with his need to find answers, to find justice."

"And you wish to save him from himself?"

She grasped Paul's hand. "Yes. Yes, exactly. But I must know how. I have failed in the past, and this is my second chance. I have seen that you have this power—"

Paul placed two gentle fingers against her lips. "There is much you do not understand, child. For now, let me only say that it is not for you to save, not for you to rescue. Only the One God can change a man's heart. This 'second chance' you wish for—it is a dangerous illusion."

She swallowed against a constricted throat. How could he ask her to give up on the man she—she cared so much about?

"But you did not come to hear such talk. What can we do for you, dear girl?"

Her lips felt stiff and cold as she blurted her mission. "Would you use your influence to help me get a teaching position in the School of Tyrannus?"

His eyes narrowed. "This is what you want?"

"It is what I need."

"Very well. I will send for you at Lucas's home if I am successful—"

"No! No, I—I cannot stay there."

"Where will you stay?"

Daria took a deep breath and looked away. "I do not know."

Timothy leaned into the conversation, as though no longer content to merely watch. "Joseph has room in his home. He and his wife would make Daria welcome."

Paul nodded and gave his protégé a slight and knowing smile. "Yes, it is a good idea." He gripped Daria's shoulder as though she was a friend. "You will like them. They also have a church that meets in their home, like Aquila and Priscilla here. You will stay with them until we find a way to help."

It was happening too fast. How could she be certain this was the most prudent course? "I do not know—"

His touch on her shoulder grew soft. "Hush, child. You are safe with us."

She resisted the urge to throw her arms round his neck and weep. Instead, she tried to smile. "I must fetch my belongings from Lucas's house."

"Good. Then return here, and we shall take you to your new home."

A moment later she was in the street, and the entire course of her life had changed.

22

"I'VE NO WISH TO SEE ANYONE, CLOVIS. WHOEVER IT is, send him away."

Lucas waved a hand at the aged servant in the doorway of his sitting room, then slumped again in his chair and lifted the terra-cotta cup of warm wine from his desk.

"Do not be hasty, Lucas." The voice at Clovis's shoulder was smooth, with a sharp edge.

"Demetrius." He did not have the energy to stand and face the metalsmith. "You have come with your *instructions*, I take it?"

"And a warning." The lean man remained in the door, trapping Lucas, cornering him.

Yes, always a warning. Lucas gave him a glance, then returned his gaze to the lion stalking its wall-flat prey.

"I told you once that you played a dangerous game, Lucas.

Now I am not certain on which side of the game your loyalty lies."

"Speak plainly, Demetrius."

"Last night's . . . *events* have gotten back to me. Did you think they wouldn't?"

Lucas shrugged one shoulder and sipped from the orange cup. "In truth, I hadn't given you a thought."

"You will give a thought—if you care anything for this city, for the goddess! I do not care if you pursue your inquiries, but the more you involve yourself with those charlatans, the less likely that the Jewish sect will accept you. And they must accept you before the Artemis Festival if we are to ensure the evidence is found with them!" Demetrius paused, then made a low, growling sound in his throat. "Are you even listening?"

Yes, he was listening. Had been listening all morning, in fact, for a light tread in the courtyard, for a voice calling a greeting to Frona, perhaps even searching for him. When none had come, he sent Frona to bring her but received only the news that she was gone.

Casting her out would be the stone lid on his sarcophagus. But Demetrius's presence only highlighted the necessity. Lucas could not afford, and did not deserve, whatever light Daria brought.

"Perhaps I do not share your patriotism, Demetrius. Though I daresay your passionate allegiance to Artemis has more to do with the wealth she brings to Ephesus. While your money belt is full, your spirit appears quite empty."

Demetrius studied him through narrowed eyes. "And are we so different? When has Lucas Christopoulos ever sung a heartfelt hymn to the Lady of the Ephesians?"

When indeed? And while all around this city there was nothing but emptiness, there *were* clusters of citizens full of some-thing . . . other.

Demetrius crossed his arms. "I swear by the gods, you have been sullen and obstinate since that woman arrived. Are you so distracted by beauty that you cannot think?"

"I told you, I brought her to teach me—"

"Yes. Language lessons. I wonder what you are paying her. Perhaps she would rather work in the house of one who appreciates her *other* talents." He glanced over his shoulder. "I have room in my staff for something so young and fresh."

"She would have no use for you."

"Ah, is that the sting of jealousy I hear in your voice? Worried that her affections might shift in the direction of more gold? I swear she is some sort of witch, to have enslaved you so. Perhaps you and she have descended together into that belly of madness beneath Hektor's shop, forgetting yourselves."

Lucas rose from his chair, turned on Demetrius, the heat of the wine pulsing his chest. The man's too-red lips stood out like blood against his skin, his expression smug. Lucas's hand formed a fist at his side. He could smash that expression.

Demetrius crossed his arms and regarded him coolly. "Almost I am coming to think you are one of them. Perhaps it is not a farce you play. Not a masquerade at all. Maybe you have been one with them since the beginning, and this woman, this witch, is pulling you deeper."

Lucas's hand squeezed the clay cup, uncaring that wine spilled at his feet. "She is nothing."

"So you keep saying. And yet she is everywhere. I am beginning to think if I want to get to you, it must be through her."

Pinned in the room by Demetrius's stance at the door, the pounding moved to his head, an angry rhythm in his veins, against his temples. The air seemed tinged with fire and smoke, the taste of charred ashes in his mouth.

"What do you mean, *through* her?"

Demetrius chuckled. "Exactly as I said. If you care little for yourself, perhaps a threat to your tutor will bear greater fruit."

The weight of the cup in his hand was heavy, too heavy, and the urge to crush the fired clay into Demetrius's face too great. He lifted it and heaved it across the room. It smashed against the wall near the man's ear.

Demetrius let out a sharp, staccato cry of rage and fear and jerked his arm over his face. But the threat was short-lived, and Demetrius's face blackened.

"Do not think that you can—"

"Get out before the next thing I smash is every bone in your arrogant face, Demetrius."

The silversmith chose the prudent course and bowed his way out of the room, a hateful expression souring his features.

Lucas paced the sitting room once, twice, three times—then stalked through the doorway and into the courtyard. The morning might be cold and gray, but the red heat in his chest was like a mountain ready to spew fire.

But even in the chill, the courtyard garden's increasing beauty could not be ignored. He drew up short, breath snatched away.

How could she have wrought such a change so quickly? Tall stalks of some kind of blue-flowered plant, whose weak stems left heads weighted and bent, now stood tall, propped with slender wooden stakes and tied with strips of fabric the color of sunshine. The scum-covered fountain water had been drained, the slime removed, and beside the chipped basin a colorful jumble of blue and green mosaic stones waited to be placed. Even the marble bench had been scrubbed white again with soda ash.

How was it possible? Did she come at night to work this magic?

She cultivated life wherever she went. She had no choice.

He drifted beyond the garden and a breeze caught his tunic, his hair, as he passed the larger triclinium. A peripheral light from the room slowed his steps. He leaned into the room, then braced a hand against the door frame.

"Frona!" His voice bellowed through the courtyard, echoed and bounced around the upper gallery, returned to him amplified. "Frona, get out here!"

The bony woman stalked from the kitchen area, clearly annoyed at being summoned. "What is it, my lord?"

Lucas still stood in the doorway, his back to the room. "What has happened here?"

"Is there some trouble?" Frona bustled past him into the dining room and he followed. "Something you need changed?"

Lucas surveyed the room once more. The heavy tapestry that had hung over the open windows for ten months was gone, light streaming to the stone floor. Bright frescoes had been scrubbed of their layers of dust and cobwebbery, colorful cushions cleaned and fluffed. Bowls of fresh flowers—red poppies—scattered across the three tables, the scent of them fresh in the air.

"What has happened here?" He asked it again, because he could think of no other words. "Why have you done this? Why have you opened the room?"

Frona straightened and frowned. "It wasn't me, my lord. I told the girl it was a terrible idea. 'The master doesn't care to use that room any longer,' I told her. But she would not listen. Insisted on cleaning it as though you would host a dinner party here tomorrow, said it must be aired, the windows opened— Are you quite well, my lord?"

Lucas sank into the couch nearest the door. "Yes. Yes, I am well. Leave me, Frona."

"It wasn't my doing—"

"I said leave me!"

She huffed and backed out of the room, leaving him awash in the light and fragrance of life, unable to hold his head upright.

How cold it had all been, all these months. The triclinium, his house, his life. And how cold it would be again, when he was once again alone.

23

DARIA'S FINAL WALK TO LUCAS'S ESTATE TOOK longer than it should have. Feet dragging and head heavy, she pushed her way through the crowded Harbor Street, without the strength to jostle those who impeded her progress.

The hillside houses seem to overhang the far end of the city like storm clouds, the mountain continuing up behind them like a wall.

She trudged up the stairs, to the street that cut a swath across the hillside below the estate, each step taking her closer to her last moments there.

She could not face Lucas this morning, not wait with patience while he apologized or explained how it would be better for her to leave, how his time was too much taken with business. No, she must slip into the house like a thief, collect her few possessions, and escape before anyone knew she had gone.

Paul's kindness, the generosity of his friends, soothed some of the rough places in her heart. She was not friendless in the world, it would seem. Perhaps Lucas was right and this was for the best.

At the entrance, she hesitated, a listening ear to the door. Hearing nothing, she opened it slightly and slid into the entryway. A few steps in she heard raised voices and cursed her timing.

Then there was the shattering of something and a cry.

Daria lunged forward. Had someone been hurt?

Across the courtyard, Lucas was growling something at another man, whose back was to her. And then Lucas spun and stalked away, deeper into the house, and the other man turned sharply toward the door and toward Daria.

He saw her at once. Demetrius's slow grin chilled her limbs.

She hustled, head down, toward her chamber. It should take only a few minutes to pack her things. Hopefully Demetrius would be well gone by the time she left.

Inside her chamber, she hurried to collect her belongings. She had brought nothing but one scroll with her from Rhodes. Was it fitting to take with her the other things Lucas had purchased? And with no pouch to pack, how would she carry anything—?

"Leaving so soon?"

Daria froze at the cool voice in the open door behind her. She swallowed against the dryness of her mouth, then forced her hands to continue folding the clothing.

But he did not leave. He was behind her, standing too close.

She straightened and faced him. He wore elegant robes in a pale green today, and his satisfied smile gave him the look of a lizard.

"Excuse me, Demetrius."

He nodded toward the heap on the bed. "You look as though you are running from Hades himself."

She gave an exasperated little snort—more confidence than she felt. "I should think you would be glad. You have clearly felt my presence here an obstacle to whatever use you have for Lucas."

"Actually, Lucas is not so useful at all. I had thought his wife's death would drive him. I did not know it would consume him." He folded wiry arms across his chest and shrugged. "But then I was one of the few who thought he might be innocent. That perhaps he did not do it."

"Do what?"

Demetrius tilted his head. "Kill her, of course."

The robe in her hand trembled and Daria pressed it against her belly to still its fluttering.

"Come, surely you know this? No? He did not tell you all before he brought you? But then, why should he? Perhaps you would not have come."

At her shocked silence, he laughed, low and prolonged, with a look of pure delight, as though he had eaten something too delicious for words. As though he would extend the moment by refusing to look away from her face, memorizing her reaction, her expression.

"Have you never wondered why no one comes here? Why there are no dinner parties, no guests? Why he has no friends but me?"

Daria tried to turn away but he arrested her flight with cool fingers on her arm. "And now you will surely flee, yes? Now that you know what he is? Because you have *principles,* Lucas says. You are *good.* But I know better."

She yanked her arm from his grasp. "You know nothing of me."

He smiled, a cold and scaly sort of smile. "I know human nature. We are none of us good, not deep inside. We pretend to be respectable, we do our duty before the gods, but it is all for ourselves, for our own interests." He moved closer, spoke with his mouth against her ear. "I was like you once. So was Lucas. Fooling everyone. Before we realized it made no difference. We could give in to our baser passions, or not give in. Could embrace the darkness we felt, or push it away. It made no difference. You will learn this one day. We all do."

The cold seemed to spread from his hand to her skin, from his lips to her cheek. She would pull away, but the fear that his words were true held her fast.

"Demetrius!"

The sharp bark from the doorway broke the hold.

Daria stumbled backward. Braced a hand against her bed.

Demetrius turned slowly to face Lucas. He should have been quicker.

Lucas was across the room in an instant, and his fist connected against Demetrius's jawbone with a terrible crack.

Demetrius went down.

Lucas's eyes were on her. He held something in his hand, a scroll of some kind. "Did he hurt you? Threaten you?"

Demetrius was scrabbling to his feet, backward, away from Lucas. He pulled himself to standing with the wall for support and rubbed his jaw with one hand, eyes spitting fire.

Lucas raised a fist again. "You were warned."

But Demetrius did not seem to care for another blow. With a last greedy look at Daria, he fled the room.

Lucas turned on her, tossed his scroll aside, and gripped her upper arms. He studied her face. "Are you well?"

She relaxed under his touch. "I am fine. He—he did nothing more harmful than spew his poisonous words."

And yet, were they not words that could destroy?

He released her and studied the pile on her mattress. "You are leaving, then?"

She drew herself up and looked into his eyes. "You made yourself quite clear."

He turned away and she thought he would leave without a word, but then he paced back to her. Then away again, like a caged animal, muttering to himself like a madman.

Yes, like a madman. One capable of murder, perhaps.

He turned abruptly. "And you wish to leave, do you?"

"No—I—I don't know. I shall miss—this house." Her voice was unsteady, a wisp of cloud against a gale wind.

"This house? Dark and tomb-like, save the garden and the one room you have brightened to match yourself? Or perhaps it is Clovis and Frona you are sad to leave. Become like parents to you, have they?"

His words were frantic, the look in his eye crazed.

Daria groped the bed for support. "Frona despises me."

"What, then, Daria? What shall you miss here in this house?"

He advanced on her, and she feared he would shake the truth from her.

"You, Lucas! I shall be grieved to part with you."

He might as well have shaken it from her, she trembled all the same.

"Ah, there it is. And why does Frona despise you, do you think?"

Daria sank to the bed. "She would hate any woman who came to this house after—"

"After my beloved wife?"

"Yes! She knows how much you loved her—"

"Do not speak of it. Of her."

Again the mad, desperate look in his eyes and the steps toward her, away from her, toward her.

Daria gripped the bedcovering at her thigh, and her hand

brushed the scroll he had tossed there. She lifted it, handed it to him. Perhaps it would bring him some measure of sanity, whatever it was.

He shook his head and held up his palms. "That is yours. It is for you. A gift."

She frowned. What sort of gift would Lucas give? She unrolled it carefully, scanned the contents. It was Thucydides. His second work.

"You said your father never found a copy before he died."

She dared not raise her head, dared not let him see her tears, the way the gift, the thought behind it, tore her apart. She held it away so her tears would not stain the papyrus.

"Thank you, Lucas." It was a whisper only. She did not trust her voice.

She stood and aligned the scroll carefully with the folded clothing. With her back to him, she breathed deeply against the pain. Spread a chitôn flat and mounded her belongings into its center. Tied the corners with trembling fingers. Even these slight efforts seemed impossible.

And then he was there behind her, as close as Demetrius had been, and yet all fire and heat, where Demetrius had been like a draft of cold air from underground.

Lucas was talking to himself again, but she understood these words.

Do I not deserve to be happy?

She released her hold on the makeshift pouch and turned a tight circle to face him.

His left hand moved to the small of her back and his right hand to her face. The madness in his eyes had turned to something other, but just as frightening. He pulled her to himself, crushed his lips to hers.

Daria breathed out the tension, the fear, the longing, and breathed in the scent of him, musky and sweet. She gave herself to his kiss even as she knew it could not last.

Too long, she let it go too long. She pushed her palms against his chest, broke the hold he had on her, and closed her heart to his moan of grief, of pain, as though someone had died.

"I must go, Lucas. It—it is not safe here—you have said this yourself—"

He dropped his arms, his head, even his shoulders seemed to collapse inward. "I do not deserve you. It is true." He turned away, crossed to the window, and stared into the gray sky. "Her blood is forever on my hands. My fault, all of it."

The face of the girl left in the brothel hovered before Daria's eyes. Her face and those strange circular markings. Like all the dead girls, Paul had said, and Lucas's wife was the first. She saw Demetrius, grinning at her. *I was one of the few who thought he might be innocent.*

Slowly, as though each moment were a passing month, Daria lifted her pouch, threaded an arm through, and secured it against her chest, never taking her eyes from Lucas's back.

She did not know what he was. What he had done or perhaps was still to do.

She knew only one thing.

She must run from this place, from this man, and she must not look back.

24

"COME ALONG, CHILD. DO NOT LINGER."

Daria scooped up the woven basket of bone needles and hemp threads from the entryway of Aquila's home and followed Paul into the street.

She'd found them all still in the house when she arrived, seated in the triclinium around tables full of food. Timothy and Paul she knew, and Priscilla, Aquila's wife. She needed reminding of the other two—the brawny men always at Paul's side—Gaius and Aristarchus. They were finishing their meal, but her hunger must have been apparent, for Priscilla seated her quickly and filled her plate.

Now she was impatiently following them to their city workshop, where they plied their trade and sold their goods and where apparently Paul worked alongside them.

"Holding court is more like it," Priscilla explained on the way, leaning in to whisper to Daria but loud enough for Paul to hear. "He pretends to be stitching, but with the parade of people through that shop every day, asking questions, seeking favors—ach! It's a wonder he gets anything done."

Paul grinned over his shoulder. "I may not produce much, but the traffic is good for business, you have to admit that, Priscilla!"

She waved him off with a dismissive hand but winked at Daria.

Daria hurried alongside, the basket growing heavy in her arms. "What favors does Paul perform?" She had only one favor in mind—that of securing a job in the school, though it was only fair that she be put to use in the meantime.

"Why healings, of course."

She said it airily, with no trace of irony. Daria watched Paul for contradiction. He did not turn.

"He—he heals people?"

Priscilla smiled. "He has the power of the Holy One, my dear. Demons flee when he commands, much to the dismay of this city full of magic and sorcery. There are even those who believe that anything he touches has the power to heal."

"But how?"

Priscilla pointed ahead. "Here we are. There is our shop." To Paul, she said, "Let the work begin, my friend!"

The tent-making business was clearly lucrative. A rectangular stall, spacious and cool in the shade of goat-hide awnings and walls, boasted piles of finished products. Aquila had arrived earlier to open, and already a cluster of young men were at its entrance.

But not shopping for canvas, from the eager looks they gave Paul. The older man quickly settled himself cross-legged on the floor of the shop, needles and threads and skins around him, and began to stitch as he spoke with each in turn.

Though the hides were tanned long before they reached the shop, occasional whiffs of the urine and animal dung used in tanning crossed Daria's nose. No one else seemed to notice. She put anxious hands to the combing out of goat hides—removing tiny burrs and bits of dried dung—and the scritch of her comb against the hides accompanied the conversation.

How long before Paul would speak with Tyrannus? While it was good of them to keep her busy, to take the sting out of their charity, she was not truly needed here and could not rely on their kindness forever. If the position at the school was not offered, she would soon be destitute. Perhaps she could find another tutoring situation, but those always came to an end. She needed something permanent. She felt the sun shift above the awning. Too slowly.

Priscilla spread darker skins on the floor and sat, her hands in a bowl of lard, coating the hemp thread. She wore a chitôn of reds and yellows today, as if to combat the drab grays and browns of her trade. Aquila sat beside her, cutting large squares for some new project.

Daria combed goat hides and watched the affectionate glances, listened to their good-natured teasing. They seemed true partners in every sense. Would she ever feel this kind of belonging?

As the morning passed and the stream of seekers flowing past Paul's feet did not abate, his answers, his challenges, his mysterious teaching began to raise questions in her own heart and mind and she listened with greater intent, despite her anxiety. Priscilla shifted her from combing to stitching, but she barely noticed the cold stone beneath her, the sharp needles that pricked her fingers, or the supple feel of hides and tug of coarse thread. Paul's teaching was like a story, well-told and captivating.

He had been ten years traveling the trade routes, he said. The list of towns he'd visited seemed endless—Antioch, Cyprus,

Iconium, Philippi, Thessalonica. Not to mention the famous cities of Athens and Jerusalem. He'd spent eighteen months in Corinth, where he had met Priscilla and Aquila after they fled Claudius's wrath against the Jews in Rome. They'd come to Ephesus together, the three of them, though Paul had left the couple here while he undertook yet another journey, revisiting many of the towns where followers had been established.

He had been in prison multiple times, been flogged before each imprisonment by his own people with forty lashes minus one. Beaten with rods, pelted with stones, shipwrecked. He had spent days in danger from nature, from bandits, from fools. Been hungry and thirsty, cold and naked and tired.

Was there any abuse he had not suffered? Who was this Messiah of his, this *Jesus*, that He could command such loyalty?

Finally Paul had returned here to Ephesus, to the western end of the Royal Road—Rome's all-important trading thoroughfare from the East—more than two years ago. He spent his time teaching and healing and helping Priscilla and Aquila build what he called the *ekklesia*, the community. It had grown to overflow the space the couple had available, and others were now also meeting in the home of Joseph, where Daria was to stay.

At a lull in the crowd, Daria slipped to the floor beside Paul. Perhaps she could redeem the time by increasing her knowledge. Aquila was haggling loudly with a customer in the shop's entrance, and Paul turned to her with a smile.

"It appears it is your turn, child."

"My turn?"

"I sense you are a woman with many questions, always. One who seeks to find the answers to all of life's riddles. You have questions for me?"

"May I?"

"Of course." He held up a needle. "But I must keep busy as we talk or Priscilla will be sewing *my* hide next!"

Daria worked as well, enjoying the far-off sounds of the harbor and the nearby buzz of pedestrians on the market street. "Your words are troubling, Paul. I have studied your Judean beliefs in the past, but what I hear you teaching is something quite different."

"Perceptive. A new way has come, you are correct."

"A new way?" She raised her eyebrows. "After so many centuries of man's good effort to please the gods? Surely you do not discard your faithfulness to your Jewish law?"

"What do you know of this law, Daria?"

She paused in her stitching, listened to the scuff of sandaled feet, studied the bright sky above the distant harbor. "People would say it is quite different from Greek thought, but I would disagree. Your 'One God' is perhaps more demanding in areas of morality than the Greek gods, and of course your law is written, unlike the Greeks'." She set aside her work, warming to her subject. "But the large portion of your beliefs is very much the same. Festivals and rituals to please your god and seek his blessing. Sacrifices for when you fail. Ritual washing to cleanse yourselves, just as the Greeks."

Paul's eyes on her glinted with flecks of blue and a hint of amusement.

"You burn grain offerings and pour oil libations as we do. You have priests that serve the people and your god, make atonement for wrongdoing. You have no statues, which is odd, but in keeping with your one god's jealousy and refusal to allow worship of any others. Your stories of the beginnings of humanity are different in some respects and alike in others, so much so that it can be assumed we all have a bit of the same story, the true story. You sing hymns of praise—"

"Child, you have made your point." Paul was laughing and shaking his head. "And if that head of yours contains such knowledge in other areas, I have no doubt you will find yourself a teaching position."

Daria shrugged and returned to her goatskin. "So are you faithful, still, to your Jewish ways?"

"I am faithful to my God, Daria. To that which He calls me to, but nothing more."

"That is not an answer."

He laughed again. "Tenacious and strong. I like that." He glanced at Priscilla, who had drawn near with her pile of threads and bowl of lard. "Reminds me of another woman I know."

The comparison warmed Daria and she smiled at Priscilla.

"It is perceptive of you, Daria, to see that the differences between the Jews and Greeks in their way of worship is so negligible that it is almost of no consequence. Most Jews would argue with me, of course, but there you have it. The chasm lies more between the purpose for the rites and rituals of each side. And of course the one great difference—that the many gods of the Greeks do not exist, and the powers that fuel their worship are demonic."

Daria's breath escaped in a rush and her hand trembled on the goatskin. Which was more blasphemous—to say that the gods were nothing or that they were the same as evil demons? How could he make such a statement without fear? A glance at his profile showed he did not flinch at his own words.

"But that aside, crucial as it is, we must examine the *purpose* of the laws, the rituals, the traditions. Do you bring offerings to your gods, Daria?"

"I—have not been as faithful of late as I ought, but yes, I try to please the gods."

"And why?"

The question was not asked unkindly, but a challenge lay behind it, certainly.

"I suppose you will call me selfish, but it is to ensure their blessing in my life."

"Good health, prosperity, that sort of thing?"

"Yes." She straightened.

"Love?"

She felt a blush and dropped her head. "Perhaps."

"Do not hang your head, child. There is no shame in wanting to be loved." He tied a knot and lifted the piece to rip at the thread with his teeth. "So. This is the purpose for your worship—to gain the favor of the gods. But what is the *gods'* purpose in it? You would say they rule from Mount Olympia, have done so since the beginning of time. What do they need with your bit of grain, your little pigeon?"

She frowned. "I—I suppose they wish only to see that I am *willing* to sacrifice. To show my humility."

"It is a good answer. Though why the gods should desire your humility is still a question. But enough of that. I will tell you where the great difference lies between the gods of the Greeks and the One True God."

Her work dropped to her lap and she studied his face.

"The One True God gives us His law expressly to show that we cannot keep it, can never earn His favor. It is impossible."

There was great sadness in Paul's voice with these words, and indeed it was sad to think of never pleasing one's god. Perhaps it was why the Jews often seemed despondent.

"That is disheartening, Paul."

"Yes, it is tragic."

"And the sacrifices?"

"Bloody reminders, each of them, that we have failed yet again."

She had no answer, and another fresh-faced youth appeared, his eyes alight with questions.

Paul patted her shoulder. "We will speak more later."

She had more questions and did not like to be cut off, but she slid aside to give the newcomer better access to the teacher, moved back into the shadows of the workshop and out of the sun that had climbed high and begun to scorch her skin.

The shop closed soon after the sun reached its zenith, and Aquila lowered the flaps to leave them in a false dusk as they shared a midday meal of roasted vegetables, sharp cheese, and olives. Priscilla and Aquila cleaned up the shop and made ready to return home for the afternoon while Paul planned to meet Timothy and a few others at the School of Tyrannus for afternoon teaching. Finally.

Daria lifted the basket she had brought and studied the man. "How do you teach all afternoon, after such a morning? Do you not grow weary of the questions, the constant conversation?"

Paul smiled and glanced upward. *"The Lord is my refuge and my strength."*

Priscilla pressed a packet into Paul's hands and smiled at Daria. "And also, he never stops eating!"

Daria shifted the basket to her other hip. Asked the one question she'd pondered all morning. "May I come with you to the school? To see about teaching—?"

"Let me introduce the idea to Tyrannus without you present, Daria. I will convince him of your qualifications before he sees how young you are and dismisses the idea out of hand."

She sighed but nodded. "Thank you, Paul." She smiled on Priscilla. "All of you, for your kindness."

Priscilla traded glances with Paul, who shook his head slightly, as though she would reveal something that he did not wish revealed. The brief exchange brought a flutter of apprehension to Daria's belly. She did not like secrets.

But it was not for her to press them when they had been so generous.

Aquila took the basket from her arms. "Will you come home with us and rest, Daria? We will take you to Joseph's house this evening."

She shook her head and eyed the street and the wide expanse over the sea beyond, calling to her. "Thank you, no. I think I will take a walk, down near the harbor." She flashed a smile at Paul. "I have been given much to think on this morning."

She left them as they set out for their afternoon pursuits and soon reached the head of Harbor Street, its columns arrowed toward the horizon, as though they met where hazy white of sky met gold glint of sea. Already the street seemed less foreign, less intimidating than it had that first night she had arrived. And the morning she and Lucas had seen the sorcerers.

At the harbor, she found a low stone wall where she could watch the dockside activity. The pleasant sound of ropes thumped against wooden decks and the horrid squeal of ships sliding into port blended to a strange nostalgia for her father and her childhood. She shaded her eyes to watch the ships, awaiting their turns to unload their crates of cinnamon and pepper from the East, or perhaps cedarwood from Phoenicia or African ivory. They would restock with Ephesian goods for faraway ports. Had any of them come from Rhodes?

Thoughts of Rhodes turned her mind toward Paul. He had spoken about sorcerers to some who sat at his feet today. It was clear that this new sect, begun in Judea, had spread to Greeks as well, that they all worshipped their One God together here in Ephesus, and that there were those in the city who greatly opposed their message. Daria saw the looks of fear in the eyes of some who came, the way they drank in Paul's words of reassurance as he spoke of their fight against the powers of darkness. She found his confidence was easy to absorb as she listened to his passionate speeches, but now, far from Paul, it drained away.

The sun warmed, but it did not loosen tense muscles. Instead, her agitation grew as the afternoon waned. Was Paul pleading her case even now, or had he forgotten her in the crush of people who sought his wisdom and gifts?

It was not only his confidence she could not retain. The logic of his words fled as well. Did he truly teach that the Greek gods were nothing? And that even his own One God could not be pleased with attempts at righteous living, with sacrifices and offerings? What was the use of such a religion, then? His argument was like something turned upside down. Like dropping a rock from a great height and seeing it rise upward rather than fall to the ground. Impossible. And dizzying.

The harbor breeze and open sky, the smell of fish and salt, the feel of sun on her face—it should be pleasant. Instead, she could think only of Lucas. She did not truly believe he had killed his wife. Nor anyone else. But did he pursue his destructive agenda today? Would there be any other to dissuade him from his course? She inhaled against the pressure in her chest and dropped her head. Had she abandoned him to whatever evil would devour him, in order to save herself? What would Paul say to such a cowardly decision?

But Lucas had dismissed her. What more could she have done?

A disturbance across the docks distracted her from the useless train of thought. She lifted her head and studied the commotion—a group of men and perhaps a few women, though she could not be certain at this distance. Shouting and even a few fists swinging. Her feet took her toward the tumult of their own accord, ignoring her usual caution.

By the time she reached the edges of the gathered crowd, the conflict in the center was difficult to see. She almost gave up and wandered away, until she heard a name she recognized, *Jesus, the Christ.*

She pushed through the crowd of curiosity-seekers, reminded of the scene she had witnessed on the Embolos on the way to the temple. Would she find another madman in the center? The city seemed rife with such evil.

The circle was widening, clearing away from one central figure, confirming her suspicion.

But this was no madman.

He is beautiful. Strange thought, but no other words could well-describe the young man in the center of the circle. Wavy hair falling against a chiseled jaw, full lips, muscular shoulders and upper arms. Had he been the one fighting? If so, it was no wonder his opponents had backed away from their own downfall.

He turned a slow circle in the center of the group, as though gathering attention, waiting for the silence that would signal a ready audience. As he completed the circuit, he raised his eyes, scanned the crowd, and found Daria's gaze on him.

And he smiled.

25

AT THE UNNATURAL SMILE, A CHILL BLOOMED IN Daria's chest and spread outward to her fingertips. Did he look at her with special attention, or was it imagined?

But no, others in the crowd were following his gaze, watching her with expectancy. She twisted her arms at her waist and dipped her chin. But she could not break the hold of that smile.

"There are some among you who doubt."

His voice was low and smooth, and the crowd seemed to lean forward to catch each word.

"But all of you"—he spread his arms to the encircled audience—"all of you have seen the power, and you know it is real."

They were eager, this group, eager to hear every word. But through a gap in the crowd a struggle was visible. Two men were being restrained by three or four others.

"But there are things you do not know!" He called this loudly over their heads, then dropped his voice to a whisper. "Secrets and answers that can be yours."

He wore a white tunic, belted in black, the loose ends of the belt swinging long at his leg in a hypnotic rhythm.

"What secrets do you desire brought forth from the darkness?"

Again he seemed to speak only to her, his eyes trained on hers, daring her to blink. She swallowed, hard, and his face blurred for a moment, indistinct and wavering, then sharpened.

He took several steps toward her, and though the crowd seemed eager to hear his words, they spread away at his approach, like ripples of water fleeing a dropped stone.

"You have questions, Daria?"

She shook her head, still clutching herself. Her fingers felt hot, so hot, against her arms. His knowledge of her name was like fire on her skin.

"Of course you do. You wish to know the future. You wish for reassurances."

As would anyone. This was no special knowledge.

"You wish to know whether you will defeat the evil that comes against one you love."

Still, it could be anyone. There was no need to fear. She took a step backward, away from those cold eyes.

He was upon her now, soft fingers with a grip of iron on her hand. He leaned in to share his secrets, and the feathery-light brush of his lips on her hair was like the touch of spider legs. The heat in her fingers blazed inward to her chest. A cloud passed over the sun and Daria shivered at the sudden cessation of warmth and light.

She passed tense fingers through her hair where he had brushed against it, and the strands caught and pulled between her fingers.

"I will give you these answers, Daria. Free of charge."

She tried to pull away, but his grip did not loosen. Did the crowd fade away as he spoke to only her?

"You make inquiries into matters beyond yourself. You tread in places you should fear and reach for knowledge you ought not to gain. Better for you to return to where you belong." He reached for her chin, turned her face toward his until she looked into his eyes. "Go back to Rhodes."

How could he know? What strange powers had given him this knowledge?

"Look, Daria." He still held her chin and turned it toward the harbor. "There is a ship bound for Rhodes now. Surely they would take on a lovely passenger." He gave her a bit of a shove toward the dock, releasing her at last.

She stumbled forward and righted herself a moment before falling.

Then she ran for the quay and the dockworkers loading the last bit of cargo onto a barge that would take it out to a ship at port.

"Excuse me, please, excuse me—" The words erupted, thick and clumsy on her lips.

A sea-worn sailor with hands as large as paddles looked her up and down with a grin. "Aye?"

"Where is this ship's next port?"

"We'll be sailing for Rhodes within the hour, miss."

Daria staggered back a step.

"Careful, there." The sailor reached to take her arm.

She pulled away, then turned and ran. But where was there to go? The strange man who had whispered her fate had disappeared, and the crowd was dispersing. Two figures ran toward her, only slightly familiar.

"Daria?"

Not again. She shook her head.

"Daria, it is Tychicus and Trophimus. Friends of Paul's, remember? We met this morning, in Aquila's home."

"Yes. Of course. I am—sorry—I—I am a bit dizzy."

Trophimus took her arm and led her to a bench, where the docks met the Harbor Street. She sat, with the two men on either side. "We tried to stop him from speaking to you, but there were too many of them."

She blinked. "You were the ones held back by other men?" Was it their voices she heard calling out the name of Jesus?

Trophimus nodded. "What did he say to you?"

Daria eyed the ship headed for Rhodes. "Who is he?"

"Only one of the sorcerers who tells fortunes for money. You didn't give him money?"

She shook her head. "He knew things. About me. Knew my name, where I was from."

Tychicus growled, deep in his throat. "There is much trickery wrapped up in it, but they *do* receive genuine knowledge from the powers of the air."

The phrase brought another shiver. "He told me to return to Rhodes. On that ship."

The two men looked to each other over her head at this, and something passed between them, like the look Paul had exchanged with Priscilla earlier.

"What is it? Why did he tell me this?"

"Will you go, Daria?" Trophimus's voice was tight. "Will you flee to Rhodes?"

"You tread in places you should fear."

Well, she did fear. But would she continue to push into that fear? Paul would say that evil could be defeated. Perhaps even Lucas could be saved. Did she have the courage to test his teaching?

"No. No, I will not return to Rhodes."

Tychicus squeezed her arm. "Come with us, then. Priscilla sent us to find you, to bring you to Joseph's house. There are others of the believers there."

Believers. Yes, that was a good name for them. They had a faith she longed for, and it gave them a strength she envied.

———

Daria slowed at the door of another stranger's house, the home of Joseph and his Greek wife.

Trophimus urged her forward. "Joseph is a Jew, but he married one of us." His voice held a tinge of pride. "There are other Jews who have married Greeks within the community. The Messiah has come for all, and we are all one in Him."

Tychicus nodded. "The believers meet together often, but always on the first day of the week, the day our Lord rose from the dead."

This was new. "From the *dead*?"

"Yes, the Messiah, Jesus, whose death atones for us—" At a look from Trophimus, Tychicus broke off. "I am sorry. It is too much. Paul says you are to be taught slowly."

At this, she bristled and stepped toward the door. "I have never needed anyone to slow their lessons in my life."

Tychicus's face flushed. "No—no, not because you could not understand—only—only because it is so important, so new, and he wants you to have time to accept."

"Why is it so important to him that I accept his teaching?"

The two men hurried her into the entryway. Trophimus called out a greeting.

A slight woman appeared in the small courtyard, older than Priscilla, perhaps in her sixties.

"Ah, is this our visitor?"

Tychicus turned her over as if she were the emperor's wife. "Here she is, yes. Daria, this is Joseph's wife, Iris."

"Welcome, my dear girl." The woman took Daria's hands and led her forward. "Let me get you away from these two eager young men. Are you hungry?" To Daria's escorts, she shook her head. "I need not even ask if you two are hungry."

"Iris is famous for her lamb stew."

Daria smiled. She could almost hear the hunger in Trophimus's voice.

"No stew tonight, boy. The others will arrive too soon."

Indeed, a crowd similar to what she had witnessed in the early morning hours soon formed in the central courtyard of the house, which was not as large as Aquila's. If this home were to hold the overflow, it appeared another would soon be needed.

As this morning, Paul arrived to the eager greetings of the community, with Gaius and Aristarchus on either side. Did the two men travel everywhere with him? Were they students, or were they protection? Perhaps both.

Daria stood aside but still found herself pulled into conversations, introduced to more new faces than she could remember. She tried to imprint each name in her memory, to drink them all in, make them part of herself. They belonged to each other. But could she belong here?

Paul taught from the far end of the courtyard, with the crowd mostly sitting or leaning against walls. He began with thanks directed at Joseph and Iris for the use of their home. "Gifts are given by the Spirit to each of us. To some is given the gift of hospitality, and none exercises it more beautifully than Iris." He directed a small bow in her direction and she rewarded him with a smile. "And I speak of more than her lamb stew. I speak of her generous heart." He nodded to her husband beside her. "And, Joseph, though you could not make lamb stew to save your life, you are a good man all the same."

The crowd laughed, Daria with them, and Joseph shrugged.

Paul grinned. "I am in jest. All of us know what a man of the Torah Joseph is. Teacher and scholar. And friend." At this there was a smattering of appreciative applause, and Joseph dipped his head in embarrassed acknowledgment.

"Tell us of the day on the road, Paul."

Daria searched for the one who had shouted the request, but the faces were blending together. It mattered little who had voiced it, for there were nods and voices of agreement all around.

"You never tire of hearing the story, do you? You must remember you each have a story. But I will tell you mine."

What followed was a tale unlike any Daria had ever heard.

He had been a teacher for many years in Jerusalem. Honored among his peers, a respected leader. When this new sect of believers in the Messiah Jesus had arisen, he had seen at once that their claim was blasphemy, that they preached the forsaking of the Law, taught that the time for sacrifices had come to an end. Outraged and zealous to protect the Law he had been raised and trained to revere, he led others in a sweep of the city, raiding homes and synagogues for these heretics.

"It was not enough that they be found and even flogged." Paul had the rapt attention of every soul in the courtyard. "I dragged them before the religious leaders to be sentenced. And to be executed." His voice broke over the final word, and the hush in the home was like deep water, still and solemn.

"Yes, executed. One after another, like lambs to the slaughter, I watched them meet their deaths. And on the day that Stephanus looked up into heaven and saw the Son of man standing at the right hand of God, I stood by and watched the stones rain down on his head and knew in my heart that he spoke the truth." Paul hung his head and breathed heavily. "That is the worst of it, my friends. You have heard it once more, you know the truth that will gnaw my soul until I stand before the throne of the Holy One myself. I knew they were right, and I denied it still, for my own pride."

Was he weeping? Daria's heart reached out to the man wrapped in his guilt.

He sniffed and raised his head. "It was I who deserved to be under those stones, my friends. It is I, even now, who deserve not your respect but your disdain. And yet, by His mercy, I stand before you. For on that day, on that singular day on the road to Damascus where I would glut my pride on more killing, our Lord spoke to me, revealed Himself to me, and called me to Himself."

Daria scanned the crowd. Paul had said that they each knew the story, but their smiling, tear-filled eyes testified that they received it afresh. She felt the power of the story in her own heart.

"Tell of the light, Paul!"

"Yes, and the horse!"

He blinked, then beamed at them with watery eyes. "Like children, all of you! Begging for another tale." But the self-conscious smile gave way to laughter. "Yes, you know what happened." He waggled a scolding finger at his audience. "You want to hear how when that bright light flashed, I fell from my horse and landed with a smack on my—pride."

The room erupted in laughter.

"But, my friends, I tell you, such a light you have never seen." His expression stilled. A far-off look came over him, and a hush fell again on his audience. "Like the light that still shone in the face of Moses when he descended from Sinai. Like the light breaking over the waters of the deep, the moment the Holy One spoke the first words of creation."

His hold on the crowd was complete. Daria could not pull her gaze from his face, which even now seemed alight with something holy.

He was silent a moment, then shook his head as though returning to them. "That I went blind for three days was no surprise. That I lived at all was the greater shock. For the veil between the seen and the unseen was torn asunder on that road.

"But, my friends, you must hear me. I have since witnessed these things again, these powers and principalities beyond our physical realm. Battles being waged and victories hard-won, and a kingdom for which we fight, that we do not yet comprehend with our mortal eyes. I say *not yet*, for there will come a day when the veil will dissolve at last and the earth and all upon it will be restored to former glory, to fellowship with the Creator as it was meant to be."

At these words, Daria breathed out tension she had not known she carried—a clenching fear that gripped her mind, her soul.

Paul continued for some time, until the lamps needed to be lit and it grew cool in the twilight. They ended with a song, though she could not catch the words because each sang in his own language, and the melding of Greek and Hebrew, Aramaic and Latin, was like a rich broth seasoned with many flavors and offered up to their One God as a sacrifice of praise.

Paul beckoned to her as the crowd emptied.

Heart racing, she weaved through the remaining assembly to the opposite side of the courtyard, smiling and nodding to those who greeted her as if she were part of them.

"Tyrannus was absent from his lecture hall today, my dear. I had no chance to speak on your behalf."

Daria took a deep breath, stilled her disappointment. "I understand. But I must find work. I have no money."

"What of your wages from Lucas?"

"I—I did not ask for wages before I left."

Paul's eyes narrowed and he studied her face as if searching for untruth. He opened his mouth to speak but was interrupted by a Greek who approached with the nervous energy of a rabbit.

"Paul, you must listen to reason. This afternoon's display—"

Paul held up a hand. "Rhesus, I know that you mean well, but your warnings will not stop me from speaking. I am not ashamed of the gospel of Christ."

"Then at least take care for your own body!"

Paul laughed. "This old body has endured more than you can imagine. And it will endure so long as He has use for it, not a day longer."

"But you are reckless, Paul! As city clerk, I hear the rumblings from all parts of Ephesus. This city is about to boil over, I tell you, and I fear you will be at the center of it!"

They argued with her between, but Daria did not move. She would hear every word this extraordinary man would utter.

"Rhesus, did you hear the story of our Lord's salvation in my life tonight?"

"You know I have heard it often—"

"Then you know I deserve nothing less than to be at the center of a boiling cauldron. Do not speak to me of quieting the message to avoid what I deserve."

Rhesus sighed and turned away, but Paul caught his arm.

"Only, Rhesus, the others are not to suffer for my sins. You will tell me if any others are in danger. This I will not stand."

Rhesus nodded and hurried off again and Paul turned back to Daria, waving to Iris to join them.

"Iris, Daria is worried that she has no money. She does not wish to be an imposition."

Daria narrowed her eyes at Paul. Was he always so transparent, even when sharing the feelings of others?

"Nonsense, girl. We have a spare bedchamber all made up for you, and you can stay as long as you like. Paul has told me what an important part—"

A little *tch* from Paul silenced the woman.

Enough of these strange comments. Daria turned on Paul, emboldened by her curiosity. "What does she mean? What have you told her?"

Paul threw his hands up in surrender. "I did not want to burden you too soon with this knowledge. It is much for anyone to bear, and you have not yet—"

"What knowledge, Paul? I feel as if I have been to the theater today, as though I have been a spectator to some great drama I do not understand. There is more here than can be understood, perhaps more than can even be seen."

He smiled. "Hmm, yes. Very well, Daria, I will tell you. There are times when I am given special knowledge. The gift of discernment, you might say, to see beyond the temporal and to understand truths and people in a special way. And our Lord has given me knowledge of you. There is a battle coming—a great and fearsome battle in the unseen realm of spirit—and you are to play a crucial part. Your special gifts of understanding and language—they have set you apart to be a warrior in this battle, though your future beyond it has not been given to me to know."

His words hung in the air, suspended and yet weighty.

That night, that last night with Xanthos, flashed before her memory. The great evil. The blood. The death.

She had run from evil ever since. But there was no running.

Not from this. She had known, always known, that it would find her. And she had believed that when it did, it would devour her.

And now at last she had found a people who seemed to have power over that very evil. Who insisted it could be defeated, not merely avoided. The claim both drew her and repulsed her at once. It was like being plunged under refreshingly cool water, then held there too long. Would she be saved, or would she be destroyed?

A question it appeared that not even Paul could answer.

26

THE PRESS OF THE STREET CROWD RANKLED LUCAS'S
tight nerves as he shoved his way along the Embolos, bumping
shoulders with more than one surprised shopper. The stink of
the crowds mingled with the odor of street-side markets cooking
meat. Too many pedestrians lingered, chattering and getting in
his way.

But at least there was the relief of motion, of a destination,
even if it did nothing to further his aims. The least he could do
was to ensure Daria's livelihood. To cast her out without fulfilling
his promise made him even less of a man.

Daria had mentioned once that Adelphos had forbidden
her to marry. Lucas must make certain nothing of the sort happened here. She must be allowed to be fully herself—scholar and
woman—and not choose between the two.

But within the hour, he was back on the street, his mission failed. Tyrannus had no use for a woman, no matter how learned.

Very well, if he could do nothing for Daria, he must do something for himself.

Hektor's shop was dim as usual, with only a young man Lucas had not met at the back of the crowded space, scraping black roots into a small pile of powder. His gaze shifted slowly to Lucas where he blocked the doorway.

"Is Hektor below?"

The boy squinted. No doubt Lucas was only a dark figure, outlined by the light from the street behind him.

"Your name?"

"He will see me." Lucas strode to the narrow doorway that led downward, but the boy reached it first.

"What is your business?"

Clearly Hektor's protégé was full of his own importance.

"You can step aside. I came to see Hektor." It took only a casual swipe of arm to knock the boy out of his path, and he hurried down the darkened steps. Let him get this over with quickly.

The underground chamber was much as it was the last time he had visited—men working at tables, women lying on mats moaning. Three torches blazed along each of the four rock-hewn walls, illuminating more of the hall than Lucas wished to see. He avoided the faces of the women on the floor. He had no wish to be burdened with their identities. If he was successful, they would soon be freed from their self-imposed prison.

Hektor glided to him immediately, hands outstretched with a welcome that did not seem sincere, given the cold expression falling over his features. His glowing hair was tied back today, and as he drew near the torch at the stairs, he blinked in seeming discomfort.

Were his eyes oversensitive to light because of living in this darkness? How often did he ascend to daylight? Such a life must change a man.

"Lucas. As usual, we were not expecting you."

Lucas did not miss Hektor's subtle shift toward the steps, as though he would prefer to rid himself quickly of his visitor.

"I was passing by, wondered how the work was going."

"Oh, as usual. Quite usual. Though Pharnaces did appreciate your . . . *assistance* with our recent incident."

"He should be more careful. The agora is no place for secrecy."

"Yes. Well. It was fortunate, then, that you were nearby."

"And how do you feel about the rumblings in the city over this new sect out of Judaea they are calling 'the Way'? It seems even Greeks are following this Jewish Messiah in droves."

Hektor's gaze lifted to the ceiling and he shrugged narrow shoulders. "It is preposterous. As though our gods, worshipped from the dawn of time, are not controlling enough, and we must submit to yet another." He sighed and pressed his fingertips together at his waist. "There are even some of our number who have been snatched up by these troublemakers."

"Indeed?" Lucas scanned the room. It seemed as crowded as ever.

"Not many, not many, thankfully. But several of our wealthier members, which is quite unbearable. It is a topic of continual debate, how best to deal with them."

"The temperature of the city seems to be rising. As though on the brink of some kind of outbreak."

"It cannot happen soon enough, if you ask me. We all have a stake in the prosperity of Ephesus, and of her Lady. This new sect teaches against our very way of life."

"I did not think you so fond of the priests and auguries."

"I am not! They bow and scrape and appease, and what does it get them? Only to live at the mercy of the gods. But in our quest for self-governance, we must not allow all we know as true to be upended."

"And the new sect condemns your practices."

Hektor lifted his chin, as though Lucas himself had been the accuser. "I care not for their condemnation, nor their praise. They are nothing to us."

Lucas bit back a rebuttal. The man's entire demeanor contradicted his words. "Until the donations disappear."

Hektor shrugged. "It is troubling. We depend upon the kindness of those of you who have done well in the marketplace in order to press forward in our work."

The obvious hint was not lost on Lucas, but he did not acknowledge it.

A young woman, perhaps about Daria's age, approached Hektor. "How long will you keep me waiting?" Her tone was bold, annoyed, and the luxury of her clothing and jewels indicated she was not accustomed to waiting.

"I will be with you in a moment, Selene. Go and speak with Numa about preparation."

The girl wandered off and Hektor turned to Lucas, his voice amused. "Fortunately, there is no shortage of rich young girls interested in . . . experiences . . . who also pay quite well."

"Who is she? She looks familiar."

"She should. The daughter of Demetrius the silversmith."

Lucas forced his expression to remain impassive. "Have you no shame, Hektor?"

"Shame? I do not force them. Besides, they live empty lives until the day they enter this place to aid our knowledge quest."

"Until your quest kills them."

Hektor sighed. "Occasionally. But they die nobly, and it is a sort of mercy killing, I believe. What else have they to live for?"

"And what will you do about your enemies, these Christians?"

Hektor raised his eyebrows. "I was unaware you were so familiar with the sect."

Lucas shrugged. "I am only curious as to how you—how we—can stop them from decreasing our numbers."

Hektor turned his face from Lucas, so only that sharp-nosed profile was evident. "You speak as though you have been accepted into our number, Lucas. I have not yet proposed such a thing to the rest. We appreciate your generosity, of course, but that is not the same as bringing you into our inner circle." He turned slitted eyes on Lucas once more. "We must be quite certain that you have no agenda of your own, no reason to expose our work or betray us to others."

Lucas's muscles tightened, his fingers curled into fists at his sides. "I can assure you, Hektor—"

He held up a long-fingered hand. "No need to be defensive. I am merely stating that we have a long way to go before you are fully trusted."

"Very well. In the meantime, then, I will keep my *generosity* to myself."

Hektor licked his lips, watched Lucas. "Then we must see to it that trust happens quickly. In fact, you, perhaps, have given me an idea of how you could prove yourself . . ."

"Name it."

"Kill their leader."

Lucas's throat seized and he forced a sputtering cough.

"The man named Paul. He has incited riots all over the province of Asia. Cut off the head and the body will die."

Lucas was left speechless, staring at Hektor.

The shop owner shrugged. "Simple, really. And when I hear that he is dead, you shall know all our secrets."

27

"I AM COMING WITH YOU."

Daria brushed the crumbs of the morning meal from her lap, then lifted the tray of remains—bits of bread and cheese and olive pits—and met Iris's frown with a look of determination.

The morning sun had not yet lifted high enough to stream into the small courtyard, and the feeble light cast a pall over Iris's skin and tinged her concern with something like dread.

"Daria, there may be trouble. You have been a help but—"

"I have been inactive too long. If anything is to change, I must do something."

The woman gave a half smile of defeat. "Almost I would think you have become one of us." She pointed to the tray. "Leave that. Keto will get it."

"I should be the one in Keto's place, serving you for the

kindness you've shown me this past week. I can take a tray to the kitchen."

In the week she had been a guest in the home of Joseph and Iris, Daria had done little more than listen to teachings and join in their meals, often celebratory events that involved many of the believers. It had pained her to leave off teaching, and she had spent sleepless nights, lying in her bed and wondering what Lucas might be doing. But in truth, the time with these people had been good for her soul. The way they shared all they had, both their possessions and their hearts, the way their singing and worship of their One God seemed a joy rather than a duty—all of it was a challenge to everything she believed.

And today, today she would test the new stirrings that grew more frequent, the feeling that she must move forward into the city, into danger even. Could she be like these people? Take on evil with nothing more than her intellect and cunning and will?

Iris's friend, Europa, was in the courtyard when Daria returned from the kitchen. She cradled her infant daughter in a sling across one shoulder, the fuzzy head and tiny feet poking from either end of the whitened linen. Daria had met Europa and her husband, Seneca, several times this week, and the woman smiled on her as she entered the courtyard.

Daria crossed to the women and stroked Flora's soft cheek. Then started back, surprised. The baby's left foot, peeking from the sling, was horribly twisted. She reached for the foot, then dropped her hand.

Europa smiled again and hugged Flora closer. "There is nothing that can be done, the physicians say." She shrugged. "But if not for this foot, I would be childless still, so I thank God for it each day."

Daria frowned and turned a curious gaze to Iris.

"I have not shared your miracle with Daria yet." She gave Europa a quick embrace around the shoulders. "They were unable to have children for many years. Then the Holy One gifted them with this special girl, whose parents did not deem worth living. She was found on the banks of the Tiber in Rome, where they were residing until a few months ago."

Daria swallowed and glanced away. The exposure of deformed children, especially girls who would likely never wed, was a common yet unspoken practice. Europa had rescued this child considered worthless and was raising her as their own?

Europa and her baby joined the two of them for the long walk to the Temple of Artemis. The crowds were sparse compared to the festival day when she'd last entered the temple precincts, and without the concern to search out Lucas and discover his intent, she was free to appreciate the wonder that lay atop the hill they approached. The warm sun struck marble and gold, and the temple precinct glowed like a snow-covered mount slashed with gleaming metal. The massive enclosure swallowed them into itself through the arched double gate, and they joined the murmuring flow of penitents, tourists, and priests spreading through the courtyards.

Iris nodded toward the long stoa on the north side of the temple. "Over there is where he typically teaches."

The same location where she had waited for Lucas, where he had appeared, intent on something still unknown. She frowned. The reminder troubled her. So many unanswered questions.

"Why does he come here, Iris? When he only intends to preach against all that is considered holy in this place?" Daria bit her lip at the question she'd asked too loudly.

Iris lifted one shoulder and smiled, searching the length of the stoa for a familiar face. "It is his way. He begins in the synagogues first, until the Jews will listen to no more of his message, then moves to the streets, the schools, the homes—wherever an audience will gather."

They picked their way through the crowd toward the stoa, the sun heating Daria's neck. "I thought that you were a Jewish sect. Why do the—?"

"We follow the Way, Daria. The New Covenant, for Jews and Gentiles alike. Although this new community still has many questions to answer. Must we Gentiles become Jews in every way before we are to be accepted? Or are the Jews to give off following the Law they have held to for millennia? Or is it neither, or both? These are the questions that Paul answers, wherever he can."

Europa pointed. "There he is." She threaded her way to a cluster of eager learners, many sitting at Paul's feet and others lingering at the edge of the crowd, curious about this teacher, whose words contradicted the very surroundings he chose as his classroom.

Iris's husband, Joseph, smiled and extended an arm, inviting all three women closer, but Daria found a place with her back against a column to listen.

The lesson had already grown warmly familiar. In a voice that would cause envy in any orator, Paul boomed his story over the people, of what he had seen while traveling to Damascus, one of the ten Greek cities of the Decapolis in Judaea and Syria. He skimmed lightly over his years in the deserts of Arabia, inquiring of the One God about his future ministry. Thumped fist against palm to reinforce his God's instruction that he was to bring the message of the Jewish Messiah to the Greeks, and that Jesus was a Messiah for all people.

It was at this place in the story that those hovering at the outskirts of the crowd grew restless, some of them calling insults across the heads of the disciples.

"Look behind us, Jew. What do we need with your god or his son? The most powerful goddess on earth visits this sacred place!"

Several catcalls echoed this sentiment. The gathering seemed to shift into two camps, those with Paul and those against. A buzz of nervous energy whooshed through the crowd, through Daria. Bystanders glanced left and right, as though they feared the goddess's retaliation for Paul's blasphemy against her.

Did *she* fear it? As these people divided, where did she belong? From her place against the column, Daria could step in either direction, join either faction. She scanned the faces of the believers. Some were fearful and some at peace, eyes trained confidently on Paul. Priscilla, trading smiles with her husband and her teacher, as if they had expected, even welcomed this moment. Beyond the Northern Stoa, a crowd of dissenters swelled. More than one bent to pick up a rock.

In the middle of this group, one stood apart, arms crossed and eyes cold. Demetrius.

Daria slid closer to Priscilla and Aquila, breath quickening. She would rather he not see her in this place.

And yet, was this not why she had come? To seek answers from anywhere they could be found? She inhaled the determination she had felt with Iris in the courtyard. Had she absorbed any of the courage of the believers in her time with them?

She leaned to Priscilla. "I will return in a few moments."

Priscilla pressed her fingertips into Daria's arm, fear etching her face.

Daria nodded. "I will be careful."

She left the portico and circled the crowd of red faces and upraised fists, then slipped through a gap to where Demetrius still stared at Paul, unmoving.

"Demetrius."

He did not shift his glance at once, and when he did drop his eyes to look at her, it was without recognition. Had he forgotten her so quickly?

"It is Daria of Rhodes, the tutor Lucas brought—"

"Is Lucas here?" He swiveled from her, searched the crowds.

"No." She waited for his attention to return. "I have some questions for you."

An amused smile tugged at his lips, condescension in his eyes. "How can I assist the brilliant tutor?"

"I want to know more about the city killings. And about Lucas's wife."

Around them, more worshippers were dropping their small cakes of grain and fruits on the altars and pressing into the commotion with curious glances.

Demetrius leaned and spoke in her ear. "So you think you have solved that puzzle, eh?"

His nearness raised the flesh on her arms. "I have solved nothing. I am still looking for more pieces."

"And you think I have them?"

At Daria's side someone yelled a vile curse in the direction of the stoa.

She stayed close to Demetrius, though he was no more safe. "Why are they so infuriated by Paul's message?"

Again the condescension, this time with raised eyebrows. "You could never understand. Not being from Ephesus. The more converts this outsider wins to his preposterous religion, the fewer devoted worshippers belong to Artemis." He glanced behind him at the temple and its outbuildings and altars, gleaming marble statuary and forest of columns. "And then what happens to

Ephesus? Everything we are is built upon this temple. It is the largest banking center of Asia, brings thousands of worshippers to buy goods in our cities every year."

"Including your silver replicas of the shrine?"

He grimaced. "Yes, I head the Guild of Metalsmiths. Since this Jew came to our city, began his teaching to the visitors who come, he has undermined our business."

Daria narrowed her eyes. "Truly? With the thousands, as you say, who come every year, you are concerned with a few who do not take home your trinkets? I should think you had larger concerns."

Demetrius's chest seemed to expand and his face harden. "It is not simply the lost revenue, woman. It is the *principle*. He speaks against all that makes our city great. Perhaps it is some Jewish plot. They are always fomenting rebellion in that backward country."

"Lucas is not a silversmith. What is his part in your concern?"

He had no chance to answer. A mighty shout of outrage burst from the crowd.

Daria jerked her attention toward her friends. The press of people was too great, already blocking the stoa, churning like foam at the lip of the sea.

Demetrius pointed toward an advancing group, climbing toward the Sacred Way from the road below. "You would be better asking your questions of them."

Sorcerers.

Their robes, their demeanor, and the swinging incense carried by the leader shouted their identity. A shudder passed along Daria's skin, a cold finger trailing from her neck to her lower back.

Demetrius was moving toward the stoa, to lend support, no doubt.

She twisted uncertain fingers at her waist. Should she regain her place on the stoa? Stand with her friends? Or seek out the sorcerers, as Demetrius had suggested? Both prospects held danger.

She pulled away from the crowd and met the group of sorcerers outside the gate, feigning confidence. Now that she was closer, she recognized the leader as the white-haired shop owner she'd encountered on the Embolos.

His eyes flicked over her as she approached.

"Lucas's friend, am I right? I never forget beauty."

The compliment slid over her like something cold.

"My friend seems unwell of late. So many things trouble him, as you know."

Hektor gave a slow nod to the others in his group. They circled him and shuffled on.

The acrid incense burned her nose and watered her eyes. She leaned from the smoke, but it enveloped.

"Indeed." Hektor watched her with squinted eyes. "Lucas is a tortured soul. I like to think we have brought him some measure of peace, however." His voice was low, as if they spoke privately in his shop.

She let her gaze drift over the temple complex, as if the conversation meant little to her. Her throat had gone dry. "I am certain you have. He is pleased to have been made one of you." She gambled, but direct questions would gain her nothing.

"Is that what he told you?" Hektor's lips twitched into a slight smile. "He is premature, perhaps. But I am hopeful that after this initial period of testing is complete, we will have the pleasure of welcoming him into our fold."

That was it, then. Some sort of initiation or mystery rites.

Daria swayed on her feet. Had she hoped for something other? Behind her, another shriek of indignation shot from the stoa area. On the plain below, a flock of black birds lifted and flapped away like a dark curtain.

Did she believe him? Black spots hovered at the edge of her vision, like the lifting birds. Lucas, a sorcerer?

No. She did not believe it. Yet she had escaped with only her life the first time. She must be wiser. There could be no returning.

"And you, my girl?" Hektor slid closer, his fingers brushing her arm. Dark eyes pulled her into his thrall, and his white hair reflected the sun like the temple columns. "From what I have heard you have an interest in deeper knowledge as well."

She pulled away. "You'll not find me so eager a learner."

He raked a measuring glance over her. "Perhaps a . . . participant, then?"

Daria's skin itched. What did he mean by *participant*?

Behind Hektor, magistrates and city officials dashed up the plain toward the temple gate. Roman soldiers accompanied them with the clink of scale armor and the iron strike of hobnailed boots against paving stone.

Hektor glided on. She stared blankly at the arriving officials, a rising tumult at her back.

There was going to be a riot.

She turned and pushed into the crowd. Where was Paul? Did he still have Gaius and Aristarchus at his side for protection? Where were Priscilla and Aquila? Iris and Joseph?

Her heart rattled an uneven rhythm, matched by erratic shouts and the thudding of those Roman boots. Her palms grew slick.

Be safe, friends.

The sorcerers joined the angry crowd. Demetrius stood a full head above most. Did he direct this river of anger? How many eyes turned to his, seeking a slight nod or incline of his head? He anchored the center of it all, arms crossed.

Perhaps they were all metalsmiths. Or their families. If so, the sorcerers joined them readily in their outcry, as each of them shoved and slashed toward the stoa.

Would Paul and the others be crushed? What could she do?

The smell of incense and altar blood mixed with the stink of too many people. The odor hovered, aggravated.

Somewhere on the stoa, pottery smashed.

A cry, like that of a child or a woman.

Daria's heart leaped and her stomach dropped.

More stones in men's hands.

Would they hurl rocks if offered a clear path to their enemy?

And he was reckless, Paul was. She had seen that in the past week. Always challenging, never appeasing. He took care that no friends faced danger. Why did he not have the same concern over his own person?

She stood on her toes, to no avail.

Could she slip through or around, get back to the stoa?

Another smash of stone or pottery. The temple complex was littered with marble and bronze statues, given by wealthy donors in honor of Artemis, hoping for good crops or healthy children. Was it one of these that toppled? What wrath would such defamation bring, from people or goddess?

Daria ran for the temple steps, hurried to the top level, surveyed the area.

It seemed as though the stoa area had sucked every worshipper toward itself. The altars had emptied, the southern side of the temple lay deserted.

And like a net of teeming fish, the mob was caught between temple and stoa, arms raised and flailing, eyes bright and raging.

What had come over the people? Religious dissent had turned

to frenzy with the arrival of the sorcerers. The crowd seethed with an anger that would soon break its confines.

She could barely see into the stoa beyond, but clearly the crowd had its enemy in sight. Paul and the others were trapped between stone walls and stony faces. Surely they would be crushed.

A tiny cry escaped her lips, lost in the din. She reached a hand toward the covered portico. Gone was any thought of pushing her way into its shadows. There was nothing she could do.

With a sudden snap of energy that shook her limbs, something broke within the crowd. What had been a tumultuous net of fish exploded, poured upward to her platform, spilled left and right.

She tried to hold her ground on the platform against the swelling tide. It knocked her backward against a statue of Apollo. She thrust a hand to keep the marble upright, then clung to its unsteady weight as though it were ballast.

She had feared for her friends.

It was time to fear for herself.

28

THE MARBLE STATUE OF APOLLO COULD NOT protect her.

Daria's fingers whitened to match the stone arm to which she clung. The swell of human tide soon overtook, dragged her along the platform toward the temple wall, then pinned her there.

Could she smack her way back down the steps, through the main gateway, and down into the city?

Soldiers like garish birds in their plumed helmets swung shields and *pilum* to clear the way, attempting to restore order.

Daria broke from her place on the wall, shoved against the flow, stumbled down the steps. Elbows and shoulders jostled and poked. A man wearing a purple-edged toga fell against her and the top of his head smacked her cheek. She jumped aside, thrust her tongue against her cheek, and tasted blood.

There was no current down here. No direction. Men and women, jumbled together like colorful pebbles, scattered and stirred.

Daria threaded through the madness, tried to swallow against the dryness in her throat, to breathe against the constriction in her chest. Waves of terror, like heat rising from pavement, spread from her feet to her face and back. How easily one could be trampled in such a fray. A slip of the foot, a stumble down to one knee, and the crowd would overwhelm like a runaway mudslide.

The crush was too much. Daria slowed, tried to catch her breath. She must not panic.

"Daria!"

She jerked her head to the voice but saw no one but the mass of faces, blended into one fierce muddle.

"Daria, stay where you are!"

She halted, feet rooted. Willing to wait, but not long.

"Timothy!"

Their hands met through a sliver of space, and his fingers were warm and solid around hers.

"Come, come with me."

He held tight to her hand and pulled her through as he had done the last time she followed him to the temple complex, creating a wake for her with his broad shoulders and sweeping arm.

They pressed through the gateway as through the neck of a jug, and the very breath seemed stolen from her chest. But then they broke free on the other side of the gate, and Timothy pulled her off the road to run lightly downhill through grass and clover.

The wind pulled at her hair, loosening it, and she tugged the comb that held it until her hair fell free and she clasped the comb in tight fingers.

They did not stop until the hillside leveled, nearly at the head of the Embolos, but at last the danger seemed behind them, and Timothy slowed, released her hand, and turned to study her face, her limbs, her hair. He grabbed her arms at the elbow and peered into her eyes.

"Are you hurt?"

Daria licked her lips, shook her head. "No. Only pushed around. Where are the others? Is Paul safe?"

Timothy huffed. "Who knows? That man knows how to bring a beating down upon himself, I will say that. He sent us all away, to slip into the crowd and return to Aquila's home. Said he would meet us there. Then turned and faced the mob as though they had paid for the privilege to hear him speak."

"I have never seen a man with more courage."

Timothy smiled, shaking his head. "Courage, or a death wish. I am sometimes at a loss to know which."

Daria scanned the head of the street, the columned end of the basilica. "I am so thirsty."

"Come, we will get a drink and you must return with me to Aquila's. We will hear more there."

After a dipperful of water from the street-side fountain, they walked slowly along the street. Hurry would only bring bad news to them sooner.

Daria watched the faces of the morning shoppers. Were they even aware of what had taken place on the temple plain above? "The city has been building to this, Paul has been saying. Some sort of clash between the believers and those who oppose the message."

"I fear this was only the birth pains of a greater crisis to come. A morning of unfocused chaos accomplishes little. They have not been content to see Paul jailed twice since coming to Ephesus. Those who fear the One God's triumph over Artemis and those

251

who are fired by the powers of the evil one will not be satisfied until Paul and followers of the Way are destroyed."

His words drove a coldness beneath her skin, deep into her bones. The hate, the rage, frightened her.

And Lucas was bent on infiltrating these sorcerers, who had set themselves against her new friends. How could she fight for him when he acted with foolishness?

"Daria, Priscilla has told me that you were married once. That you are a widow."

His words brought a sharper point to her thoughts. "Yes. Yes, my husband died several years ago."

"And—and you have never thought of marrying again?"

She glanced sideways at Timothy as they walked. The unexpected question fluttered against her nerves.

"I have thought of it, of course. There is great security to be found in marriage. But I have not been willing to give up some things that I deem important in order to gain that security."

"Perhaps marriage to a man who cared for you, who understood you, would not necessitate relinquishing these things."

She smiled. "Perhaps. You must tell me if you meet such a man."

At his silence, she glanced at him again and found his face flushed and jaw set.

Oh, Timothy. She had not even realized.

And was it so preposterous? He was about her age. It was only in comparing him to . . . someone else . . . that he seemed so young. And he was a good man, that was certain.

Not knowing how to rectify her foolishly casual words, she remained silent, as did he, for the rest of the walk down the Embolos, along Marble Street to the merchant district and finally to the door of Aquila's home.

Inside, the courtyard was buzzing. How had so many reached the house before Timothy and her? She had seen no one pass.

They were pulled into the crowd, with back slaps for Timothy and cautious nods for her. She still had not been fully accepted into their number, not surprising since she worshipped Greek gods.

In the center of the courtyard, amidst the small plot of greenery, Paul was pacing. A purpling bruise and raised knot on his forehead told much of the tale.

"Have they not suffered enough, even at my hands?"

The words were muttered, fists clenched, his eyes barely open as he crossed the stones. Did he speak to his One God? Those who surrounded said nothing, only watched.

"For me it is fitting, Lord. For me it is fitting. If I should take unnumbered blows upon my body, it still would not atone for past sins. But these precious ones—"

At this, he seemed to remember his audience and lifted stricken eyes to the gathered community. Tears welled and spilled, and his words ceased. Continued, perhaps, only between him and his God.

Priscilla stepped forward. "Paul, you have had a jolt. You should sit, take some wine—"

But Paul lifted his eyes to the woman and saw what they all did—the deep scratch across her neck, angry red bordered by a whitening welt. At the sight of it, the man cried out and reached gentle fingers to her neck.

"It is nothing. Only a scratch. We have seen worse, my friend, and will no doubt see worse again." She waved a servant forward bearing a sweating jug and an earthenware cup. "Sit now, take some refreshment."

He allowed himself to be lowered to the bench but spoke to

all. "It is the sorcerers. They are crazed by the conversion of their own numbers."

Many of the believers glanced around the courtyard at this statement. Were they searching for the new converts who had caused the trouble? No one stepped forward, no one made accusations. More than one suspicious eye turned on her. She felt the stain of her contact with Lucas as a nearly visible thing. Did all see it?

And what was the use of fighting any of it? She could do nothing for Lucas, nothing for these people—even Paul, who had grown dear to her in the short time since she met him, and Timothy, who watched her with fondness in his eyes.

A shout from the street turned the attention of the group. Someone ran through the front door—Tychicus, wasn't it?—his face red.

"In the square!" He was panting and bent double to brace his hands against his knees. "I've come from the square outside the theater. They are burning their books!"

Paul pushed through, creating an aisle through the gathered. "What is it? Who is burning?"

Tychicus grabbed Paul's arms. Beneath the bluster his face lit with some kind of joy. "The new believers—the ones who have come out of the dark arts." He met the glances of many in the house. "They are burning their books of sorcery. Hundreds of them!"

Daria stood her ground longer than most. The rest rushed from the house, as if they had not just escaped one threat and were running toward the next.

And it was Paul who led the way.

In the end, Daria ran as well.

She reached the square behind most of the others, and a crowd much larger than only the believers had already gathered.

In the center of the circle a bonfire had been lit, much larger than necessary to burn a few scrolls, certainly. Had the ex-sorcerers created the spectacle to draw a crowd? To declare themselves? Did they know about the morning's temple fiasco and foolishly seek to add to it, or was it merely a terrible coincidence?

They were fighting their way through the crowd, one at a time, arms laden with scrolls.

Men shouted around them in protest. Some tried to pluck the valuable scrolls from their arms but were dashed backward by others.

Such anger, such hatred. Why? Where did it come from?

A man ran circles around the fire, his expression wild, mouth flecked white at the corners as he screamed curses at those who came.

Daria stared. Was this the shopkeeper Hektor? Always so cool and guarded?

He darted toward the fire as if to pluck burning papyri from the flames. The scrolls hissed and curled and charred on the great fire. Orange-and-black fragments twisted upward on the breeze, grayed to ash, and floated toward the sea.

It was a strange procession, this marching of the new Christians through the crowd with their arms laden with evil. Did their supply have no end?

And how, when their actions caused the absolute fury of so many, did they continue unaccosted?

A dozen or more sorcerers crisscrossed the open space around the fire now, tearing their hair and shrieking with sounds terrible enough to wake the dead.

And then she saw him. Paul, at the opposite side of the circle, arms raised over the unholy fire, his bruised forehead sheened with sweat and glowing unnatural in the orange light.

Somehow, in some unearthly way, he was holding back the crowd with those arms.

His lips were moving, though she heard nothing. Some kind of silent prayer of power, it created this channel of safety for them to come, to leave their past behind, burned and purged in the fire to be remembered no more.

He stood against the evil, and he was not destroyed.

But his protection did not extend to the other believers. Behind him, the huge Gaius was struck on the head and went down. His partner, Aristarchus, swiveled to find the attacker and himself was pummeled by fists.

She scanned the crowd for other faces, and the repeat of this morning's violence sickened her.

There—there was Timothy, like a young Hercules fighting the nine-headed Hydra, brash and bold and foolish. A dozen fists rained down upon him until he was lost to her in the crowd.

At the vanishing of Timothy, something rose within her, some former sense of herself that had lain dormant, perhaps since the morning she ran from Lucas.

These were her friends. Her people. She must do something to help, to rescue.

Her chest expanded with the knowing, like a new thing awakening, or perhaps an old thing brought back to life. Her arms extended from her sides, the protective feathers of a mother bird, fists balled in the passion of a warrior.

She would be a spectator no longer.

She searched the crowd. Who was it she was to protect? Who needed this fire that had lit within her chest?

She heard a shriek, that of a girl, and pivoted to the sound.

There, across the fire, a girl writhed and screamed, held fast by the grip of a man whose face hardened with a crazed anger.

And that man was Lucas.

29

THE GIRL HAD LOST HER SENSES.

Lucas kept a firm grasp about her waist, despite her struggling shouts. This was what Hektor's influence brought them to. All of them. The thought filled him with a fury nearly as wild as his captive.

He should have expected such trouble. Should have seen it in the pall of the city this morning.

He had emerged from his estate into morning air charged with energy—a nervous excitement like a stallion pawing the dust before a race, like a thundercloud rolling in over the distant hills ready to unleash.

And empty. The streets, the shops along the Embolos lay quiet, waiting. As though its citizens had been spirited away and the city were only a shell.

He had avoided Hektor this past week. Avoided his foul suggestion to murder Paul, though he let the man believe he was considering the plot. Instead, he had tracked down some who might better assist him.

Lucas approached the early-morning appointed meeting place—the Augusteum—glancing left and right before ducking under the temple's lintel.

In the dim interior, his eyes sought the only light—a lamp at the far end of the temple.

"Lucas."

One voice, but he sensed there were several waiting. He strode forward into the darkness. He must appear confident, sure of his purpose.

Several pairs of eyes set in pale faces materialized. He focused on Vettias, a lawyer who had always seemed the leader of the group. "Well, Vettias? Have you made a decision?"

Vettias's face was unreadable, but set in its firmness. "We want to do all we can to end this, Lucas. But you ask too much. We have families to think of, businesses that rely upon us—"

"And I do not?" He battled to keep his tone even.

Vettias sighed. "Lucas, you know what it means for us to have made this shift, to have turned our back on one secretive sect and embraced another group that is even less approved. We risk everything already. To also open ourselves to suspicion—"

"So you will do nothing. Is that it?"

Another stepped forward, younger, his face afire with passion. "No! We will decry their deeds, their beliefs, publically shame them if we can. But do not ask us to bring incrimination upon ourselves."

Lucas cast about for another argument, but what more was there to say? He could not ask these wealthy men to possibly give up their livelihood, their freedom. They did not share his desire for justice. Though of late, that desire had bloomed into something fired more by hatred than integrity.

"Publically shame them?" He rubbed at his jaw, eyes on the floor. It would be a beginning.

The third man of the group, silent until now, spoke from the shadows. "We could burn the scrolls."

The other two focused on Lucas, as if to watch his reaction. "The scrolls?"

"Our books of sorcery. Between the three of us, we have a highly valuable collection."

"And we could get others!" Vettias's eyes lit with something like excitement.

Lucas shrugged. "Such an act would infuriate them, certainly, but—"

"We could do it in the city. In front of the theater. Draw a crowd."

"There might be danger in this." Lucas searched their faces for fear.

Vettias held up his hands. "We are not afraid of danger, Lucas. Only prosecution."

Lucas laughed without mirth. "This I understand. To be suspected, to be imprisoned for the deeds of another—there is not much worse."

"When?" Vettias turned to his friends. "When shall we do it?"

The youngest of them pounded a fist into his palm. "Today." He surveyed the others with wild eyes. "Why not? Why should we wait to shame them?"

The others nodded their agreement.

"We will be there well before midday." Vettias clapped Lucas on the shoulder. "When the square is crowded with shoppers. Have someone prepare a fire. We will bring all we can collect and make certain the city knows that evil is today being purged."

He had left them there, still plotting. Only a beginning, but still worthwhile. He retraced his steps along the street. The city was refilling from the direction of the Magnesian Gate. Had there been a minor festival at the temple he'd forgotten?

But if so, the mood of the returning worshippers was anything but celebratory. Pinched faces, hands of children tightly clasped, hurrying feet.

It did not take long to hear the story. An angry horde, churned up over the teachings of the man Paul, venting their fear and aggression on whomever was near.

It was the perfect morning for what was yet to come.

And by the time he had enlisted and paid a few dockworkers to build a bonfire in the square outside the theater, the streets were jammed with citizens, in the way that a common threat, a scandalous event, brings commoners and wealthy together to discuss and react. The fire fueled their curiosity, and long before the sun crested in the sky a crowd had gathered.

Lucas kept to the fringes.

Here they were. The three he had met with in the Augusteum, and several others besides.

They carried armfuls of scrolls, with slaves wheeling small carts alongside, overflowing with more of the offal destined for the bonfire.

They were recognized, their names whispered and passed through the crowd like a trickle of water running downhill, gaining force.

The crowd split to allow them entrance.

Vettias spoke first, his arms loaded with scrolls and his voice carrying over the murmur of the crowd and the hiss and spit of the fire. "Citizens of the great city of Ephesus! There is a plague among you, an evil that is sucking the life from this city! Too long we have been part of it, willing to trade our souls for a bit of secret knowledge, our hearts for the illusion of control. Our very destiny for a taste of power. But no longer!"

He dropped the scrolls at his feet, then picked up the first of them.

From behind him, another stepped forward, scanned the crowd, and captured the gazes of all who had gathered. "We have brought scrolls of magic." He waved an arm over those at Vettias's feet and those in the arms and wagons at his back. "Within these pages are all manner of dark secrets that call upon the powers of evil, that enlist demon forces to do our bidding. But it was we who did their bidding, we who were controlled, and we declare to you today that we have been set free!"

Their words riveted. The crowd watched, open mouthed and wide eyed, as Vettias tossed the first of his scrolls into the fire.

A hideous screech reverberated in the square. The hair on Lucas's arms prickled. Impossible to say where the sound came from. The crowd? The burning scroll as it caught with a burst of flame and the fire greedily consumed it?

Across the circle, the crowd opened again for a newly arrived group. The Christians.

Paul led them, with a pleased, if curious, expression.

Vettias raised his eyes to Paul and seemed to draw strength from him. "Yes, set yourselves free, fellow Ephesians!" He tossed several more scrolls into the fire. "Not only from the demonic plague that enslaved us, but also from the Lady herself, who could never be our salvation!"

At this the crowd seemed to shudder as one, and glances shifted to the temple plain and its unseen goddess, ever present above the city.

Another gathered an armful of scrolls and added them to the

blaze. "There is but One God! One God who declares to you that your sacrifices and offerings cannot atone. Only the blood of His Messiah, sent for the salvation of all men, can save!"

The fire-blackened fragments were rising like an offering now, and the smell of it pleased Lucas. The licking tongues of fire consuming the valuable scrolls, the roar of the crowd at the ex-sorcerers' words, like spectators at a sporting match, all of which sent waves of cold pleasure through his limbs.

The sorcerers had arrived now, inevitably. They came roiling and agitating and stirring onlookers to outcries of indignation as they came.

"Treasures of the city!" a woman cried from somewhere within the crowd. "They are burning our most precious treasures!"

Like two armies flooding toward each other on a plain of war, the sorcerers and the Christians faced off across the bonfire. All the while Vettias and his colleagues fed the flames with the crackling papyri of spells and incantations.

The heat of the crowd built as surely as the blaze. Restless, anxious eyes. Rude shoves and angry retorts.

Screaming. A young woman—perhaps the same who had cried out a moment ago.

Where was she? Impossible to tell.

To his left, people rippled away from some disturbance.

There, there was the girl. That awful shriek, tearing at her hair.

Selene. Lucas's heart lurched.

He had been watching the daughter of Demetrius all week, gambling that she was not yet fully in the sorcerers' grip. He had said nothing to Demetrius. The girl could prove to be leverage later, when Lucas might need it.

But here she was, clearly intoxicated with one of their foul potions, screaming curses down on the heads of those who burned the scrolls.

Lucas moved through the crowd, jostling others aside, and reached her in moments. He tightened a grasp around her arm.

"Selene. Come away."

She turned wild eyes on him, eyes without recognition. "We must retrieve them!" Her voice was low and guttural, like something from the grave. "We must save the scrolls."

She tore her arm from his grasp and plunged forward, through the crowd. Toward the fire.

She was going after the charred remains!

Lucas shoved through, shouting her name.

She hovered at the edge of the blaze. Could he reach her in time?

Step away, Selene!

Arms reaching, reaching toward the flames.

Did no one else understand her intent? She leaned impossibly far.

And so Lucas had grabbed her from behind, locked his arms around her waist, lifted her feet from the paving.

She screamed, kicked against his shins.

"I have you, Selene." He called it into her ear, but she was senseless.

Fragments of memory floated, like the ashy remnants of the scrolls. Another woman, thrashing in his arms. Beyond redemption.

He dragged her backward, still screaming her curses, now directed toward him.

The crowd parted for them, fearful of both captor and prisoner. He pulled her through the sea of startled faces, beyond the chaos. The gap closed itself, people's backs to them, their passing interest already moving to something else.

"Lucas!"

The girl still struggled in his arms. It was another female voice that called his name—a voice as familiar as the blood in his veins.

Then the body, the face, to match the voice.

Daria.

He froze, his desperation nearly forgotten, and drank in the sight of her. Felt his heart tumble across the square to her, as though she had tossed a coil of rope over him and yanked. She wore a lavender robe, pinned in gold at the shoulders and braided gold at her waist. She was like a cool spring flower dropped into the boiling cauldron of the square.

She ran, her glance trading between Selene and him, concern etched across her forehead.

"Help me, Daria. I must get her away from here before she hurts herself."

Did he truly dare to speak such words? Involve her yet again without so much as a thought? His only consolation this past week had been that she had been safe. How quickly he discarded her safety for his own ends. The shame of it swamped him.

The girl in his grasp kicked out, connected with Daria's legs.

Daria jumped out of range of the girl's feet, circled to her side, laid a hand on her face. "Sshh. He will not hurt you."

Selene calmed for a moment, breathing heavily.

It was enough. Lucas pulled her upright, lifted her easily, and put her over his shoulder.

"Keep her calm, Daria. We must take her somewhere safe."

It was a strange repeat of that night in the agora, but they would not go to the brothel again. He must take Selene to his own home.

Fortunately, the Marble Street pedestrians were focused on the smoking bonfire at the end of the street and ignored the merchant hurrying in the other direction, a muttering, hysterical woman over his shoulder.

Daria ran alongside, whispering words of comfort and reassurance to Selene. How could she step in so quickly, so readily, without any knowledge of what was happening? Implicit in her actions was a trust in him, an undeserved trust that thickened his throat with emotion even as he ran with his strange burden.

By the time he reached the steps leading upward to his estate, fatigue was gnawing at his muscles. He set the girl down with a jolt and tried to catch his breath.

Daria instinctively moved in to slip a comforting arm around Selene's waist and lead her upward while maintaining a steady stream of trivial conversation.

"Wait until you see the view from the estate. It's like taking a breath for the first time. Have you been up here to these homes? They are just magnificent. You'll be able to see the harbor and the water from the terrace. It's so beautiful."

The girl was following, miraculously. Lucas lumbered behind the two women, shoulders and arms prickling with exertion.

When they reached the interior of his house, Clovis met them.

Lucas waved the servant over. "Hurry down into the city." He pulled some coins from the money pouch at his waist and pressed them into the old man's palm. "Take this. Pay a few boys to search the city. Find Demetrius the silversmith and bring him here. Tell him I have his daughter and she is unwell."

Clovis nodded, and Lucas noted the surprise on Daria's face. But she led Selene forward, toward the triclinium where they had spent mornings in lessons.

Lucas hurried Clovis to the door. Should he go himself? The old man moved too slowly. But no, he dared not leave Daria alone with Selene in her condition.

He found Selene already stretched on one of the couches and

Daria bathing her forehead with a wet cloth. A pitcher and water basin stood on the floor at her feet.

The effects of whatever potion the sorcerers had fed Selene must be wearing off. She was restless but limp. Her head lolled on the couch, eyes unfocused.

Daria raised her gaze at his entrance. "What has happened to her? What was she doing down there?"

"She has gotten involved with sorcery, I'm afraid. They gave her something. To alter her mind, I think. She was going to leap into the fire to save those cursed scrolls."

Daria opened her mouth as if to question, but the girl suddenly sat upright and started to yell.

It took both of them to restrain her, to soothe her into some semblance of peace. She fought with an uncanny strength. They were still pinning her arms when he heard Demetrius shouting at the front door.

"In here!" Lucas eyed Daria. She hated the man, he knew. But her face showed only concern for Selene.

Demetrius trotted into the triclinium, his face an angry red. "What do you think you're doing with her?"

He crossed to the couch in one stride and threw Lucas from his daughter.

Daria rose, her lips whitening in outrage. "He was saving her life, Demetrius!"

Father held daughter in a tight embrace, but he turned his head to Lucas. "What is she saying?"

"The sorcerers gave Selene some kind of pharmakeia. She ran at the fire. She was going to plunge into it, to save their spells."

Demetrius seemed to deflate. "But why?"

"She has fallen under their influence, I believe." No need to confess that he'd seen the girl with them a week earlier.

"No." Demetrius shook his head. "No, it is those infernal Christians who have caused this. They set that blaze—that hate-mongerer Paul who stood with his arms raised calling down some kind of curses from his god over the people." Demetrius clasped Selene tighter to his chest. "Over my daughter."

Daria stepped forward, hands balled into fists at her sides.

Lucas shook his head. *Remain silent, Daria.* He circled the couch and grabbed her arm as she opened her mouth to speak.

She glanced at him. But she would not be so easily dissuaded. And he could not have her revealing information that would endanger them both.

She turned to Demetrius, but Lucas spoke first.

"Take Selene home, Demetrius. Let her sleep it off, then talk with her. It is not too late, I am certain."

Demetrius gathered the girl in his arms and lifted her.

Lucas went to the door, called out to Clovis hovering in the courtyard. "Fetch a horse and cart. Bring it around to the front for Demetrius and his daughter."

Demetrius nodded and carried the girl to the front door.

Behind Lucas, Daria was still geared for an attack. She strode from the dining chamber, face flushed.

"Demetrius, it is the Christians—"

Lucas wrapped an arm around Daria's shoulders and steered her from the doorway. "Excuse us." He gave the man a nod, directed a slight smile toward his daughter. "It seems my tutor is in need of a lesson."

He pushed her toward his tiny sitting room, ignoring her sputtering protest. He heard the front door slam behind the two leaving, but when he had Daria in the sitting room, he closed the door all the same, trapping her inside.

It was time for the truth.

30

DARIA RECOILED FROM LUCAS'S HAND, URGING, pressing her into his sitting room as though she were his to command. He had silenced her when she would speak a defense of the Christians. This, after his own actions in the square. She turned on him, face hot with indignation.

She was torn between two truths, paradoxical and overwhelming. To be conscripted into yet another of Lucas's rescues—how was she to reconcile the dark and brooding silence of the would-be sorcerer and the compassionate risk taker who would carry a woman across the city to save her from herself?

That the girl was Demetrius's daughter only deepened the chasm between logic and fact. Lucas hated Demetrius. She had seen it on his face, heard it in his voice. Why help his daughter?

She pointed a stiff finger toward the door. "He knows nothing of the Christians, if he blames them—"

Lucas held up a hand, silencing her once more.

"I do not work for you, Lucas. Not any longer. And I will not be treated as a servant!"

In the close intimacy of the sitting room she could hear the cadence of his breath, see the pulse pound in his neck. The tiny lamp on his desk left half his face in shadow, and he turned from her, away from the light until his expression was lost.

"No. No, I shall not treat you as a servant. But there are so many things you do not understand."

"I understand more than you know. I have been to Hektor's shop. Have spoken to him about you, even."

He whirled, grabbed her arms. "Foolish woman!"

Her chest thudded. "He knows only that I am a . . . friend . . . of yours."

"You should not have done that, Daria."

"Should not have discovered that you are letting them pull you into their mystery rites? Or that you also blame the Christians for what happened to your wife—?"

"Aagghh!" Lucas ran both hands through his hair, then beat the wall with a fist.

Daria inhaled sharply and swayed backward.

But he advanced on her, eyes boring into hers, as though to pry out every secret. "This is what you think? This is what you fear?"

She lifted her chin, narrowed her eyes at his penetrating gaze. "Tell me otherwise, then, Lucas. Tell me the truth."

She did not expect him to take her face in his warm hands. Did not expect his eyes to fill with tears.

"This is the truth, Daria."

His lips on hers were hot, feverish. The honeyed scent of him filled her senses.

"This is the truth." He kissed her eyelids, her forehead. "And this. And this." His voice was like gravel, pain edging every desperate word.

He kissed her lips again, his hands still wrapped around her head, and she returned the sweet pressure of his mouth on hers, dug her fingers into the fabric at his shoulders, and clung to his strength, to the knowledge that he cared for her like this, that he wanted her for himself, regardless of the memories that haunted them both.

He broke away at last, and still she clung to him. But he was receding from her. Too soon. Too soon.

"You deserve the entire truth, Daria. All of it."

He rubbed at his eyes, at his forehead. Was he ill? Even to utter words seemed to bring him pain. He crossed the tiny room and sank into the chair beside his desk.

She would not sit, not across the room, even though the separation was slight. She stood at his side, her right hand worrying the wood of his desk, her left hand restless at her side—for she would soothe that furrowed brow if she dared.

He stared into the flame of the lamp and his words were hushed, the single, flat tone of a man recalling what he wished left forgotten. "It seemed the best way when it began. I was so—so *guilt ridden* over what had happened to her. That I saw it coming, but did nothing."

"Your wife?"

"She was never happy here. I tried, I tried to give her all she wanted, but it did no good. I could not give her the one thing she truly desired."

What could she have wanted that Lucas's money and influence could not have procured for her?

Lucas's fingers curled into a fist and he rested it on the desk, tight and controlled. "I could not give her my love."

Searing heat, like a wave dousing her from above, traveled from Daria's hairline to her toes. "Wh-what? You did not love her?"

"No, I did not love her. Not like I should have. I did my duty and little more. When we married, her fortune meant more to me than her person. There! Does that shock you? It should."

"How—how can this be? You are so angry. So tortured, heartbroken over her death!"

His eyes were trained downward. If only she could see his eyes.

"Not her. It was never her. But she carried my—" He shook his head, a flutter of movement that seemed to cost him. "I tried. But I could not love her. She was—she was not good."

"Not good?" Daria leaned toward him, tilted her head to better see his face. "What does that mean, *not good*?"

"I do not know how to explain it, Daria." Finally, his eyes lifted to her. "She was always searching for something, always needing and wanting something more, something that would fill her somehow, and it—it made her grasping and ruthless. Deceitful at times, and always manipulating."

Now that he had begun, the words tumbled out in a rush, like a foul river cresting its banks.

"When she saw that I did not—could not—love her, she turned to others. Other men at first, as if I did not see. But even that was not enough. Perhaps they did not love her any better than I. Soon it was religious acts. She became obsessed with the temple, with Artemis. She brought sacrifices daily, prostrated herself before the statues and altars, tied charms to trees and whispered constant prayers. That lasted perhaps a year, but she grew discontent even there. It was then that her tastes took a darker turn. She met Hektor. Began to dabble in his spells and his promises."

Daria's breath had grown labored, her hands clammy. Too familiar. All of it, too familiar. She crossed the sitting room on shaky legs, grasped the narrow chair against the wall, dragged it to Lucas's desk, and sank into it, no longer able to remain upright.

He glanced at her, then away. "You must think ill of me, that I could not make her happy. Could not prevent her from seeking out such evil."

She shook her head, the motion jerky and unnatural. "No." Her voice was not her own, raspy and thick. "No, I understand. I understand too well."

At this, he grasped her hand where it lay on her lap and nodded, as if inviting her to speak of the past. But it was his story to tell, and it was not yet told.

He began again, his voice a murmur. "Where once she had been unkind and selfish, she now grew hateful and cruel. The sorcerers gave her potions and spells, they included her in their strange and sick rituals, they foretold her future—things she wanted to hear, and perhaps they were true, I do not know. I begged her to stop, to keep away from them. And for a while, I grew hopeful. She started spending time with others. With Christians."

Daria sucked in a breath. She had not breathed in too long. Her chest was tight and hot.

He nodded. "I saw a change in her and dared not criticize this new sect she'd fallen into since it seemed to improve her. We—we grew closer for a while." He dipped his head, exhaled. "When I learned she was with child, I believed that all would be well. Surely she would not return to Hektor while carrying our child." He rubbed at the back of his neck, eyes closed. "But she did. She did."

He lapsed into silence, as though he had forgotten Daria. Forgotten his story. She let some minutes pass, then could wait no longer.

"And she died soon after?"

Lucas inhaled and jerked his head upright, as if she had roused him from sleep. "What? Yes. Yes, she was dead within the week. I—I did not know who or how or why. Had the Christians learned of her return to Hektor and killed her to protect their secrets? Had her involvement with Hektor been fatal in some way?"

"And you were suspected."

He laughed without humor. "You *do* know more than I realized. Yes." He hit his fist lightly against the desk. "Yes, the city magistrates, Zagreus especially, believed that I killed her. Perhaps they still believe it. Though I know otherwise."

"Because you went to the sorcerers, became one of them."

"No! Not one of them, never one of them." He took a quill from the desk, rolled it absently between his fingers. "That was when it all began, when I devised this plan to discover who was responsible and to make them pay for what they had done to her. To my child." At this last word, his voice broke and the quill snapped between his fingers.

"I went to them all—the Christians, the sorcerers, even the society of wealthy wives that knew her well—and began to gain the confidence of each group, trying to search out the truth. The sorcerers insisted that it was the Christians who had killed her, and the Christians pointed to her obsessions with evil. It was in my inquiries with the wealthy wives and daughters of the city that I met Demetrius, and when he learned of my situation, he conscripted me to help rid Ephesus of the Christians, for the threat to Artemis worship they have become." He propped his elbows on his desk and dropped his head into his hands. "I pledged my loyalty to all of them, Daria. One against the other, with none of them knowing, so I could learn the truth. It seemed wise at the time. But now I see that I have been a fool."

She risked a light touch of his arm. "Why? What has made you a fool?"

He did not react to her touch. Did he even sense it?

"I thought I could control my own heart, my beliefs, my philosophy. Not get pulled into any of it. Instead, a fierce war is waging in my soul, and I understand now how she fell into it so easily, how she became deceived."

"You still seek the truth?"

"Yes, truth. But not simply about what happened to my wife. I seek the Truth that is all, that answers all the questions of man's heart, that draws us to the divine and makes it possible for us to know." He licked at dry lips, swallowed with effort.

She wished for a pitcher of water and a cup but dared not walk away from his confession.

"They are so alike, Daria. So alike and yet so different. What the Jews believe, and the Greeks, and the Christians. Even the powers that pull at me from the darkness of sorcery. So many promises. All the same ways to please the gods, except for the Christians."

He still held her hands, his thumbs caressing her wrists. The connection felt tenuous. Temporary.

"I have been with them as well, Lucas." She whispered the words, afraid to break the link. "And they are different."

"Yes, you see it too! They have their rites and rituals just as we do, but what of this insistence that sacrifices are no longer needed? That their One God has made a single, final sacrifice of Himself? How could any god be so gracious?"

He leaned back, studied the raftered ceiling as though answers could be found there. "It speaks to something opposite of all I've ever known. I want to believe it, to believe that there are not a dozen gods, not a hundred gods, and a thousand requirements to please them, but only One God who offers redemption."

She inhaled the room's balmy air, let the softness fill her

chest. "Yes, I know this desire. This desire to believe, and yet a resistance to the unvarying, scandalous simplicity of it."

"And the darkness, it has sunk its teeth into me as well." He whispered the words, shame-tinged and sorrowful. "I—I have longed for its promises of blunted pain and sharper ecstasies. I have let them take me to places a man ought not to go. Just as she did. Even knowing that it killed her, I have followed in her condemned footsteps."

"It is not too late, Lucas." Daria spoke the words in a rush, words she had longed to speak for weeks. "You are a good man, with a good heart. You can turn away from their power, from their appeal. I know you can."

He tried to smile. Reached his hand to her cheek and wiped at the tear she had not known she shed.

"This is why I brought you to Ephesus. I saw this in you, even from the beginning. This belief in people, this passion to see them released from their bondage. I believed, I hoped, that it was still possible for me. But I think that this also was foolish. I must finish what I began. Restitution must be made. Payment and justice must be exacted."

A chill breeze seemed to slink through the room at his words. Daria wrapped her arms around herself. "But not by you, Lucas. Not by you."

"I am all there is. I am the one who must make them pay."

She clutched at his hands. "It will destroy you. Trust me, it will."

"I know."

He was everything that terrified her, this man. And everything she needed. But she could not be part of his vengeance or it would annihilate them both. Perhaps he was the antidote for her disease, but it would kill before it cured.

The silence between them stretched, not taut and ready to snap, but a slow drift, as if he watched from a riverbank and she from a boat while the lazy current lengthened the distance between them until she should never see him again.

And in the silence, the shout from the courtyard startled all the more.

Frona. It was Frona shouting outrage at an intruder.

Lucas's eyes met Daria's. What was this knowing she saw in them? As if he had been waiting for this moment, had known it would come?

He stood slowly, pulled his hands from hers, and turned to the door.

It burst open a moment later. Three men stood in the corridor beyond, and one stepped into the sitting room, his mouth a tight slash and his eyes cold.

"You will come with us."

Lucas bowed his head for only a moment, reached a hand out to clasp hers, to squeeze her fingers and then release. "Daria, this is Zagreus, the city praetor."

The man ignored her. "Do not make it difficult."

"What is this, Zagreus?"

"There has been another murder, Lucas."

Daria put a hand to her belly, insufficient to quell the nausea and foreboding.

"You weren't so careful with this one, were you? She wasn't dead when we found her." Zagreus advanced into the room. He wore a daunting sort of club strapped to his waist. Two Roman soldiers accompanied him.

"I thought you said it was a murder."

"Yes, she's dead now, that is certain. But she had time to speak before she died. She was questioned by those who found her, asked who had done this thing to her, who had burned these strange markings into her arm. She died with one name on her lips." He sneered, as if the revelation brought him pleasure. "Lucas Christopoulos."

Daria sank into her chair, breath expelling and muscles weak.

Lucas nodded, his eyes on the mosaic floor.

A moment later they were gone and the lamp flickered and went out.

31

IN THE DARKNESS, DARIA GRIPPED THE EDGES OF her chair until the wood bit her fingers and numbness crept in.

She tried to sort emotion from logic, feelings from facts. Tried to fit the pieces of this jagged, sordid puzzle together in some way that answered more questions than it raised.

Lucas, involved in another killing? Accused by the dying girl herself? How could Daria continue to cling to his innocence when she was presented with his guilt at every turn?

She *would* hold on to it. Until she heard otherwise from his own lips.

In the meantime, she must pursue the truth, first with those Lucas claimed to have been part of.

She stood in the sitting room, legs shaky, and took a deep breath. She'd given enough time to emotions and fear. It was time to act.

From the front of the hillside estate she could see much of the marble street leading off to the amphitheater in the distance. It had emptied since their headlong rush to Lucas's house, with Demetrius's daughter in tow.

In truth, the whole city seemed vacant. A fearful silence had fallen over the streets. Daria hurried through the weighty emptiness. Even the agora was nearly deserted. Somewhere beyond the street, a bird chirped a lonesome call.

Had everyone fled to their homes after the events of the morning? With escalating violence perhaps none felt safe.

Daria flexed tense shoulders at the thought and continued on, pressing toward the merchant district. It was not yet midday, the time for Paul's teaching in the lecture hall. Would she find him at Aquila's shop? Their home?

When she reached the shop, the flaps were already lowered. She called beyond the leather, but there was no answer.

She hurried on to their home, heart pounding now with exertion. And more than physical, the fear she had refused to acknowledge had a grip on her chest, her lungs.

What justice would be enacted if Lucas were declared guilty? And how soon?

"Aquila? Priscilla?" She began calling before she was even across the threshold. Her voice was tight, strained.

A young servant girl appeared at Daria's bold entrance—one of the poor girls they'd rescued from the streets.

"Are your masters at home?" Daria pressed slick palms against her robe.

"They are resting—"

"Daria?" Priscilla's welcome voice carried from the balcony above. "What is it? What has happened?"

Daria shielded her eyes from the sunlight slashing harsh

stripes across the courtyard and peered at her new friend. "I—I must speak with Paul. Or you, I could, perhaps, ask you as well." She was out of breath. She must sound hysterical.

"Stay there, girl. We'll be right down."

Aquila trotted across the courtyard first, followed by his wife. He pointed to a stone bench beside the spurting fountain. "Sit, Daria. Sit."

"I can't. I can't stay. I just have to ask a question. It is about my employer—my former employer—Lucas."

The couple exchanged glances, and in this, Daria read much.

"What have you not told me? What do you know?"

Priscilla sighed. "He did not want you to know."

"He did not even want you involved with us, at first." Aquila shook his head. "Stubborn fool."

Daria sank onto a bench after all. "Tell me. Please, tell me."

Priscilla edged beside her and clasped her damp hands. "Lucas has been a questioner for a while now."

"Questioner?"

She half smiled. "Rather like yourself, Daria. Listening, learning, being drawn, perhaps. But not yet ready to claim the Messiah as his own."

Aquila paced before the two women, the heat of the day building beads of sweat across his forehead. "Almost he has seen the light, I would say. Almost. But his anger and his guilt hold him back. And his mad ideas of justice."

Priscilla studied the blue-and-white mosaic that ran the length of the courtyard walkway. "He is determined to find guilt somewhere."

"So he is not a sorcerer? Not training to be one of them?"

"No!" Priscilla's eyes went wide. "No, he is only gaining information."

"Foolish *and* dangerous." Aquila's brows drew together over his eyes. "He has little idea of the evil to which he draws near."

She refused to shudder, to react with weakness at all. "I believe perhaps he knows."

Priscilla swept an errant hair from Daria's eyes. "What has happened, Daria? You are overwrought. Is it the new believers and their burning scrolls today? You must see that it was a mighty act of the One God, to defy the sorcerers in such a public way, to bring shame upon them and to lift up the name of the Messiah—"

"Lucas has been arrested."

"What?" Aquila turned on her, as if she were to blame. "Where? Why?"

"I have just come from his home, where Zagreus came for him. There has been another murder."

"Help us, Jesus." It was a whispered prayer, escaping from the lips of Priscilla.

"They believe Lucas killed the girl."

Aquila's nostrils flared and the cords of his neck bulged. "Why would they possibly—?"

"Because she told them so, before she died."

"This is ludicrous." Aquila called for the servant girl. "Bring my outer tunic." He turned to Daria. "I am going to straighten this out. He is at the prison?"

"I—I do not know where they took him."

"Of course, the prison." Priscilla nodded. "Where Paul himself has often been chained. Even the innocent sometimes see its bowels."

This news did nothing to cheer Daria. "I am coming with you."

Aquila opened his mouth as if to protest, then clenched his jaw and nodded once. "Very well."

Daria struggled to keep pace with the large man, through the merchant district, out to the theater square where a sooty splotch was all that remained of the morning's commotion, and down Harbor Street.

Harbor Street, where she'd first seen the group of sorcerers and worried that evil had followed her from Rhodes, that it would claim her still.

If anything, that fear had only increased.

The prison was little more than a narrow-doored entrance off Harbor Street, compressed between a perfumery, of all things, and a wool-dying enterprise. The scents of perfume and odor of dye hung heavy outside the door, watering Daria's eyes and thickening her throat.

She followed Aquila's wide figure into the shadows of the prison entrance and took in the meager furnishings at once. Rickety steps led to a narrow loft, and the tattered edge of a ratty blanket hung over its splintered edge. It was a shack built over a hole, nothing more. In the center of the floor, blackened chains secured a square trap door.

The heavy tread of feet on the steps greeted them. "Who is it? Who is there?"

Aquila's voice was a snarl. "What is this about Lucas Christopoulos being jailed? We have come to see him."

The jailer, a man of about sixty, with sparse drifts of ash-gray hair barely clinging to an oily head, squinted down at Aquila. "I've got him, yes. But you're not going to see him."

"Ridiculous! You have no reason to keep him—"

"I have every reason—the city magistrates brought him here and threw him down." He jerked a thumb toward the door in the floor.

He was down there. Daria swallowed against the growing tightness in her throat and the peculiar smell of the place, a mixture of waste and mildew. She could not think of Lucas in that hole. Only of how she would somehow get him out.

The jailer crossed his arms. "You seem to think I make the decisions about who is guilty. I'm here to keep them locked up. If you have a problem, take it up with the city officials."

"We shall do that!" Aquila spun on his heel and nearly bowled her over in his rush for the door, perhaps as anxious as she to avoid thoughts of that hole.

In the street, Aquila was not so confident. "There are a few who are sympathetic to the Way. But I am not certain they can influence others." He straightened. "But we will try."

Daria chewed her lip and scanned the street. "I thank you for whatever you can accomplish, Aquila. But I am going to work for his release in other ways."

Aquila squinted, the concern of a father crossing his face, but then patted her shoulder. "Be safe, my friend."

———

Daria picked her way across the yard of the Metalsmith Guild, ignoring the stares of workmen returning from their afternoon breaks.

Demetrius's penetrating look, however, she could not ignore.

He stood at a squat furnace, holding a metal stake whose tip glowed red. An iron pot lay half-buried in the furnace's charred embers.

"The tutor has come for a visit." He wagged his eyebrows, but his usual leering grin was absent.

"I must speak with you." She stepped to the furnace, and the heat lashed her legs.

Demetrius retained his hold on the fiery rod. "What can I do for you, Tutor?"

"Lucas has been arrested."

He shrugged a shoulder. "So I have heard."

"They say that a girl named him as her attacker. I must know more of this girl. Her background, her family. What do you know?"

Again the raised eyebrows. Demetrius glanced sideways at his colleagues, as if to check whether they listened. "And you think I have—"

"Do not pretend with me. I know you have involved Lucas in your plans, have pressured him and perhaps endangered his life. Tell me what you know!"

Demetrius shifted to lay the heated rod across the furnace's roof, wrapped leather strips around his hands, and reached for the pot in the heat. Slowly and methodically, he poured molten silver into a plaster mold.

Daria had seen the process once before. An item was created out of wax, then the plaster poured over and the wax melted out to form the mold. She had no patience for artwork today.

"Demetrius—"

"You are meddling in dangerous matters, woman. The dead girl was involved in some dark practices, ones best left alone."

"Like your daughter? And how is she?"

His face darkened.

Was that remorse painted on his expression? Perhaps even fear? If so, it was the first she'd seen of such weakness.

"She ran off as soon as I left her at home. I do not know where she is."

Daria clutched his arm, bare above the leather straps. "Then you understand the danger. I am trying to discover what is truly going on. What do you know?"

He eyed his coworkers at similar furnaces. "I know that we are all in danger—what we do here. Who we are." He exhaled heavily. "The dead girl who accused Lucas—her name was Maia. That is all I know."

Maia. The girl they had helped in the agora. But how could she—?

"Get out of here now, woman." Demetrius lifted his metal rod again, still a fiery red, and gave her a little shove with the other hand. "I want nothing more to do with you."

Daria stumbled from the furnace yard into the street, and her feet turned of their own accord toward the brothel. Surely the prostitute they had encountered that night would testify that Lucas had only tried to help the girl. That he had left her well tended by a physician, even paid for her care.

She was footsore and heart-weary by the time she reached the brothel and braved its entrance. The overpowering scents assailed her in a wave, blurring her vision so much she could barely make out the obscene pictures on the walls.

A very young woman, a girl really, caught sight of her and stopped in the hall. She ran a glance over Daria's clothing— respectable, though not wealthy, and the question was plain in her eyes.

What had been the woman's name who had met them that night?

Leto.

"I—I am looking for Leto. I met her once—"

The girl shook her head and hurried forward, her eyes sparking in fear. "You cannot be here. The evening is beginning, and good women are bad for business." She turned Daria toward the door and pushed against her shoulders. "You must go."

Daria planted her feet. "It will only take a moment!"

"No. You must go." The girl's voice seemed desperate, as though she would be blamed for any lack of business due to

Daria's interference. "Come back in the morning if you must. But not now. Not tonight."

She shoved Daria into the sunlight, then drew back and disappeared within. An older man, hunched and wrinkled, approached the doorway and slowed when he saw Daria.

She fled, frustrated. Angry. Back to the home of Joseph and Iris, where she would be welcomed and not questioned. But where she would not feel peace until Lucas was safe.

———

When the sun had barely crawled above the horizon, she was back at the brothel, pushing through its reeking halls, asking questions, asking for Leto.

"You are looking for me?"

The nasal voice at the end of the hall was the most welcome she'd heard in a long time. Daria turned and smiled. "Yes. Yes, I need your help."

Leto wore an elegant chitôn, but one that had seen better days, perhaps discarded by a wife of a patron. Pinned at the shoulder, it nevertheless slipped down to reveal bare skin. She pulled it up self-consciously at Daria's smile.

It was a simple matter to explain what she wanted. Not so simple to convince.

"I cannot have any trouble brought on the girls here. I keep clear of those in power. Except when they are customers, of course." At this, a little grin, less lighthearted than the words tried to convey.

Daria gripped the woman's hands. "Please, I will explain your help in the most flattering light. Who knows? Perhaps it will even earn you favor. You did a good thing that night, and it would be a good thing today, to tell the truth."

The woman's eyes flickered at this, the cunning expression of a seasoned businesswoman who saw an opportunity.

"All right. I will go."

Daria exhaled her relief. "Thank you."

The cool interior of the magistrates' offices at the head of the city was a welcome change from the hot climb. Daria led the way inside, asked several questions, and was given unwelcome information.

The magistrate Zagreus who had arrested Lucas was now at the prison, questioning him. If they wanted to speak to the man, they would have to wait. As to when he would return, no one seemed to know.

Daria turned hopeful eyes on her companion. "Will you come to the prison with me?"

She sighed, then extended a hand toward the door, inviting Daria to walk ahead.

They retraced their steps, then proceeded farther to Harbor Street, to the narrow prison doorway.

Zagreus stood inside, speaking with the jailer. There was no sign of Lucas, only that awful door in the floor, looped with iron chains.

Zagreus raised his gaze to her, then to her companion, where it lingered.

"We have come to put these ridiculous accusations about Lucas to rest." Daria pushed forward, pointed to Leto. "Tell him. Tell him what Lucas did for the girl, Leto."

The woman from the brothel shrugged and told her story. Told how Lucas had brought the girl, had paid to have her looked after and for the physician to be called.

"He even came back the next day. Wanted to make sure he knew where the girl had gone, where she could be found." She smiled. "I suppose he was looking for some gratitude."

Daria frowned. Lucas had returned and asked for the girl's whereabouts?

Zagreus shrugged. "I am hearing nothing that changes my opinion here. In fact, you have brought me proof that Lucas was indeed involved with this girl."

Daria stepped forward, spread her hands wide. "But why would he have helped her, then later killed her?" She fought to retain a respectful tone. Antagonizing the praetor would do little good.

Zagreus studied her, paused before answering. "Perhaps because you were with him the first night. He did not want a witness."

"No! Maia knew he would help her, that he did help her. That must have been why she asked for him as she was dying."

"I admire your loyalty, woman. But I am afraid it is misplaced. More evidence has been found."

Daria's heart stuttered and she looked to Leto, as though she were a sympathetic friend. "What evidence?"

From the pouch at his waist, Zagreus produced a small metal object and held it out to her on his flattened palm. A strange iron star inscribed inside a circle, with a protruding wooden piece.

She recognized the symbol at once and lifted her eyes to Zagreus's.

"It is a sort of *brand*." His lips curled over the distasteful word. "Heated and then burned into the skin." He closed his fingers around the object and studied Daria as if to gauge her reaction.

"We found it in Lucas's home."

32

THE INFERNAL DRIPPING REMEMBERED FROM HEKTOR'S underground lair of sorcerers had its echo in the prison hole of Ephesus. Lucas shifted his position on the muddy floor and let his chains clank together, simply to drown the infuriating constancy of that dripping.

Across the single cell two others leaned their backs against the damp wall, each with wrists and ankles bound by iron, as he was. Neither was conscious. Whether drunk, sick, or sleeping he could not say, but neither had acknowledged his rough entrance, the irons clamped around him, the barked warnings of the jailer, or the clunk of the trapdoor.

One small oil lamp burned in a gouged wall niche and did little to overcome the grimy blackness. No doubt the shadows hid creatures unaccustomed to light. Would they visit him in the night, chew at his flesh while he slept? The stench of unwashed, untended men with no latrine burned his eyes.

It had not surprised him when Zagreus came for him. Somehow it seemed a fitting conclusion to unburdening himself to Daria, to letting the past flow out with all its failures and guilt. He had confessed. Why should he not now be punished?

The door above yanked open and feeble light fell across the mud, illuminating his lower leg, already dirtied by his imprisonment.

A pair of feet began to descend the ladder, the calves too large to be the jailer's.

"Aquila." Lucas called the man's name, but his voice was muffled, deadened in this place.

After Aquila, another pair of feet, presumably his wife's. They were known to visit those in prison. But when the shoulders and head appeared, Lucas closed his eyes. Daria should not soil herself in a place like this, nor see him here. It was unjust.

"Why have you come?" He did not, could not, look at Daria.

Aquila took in Lucas's fellow prisoners, the chains, the mud. "To try to get you out of here, man. Why else?"

Lucas lifted a manacled hand toward his fellow prisoners. "There is no getting out of here."

"Well, we shall see. Not today, at least. But you're strong enough to survive a day in the hole, I daresay."

Lucas could ignore Daria no longer. She was there beside him, kneeling in the dirt in her untarnished white robe, pushing the hair from his eyes and studying him with tender care. His heart reached for her, but he kept his hands on his thighs.

She didn't speak. There was nothing to say. How could she even be here after the accusations she'd surely heard?

The jailer's voice shot from the square of light above. "That's enough now. I shouldn't even be allowing—"

"We are coming, we are coming." Aquila nodded once to Daria and started up the ladder, moving slowly.

Daria turned her full attention on him, looked into the depths of his eyes. "Stay strong, Lucas. We are doing everything we can to find the truth, to secure your release."

Her hands on his arm, on his face, were warm and pure. How could he tell her he did not deserve her pity, nor her help?

"Tell me you will be well, Lucas. Tell me you will be strong until we come again."

"Listen to me, Daria. You must leave this place. This city. It is not safe for you here. They are trying to destroy me, and you have gotten too involved. You know too much. You are a danger to them. You must flee."

Somehow the jailer had already descended. He pulled on Daria's shoulders with rough hands. "Time to go, girl. Let's go."

She clung to Lucas, her fingers burrowing into his arm. He watched the tears slide down her pale cheeks, watched them drip from her chin.

The jailer grew rougher. Lucas did nothing to stop him. Better that she should go.

He shoved Daria toward the ladder, then began to ascend behind her, urging her forward. "You'll get to see him again." He chuckled. "If nothing else, at the execution."

At the word her foot slipped and Lucas heard her suck in a breath. But then she continued, up and through the patch of light, and was lost to him. The trapdoor slammed.

The hole was empty now. It mattered not that three shared the space. The life had gone out of it, gone out of him, when she left.

Time passed, he knew not how much. Impossible to tell. The oil lamp sputtered and died, his cellmates moaned in their stupor, and Lucas's belly rumbled with hunger.

The jailer came, relit the lamp, left dishes of cold slop for him to suck up as best he could with his manacled hands. The other two stirred at this offering, perhaps the only time they roused themselves. They ate in silence.

When the chink of light around the trapdoor widened once again, he could not have said if it had been a day or a week. He hoped for a better meal.

Instead, he got Demetrius.

Truly? Even here the man would hound him?

But when Demetrius dropped to the mud, it was the silversmith who appeared hounded. Even in the cell's murky light, the shadows that ringed his eyes spoke of sleeplessness and worry.

"Where is she?" Demetrius clenched his fists, towered over Lucas as though he would strike.

A bolt of dread shot through Lucas's body. Had something happened to Daria?

"Where is Selene?"

Lucas blinked. "Your daughter?"

"Do not feign innocence, Lucas. Innocent men do not end up in holes such as this. Tell me where she is."

Lucas licked his dry lips and shook his head, heavy with the lethargy of inaction. "I—I do not know anything about—"

"You must! She went back to you, to all of you!" His eyes were white, frantic. "What have you done with her?"

Lucas felt the man's pain, understood the danger to his daughter, and somehow pitied him in that moment. "I am not one of the sorcerers. I never was."

Demetrius lurched to his knees, grabbed Lucas's shoulders,

and shook him. "Not the sorcerers, fool! The Christians! They have taken her."

Lucas let his head loll back against the stone wall, drained. "If that is true, then she is well. They will care for her."

Demetrius shoved Lucas's shoulders and sat on his heels. "Are you mad? They are destroying our city. Will take away everything that is both sacred and secure about Ephesus. And their mystery rites are an abomination. You defend them?"

"There is much you do not understand, Demetrius."

"I understand enough. And the guild's purpose in this continues, with or without you. The robbery of the temple will take place on the day of the Artemis Festival as planned. The Christians will be blamed, and their leader, Paul, will be arrested."

Lucas huffed a half-amused laugh. "Then I shall be in good company."

"Do not count on that. He will be dead before he reaches the jail. We will make certain."

Yet another plot to kill Paul? "You do wrong to accuse or condemn him, Demetrius. He is a good man."

"A good man? Like you, Lucas?"

"Nothing like me."

Demetrius stood, brushed at the muddy knee prints embedded in his tunic to no avail. "Will you not tell me where my daughter is?"

"Truly, I do not know. But I will pray for her safety."

"Pray? To whom?"

The question hung unanswered.

Demetrius climbed and again the trapdoor sealed off the cell from the world. His cellmates did not stir.

What was Daria doing out there now? Searching for a means to exonerate him, no doubt. How long until he was tried and executed? Perhaps they would rush the trial to set the execution for the Artemis Festival. The city officials were always looking to increase the entertainment value of the day's activities.

Would he speak in his own defense? What defense did he have? He had not killed that girl, it was true, but he might as well have.

How many women had perished while he continued in his stubborn plan? Was not each of them also someone's wife? Someone's child? Did he not bear guilt for every one of those innocents?

He had sworn it would be better not to speak. His accusations would have done nothing, he told himself. Better to continue to ingratiate himself into their midst and then get proof of their guilt. But how many nights had he lain abed and envisioned them, trapped in that sick dungeon below Hektor's shop, screaming out their fear as flames annihilated their scrolls, their instruments, their amulets, and their very bodies? Somewhere in his search for justice for the death of his wife and child, he had crossed the line to vengeance.

And now not even his precious vengeance was left to him. He was to die as well, another victim in their long line of victims, without any justice meted to those who killed with impunity. Perhaps someone would find a way, someday, to strike back. But it was not to be him.

The vengeance he sought had turned back on him, to bite him like a serpent devouring its own tail.

The self-admittance was like a release. He had held tightly to anger for so long. He let it go with a heavy sigh and a loosening of muscles that left him fatigued and weak as a babe. His arms rolled outward at his sides with the weight of his chains, and the scarred-over wound on his arm glowed pink in the lamplight.

So much pain for nothing.

Daria's stricken eyes seemed to appear in the gloom before him. Pain there as well. He had brought only pain to her, when she deserved so much more.

His gaze fell upon one of his fellow prisoners, slack-jawed and slumped against the opposite wall.

Or was it only a mirror in which he saw himself?

33

AQUILA HELD HER ARM AS DARIA STUMBLED FROM the prison. Where should she go from here? What could she do for him? Heavy folds of wool seemed to darken her thoughts, though she tried to claw them back into the light.

Aquila pulled her to Harbor Street toward the theater, and she fell into step until he stopped.

Daria raised her eyes, but his attention was farther up the street, nodding to a cluster of people headed toward them.

"I hoped we would see you pass."

Paul walked at the head of the little group with his protectors, Gaius and Aristarchus, on either side. Priscilla smiled at her husband, but behind her, the faces of the others were more solemn. Timothy, and the two friends Tychicus and Trophimus. Joseph and Iris. Europa and Seneca and poor little Flora. She had met so many in recent days. All of them, somber. Did they believe that Lucas would surely be executed?

Paul reached Aquila, clasped his arm, and inclined his head toward the harbor. "Their boat sails within the hour."

Timothy circled those blocking him and came to take Daria's hand. He carried a large pouch over one shoulder. "I heard about Lucas. I am very sorry."

"You are leaving?"

He nodded, lips pressed together, and blinked several times. "Paul thinks it best if Erastus and I head to Macedonia a little ahead of him, to ensure things are prepared there."

"Ahead of him?" Daria turned a heavy head to Paul, her gaze probing.

He gave her a slight smile. "I am leaving after Pentecost. It is time for me to move on from here. The message is needed in Macedonia as well." He gripped Aquila's shoulder. "And I am leaving the work in good hands here."

Timothy leaving. Paul leaving. Lucas executed. The leaden feeling in her chest multiplied.

"Come with us to the harbor, Daria." Timothy tugged on her hand. "See us off."

She shook her heavy head. "No. No, I—I must—do something else. I will say good-bye here."

Timothy bowed to her, kissed her hand, and released it. She gave him the best smile she could. "Be well and safe, Timothy. I thank you for your friendship."

"You shall always have it, should we meet again, Daria." His voice caught on the final words.

She squeezed his arm, gave another smile, but then turned from the group and drifted up Harbor Street, leaving them to their farewells. She did not belong to them, or with them. And she must think. Think of how to help Lucas.

Her steps were slow along the shadowed colonnade, and the crowd jostled and redirected her uncertain steps.

The dark wool that had blanketed her thoughts seemed to spread and enfold every part of her, body and mind, until she had to pause, had to clutch at the coolness of a stone column and breathe.

When she lifted her bent head once more and let her gaze drift across the street, it fell upon a pair of watching eyes.

Hektor.

A wicked chill ran from her chest out to her fingertips.

The white hair, pulled tight against his scalp, those hooded eyes, that full-lipped mouth. He did not even attempt to conceal his scrutiny. Why did he watch her? Follow her?

"You know too much. You are a danger."

Lucas's warning. She had barely heard it, so taken up was she with seeing him, hearing his voice. But had his warning been well founded? Did they see her as a threat to be eliminated?

She must get away. Get away from the evil that stalked her in the streets, that would steal her mind and soul.

Ahead, the shops of Harbor Street gave way to the huge open square of the commercial agora, penned by countless merchant stalls, crowds buzzing like a nest of angry hornets.

Those eyes. Hektor's eyes. Even across the street she saw something so familiar in them. A look she would remember no matter how many passing years intervened.

The look of evil, hunting for prey.

With a last glance at Hektor, Daria darted through stone columns. She paused at the vastness. She could scream across this marketplace and never be heard. Better to lose herself in the chaos.

The morning's soft haze had been scorched away, and the white-hot sun struck marble pavers and pained her eyes. She ran past a fabric stall and gauzy fabrics snaked out in the breeze like shrouds to entangle and suffocate. A snatched look over her shoulder—Hektor still followed. Hair whipped into her mouth and she spit to clear it.

Could she hide? Her chitôn stuck fast to her damp skin and an occasional hiccup of breath was all she could marshal.

She spotted a butcher stall ahead, with knives jutting from wood blocks and hanging sheep staring with liquid eyes that made one shudder and blink away.

But he was too close.

She darted through the thicket of bloody-white wool to a stall of exotic spices and perfumes that choked the air. A seller barked an offer for his heavy chained jewelry as she ran, a stabbing at her ears she ignored.

And then he was somehow, impossibly, at her side. Circling her waist with an arm, dragging her into a dim enclosure, ordering a boy to drop the awning.

She tasted bile in her throat. A surge of anger sent strength to her arms and legs, and she kicked and swatted even as she was swallowed into the stall.

The canvas unrolled with a heavy thud to the stones, sealing her inside with Hektor and a table of his charms and amulets and potions.

He held her from behind, and she sensed him jerk his head toward the boy in dismissal.

And then they were alone.

She beat against the sinewy arms locking her against his body.

He made a sound low in his throat, a satisfied sort of growl.

"And *this* is precisely why I must have your help, Tutor."

She stopped struggling at the title. Her pretense of being Lucas's visiting friend was clearly at an end.

"Just listen a moment, will you?" He shook her body, rattled her teeth. "They say you are a knowledge-seeker. What we could do together! Rise up and take control for ourselves. You do not want to live at the gods' mercy any more than I do."

Her eyes were adjusting to the shadows. She focused on amulet stones strung across the table, painted with the evil eye in hopes of warding it off. He would not have his illicit charms here, only those deemed acceptable by good, religious Greeks and Romans.

"Do you not want to assist me? Refuse to submit, pass the boundaries—"

"I want you to let me go." She spoke the words as a command, cold and firm.

He did not loosen his grip.

"Do not think you must be willing, woman. There are many ways to gain your aid without your accord. And if you are not a help to me, then you are a danger."

That was what he had said, that terrible night. Her husband, Xanthos.

"You are a danger to them."

"You are to be a warrior in this battle."

She had asked for none of this. Wanted no part in this fight. Why would evil seek her out, try to destroy her?

The darkness had claimed her husband . . . it had somehow claimed Lucas.

She should have run, not tried to fight.

She relaxed against him, too tired for the moment to resist any longer. Would he force something on her, as he had Selene?

Would she lose her mind, the only thing she had left? Her insides trembled, the flutter working its way to her limbs.

A slivered triangle of light opened at the face of the stall, then darkened with the silhouette of a man.

Hektor's grip loosened a bit.

"A private showing of your abominations, Hektor?"

The voice, the stature. Even with the light at his back, Daria knew him.

Paul.

Hektor yanked her toward the back of the stall. "This is none of your concern, Jew."

"Ah, you are wrong. Daria is a great concern of mine. And so are you."

She still could not make out his features, but the voice, it was the same he used while praying, the same he used while easing the demons out of a tormented man on the street. Effortless and persuasive.

And as easily as the chains had fallen from the man in the street, Hektor's arms fell away from her body. He still stood behind her, and she dared not turn.

"Come, Daria." Paul held out a hand. "It is time to leave."

She stumbled forward with one hesitant step, then rushed to embrace him.

A little chuckle in her ear, a hooked arm around hers, and he was leading her into the light. The canvas fell closed behind them, secreting Hektor inside.

"H-How did you do that?"

He wandered through the stalls and tables, still guiding her with his hand over hers, clutching his arm.

She risked a look backward. They walked alone. "Thank you, Paul. I could not have gotten away. I do not have your power."

He laughed. "Even I do not have my power, Daria." He slowed at a table piled with turnips and artichokes, then continued toward the agora's end.

"I do not understand."

"You are trying to be victorious in your own strength. And no matter how formidable a woman, you are still only human."

She bit her lip, kept her eyes trained away from the bright sun. "Nothing compared to the gods and demons, you mean."

He turned on her in the square, grasped her hands, and looked into her eyes. "You are a beautiful, exceedingly gifted, and highly prized instrument. But you are an *instrument*, to be used and played by the Master. Only in submitting to this truth will you find freedom and any success."

She stared along the edge of the agora, toward the hillside estates. "I wanted to help him. To succeed where I had once failed—"

"This second chance you long for, Daria, is only another attempt with the same failed reasoning. You do not need a second chance to redeem yourself—you need a *Redeemer*. And Lucas does not need you to be his savior. He needs Jesus."

She shook her head to clear the muddle of confusing messages, to no avail. How could this be true—that her intellect, her strength of will, none of it was sufficient to set things right?

She pulled away from his handclasp and tried to smile. "Thank you for the rescue, Paul. But I must—there is something I must do."

34

HIS JAILER MUST BE A ROMAN.

Nothing else could explain the neglect, the hostility with which the man shoved his excuse for food at his prisoners, the way he seemed to delight in their misfortune.

Lucas tried to count the meals as a means to keep track of time, but it was soon apparent that there was no regularity nor guarantee that food would arrive at all. The prison had been dug too near the harbor's low water table, and the mud softened then dried in tidal regularity.

And so he assumed day melted into night and awoke again, but he could not be certain. The trapdoor allowed not even a breath of light past its chains to signal the dawn.

He slept. He attempted conversation with the two who had been here longer. He tried to think, to plan. But there was nothing to think about, nor to plan. He was at the mercy of the gods now and could only await his destiny.

But a sure and certain feeling began to take root, a knowledge that he did not have long for this world. That he must make his peace with the divine before it was too late.

As if in answer to his thoughts, the trapdoor opened and the jailer's harsh voice marshaled someone else down the ladder. Then another. The door snapped its jaws on the newcomers only an instant after Lucas had seen their faces.

"Gaius? Aristarchus?"

Kind of Paul to send his friends, but even these two could do nothing.

But then the door was open again, the jailer was descending, an iron key in hand.

A lift of hope leaped its way across Lucas's heart. They had secured his release!

"Sit." The jailer shoved Gaius's shoulder, and the man dropped to the floor in obedience. Aristarchus joined him in the mud, legs extended for the chains.

The jailer's key did not move toward Lucas's bound wrists. It was inserted into another lock, chains twisted around Gaius's arms, fastened down with a sickening clang. He moved to Aristarchus, repeated the lockdown. And then he was gone without a word.

The two men turned their attention to Lucas immediately.

"How are you, brother?" Gaius's natural smile seemed as out of place as fine wine dumped in a gutter.

Brother. He was not their brother.

"I am alive. But what terrible turn has brought you two here?"

Aristarchus shrugged. "Everyone is still in madness over the sorcerers' bonfire a few days ago. People are blaming the believers for the loss of property and power."

"They say the scrolls were valued at fifty-thousand pieces of silver!" Gaius's voice chirped with the elation of a young boy. "It is a great victory for the One God. Proof that even the demons cower before the name of the Messiah."

"Now if only the people would see the worthlessness of their Lady so easily." Aristarchus did not share his friend's constant optimism. "The upcoming Artemis Festival is bringing out even those who rarely see the need to worship. The whole city is in a frenzy of preparation."

Lucas rested his head against the wall. The short conversation had already tired him. "But I do not understand why you two—"

"Charges of blasphemy against the goddess. Of inciting a public disturbance." Gaius grinned. "The usual. Only difference is that this time, Paul's not with us."

Aristarchus sighed. "He deserves a respite. The man's taken more blows than I can count."

"Will you have a trial?"

"Probably. This is a Roman province and we are Jews." Aristarchus smiled. "As much as they might desire it, they cannot simply take us outside the city and stone us without causing more upheaval."

"You seem unconcerned, for two men in a hole."

Gaius rattled the chains around his wrists. "It is a privilege to suffer for the Name, Lucas. To be chained for the sake of the message that sets all men free."

Lucas turned away, pretended to fall asleep to avoid more conversation. Words he did not want to hear.

But there was no avoiding their message when sometime later they received another visitor.

Paul.

Lucas half expected to see the jailer follow and place Paul in irons, but the door closed above him, and he turned to his friends with outstretched hands filled with fresh bread.

Lucas accepted a loaf gratefully, eyed the two who had not spoken since he arrived. He did not trust their greedy hands. But with heads lolling against the water-rivuleted wall, they were insensible to Paul's presence and his gift. He tore a chunk of the yeasty bread with his teeth and chewed hungrily.

And cheese! Produced from a pouch at Paul's waist. The sharp taste and soft texture were the finest things he'd ever tasted.

"You must stay strong, boys." Paul's eyes were somber, his voice low. "I am so sorry I was not able to keep you from this. I wish it were me in these chains rather than you two." He turned to Lucas. "And we are all convinced of your innocence as well, my friend."

He dropped beside the three of them, willing to sit in the muck. "I cannot tell you how much it pains me to see you all here. I have sought the Lord several times, to ask why He allows the innocent to suffer."

Aristarchus patted Paul's leg. "Do you ask this of Him when *you* are the one in chains?"

Paul dropped his head. "I am not innocent, as you well know. But others should not suffer in my place."

"Is this why you sent Timothy ahead to Macedonia?"

He nodded, not lifting his head. "The boy—the boy has been with me for some time now. He has become my son in the faith. And he is not strong, not like the two of you. Not yet. He has much growing to do before he will be ready to take the place set out for him. I could not bear to see him harmed. Though to part from him was nearly as painful."

Paul focused on Lucas, his brows drawn together. "And what will we do to assist you? These strange charges that you have been responsible for the terrible murders in the city, it is more than any of us can believe."

Lucas shrugged. "I have been gambling, Paul. And I have lost."

"What does that mean?" Paul's eyes were clear and focused, his voice warm.

"I believed I could punish those responsible for my wife's death. Could see justice enacted against them. But in the process I have brought guilt upon myself. And now it is I who will suffer for their actions."

"You know this has not been justice you have sought, Lucas. Vengeance is better left to God."

Lucas shifted, chains chafing at his ankles, grinding against raw skin. "Your god?"

Paul chuckled. "Still resisting, I see. Yes, my God. The One God. He will make all things right. If not now, then in the end, in His kingdom to come."

"How can I believe this?"

"You must have faith. You have seen the power on both sides. You know that the One God makes war against all the other gods, who are not gods at all but demons in disguise."

"You are telling me that I am not to protect those I love?"

"Of course we protect. But we must always remember that true security is found only in God's hands. We cannot arrange it for others."

Lucas glanced at Gaius and Aristarchus, then back to Paul. "And do *you* believe that?"

Paul fell silent, his eyes softening, his gaze drifting to the back wall. "You have spoken truth to me, Lucas. I thank you for that. I must seek the Lord on this matter."

With that, he stood, mud sucking at his feet, and clasped their hands all around. "I will return. I will do what I can."

He climbed the ladder, banged on the underside of the door, and when it opened, disappeared through it.

They left him alone, thankfully. Gaius and Aristarchus carried on their own conversation and left him to his jumbled thoughts.

In all that he had seen, all that he had heard since meeting the Christians, one thing had become clear: they worshipped a God of great power.

He had seen power elsewhere, true. But the Hebrew God whom the Christians—both Jews and Greeks—claimed as their own was the greater, as well as righteous.

And if the greater power, was it not possible He was the only God? The One God, as they said?

Could Lucas give up vengeance to this One God? Allow Him to repay the guilty ones?

He asked himself the question, let the uncertainty hang in the dark air above him.

Yes.

It was another letting go. This moment of faith, whatever it meant. Like a child giving over his broken toy to his father for repair, Lucas gave the desire for justice and the anger that had accompanied it to Paul's One God.

Let us see what He does with it.

But there were things that could be done to arrange for others' safety.

If he were to be executed, there was only one person whom he desired to protect before his death. There must be a way to keep her safe, to provide for her future.

But he would need help. There were letters that must be written. Arrangements made.

How could he act from a hole in the ground?

35

SOMETHING SHE MUST DO, SHE HAD TOLD PAUL.

Nothing more, for he would not approve.

She had some money with her. Not much, but almost all she had. It seemed only fitting that her sacrifice would require a surrender of nearly all her resources.

A few weeks with the strange sect had confused her thinking. She needed to return to what she knew. She had displeased the gods, and they had lifted their protection. And for this there was only one remedy—she must make amends, pledge her devotion. Seek their blessing.

The climb to the temple plateau took the better part of two hours and sapped her strength. The sun-soaked temple precinct overflowed with sweating, anxious celebrants, their efforts to please ridiculously early, since the Artemis Festival did not begin for two days. Daria sagged against a stone column just before the gateway, and even the stone had absorbed the heat and hum of the crowds.

But she would fight the madness to do what she must. What choice did she have? She could not expect protection, or release for Lucas, if she did not offer proper worship.

Inhaling resolve, she forced sluggish feet up the wide stone steps, in company with revelers and penitents. Under the double-arched gateway and its carved reliefs of gods and animals, through three pairs of columns supporting the arches, and into the vast temple precinct. Ahead, behind the towering statue of the goddess that greeted worshippers, the Altar of Artemis already smoked with morning offerings, no doubt more lavish and abundant than any Daria could bring. She touched a hand to the pouch secured under the folds of her robes.

A tall man, talking and laughing with another at his side, knocked against her shoulder as he passed but acknowledged nothing.

Best to keep moving. It was not the place to stop and gawk.

Off to the right, before the grand staircase to the temple, several merchants shepherded pens and cages of small animals at the ready for worshippers in need of a purchase. Daria nodded a greeting to one of the men. His calculating gaze sized her at once, and he jerked a thumb toward the cages of turtledoves, scrawny and inexpensive.

Daria traded away most of her coin for two of the birds and looked away as he stuffed them into a sack, their feathers flapping a protest. Did they sense what was coming? Realize that even a merchant's captivity was better than the fate that awaited?

The temple crowd seemed to flap and squawk as much as the birds, their many-hued robes and tunics darting through the courtyard, up and down temple steps, in and out of the stoa, the treasury, the meeting halls. Hurrying, chattering, fluttering crowds, all anxious to please the goddess and find favor in these hours leading to her great celebration. She must watch with pleasure.

The merchant tied the sack with a bit of frayed knot and handed it to Daria. She grasped the squirming sack at the gathered twine and held it from her body. Tried not to think of its contents. Began the trek toward the great altar, toward the line of others who came for duty and for love.

Had she come for love?

All her life she had sought to please the gods, done the right things to have a blessed life. Sometimes her actions seemed to bring favor. Sometimes they did not. *"Rise up and take control,"* Hektor had said. No, safer to follow. But with such vagaries of the gods' whims, how could she even be certain they listened?

Or that they existed?

Perhaps all was random chance, and the earth crawled with meaningless creatures seeking only to find significance in worship, in a grasping belief that something, someone, greater than themselves held destiny in divine hands.

Her feet were leaden and her tread halting. The birds calmed, perhaps reconciled to their fate.

She found her place in the line. Tried to keep her eyes focused on the calves and sandals of the young man in front of her, but the frenzied activities of the sacred space of the *temenos* seemed to escalate with every breath.

Nearby, a woman screamed and fell to the marble paving, writhing and shrieking. At the same moment, unseen musicians began a flurry of drumbeats and a horn signaled a processional.

Another woman dropped with a scream, then another.

Daria held her sack against her body, kept her arms tight,

but her gaze scanned, watched. Would she be next? Some sort of powers snaked through the courtyard, claiming victims. Surely the goddess would intervene and protect.

Her mind tumbled and pounded in rhythm with the drum-beats. Did Artemis hear their prayers and laugh? Was their submission, their groveling, insufficient? Was it even possible to earn her favor?

The line edged forward. Another throat slit, sacrifice offered. Another penitent leaving the altar, believing he had sated the god-dess's bloodlust and curried blessings for his crops, his health, the fertility of his wife.

In the stillness of the chill damp, the smoke rose from the altar without drifting, but Daria was close enough for it to fill her nostrils, burn her eyes. She lifted her gaze to the heavens. How far must the sacrificial smoke rise for Artemis to sense it? Above Daria's head, the iron-gray of heavy clouds seemed impenetrable. As though the sacrifices and the prayers must be returned to them unheard.

Perhaps this was the true state of worship every day, not only when the sky sealed itself.

Another step toward the altar. A moment later, the death-squeal of a small animal. So many sacrifices today. The altar must surely gush with blood. She could not bear to look.

It must be right, this way of sacrifice. Did not all mankind bring offerings to altars? The Greeks, for untold centuries. The Romans, with their jumbled pantheon assembled from the myriad of conquered gods. Even the Jews, with their One God, brought sacrifices.

Not the Christians. Greeks and Jews worshipping the Jewish God but without sacrifice. Their Messiah, a once-for-all sacrifice. Too simple.

Beyond simple, was their claim not madness? To teach that rather than requiring His followers to ceaselessly offer sacrifice, He instead had provided the sacrifice for *them*? That He wanted children to love, not slaves who would serve?

She was nearly to the altar now. Nearly her turn to shed blood for the goddess, to whisper prayers and pleas, to hope to be heard. Relief would come with the wringing of birds' necks. It must.

But her assurance had been sucked away by the questions within and the chaos without. All around her, citizens of Ephesus were roused into religious ecstasy that seemed hollow, ineffective. The sky unyielding and the darkness hovering at the edges of the courtyard, seeking to devour.

The birds fluttered again in their woolen prison, wings worrying the fabric, and her soul fought its own confinement, the rigid beliefs that had strapped her in ritual and guilt for so many years.

Freedom. This love of a God rather than petty and capricious demands.

But where was the logic? The proof? Her systematic pursuit of answers that led to only one solution?

"Your sacrifice."

Daria lifted her head. She had come to the front of the line. A priest, his costly robe spattered with blood and gore, held out a waiting hand and eyed the wriggling sack.

Caught in the suspension between calculated logic and blind faith, Daria clung to the knotted fabric. The charred remains of obedient worshippers smoked and glowed on the altar and the priest's knife glinted, refracting the orange ember-light.

She leaned away, backward, until the man behind her grunted.

And then she turned and ran.

The slap of her sandals disappeared in the clamor and tumult of the surging masses, and she ran a jagged path through the crushing crowd, across the stones, under the arch, down the wide steps.

She ran down the hillside toward the city, and as she ran, she untied the twine that cinched her woolen sack.

Halfway to the Embolos, she stopped, opened the sack, and watched the tortured birds soar to freedom.

36

DARIA PUSHED HER WAY THROUGH THE EMBOLOS IN the opposite direction of the throng. Did the Lady of the Ephesians even now frown on her from the slate heavens for her lack of piety? There was no way to be certain, not before action was taken. Her insistence upon clear thinking before every decision had failed her in matters of faith. She could no more be certain of Artemis's displeasure than she could of the Christian's One God.

But the flicker of rebellion that had ignited at the foot of the altar grew as she fled the temple plain. She passed the house where she had first seen Paul's God drive evil from the heart of a sick man.

Hektor's bid to gain power and control the gods was a failed one. He had some power, it was clear, but everything Daria had seen of Paul proved his One God had more.

With her growing doubt of the gods came another, stronger,

determination. She would fight a battle, as Paul had said. But it would be a battle for Lucas's freedom.

She crossed into the street to speed her progress and jumped to avoid an ox-drawn cart that swerved unpredictably.

He would be brought to trial soon. What could she do to counter any evidence?

The city praetor had discounted the prostitute's assertion that Lucas had helped Maia that night, believing instead that Lucas had concealed his true intent because Daria was present and had found the girl to finish the task.

And that iron symbol, used to brand the women, found in Lucas's house. It was particularly damning. Did she not have a moment of doubt herself when she heard of its discovery?

She slowed along the street, letting the shoppers and pedestrians jostle around her. How had that monstrous object found its way to his house? And why?

If it did not belong to Lucas, then someone had placed it there to be found. Someone who desired to see Lucas blamed for the killings.

Who had cause for such a thing? Lucas had allied himself with Christian, sorcerer, and Metalsmith Guild alike. She finished the trek down the Embolos, then up the steps and along Hill Street to the flat-roofed line of estates built into the hill.

At Lucas's lofty entry, she lifted the latch with a careful hand and slid the door inward a crack, then wide enough for her head and shoulders.

There was no sign of either Frona or Clovis. Holding her breath, she slipped inside, closed the door, and tiptoed to Lucas's sitting room. No lamp had been lit, so she left the door open and searched the contents of his desk with what little light eked in from the courtyard.

There was nothing here to exonerate or incriminate. A feeling of hopelessness, pointlessness, stole over her.

Little as she relished confronting the two old servants, if she wished to get information, they were the only two likely to possess it.

She crept from the sitting room into the courtyard. Why had she not knocked? Now she was an intruder, no doubt an unwelcome one.

Should she slip back outside, approach again, this time waiting at the door to be invited?

"What are you wanting?"

Daria startled at Frona's harsh voice, issuing forth from the back of the house. She frowned and squinted into the darkness. "Frona? I—I came to speak with you."

"We've had enough speaking to us these last days."

The woman materialized from the shadows, her lined face puckered with disapproval. But something else as well. Her gaze darted past Daria and back.

Daria turned to follow Frona's glance, but the courtyard was gray and silent. "You have been questioned? By the city magistrates?"

"Aye, they've tracked their mud through here more than once since the master was taken."

"And searched the house?"

Frona's eyes narrowed. "What does the tutor need with such reports?"

Daria tried to smile. "I want to do all I can to prove the master's innocence. Will you help?"

Frona twisted bony hands at her waist. "Perhaps he is not so innocent as you think."

The woman's words were like cold water poured down Daria's

back. She crossed her arms, suddenly chilled in only her thin robe. "He is a good man. Surely you cannot have worked here so long without seeing this truth. Tell me, Frona, who else has been here? Someone who might have reason to leave something behind for the praetor to find?"

At the question, Frona's lips tightened and a furrow formed between her brows, as though Daria had accused the woman herself.

"There is no one here! No one has come. And you are not welcome!"

Frona crossed the empty space between them, her skeletal frame bearing down on Daria like a ship dispatched for warfare.

Daria held her ground.

"I am not leaving, Frona. Tell me who has been here."

Frona drew up short in front of her. She breathed heavily through flaring nostrils and looked on Daria as though she would strike her down with hatred alone. But she did not touch her.

And Daria would not back down. "Someone placed an object in this house, Frona, where the magistrates would find it and believe it belonged to Lucas. This object has connected him with the city murders."

From the quick twitch of her lips and widening of her eyes, this information seemed to be a revelation to Frona.

Daria pressed the moment. "Who would have been here to leave such a thing? No one comes or goes without your knowledge. Surely you know who—"

"No one has come, I tell you!"

The sharp protest echoed off the peristyle walls and columns, and in the echo another sound mimicked, this one like the cry of an animal.

Daria lifted her head toward the noise, startled, then looked to Frona. The woman's eyes shone with terror.

"What was that noise, Frona?"

Memories of the morning at the temple, of the anguished squeal of sacrificed animals, made her stomach churn. What was the woman doing back in that kitchen?

Frona rubbed at a spot on her chest, just below the hollow of her throat, and shook her head. "Clovis has bought a pig at the market for butchering. That is all. Nothing more."

Her skin washed gray, then pink. She was a terrible liar.

"Fresh meat, when the master is not at home? I would see this pig." She pushed past Frona, but the woman grabbed her wrist with fingers like birds' talons. "We have no need of you in the kitchens—"

Daria jerked her arm free. "I have need."

Frona's scuffling sandals followed, but Daria ignored her and pushed toward the kitchen. If it were only a pig as Frona said, there was no real concern. Perhaps the old couple had taken a few liberties in their master's absence. It would explain Frona's nervous desire to be rid of Daria.

But the premonition in the pit of her stomach told Daria otherwise. All was not right here. Perhaps it never had been.

Behind her, Frona called out over her head, "I am not accustomed to having intruders in my kitchen!"

An empty threat. And one that seemed intended to warn someone else of Daria's approach.

She rounded the corner into the kitchen and was met with the immediate warmth of the cook fire and the smell of roasting meat. A haunch of something, impaled on an iron rod over the fire, sizzled as the fat dripped from the skin.

"You see?" Frona bustled past her into the smoky chamber.

Daria laughed, a short humorless laugh. "I am expected to believe this roasting meat was crying out only a moment ago?"

Frona lifted her chin. "You are not welcome here. The master released you from service."

Another small cry, this one from the corner of the kitchen.

Daria eyed Frona, whose mouth had twisted in hatred.

Heart pounding, Daria crossed the kitchen in two strides, to the dark corner where a flimsy basket was pushed against the wall, half-covered with a ragged blanket. She snatched the fabric from the reed basket and tossed it to the tiled floor.

Daria gasped.

Whatever she had been expecting, it was not this.

A baby, dark-eyed with a shock of black hair. Pink lips in a pout. Tiny arms waving, legs kicking. Swaddled in rags.

She spun on Frona. "What—whose baby is this?"

Frona's head jerked back and forth, denial and refusal mingled.

"What have you done, Frona?" Again, images of the morning's sacrifices played across Daria's thoughts, and the emanating sense of wrongness she felt from the old servant. And the acrid smell of that roasting pig did not help. "What are you doing?"

The baby cried out, and Daria's heart lurched in pity. She bent to the basket.

"No! Do not touch him!"

A boy. How old? Daria did not have enough experience with such matters to guess. She hesitated.

In that moment, Clovis entered, wary eyes on Daria.

"Who is this child, Clovis? What is he doing here?"

The old man glanced at his wife, then back to Daria.

Frona stepped between them. "Why ask this old fool? He knows nothing of babies."

Clovis's shoulders sagged as they always did under the weight of his wife's censure. But he spoke anyway. "He is the child of a neighbor's kitchen slave, my lady. Suffering from a bit of congestion."

Daria did not miss the respectful title. The man knew the right moment to flatter.

He gave her a lopsided smile, as always a bit slack on the left. "Frona has a touch with the young ones when they get like this. The slave begged Frona to take the child, nurse him back to health."

Daria looked to the baby. He rewarded her glance with a toothless smile. He did not look ill. She studied Frona's face, whitened again and hardened with fury.

"Is this true, Frona?"

"Slave dealings are none of your concern."

Frona clearly did not share her husband's diplomatic skill.

Daria bent to the baby. Nothing appeared amiss. She had no reason to think the child in danger. No reason but her own suspicion that there was some deceit.

Daria chewed her lip. She must leave, and leave the baby to their care.

She stood and peered at Frona, watching for any sign of deception. "Will you not tell me who has been in this house?"

"I *have* told you. All manner of intruders. The last of which still remains." Frona curled her lip over the last words and looked Daria up and down like the distasteful leftovers of a day-old meal.

She glanced at Clovis, but he seemed to shrink into the shadows.

Nothing more could be accomplished here. The days and hours until Lucas's trial ticked away, and thus far Daria had done nothing to procure his release.

She left the house feeling the malice of Frona's scowling gaze against her back.

Hungry and bone-weary from the day's confrontations, Daria trudged back through the city to the home of Iris and Joseph.

She found Iris teaching the Scriptures to a group of eager

young women, circled around her in the breezy courtyard. The older woman broke off at once, despite Daria's protestations, and scurried to settle her with food and drink in their spare bedchamber, then stood at the door, hands tight at her sides.

"What is it?" Daria sat upon the bed, her eyes on Iris's somber, downcast face. "What do I need to know?"

"There has been word."

"Of Lucas?" Daria stood.

Iris nodded.

"Tell me."

The kind woman raised her eyes to Daria. "He is to be tried tomorrow. And if found guilty, executed at the Artemis Festival on the following day."

37

THE CITY CHURNED WITH PEOPLE. THE ANNUAL
Artemis Festival brought thousands upon thousands to celebrate,
pouring into the city like grains of sand, filling every crevice, clog-
ging the streets. It brought prosperity to the citizens of Ephesus
in the pockets of its visitors. Gold and silver coins ran through
the hands of merchants and shop owners, a river of new wealth
to feed families for months. Even Aquila and Priscilla showed
grudging appreciation for the goddess's celebration and the business it brought to their little tentmaking shop.

Daria pushed toward the upper city, to the basilica alongside
the state agora. There in the domed Council House, a half circle
of cold seats around a vacant floor, a man would stand accused of
atrocities today and would plead for his life before city magistrates.

Or would he?

A vision of Lucas, standing proud and silent, unwilling to provide a defense, invaded her thoughts, gripped her with foreboding.

She passed the School of Tyrannus and glanced at its inscribed entrance. She had never even been inside. Her passionate desire to teach in the school seemed a lifetime ago.

If Lucas were executed, would she—?

No, it did no good to think in such terms.

The Prytaneion's open entrance beckoned as she passed, its warm hearth fire always burning, symbol of the city's hearth and hospitality. Countless dignitaries must be entertained inside during a week such as the Artemis Festival. Smoke ascended from the open-air altar in the colonnaded courtyard dedicated to the worship of Artemis and Augustus, tucked beyond the basilica's long line of columns. Though nothing in scale compared to the Artemision, this temple dedicated to the Roman Caesar-declared-god was one of the first to greet visitors in the city's official precincts, and any good Greek would cast an evil eye on the empire that had insinuated itself into worship in its conquered lands here and in every Roman province. The temple made Augustus a sort of partner with Artemis, and another smaller temple in the center of the paved agora paid homage to the first divine Caesar, Julius, and Dea Roma.

Daria had no time for political concerns. The edges of the agora were marked by monuments dedicated to important city figures, but it was the basilica stoa with its forest of columns lining the north side of the agora, whose steps she climbed, already warmed by the rising sun and protected from the wind. A favorite gathering place for businessman and philosopher alike, the long stoa's three aisles were clustered with men discussing business and politics and teachers who had gathered students to hear their wisdom. Between columns, statues of the Roman imperial family reminded citizens at whose beneficence they lived and worked and philosophized.

Daria jostled through groups of chatting men, ignoring glances. Her destination was the east end of the stoa, where the Council House held court.

Two Roman soldiers stood on either side of the wide entrance, their leather and metal uniforms gleaming in the sunlight.

Heart pounding, she kept her head down like she belonged inside and headed between.

The soldier on the right stepped into her path.

"I have come for the trial. I—am needed to give evidence." She stared them down and scowled.

Her confidence won out. The two exchanged glances and a shrug that seemed to say, *What harm could a woman do?* and the soldier barring her entrance stepped aside.

The interior of the Council House was cool. The smooth rounded sides of the building, extending above the gallery of seats, held no windows. Instead, the oculus above opened to the sky. Sunlight shafted through its staring eye and lit white sparks of dust. Niches set high in the walls held braziers, lit even in the day, and the combined effect danced light and shadows along the rows of marble seats.

The house was more than half-full of spectators, and more still pushed in behind her, elbowing her to the side. She slipped to a row to her right, climbed a few steps to reach a higher seat, and squeezed in beside a man who looked more farmer than politician.

The trial of the supposed city murderer had drawn a crowd.

The gallery continued to fill and buzzed with anticipation. Daria studied the faces of the men seated in the lowest row, facing the wider marble seat where the proconsul Sophanes presumably would listen to testimony. Would they be impartial? Show leniency? She forced her hands to relax in her lap, tried to stabilize her breathing.

And then Lucas was there. Dragged in, half stumbling and grimy, bound at the wrists with a blackened rope.

At the sight of him, unwashed and already gaunt with lack of food and clean water, Daria's throat went dry and her pulse stuttered. He had been mistreated.

Lucas scanned the council house as they pushed him forward, as if looking for an ally.

Daria leaned forward.

His eyes found hers and he ceased searching.

She could not read his face. Pity? Remorse?

Her hand stretched toward him, as though she could tend the wounds and dirt from her perch on the upper row of seats. Her throat felt swollen and hot.

He gave her a smile, meant to reassure, but somehow it seemed like a smile of defeat. Of farewell.

Daria shook her head. No. She would not let him go without a fight.

The proceedings began with a thump of a Roman spear on flagstone and a call to order. Sophanes entered, his bearing proud and magisterial. He was a huge man, swathed in a Roman toga, edged in purple, and he lowered himself to the marble seat as if he were Nero himself.

Some formal reading of official statements was made, but Daria heard little. Her eyes and attention were on Lucas, whose profile as he stood before Sophanes betrayed little of his thoughts.

And then the charges.

"Lucas of Ephesus, son of Christos, you are charged with nine counts of torture and murder."

Daria cringed at the number. Had there been so many?

"This court will now hear evidence."

Did Lucas have anyone to speak on his behalf?

Zagreus came forward first. His easy stride exuded confidence, and he examined his fingernails while stating his name and position.

"What evidence do you bring?"

"Esteemed Proconsul, as you know these murders have been of chief concern to the city for some months now, beginning with the death of Lucas Christopoulos's wife and leading to the death of Maia, daughter of Dymas the Publicanus, only days ago. It has long been our belief that the prisoner before you is guilty of not only his wife's death but those that followed. Only in recent days have we acquired sufficient evidence—"

"Yes, yes, what is this evidence?" Sophanes rolled his eyes toward the roof. He spoke with a pronounced lisp, high-pitched and light. "Save us from lawyers who love to hear the sound of their own voice."

Unruffled, Zagreus cleared his throat. "As you may or may not know, Sophanes, each of the women was tortured before her death with various horrific practices, not the least of which was some sort of branding, the burning of a strange symbol onto her inner arm."

Sophanes betrayed no surprise at this information, only waved a hand as if to speed up the proceedings.

"Yes, well, this symbol, and the very iron piece used to inflict it upon the women was found in Lucas's home when it was searched after his arrest."

Sophanes leaned forward, his brow puckered. "After his arrest, you say?"

"Yes, Sophanes."

"Convenient."

Zagreus frowned. "I would not call it convenient, only incrim-
inating. As it matches the burn found on each of the women—"

"Not my wife."

Daria straightened. Lucas had spoken!

Sophanes gave Lucas a heavy-jowled sneer. "You will have an
opportunity to speak after Zagreus has finished." He jutted his
chin toward Zagreus. "Continue."

"Yes. The presence of this piece in his home certainly
confirms—"

"Not with that bit again. Why was he arrested, if this evidence was not found until after?"

Zagreus squared his shoulders. "With his wife's suspicious
death some months ago, and these new killings, we have been keeping a close eye on the prisoner for some time, Sophanes. It would
seem that each time he leaves the city on business in foreign ports,
we have no killings. Each time he returns, the killings begin again."

Zagreus puffed out his chest and delivered another blow
with a lifted voice. "Several weeks ago Lucas Christopoulos was
observed at night in the harbor agora, carrying the body of a
young girl."

As one, the gallery spectators gasped.

"No!" Daria was on her feet. "No, he was only helping that girl!"

Heads and eyes turned toward her, and she felt her skin grow
hot and her voice fierce. "We have brought you proof that he took
the girl to the brothel and had a physician tend her wounds!"

Sophanes looked to Zagreus, his eyebrows raised. "Who is
this woman?"

Zagreus sighed. "Apparently she is his tutor."

"Tutor?" Sophanes chuckled and spoke to Lucas. "Did your
father not provide such when you were of age?"

Lucas answered the proconsul, but his eyes were on Daria. "She has supplied me where I lacked."

Daria's legs wobbled and she sat. Memories of that last afternoon in his sitting room, before Zagreus came with the soldiers. The stalking lion and the unwary bird watching from the frescoed wall. His desperate kiss, his tortured confession. She would have that moment back again, even knowing it would not last.

She fought the tears. If she was called to testify it would not do to show emotion. If ever there was a moment to rely upon her calculating intellect, it was now.

And yet, a pulsing sorrow beat in her veins, weakened her limbs, and thickened her throat until she feared she could not speak if they called.

"Is this true, Zagreus, that you were given evidence the girl was not dead?"

"She was, perhaps, not dead that night, Sophanes. It would appear that the accused did bide his time and appear to help the girl." Zagreus turned a pointed look on Daria. "No doubt to deceive his tutor. It is plain to see there is a certain . . . fondness . . . there." He returned his attention to Sophanes and shook his head as though the truth pained him. "But within two days she was found, burned and branded as the others, and she lived but a few minutes longer. Long enough, Sophanes, to be asked to name her killer. She died with the name Lucas Christopoulos on her lips."

The spectators sent up another round of murmurs and gasps.

A figure to her left, entering the council house late, caught Daria's attention.

The physician!

"May I be heard, Sophanes?" His voice bounced from the stone roof and stopped the murmuring.

The proconsul raised his eyes. He was sweating profusely

by now and looked as though he would not suffer to extend the proceedings.

"I am Pollio, the physician who tended the girl, Maia, Lucas brought to the brothel."

Sophanes fluttered a hand of bored acquiescence once more, and Pollio strode to the center of the open floor.

Daria gripped her robe between tight fingers, crushing the fabric in her damp grip.

Beside her, the farmer opened an oily leather-bound packet of dried fish.

"Lucas paid me well to tend to the girl, not only for the few minutes while he remained, but for time after. I had the girl removed to the quarters where I tend patients and cared for her wounds until the next day, when she insisted upon leaving."

"And when she left, Pollio, did you expect her to recover from her injuries?"

"I did. Certainly if complications had set in to an extent that would cause her death, it would not have happened so quickly. For her to perish within the following day, I can only surmise that further injuries were inflicted upon her."

Sophanes jiggled against the back of his seat and folded fleshy arms. "And why, Physician, do you believe she would name the accused as her killer?"

"She was grateful, Sophanes, when I informed her that Lucas had paid for my services. I believe she saw him as her savior of sorts. If she called his name in the pangs of death, I believe it was to save her once more."

Zagreus stepped forward, hand waving. "Sophanes, this is a ridiculous statement. And as Pollio was not present at the girl's death, I must insist that his speculations not be considered."

"Only *your* speculations, eh, Zagreus?"

The crowd tittered and Zagreus's face reddened, a sheen of sweat glowing along the ridge of his hairline.

"I am still curious, Zagreus, what motive for these vicious deaths you ascribe to the accused. He does not appear to be, nor have the reputation of being, a madman."

"Perhaps I can shed light on this matter, Sophanes."

Daria's blood chilled at a fawning tone she well recognized.

Sophanes huffed. "Another surprise testimony, Magistrate? It seems the city is doing your job for you today."

But Zagreus's attention was on Hektor, and from the calculated look in his eyes, perhaps Hektor's interruption was no surprise.

Hektor did not introduce himself to Sophanes. Was he so familiar to the entire city?

"I have had some dealings of late with Lucas Christopoulos. I believe I have information that will illuminate the vile actions here in our city we are all so anxious to see terminated."

No one spoke and Hektor smiled, a smile that took in the entire gallery, his audience, and chilled Daria's blood.

"It has come to my attention, Sophanes, that Lucas has aligned himself with that sect of godless people known as the Way."

Silence reigned in the council house. No gasps, no gossipy trading of opinions. As if Hektor's proclamation had dropped heavy wool over the proceeding, muffling sound and thought. Daria gripped the edge of her seat.

Sophanes alone spoke. "Do you speak of those responsible for the fire that damaged the theater square and sparked panic among the people?"

His voice was smooth, hypnotic. "Exactly. These Christians speak against all that is sacred in Ephesus. They do not worship in a temple, do not offer sacrifices, do not provide offerings to create wealth for the goddess. They do not participate in the public rites and festivals we hold so dear. And they encourage others to rebel also. But there is more than this, Sophanes."

Hektor let the silence hang for a moment, until it seemed the entire gallery leaned forward, lips parted and eyes wide.

Could they not see that he was a liar?

"The Christians practice abominable mystery rites. Eating flesh. Drinking blood." He turned a dark eye on Lucas, then to the crowd. "For the sake of the families of the poor women murdered, I will refrain from speculating as to what they have been doing with these women before killing them. Needless to say, their practices are blasphemous. Hideous." His voice rose in pitch and volume. "One might even say barbarous."

The sound of Sophanes's questions and Hektor's answers began to blur in Daria's ears, as though the conversation moved away from her, or she from it. Sophanes asked for confirmation of Lucas's involvement with the Christians, and several around the ring of marble seats stood in their places and swore to it. The mood of the crowd grew ugly, a hissing of angry threats and censure of any who would blaspheme the goddess.

And then Zagreus was backing away from Lucas, as though to avoid contamination by the condemned, and Lucas was swaying on his feet in the center of the council house while Sophanes pronounced his verdict in a voice that might have carried to the goddess herself.

"As one found guilty of unlawful death, you are condemned to death yourself, Lucas Christopoulos, and sentenced to die in the arena during the period of executions scheduled for tomorrow's festival."

She could retain her seat no longer. Her feet took her down the few steps to the floor level, and she was nearly to the door when they dragged him to it.

"Lucas!" She lunged for him, arm outstretched to catch any part of him.

He lifted his bound wrists to her, raised grief-filled eyes.

She reached him at the door.

He laid the back of one dirt-caked hand against her cheek. "Daria." The word was a whisper, like a prayer.

She clutched the offered hand, would not let go, even when the soldiers pulled him toward the door.

And it was like that moment on the docks, with Lucas's arm outstretched across the water, his eyes inviting her to leap. Fingertips grasping, a fragile connection. She had known in that moment somehow, and perhaps he did too, that when he made the offer and she accepted, that they reached for everything each had ever wanted or needed in another.

And then he was yanked through the door, into the unblinking sunlight. The two soldiers filled the square of the door frame.

She shoved against them. "Let me pass!"

She might as well have thrown herself against a stone wall.

Through a gap between their shoulders, Lucas's gaze found hers again, and then he was lost.

38

WORSE THAN THE BEATING, WORSE THAN BEING paraded through the city filthy and bound at the wrists, was the sight of Daria reaching for him, yelling at the two Romans in her path, standing on her toes to catch a last glimpse of him.

He stumbled through a clot of onlookers, their jeers and insults a hazy background to the accusations of his own blaring thoughts.

What had he done? He should have left her in Rhodes. She could have found a position somewhere, a future. What arrogance, to think she would be better off with him.

Or had he even thought of her at all?

The grip of the guards on his arms was unsympathetic and impatient. He held back. Would Daria break through her captors and reach him in the street?

"Move along!" The blunt end of a short sword met his kidneys, knocking the air from his lungs. He staggered and pebbles jammed his sandals.

The walk to the prison would have been a long one, but they shoved him into the back of a cart and the two guards jumped in behind. One looped a rusty chain through his roped hands and secured it to an iron hook in the cart floor. They sat with their backs to him, legs swinging off the cart as the driver clucked to the horse and it jostled along the rutted street.

Lucas eyed the street, the chain, his captors. Any chance he could escape?

He snorted a small laugh at his own foolishness. Where would he go?

The city's mad excess of people lined the streets like spectators at the parade leading to gladiator games. He lowered his head to the raised fists, taunts, and name-calling. Word of his condemnation and his sentence must have exploded through the city. They had all turned out to see a killer.

A glob of wetness struck his cheek. He raised his hands to wipe the spittle with the back of one hand. His cheek and jaw scraped his skin with the unshaven growth of the prison hole.

They turned the corner at the bottom of the Embolos, and he trained his eyes away from the hillside terrace, the estates overlooking the city. The sun bore down hot on his head, and straw in the wagon bed poked at his thighs.

Past the brothel and shops opposite the agora, the cart clattered over the burnt stones of the theater square, took a sharp turn at the agora's end, and bounced toward the Harbor Street prison. His neck ran with sweat but he could not reach manacled hands to swipe at it, and the perspiration chased down his spine.

The soldiers told coarse jokes and ridiculed the peasants they passed.

They reached the prison and the two jumped from the cart.

"Move it, prisoner."

Lucas shimmied along the cart floor and held out his hands to have the chain unfastened.

"We got ourselves a nobleman here, Cellus." The soldier yanked the chain through Lucas's arms and it bit into his shin. "Thinks he's better than us, I imagine."

"That true, nobleman?" Cellus grabbed Lucas by the hair and pulled him from the cart.

He regained balance, but the pebbles in his sandals cut his feet.

"Nobleman or not, he'll die like any man, I would guess."

The first soldier barked a laugh. "We shall see. He may die whimpering like a dog."

Cellus shoved Lucas toward the prison. He stumbled and went down. Without his hands free, the stone walkway rose up to smack his cheek.

Cellus completed the humiliation with a kick to his midsection. "Get up, dog."

He pulled his legs under himself, scrabbled to standing, and staggered through the prison door before the two thought of further indignities. A week ago men nodded in respect when he walked this street.

Inside the prison, Lucas stayed the jailer's hand before he shoved Lucas into the square of darkness at the floor.

"Neritos, you know I am a man of means. I can pay you—"

Neritos scowled. "Nothing you could pay me would be worth my life, which would surely be forfeit if I released you—"

"No, not that. I need parchment. Or papyrus only. A quill or reed to write with. Important documents I must create before my execution."

The jailer hesitated, lips puckering.

"Please, Neritos. When I am finished you can carry the papers to my estate, and I will send instructions in my own hand that you are to be well paid."

Neritos glanced toward a chest in the corner, latched and dusty.

Moments later Lucas was knocked into the hole but with supplies in hand.

At least he still had Gaius and Aristarchus for company.

"What happened?" Gaius's face appeared hovering over his after the jailer had thrown him down the ladder to land on his back in the mud.

"Were you tried?"

Lucas closed his eyes. "Tried. Sentenced."

Gaius sat back on his heels and Aristarchus let out his breath in a low whistle. "That is not good."

Lucas managed a hollow laugh. "No, my friend. It is not. But it is not surprising."

"When?"

"The Festival tomorrow. It would seem that my death will be quite entertaining. A fall from grace, and all that."

The two men exchanged looks over his head and he sat upright, set aside his writing supplies, and rested forearms on his knees.

"Lucas, you need to fall *into* grace. Now more than ever."

"No more of your Messiah talk, Gaius. I am too tired." He repositioned himself against the slimy wall. The jailer had not secured him in irons this time. Perhaps it was a reprieve for a dead man's last day among the living. Or to leave him free to write his documents.

"It is more than talk, Lucas. And a man about to face his eternity should find motive to ask questions, and to listen."

"You say that your Jesus died a condemned man, yes?" Lucas

kept his eyes closed and head back, but Gaius was right. He had important matters to attend, but the time for postponing thoughts of his destiny had also ended.

"Condemned for the sins of all mankind. Yours and mine."

"But this is where I cannot join you. For I am going to die for my own sins tomorrow."

Aristarchus's voice was tight, tense. "You are not a killer, Lucas. We know this."

"Perhaps I am not guilty of their accusations. But I am guilty, nonetheless. And in this I find my redemption. My death tomorrow in payment for my wrongdoing."

"But, Lucas, you mistake the death of your body for the death of your soul. A man's eternity cannot rest on the merits of his actions. Not if he hopes for eternal life. The One God provides atonement for your sin that will carry you beyond the grave and into His arms."

Lucas sighed. They were a strange bunch, these Christians, with a strange faith that took all he knew to be true about the gods and somehow turned it on its head while retaining such similarity. Their words seeped into the cracks of his soul and took root, but he could think no longer about such matters. The sputtering wall torch could leave them in darkness at any moment.

The men lapsed into silence, each to their own thoughts, as the day wasted. In the meager light of the torch, Lucas scribbled his final instructions on the ragged papyrus Neritos had supplied.

Daria would be cared for. Perhaps she would return to Rhodes, but it would not be as a penniless tutor. And his estate, it was to be given to the Christians. He glanced at his two sleeping companions and smiled sadly. They would be pleased. But perhaps they would not even know of the gift. Tomorrow's festivities could well be their end. But the others. The others could sell his property and use the proceeds to benefit the poorest among them. Or perhaps they would retain the estate and use it for a meeting place. The last time he had attended one of their early morning gatherings, the courtyard had been crammed with followers.

Something for Clovis and Frona, still faithful even as he had grown more difficult to serve and had dismissed all but them. They would not want in their old age, would not need to find service elsewhere.

As if to punctuate the completion of his scribbling, the wall torch extinguished.

Lucas knew not how many hours had passed when the door above opened again, but he had trouble lifting his head, and in truth cared little to see who climbed down into their abyss, so he kept his eyes closed.

"Lucas."

It was a mere whisper, but he knew that voice. "Daria, how—?"

"I only have a few moments. Joseph gave me money to bribe the jailer." She carried a small lamp and set it on the floor beside him, then fell to her knees and grabbed his hands without even a glance at Gaius or Aristarchus.

"Why, Daria? Why have you come? There is nothing you can do."

Tears pooled in her gray eyes and spangled her lashes. "I am sorry, Lucas. I tried—to bring the physician, to find a way—"

"Ssshhh." Lucas placed his hands over hers. "It was not your fight to win."

She curved her warm grasp around his cold one. Her lip quivered and she tried once to speak, hitched her breath, and tried again. "I fought for us both."

He smiled on what might have been and looked away to hide

the emotion in his own eyes. The heads of his companions were bent, their eyes averted.

"This is how it must be, Daria. Can you understand? I have spent too much time tortured by remorse and guilt. In this I find release. It is good."

She leaned forward on her knees. "And what of me? What good can you find for me in your death?"

He could hear every modulation of her voice—the frightened tremor, the angry iron underneath, the warmth and passion. He touched a fingertip to her face, traced a line from eyebrow to lip, lingering there. Then took up the rolled papyrus. "You must take this and place it with my private papers, in my sitting room. Later, after I am—after the festival—when the city magistrates look through my belongings, they will find it and know what to do."

She took the papyrus, her face grave. She said nothing more of her own future. No doubt she suspected what he had written. Pride, or perhaps denial, would cause her to object. But she would see the wisdom in it later.

Time was closing in upon them, he could feel it. The jailer would return for her, and there were things he must say.

"Daria, listen to me."

Her eyes lifted, but her thoughts seemed elsewhere. She was drifting from him already.

He pulled her chin to face him. "Daria, I owe you much, but most of all my regret over bringing you to this foul city. It was selfish of me. I believed you would do me good, and I was right. But in bringing good to me, you yourself became tarnished. I had no right to do this, and I must know that you forgive me before I die."

She looked away, toward Gaius and Aristarchus, though she did not seem to see the men. "There is nothing to forgive, Lucas, but if you need to hear it, then know that I hold nothing in my heart against you." She gripped his hand. "In truth, my heart is only for you."

"I know." He cupped her cheek with his hand. "I know. But I will not speak of what cannot be."

She leaned into his hand and closed her eyes.

He inhaled the scents of her—garden soil and flowers, papyrus and ink. Everything he loved about her.

The moment was cut short by the yanking open of the trapdoor above and the harsh voice of the jailer declaring that her aureus had not purchased her any more time.

She was breathing hard now. Would that he could share the quiet certainty in his own heart that what was to come had been decreed for him, that she would go on and she would be well. He grasped her hands a final time, sending peace to her through his hands, quieting her with his thoughts.

She leaned forward and grazed his lips with her own, a soft kiss of good-bye.

He watched her go, papyrus in hand. Watched her feet disappear into the fading light above, watched as the door was dropped into place.

"The sun is setting." Gaius's voice was hushed, reverent. "It is the beginning of Shabbat."

The two huddled around the lamp Daria had left behind, their heads bowed. Both rearranged their tunics to pull the back of the fabric over their heads, a makeshift covering, and brought in Shabbat with quiet songs of prayer, mournful and low and filled with all the yearning of a people who had spent most of their history longing for a home.

Though he did not understand their Hebrew tongue, the sadness of the minor tune worked its way into Lucas's heart, wedged an opening there until it was raw and bleeding, laid bare before their God. A God whom Paul insisted loved him with an everlasting love.

Lucas had let go of vengeance. Even released the need for justice by his own hand. Given up Daria for her own good. Nothing was left, nothing but a wide, vacant place in his heart that seemed only fitting for Paul's God, who whispered that Lucas was not worthless, that he could be redeemed not by his own actions, but by the actions of another condemned prisoner who had gone before to pay the price.

And in the darkness of the falling Shabbat, Lucas made his peace with the One who would welcome him home.

39

THE LIGHT IN THE WEST WAS GONE WHEN DARIA lurched from the prison house, clutching Lucas's rolled papyrus.

She nearly thrust the scroll from her hand, trampled it underfoot. It was a vile thing, proving that Lucas would indeed be executed, that a document was necessary to secure his estate.

But she took to Harbor Street, still crushing the papyrus in one hand, using the other to dash away useless tears.

Once more to Lucas's house. Once more, then she would retreat to the home of friends and wait out the long night before tomorrow's horrors.

That she would attend the execution was a given. Though it would tear out a part of her soul, she would not let him go to his death alone and unfriended.

Every step away from the prison was a small good-bye. Her heart dulled as the distance between them grew. Would it remain numb tomorrow when she watched him thrown onto the stage?

The festival's religious activities would center around the Temple of Artemis, but the theater would hold the entertainment. It was not an arena, not large enough for pairs of gladiators to battle in the sand nor wild beasts to tear at each other while spectators watched from the safety of raised seats. No, the Ephesus amphitheater was designed for drama, for music and speeches. What kind of execution, then, would it be?

Perhaps the condemned prisoners would be given dull swords and pitted against trained soldiers. The Romans favored crucifixion, but such was a slow way to die, and not the least entertaining.

There was always beheading. Swift and dramatic.

A slick sweat formed on her skin at the dark turn of her thoughts. She reached the end of Harbor Street and turned the corner at the theater but trained her eyes away, toward the emptying agora. Strange that her first entrance into the city's colossal theater would be for such gruesome amusements.

And her last. She would not enter the theater again after tomorrow. No matter how long she remained in Ephesus.

To her right, far beyond the agora, the setting sun hung heavy and low, lighting the harbor waters with a fiery glow. Far ahead, lamps and torches blazed one by one from the hillside estates, as though returning the sun's dying light with a pale imitation.

How would she place the papyrus in his sitting room without encountering Frona? The woman would, perhaps, call Roman soldiers if she found Daria in the house once more.

What of it? Daria would complete her errand and be gone before anyone came to see her out.

The cool of the evening drew citizens from their homes to begin the darker pursuits of the night. Leisure and drinking, brothel and tavern visits, beggars on corners hoping for inebriated passersby to part with coin. And with the city glutted with visitors, even the alleys seemed crowded this night. On the eve of the festival, with their sacrifices ready and their hearts full of duty to the goddess, the celebrations had already begun.

Did those who came from outside the city, across the lands of Anatolia, or across the sea from islands and distant ports, sense the undercurrent of evil that ran beneath Ephesus like its drainage pipes—snaking under the feet of poor and wealthy alike, flowing with a secret taint and boiling up, uncontrolled and grasping at the minds and hearts of the people?

She reached the steps leading to Hill Street and paused at the base, running her gaze over the line of estates. Was this one such place where evil had erupted like a hot spring of death?

She took a deep breath. She would complete this task quickly and be gone. Lifting the hem of her robe, she hurried up the stone steps, then along the street to Lucas's home. She opened the door slightly, then entered fully, silently, with eyes scanning the courtyard and corridors beyond.

Conversation. Muted by stone walls, somewhere beyond the courtyard. Was it safe to slip across to the sitting room?

There would be no lamp within. She would have to place the papyrus with his other important documents, using memory and touch alone.

The voices grew louder. If she was to do this, it must be now.

She ran across the moonlit courtyard on her toes, breath tight and pulse beating in her ears. The sitting room door was closed, latched, and it grated and squeaked as she slid it open. Daria cringed at the sound and paused.

Two women.

Not Clovis and Frona as she had assumed. She heard Frona's harsh tone, but the second voice, nasal and strident, was certainly not the servant's husband.

Daria edged the door inward enough to slip through and hid herself in the sitting room only a moment before the voices breached the courtyard. She could not make out the words, but it seemed the two had slowed. Perhaps were seating themselves on the stone bench, not passing through.

Daria flattened herself against the frescoed wall, though there was no chance of their seeing her unless they entered the room with a lamp. She took gulps of the dark air, forced her breathing to slow.

What was it about Frona that so terrified her? This unreasonable fear at being apprehended by an elderly servant made no sense. It was the same sort of fear that being near Hektor built in her chest. That otherworldly pressure, cold fingers reaching at her from beyond what was seen, pulling her toward the unseen.

At the thought, her fingers convulsed, crinkling the papyrus. The sound seemed to bounce around the room and amplify.

Daria slid along the wall, the fingers of one hand tracing her movement, until she reached the corner, then crept another length of floor until her thigh bumped Lucas's desk.

Like a blind woman, she caressed the surface of the desk with a light touch, locating his reed pens and quills, a few coins. Her hand brushed a small jug of ink and she grabbed its neck to keep it from tipping.

The desk was cluttered and confusing in the dark. In Daria's absence, Lucas had reverted to his habit of chaos. Something in this small fact clouded her eyes with tears. She blinked them away, though in the darkness it mattered little.

There, in the far corner of the desk, her probing fingers found the small chest she had remembered seeing. She cleared the lid of its untidiness and lifted it carefully. Inside she touched several scrolls, rolled tightly and sealed with cool discs of wax. She dropped the newest into the chest.

With her fingers still brushing the surface of the scroll, she breathed out yet another small good-bye. The last connection of touch with him. Then removed her hand from the chest and lowered the lid.

She retraced her slide along the walls, back to the door.

The women still conversed in the courtyard. How long would she need to wait before her path would be clear?

Must she wait? She need not cower in fear of a servant and her visitor. She could simply stroll from the room and leave without a word.

But there could be no question of what she had been doing there. No hint that she might have left something or taken something of value. Lucas's final document must be found after tomorrow, without any questions raised about its placement or its authenticity.

And Frona was not to be trusted.

Curiosity drew her to the edge of the wall where the open doorway began. She inclined her ear toward the door, focused on the low tones of the women.

"Where will you go?"

It was Frona's voice asking the question, but Daria did not hear the answer. Perhaps there was none.

Frona spoke again. "Why can you not stay in Ephesus? After tomorrow, there will be no danger."

"Have you understood nothing, Frona? The danger only increases after tomorrow. And my reason for coming will be gone."

"I thought you came, at least in part, to see me." Frona's

voice was softer, wounded even. A strange inflection for the cold woman.

"I knew you would keep my secret. But there is nothing for me here. I took a great chance in coming at all, and now it is useless." She paused, then spoke again. "I should have made myself known to him sooner. Now there is no way except in the public theater, and that is much too dangerous."

"Perhaps if you spoke to them, he could yet be saved—"

"No." The woman's voice chilled. "I will tell no one else, not even to spare him."

Daria's every muscle tightened. Did they speak of Lucas?

Frona answered. "I understand. There is more than your life to think of."

She laughed. "Oh, but it is my own life that chiefly concerns me."

"Yes, as it always has."

Did Daria detect a note of bitterness in Frona's voice? Until now, the servant had seemed almost doting on her visitor.

Another sharp laugh. "Does this trouble you, Frona?" Sandals scraped stone as if the woman had stood. "You have always known what I was. Since the day I married Lucas."

Daria's intake of breath was sudden and rasping. She clamped her lips against her teeth, breathed fitfully through her nose. The shock passed, her body shook with something akin to anger. Every muscle hardened, as though she had gazed upon Medusa and been turned to stone.

In the beat of silence she lost concern for Lucas's private papers, for the truth of her visit becoming known. All that mattered was the woman who spoke with Frona in the courtyard.

Lucas's wife.

Daria stepped from the sitting room, into the torch-lit corridor along the courtyard.

Her presence caught Frona's immediate attention. She hissed and shot to her feet.

The other woman, his *wife* whirled to face Daria. "Who is this?" Her face flamed and her eyes went cold. "You said he had retained no other servants!"

Silvery moonlight fell through the open atrium and across the woman's shoulders. She was tall, with voluminous black hair piled atop her head making her appear even taller. She wore a mass of jewelry—thick gold bracelets, earrings that nearly brushed her shoulders, and a heavy ruby pendant that nestled below the neckline of a pale green chitôn.

Frona stormed toward Daria. "What are you doing here?" Over her shoulder, she spit out, "It is the tutor he brought from Rhodes."

The wife's narrow lip curled. "So, the tutor is still learning, is she? Creeping around, searching out secrets?"

Daria lifted her chin at Frona's angry approach. "Lucas asked me to come."

Frona stood too close, glaring.

But it was the other woman who circled, sizing up Daria. "Did he? You are quite . . . friendly . . . with him, then?"

Daria stared at her, back from the dead. How was it possible? Was it some trick of sorcery? Did Hektor have the power to summon spirits from the underworld? She pressed slick palms against her robe, and a chill rose on her flesh.

"Does he know? Does Lucas know you are alive?"

Frona jumped between them, lips twitching. "Apphia's return must be kept quiet!"

Apphia. She had never known the woman's name until this moment. The thought gave her courage. How powerful could she be, when she had gone so long unnamed?

"Why? Why does he think you are dead? Why have you not—?"

"So many questions." Apphia's eyes on her were still cold and unfeeling. "Frona said you never stop asking. And the garden"—she extended a hand to the dark greens and restored fountain—"quite a transformation you have wrought here. I never did have the skill for it."

Frona huffed. "Thinks she can grow all manner of herbs for medicine, and for cooking in my kitchen."

Daria shook her head in amazement and fisted a hand at her side. "Why are we talking about the garden? Lucas is to be executed, and none of this would have happened if you were not believed dead. He would never have been suspected of the murders!"

With the declaration came a surge of hope. Perhaps it was still not too late! If Apphia were to appear before the magistrates, explain whatever bizarre circumstances had led to this horrible misunderstanding, perhaps the sentence could yet be reversed.

Daria charged across the stones to the woman, reached to grab her arm. "You must come, we must tell them—"

Apphia yanked her arm from Daria's reach, bracelets clinking. "Foolish servant! Do not touch me!"

Daria was near to panting now with hope and desperation. "You cannot let him be executed!"

"That is not my concern. What will be, will be. I will not endanger myself."

"Then why did you return? And where have you been?" Daria looked between the two women. "Servant or not, someone must explain this to me!"

Apphia sighed, an impatient, condescending little sound. "Very well. But can we at least sit?" She returned to the stone bench, lowered herself to it, and smoothed the pale green fabric around her. In the moonlight she appeared a garden spirit, come to make the courtyard her nightly home. Had she been the one stealing through the house at night, making Lucas believe his house held spirits of the dead?

Daria's feet remained rooted to the paving stones, but she allowed herself to take in the woman now, to try to understand this unlikely moment.

Apphia was beautiful, as Daria had known she must be. But it was a beauty like cold marble, smooth and polished, unflinching. She had been born to wealth and it still rested on her like a silk mantle, creating that haughty look in her eyes, that slow and deliberate way of moving, as though she had never been forced to hurry.

"You search me with those inquisitive eyes, Tutor. I am no scroll that needs deciphering."

"Oh, but you are." Daria stepped backward, chose to lean her back against the coarse trunk of the cursed orange tree with its swampy roots and sooty mold-spotted fruit and leaves. "You are a greater mystery than any I have yet encountered."

Apphia ran a long-fingered hand through her hair and turned a self-satisfied smile on Frona. "Do you hear that? I am a great mystery."

Daria rubbed fingertips against the tree bark, gained clarity from the bite into her skin. "Why does he think you are dead?"

Apphia sighed and shrugged one shoulder. "All of that has been newly given to me by Frona. There was some misunderstanding."

"Misunderstanding?" Daria's voice had grown cold, but the time for coldness had come. "Your death has haunted him all this time. Tortured him with guilt."

"That was not my doing. I had to leave, and I left word for him, explaining everything."

"Explaining what?"

"My departure. He did not love me, Tutor, if that is what concerns you."

"It is the rare marriage that is built on love. You did not leave for lack of it."

Apphia tilted her head and studied Daria. "Perceptive. You are correct. I left because I feared for my life."

A bit of heat sparked in her voice again. "Lucas would never—"

"Not Lucas, silly girl. Someone with far more power than he."

"Hektor." Daria could not say how she knew this, but the knowledge was there, solid and certain. She drew strength from the possession of at least one answer.

Apphia's eyebrows shot up and she glanced at Frona, who shook her head as if to deny that she had shared secrets.

"Yes, Hektor. His . . . fondness . . . for me had grown to be a problem."

Daria rubbed at the tightness in her neck with tense fingers. "Lucas said you became involved with the sorcerers."

"With one sorcerer in particular." She half smiled and gazed into the flame of a corridor torch. "There was something so attractive, so seductive about him. I believed his affection was harmless. I enjoyed it."

"Hektor is far from harmless."

Her eyes returned to Daria. "Ah, I see you have fallen within his spell of influence already. Yes, he wields a power stronger than most."

"Or it wields him."

Again, the grudging admiration in Apphia's eyes. "Regardless,

I chose to escape rather than continue my relationship with him. It was the best thing—for both of us."

"Both of you? You tore Lucas's heart out when you left—"

"Not Lucas."

The best thing for both of them.

Daria's heart stuttered an uneven beat.

The baby.

The baby in the basket in the kitchen, under Frona's watchful eye. Frona, who had adored her mistress, mourned her death, would do anything to protect her.

Daria's fingernails dug into the flesh of the tree. "Lucas has a son."

The first flutter of humanity touched Apphia's lips. "Yes. And now you know why I returned."

"To give him his son?"

Apphia sighed and rolled her eyes. "Do not be ridiculous. It takes money to raise a child, if one does not want to beg for food. And Lucas has more money than he needs."

Daria set the unbelievable selfishness aside. Too many questions, still.

"This does not explain your supposed death."

She shook her head. "I cannot explain it either. Frona tells me that my letter to Lucas was never found. That the mutilated body of a woman wearing my clothing and my jewelry was found in the harbor water, that everyone assumed I had been murdered. I knew none of this until returning a week ago."

"A week! You have been in Ephesus a week and yet when Lucas was arrested you did nothing?" Her fingers unwrapped from the tree, curled into fists.

"Calm yourself, Tutor. As I said, I have safety as my first concern. For the child, of course."

Yes, for the child.

"As you have said, Hektor is not a man to be trifled with. Clearly the poor woman whose body was mistaken for mine was an intentional mistake. Someone wanted Lucas to believe me dead."

"And you think it was Hektor?"

Apphia shrugged. "Who else? And until I understand his motive, I cannot believe it safe to reveal that I have returned."

Her nonchalance infuriated Daria. "I can tell you his motive." The pieces were beginning to fit now, the puzzle coming together at last. "He wanted to set Lucas up as a murderer. He hates him, perhaps because of you. When Lucas was not found guilty of your death as Hektor hoped, he began to arrange a new and better way to see him tried and executed."

"And it would seem he has been successful."

Daria pushed away from the anchor of the tree and crossed the space between them to stand in front of the woman, finger jabbing the air. "That is why you are going to present yourself to the praetor and set this thing right."

A loud cry from the kitchen followed Daria's declaration, like a dagger driven into the words. Frona hurried off.

Apphia stared at her. "You would see me and my baby dead, to save a man who employs you as a servant?"

Daria blinked, exhaled. "I wish to see no one dead—"

But Apphia had stood and was peering into Daria's eyes, into her soul. "You are in love with him?" She laughed, short and bitter. "And I suppose he loves you as well, with that sweet demeanor and exceptional mind. Yes, what I could never accomplish, the tutor has done."

Frona appeared with the babe in her arms.

At the sight of the child, Lucas's child, Daria's anger and indignation deflated.

He was all chubby roundness now. Would he have Lucas's square jaw as he grew?

Apphia glanced at the baby but did not take him from the servant.

"For the child, Apphia." Daria let a note of pleading creep into her voice. "For the child, you must save the father."

40

THE MOON CLIMBED HIGH AND FULL OVER THE courtyard, poured down on Daria where she sat on the lone bench.

Apphia had gone to tend to the babe, and to sleep somehow in peace.

Daria would wait out the long night here, then work again in the morning to convince the selfish woman to do what was right.

A soft night breeze and the gentle whir of insects did nothing to soothe Daria's spirit. Her mind tumbled with a thousand thoughts—of Hektor's spells and Paul's teaching, of Lucas still married and the son he did not know.

The night sky was a deep black when a restless defiance of inaction drove her to her feet, sent her searching for the tool she'd once seen among Clovis's storage at the back of the house.

Minutes later she was back in the garden, ax in hand.

The anger and the questions strengthened her arms and she attacked the orange tree's diseased limbs with malice—something she'd wanted to do since arriving. Her feet sank against the tree's soggy roots and the ax chunked through one quivering limb after another, their black mold-spotted leaves and fruit dropping at her feet. She felt the fungus on her sweaty skin, tasted it in the air.

Hack. Chop.

The crack of the ax punctuated her jumbled thoughts. Hektor and his insistence that they not submit to the gods but instead find their own strength. But Hektor's power was lesser than Paul's.

Paul, teaching that his strength was not his own, and that she could only be strong *through* his God, through submission.

Arms prickling with exhaustion, she finally dropped the ax and fell against the bench.

Wherever strength was to be found, she needed the answer quickly. It would soon be dawn.

Daria ran a frantic hand through her loosed hair, found her comb tangled in its midst, and resecured it. She had fallen into bed in her former bedchamber sometime in the early hours of morning, and now the sun was too bright, too high.

She yanked the bedchamber door open and strode into the courtyard, searching the greenery, past the fountain, the gallery above where Apphia's former chamber lay.

"Frona! Apphia!"

The old servant appeared at once, as though expecting Daria's call.

The executions were no doubt held early, before the main

entertainment of the day. A macabre prelude to the more enjoyable theatrics. Daria's belly lurched at the thought. Was Lucas
already dead? Had he gone to his death without her there to give
him strength?

"Where is she, Frona? Where is Apphia?"

"I am here."

Daria jerked her head backward, to follow the voice above.
Apphia stood with hands gripping the rail, looking down on
Daria in the courtyard.

"We must go, Apphia. Now."

The woman's face was unreadable from this distance, but
after a slight hesitation, she nodded once. "I will come."

Frona hissed her disapproval. "Let us at least cover your face."

They left within minutes, Apphia's face and head swathed in
a pale blue silk like a Persian and Daria prodding her from behind
to speed her progress.

Gone was the fear that had held her captive for weeks. There
was action to be taken now, action that could save Lucas's life,
and she would not stop to think it through, to wonder if her task
was the safest course. She also would not acknowledge the biting
truth—if she were somehow able to save him, he would belong to
Apphia. That did not matter. It did not.

Apphia kept her head down and eyes hidden as they pushed
through the crazed city.

Daria had thought the preceding days crowded and unruly,
but she had seen nothing. The throngs of citizens and visitors,
carousing though it was not yet noon, shoving toward the temple
plain above and the theater below, left no room to move, no room
to breathe.

They passed Hektor's shop on the opposite side of the street,
and neither looked that direction.

On past the Prytaneion, past the temple to Augustus, into the agora. Apphia lagged at the base of the basilica steps.

Daria took the steps ahead of her, then stopped, raced backward, and grabbed Apphia's arm.

"The afternoon is nearly upon us, Apphia. They will be returning from their worship at the temple, filling the theater for the day's entertainment. We must hurry!"

Whatever strength or generosity of spirit Apphia had summoned to bring her out of Lucas's house seemed to be fading. "I cannot do it. Once he knows—once he knows I am alive, Hektor will come after me. I—there are things I have not told you."

The woman was beyond infuriating. "And there is no time to hear it now. Come!"

They ran up the steps, under and along the stoa, and reached the offices of the tribunal. Daria pushed Apphia through the door ahead of her.

An old man looked up from a table spread with some documents.

"We must see the praetor. Where is Zagreus?"

The man grinned a half-toothed smile. "Zagreus? Where would you expect? He is at the theater, preparing for the executions."

Daria pressed a hand against her chest to control her breathing. "When? When will the executions take place?"

He shrugged and squinted toward the door, as if to ascertain the sun's position. "I cannot say. Soon, I should think."

Daria pulled Apphia outside and started along the stoa.

Apphia held back. "I cannot do it, Daria. I cannot—"

Daria turned back and stormed up against the other woman's body, her face a breath away from Apphia's. "You can do it and you will do it. Your husband is a good man, about to die for something he did not do, something for which you are to blame. If you let that happen, you will not have a moment's peace for the rest of your life. If your own conscience does not plague you, then be assured I will do it myself."

Whether it was her impassioned speech or some innate sense of duty, Daria could not say, but Apphia sighed and started walking.

Daria hooked her arm and pulled her faster.

They reached the theater sweating and breathless and merged with the thousands who poured in from Harbor Street and from all directions of the city. A sea of bobbing heads—dark and light hair and a rainbow of headcoverings—straining forward to be first. A little boy chewing on a skewer full of blackened meat darted in front of her. Daria tightened fingers around Apphia's wrist. She would not lose her now.

The lofty theater entrance, two massive columns with a carved lintel astride, for all its height was much narrower than the public square that teemed with citizens, and it allowed only a relative trickle of people through its neck before releasing them to the curved bank of stone seats. Daria craned her neck to see over heads. Would she spot Lucas as he was brought from prison? Was he already inside?

Someone was shouting in the theater. From the stage, it would seem, if the carry and echo of his voice was an indication. Daria could not make out the words, though the tone was angry, accusatory. Who would be mad enough to incite a crowd of this size, for any reason?

Again she scanned the tops of heads, the gaps between clusters of people. With her attention to the left, it took a moment to realize that on her right, Apphia had disappeared.

"Apphia!" She shoved through the confusion, against the flow of people. "Apphia!"

A hand shot out from the crowd, wrapped around her wrist, and tugged.

She breathed in relief and let herself be pulled by the arm, through scowling faces and past sharp elbows.

She burst from the crowd like a stopper from a jug, into a darkened doorway that led to rooms behind the theater's stage, where the actors would amass before a performance. In the sudden shadow she blinked, peering into the corridor.

It was not Apphia who held her wrist.

She tried to pull her arm from the man's grasp, but he did not release her.

"What is going on? Who are you?"

In answer he dragged her down the inner corridor, sloping deeper behind the stage.

Daria shot a frantic look backward at the sunlit door, where the throng still eddied past, eager to reach the best seats in the theater, oblivious to her. "Someone, help!"

The man dragging her chuckled.

Down a long flight of steps, into the bowels of the theater, damp and musty and dark. They continued along a corridor, only one torch thrust into a socket at the end to light their way.

"Where are you taking me? Who are you? Where is—?" She broke off, unwilling to share Apphia's secret with this stranger.

They reached a doorway and the man swung her around himself and through it. She ducked just in time to avoid smacking her head against the low frame, stumbled through, regained her balance, and glanced into the room, eyes wide.

The room smelled of actor's chalk worn under their masks, and a powdery haze of chalk coated the air.

"Ah, the tutor."

"Hektor!"

The shop owner-turned-sorcerer braced against the back wall of the lamp-lit room surrounded by propped-up wooden theater masks. The masks grinned and cried, their oversized eyes and mouths grotesque.

In a chair at his side sat Apphia.

Anger at the betrayal shot through Daria.

But the woman's eyes held all the terror that Daria felt in the man's presence. This had been Apphia's greatest fear, to have Hektor learn of her presence in the city. He had some strange hold on the woman. Even now, why did she simply not bolt from the room? She sat as though bound to the chair, teeth clenched and jaw muscles working, but no ropes held her fast.

"Do not interfere, Hektor." Daria advanced into the room. "We have business to attend. Come, Apphia."

Apphia did not move.

"So, the tutor and the wife have become acquainted." Hektor smiled and lifted his hand before his body, chest high. A blade, wickedly thin, glinted in the lamplight.

"What do you want with us? We have nothing for you." Daria's inner sense of wariness, always on alert, screamed at her to back out of the room and run. He was one man. She had never seen him move any faster than a slow crawl. Would he truly chase her? She would be in the theater in a moment, lost in the crowd or finding Zagreus and alerting him to Apphia's captivity.

But Apphia's eyes—the woman begged with a silent intensity not to be left with the sorcerer. Last night she had seemed larger than life itself to Daria. Today her skin had drained to white and her blood-red lips trembled.

It was no wonder she had fled Ephesus. What kind of man was this?

"Two women." Hektor rotated the blade to catch the light,

watched the reflection play against the stone ceiling. "Lucas has two women willing to run through the city to save him. And yet he is not worth saving."

"That is not for you to say." Daria leveled a gaze at Apphia, signaled the woman with her eyes. Would she understand that they must run?

"Lucas dies today, Teacher."

Daria shuddered at his words, delivered with a cold finality.

He tilted his head. "And though I once thought you a worth-while asset, you are free to leave, if you wish."

She frowned. His smile was placating and insincere.

"What will you do with Apphia?"

Hektor still held the knife in one hand but trailed the fingers of the other along her neck, dragging wisps of hair. "We will get re-acquainted. She seems to have forgotten how much I care for her."

"And Lucas?"

His head jerked toward her, eyes black with malice. "Lucas can go to Hades."

Daria took a step backward. Dare she leave Apphia? She must choose between trying to stop the execution and protecting this terrified woman.

"You can protect no one."

She felt Hektor's words within her body. Had he spoken them aloud? Did he hear her thoughts?

"You are nothing, Teacher. No one wants to be instructed by you, no one will listen to you. You cannot solve every problem with the strength of your intellect and will alone."

It grew cold in the room. A cold that stole up from the floor, through her limbs, reached for her heart. Hektor's lips moved, he spoke as a mortal man. Then why did the words seem to etch themselves on her heart, scratched there until she felt raw?

"I am going, Hektor. You will not succeed."

"Go, then, Teacher. Go."

She wanted to go. And despite Apphia's pleading eyes, she would go.

But she did not.

Something was at work here, something unnatural. Her feet, rooted to the floor. Her limbs, weighted like the ice of mountain rivers.

Her mind, her thoughts, solidifying.

Irrational thoughts, spinning in orbit around the parts of her mind that grew hard and impenetrable.

Daria looked away and shook her head, once, twice. It would not clear. This strange congealing of ideas.

Her breath came short and choppy, as though it were her lungs turning to stone, but it was fear that left her panting.

Had she not always known that evil would someday claim her mind?

She had believed she would rave and scream, cut at herself and flail upon the ground. Not this. Not this slow betrayal inside her head, this separating of body and mind. She would be nothing but physical body soon. And was that not the same as death?

She had tried but she had been wrong. Evil could not be defeated. Only avoided.

And she had not kept her distance.

41

SO MANY.

Lucas had not expected so many to witness his execution.

The slow and methodical walk from the prison, accompanied by a Roman *contubernium,* took them past hordes of onlookers. The eight legionaries, a column of four on each side of the three prisoners, marched in step. Lucas and his two friends shuffled. The days of cramped quarters and meager food had sapped their strength.

To Lucas it seemed a day's walk down Harbor Street, with the theater rising in the distance ahead. He smelled every scent in the wind, from the festival day's meat vendors to the copious amounts of wine already drunk. He felt every ray of the sun on his face, every hair lifted by the harbor breeze. The reds and yellows and blues of clothing, the blacks and browns of pawing horses, the white of the stone bowl of seats filling ahead, all seemed sharper and brighter today.

The crowd seemed excessive even for the Artemis Festival. What had brought them all to the theater? Surely not the execution of a few random prisoners.

Gaius and Aristarchus plodded on either side of him like twin oxen. Hands bound and eyes on the theater, their lips moving in prayer. *"A privilege,"* Gaius had called it. A privilege to suffer for the Name.

They reached the theater, but not even their escorting soldiers could create a break in the crowd to get them through. The soldiers flanked the prisoners and held them in the square.

"Paul!" Gaius's voice and face lit with a strange joy.

Lucas followed his gaze and saw Paul, surrounded by others of the Way, also straining to move forward. At Gaius's call, their group surged toward the prisoners, though was held back by the pointed ends of Roman pilum.

Aristarchus leaned around a soldier. "What is happening in there?"

"I must get in!" Paul's attention was on the entrance. "I must speak to the people!"

Lucas glanced at Aquila in inquiry. The big man seemed to have assumed Gaius's position as protector.

"There's been a robbery in the temple." He glanced left and right, as if unwilling to spread the news, though he needed to shout to be heard. "The Metalsmith Guild—that snake Demetrius who leads it—he is accusing the Christians of the desecration, and all manner of other crimes." At this, his eyes flicked to Lucas, the meaning clear, then shouted again. "It would seem he is trying to incite a riot, with Christians and Jews alike vilified."

So Demetrius had accomplished his goals without his help. Lucas shouted Aquila's name. The man must be told of Demetrius's plan to hide evidence of the robbery in his own home. But Aquila had moved too far to hear, dragging a protesting Paul with him.

The crowd within and without the theater suddenly quieted, as though actors had stepped onto the stage.

But it was Demetrius's voice that rang out, filling the amphitheater and reverberating back to where they stood outside. Lucas barely recognized it, so fueled by hate.

"How long, fellow citizens, will we allow this godless sect to attack our way of life? To attack the very goddess herself? Even today, one of these Christians will be executed before you for the hideous murders that have long befouled our city. Women, all of them in their youthful prime, your daughters and sisters and wives—slain in such a shocking manner."

The heads of those still outside the theater were turning toward Lucas, toward the cluster of Christians behind him.

Ironic, that until yesterday Lucas would have denied the association with the followers of the Way. But today, Demetrius spoke truth in at least that detail.

But Demetrius was not finished. "My own daughter, fellow citizens! She has taken up with these Christians, most of them Jews, and is now missing. I fear for her life!"

"That is not true!" Lucas shouted over the heads in front of them, though his voice went nowhere. "It is the sorcerers she has consorted with!" His defense did nothing.

"Let us bring their leader before us!" Demetrius's voice rose in pitch, the voice of a desperate man. "Bring Paul into the theater, to make his defense!"

Lucas glanced at Paul, who ran forward at once. The hands of

Aquila and others grabbed his arms, his shoulders. He outran them for only a moment, then strained at their hold. "Let me speak to them! I can explain—"

"No, Paul." Aquila's voice brooked no argument. "Your life will be forfeit if you step into that theater."

Inside the theater, another man shouted to the people. "Do not condemn all the Jews along with these Christians, Demetrius. We want nothing to do with them."

Paul's face contorted with anger. "Alexander."

Joseph stood nearby. Lucas inclined his head toward the man. "Alexander?"

Joseph nodded. "Another of the metalsmiths. A Jew. He has been very vocal in the synagogue, denouncing the Way. Forced Paul to move his teaching to the lecture hall of Tyrannus."

But it sounded as though the people would have none of Alexander, perhaps because he was a Jew, whose defense of his people and their One God meant little to those dedicated to their goddess.

A chant began somewhere in the upper tiers of the theater, and it built and carried even to those outside.

"Great is Artemis of the Ephesians! Great is Artemis of the Ephesians!"

More than a shout of devotion, the words seemed to call upon the very powers of the earth, of nature, and of the moon goddess herself and all the gods who reigned with her from Mount Olympia.

The wind rose, the sky darkened. Storm clouds rose in the west, roiling over the horizon.

The crowd outside the theater, so anxious to get inside, to be part of the action, began to break apart, to spread away from the little knot of believers.

Lucas watched, confused. Until the crowd isolated another small group.

Sorcerers. He recognized them all from the belly of Hektor's shop. They stood in a half circle, twelve of them, missing their leader.

On his left the Christians massed as one. On his right, that eerie half circle. The two groups faced each other like opposing gladiator troupes, their only weapons those they could call upon from the air.

All the while, that endless chant from the theater picked up even by those outside. *"Great is Artemis of the Ephesians!"*

From the center of the Christians, Paul's face shone like the hidden sun, like it had reserved its rays for only him. In truth, a power radiated from him that Lucas could feel in his chest, on his skin, hot and bright.

And across, swirling unseen but as real as the stones and the noise, a loathsome darkness within that half circle. It shot from sorcerer to sorcerer, lightning strikes of evil.

They said nothing, none of them.

Lucas watched, left to right, as a battle more intense than any fought on a field happened before his eyes.

Lips moving, eyes raised to the heavens or leveled at enemies, praying, all of them. Some to the powers of darkness and others to the One God, in the name of His Son Jesus. Lucas swayed on his feet, caught between, pulled in, trancelike.

There was a push and pull to this invisible, near-silent battle. Somehow the chants of the people seemed to strengthen the sorcerers. But the cluster of Christians was growing. From side streets, out of the crowd, exiting the theater, coming up from the harbor. Dozens of them, hundreds perhaps, joining the huddled group behind Paul, swelling their numbers.

The air grew thick, hot, choking. Lucas's knees buckled.

A soldier caught him under the arm with a rough hand, then jerked him toward the theater entrance. "Time to go."

Whatever was happening inside, someone must have thought that a few good executions would calm things down.

———————

In the depths of the theater, the wide-eyed, gap-mouthed masks sneered and laughed at Daria, joining with her to cry in fear, mocking her with empty laughter.

From above, the pounding rhythm of voices beat against their heads.

"Great is Artemis of the Ephesians. Great is Artemis of the Ephesians."

Steady and insistent, full of rage and local pride, the words bore through the tunnels and into the dark room where Hektor stood behind Apphia, his hands possessive and tight on her shoulder, smiling at Daria like one of the monstrous masks.

The chanting voices seemed to poke holes in the strange and solid feeling in her mind.

Or was it something else?

Some other sort of power that swept into the room on a clean breeze, as though she had allies outside the room, who poured their own strength through the open door and swelled at her back. Her body—a dam holding back an unconquerable force.

A vision exploded across her mind. Turtledoves, set free. Soft gray wings against a blue sky.

She faced Hektor, lungs filling with hope.

Hektor seemed to grow taller, to fill the room, to dwarf Apphia. He drew strength from somewhere as well. Perhaps the chanting, perhaps somewhere beyond the theater. Dark forces, clawing their way through the tunnels. His eyes rotated in their sockets, unhinged from his mind.

He still held the knife in one hand, its tip near Apphia's throat. The woman was motionless, eyes staring without comprehension.

Time was running out. She must get Apphia to the praetor if the execution was to be stopped. Surely the screaming mob would soon call for their entertainment.

Hektor inclined his head toward the door. "Shouldn't you be in the theater, watching Lucas die?"

"You knew what he was doing all the time, didn't you? Did you always plan to place the blame for the killings on him?"

His gaze shot to the ceiling. "For one supposedly so brilliant, it took you a very long time to come to that knowledge."

"It is over, Hektor."

Daria spoke the words with a confidence that held no logic, no sense. He had the knife, he controlled powers of which she knew nothing. Where did such words come from? Her head and heart beat with the chant of the mob.

"Apphia does not want you. She never did. Why do you think she fled Ephesus? She preferred exile than a life with you."

Hektor's face whitened, the grip of his open hand tightened on Apphia's shoulder, then moved closer to her throat.

Apphia winced, a welcome sign of life.

Daria pressed into Hektor's weakness, drew strength from it. "Tell him, Apphia. Tell him the truth."

Confusion crossed Hektor's face, usually so confident. After all his boasts of control, was he weak after all?

Apphia swallowed, and the muscles in her throat convulsed with the effort. She turned her head slightly, away from the knife-point, but did not meet Hektor's eyes. "I—I must save Lucas." Her voice was half strangled, though if her air was cut off, it was not by Hektor's hand.

"Lucas?" Hektor bore down on her like a charging ox. His

voice pitched upward, near hysteria. "Lucas! After all this time, after all I have done for you, all I have sacrificed for you, still you are loyal to him!"

Daria saw it before Apphia did. Saw the knife twist in his hand. Heard her own voice cry out, felt her limbs go weak. Another vision, another memory—a bowl of oranges—she lunged toward the man, toward the knife, without thought, her scream matched by Apphia's.

Her hands fell upon his arm, yanked it from Apphia, and he fell away with the force of Daria's body slamming into his.

But it was too late.

The knife had made its cut, precise and practiced.

Apphia's hand went to her neck and blood poured between her fingers.

"No!" Daria shoved Hektor backward against the wall, ran to Apphia, who was already leaning in her chair, falling, falling toward the floor. Daria caught her upper body, laid her gently on the stone.

"Be strong, Apphia!" She searched the room, frantic for something to bind the wound, ignoring Hektor where he slumped against the wall. This could not be happening.

Apphia's hand clutched Daria's robe. Her lips worked in silent effort.

Daria leaned close, sobs catching in her throat.

"Letter." The word rattled in her throat. "Get the letter. For Lucas. For Kallon."

Apphia's eyes widened, as though she saw something beyond Daria. Beyond even the mask that stood at her head and was still laughing as she died.

The contingent of Roman soldiers shoved Lucas, Gaius, and Aristarchus into the theater, forcing them through the crowd like needles through stubborn wool. Faces turned in anger at being prodded aside, expressions turning to anticipation as they saw that the offenders were prisoners being herded.

They burst onto the open staging area at the feet of twenty thousand or more spectators, still chanting to their goddess.

Only one man stood on the stage, shouting to the people, his hands outstretched, palms down, as if to quiet them. But even from only a stone's throw away, the words were lost in the deafening roar.

The screams grew louder at the sight of the condemned.

The man failing at his task crossed to the group of soldiers. "We're going to have a riot on our hands if something is not done."

The centurion in charge jutted his chin toward Lucas and the other two men. "Give them a few rolling heads. Something else to think about."

The man, a city clerk if Lucas recalled correctly, rubbed at his jaw. "Or will it inflame them further? I have seen the games you Romans put on. Blood rarely calms a crowd."

The centurion shrugged. "Then let me call the rest of my unit from the barracks. They know how to put down a riot."

The clerk's face paled. "And then we will surely have a blood-bath! No." He glanced at Lucas and the others. "Take them aside for now."

The centurion raised an eyebrow at the superior attitude of the clerk but jerked his head at his soldiers, and the prisoners were taken back to stand near the theater entrance. Perhaps the centurion was no more interested in quelling this uprising with violence than the clerk.

A voice at Lucas's ear, familiar and angry, turned him toward Demetrius.

"Is this what you imagined when you aligned yourself with them, Lucas? Your head on a block in front of the city?"

Lucas faced the silversmith once more. Behind him, Joseph and his wife, Iris, reached out to grasp the arms of his two fellow prisoners. "I would sooner die innocent than live guilty. What you have done here today is vicious and evil."

"I have done what I wanted to do, just as you have always done."

Lucas nodded. "My reckless actions have brought me to this place. But I have no further need of death and vengeance. You, I fear, will be consumed by it."

Demetrius laughed. "Do not fear for me. Fear for your leader, the little weak-eyed Jew who brought destruction on himself."

Lucas kept his eyes on Demetrius, did not give a glance to the couple behind him, who had drawn close enough to hear. "You still think to kill him? He is not coming into the theater as you demanded. Your plot is thwarted."

"Ha! You must think me simple to have relied on the whim of the mob for success. No, I have men in place all through the square, watching for their opportunity. Perhaps even now a knife has already slipped between his ribs."

Lucas risked a glance at Joseph now. The man's eyes were somber, comprehending. He gave Lucas a slight nod, wrapped an arm around his wife's shoulder, and the two disappeared, melting into the crush of people at the entrance, back toward the square.

Daria backed away from Hektor, one slow step at a time.

He had lost control of whatever powers he believed he could manipulate. He scrabbled along the stones toward Apphia's body, his mouth agape.

374

She saw something of herself in that moment—the shock of realization that one's knowledge and answers have proven insufficient. He believed he controlled the powers of the universe, and yet he was being destroyed by simple human passion.

"We live at the mercy of the gods."

The words of Paul flowed over the words of Hektor.

Yes, and if there is only One God and He is all-powerful, then of course we live at His mercy. That is how it must be for created beings.

But what mercy it is! Not capricious and vengeful, not petty nor scheming. A God who loves and provides, sustains and forgives. Strengthens. Who gives us calling and purpose and then gifts us for it.

All of this she saw at last with clarity.

God of the Christians, One God, help me now.

The images of blood and death that would swamp her mind and drive her mad receded.

And then she ran.

Up the stone-hewn stairs, along the smoky corridor, toward the square of light, still clogged with people.

But it was easier to shove one's way *out* of the theater than in, with everyone pushing for a place in the seats. Each fraction of space she vacated was immediately filled by someone wanting to get closer, and breath by breath she slipped through the crowd, until she was loose on the other side of the square and running down Agora Street toward the hill.

She did not pause at the steps, did not stop to even breathe along Hill Street, did not enter Lucas's home tentatively as she had so often done.

She burst into the entryway, swinging the door wide.

"Frona!"

Her frenzied call filled the courtyard, and she ran for the steps in the corner.

The servant appeared when she was halfway up the stairs.

"A letter, Frona! I must find a letter that Apphia has written. Show me where she would have left it."

Frona's eyes widened in horror, focused on Daria's chest, her hands. "What has happened? Whose blood covers you?"

She clutched at her robe, spattered crimson. "There is no time, Frona. Apphia sent me for the letter. Quickly, help me find it!" Tears hovered at the edge of her voice, but she would not give in yet.

Frona crossed her arms over her tunic, her lips a tight slash.

From a darkened doorway behind Frona, a voice, strong and solid, spoke. "Give her the letter, Frona."

It was Clovis, standing straighter than Daria had ever seen.

Bless you, Clovis.

Frona slumped at his command and trudged to the steps.

It was in that loathsome trunk that Daria had so long ago uncovered. She should have known. Daria unrolled it, glanced at its contents only long enough to be sure of what she'd found, then rerolled it and ran for the steps.

Frona called something after her, but she did not stop to answer.

Across Hill Street, down the steps into Agora Street. She flew toward the theater, the rolled papyrus clasped in her trembling hand.

She must find the praetor, show him the letter. Take him to Apphia's body if Hektor had not moved it.

Pushing with the masses now, trying to get into the theater.

Angry faces at her presumption raised fists, and bony shoulders thrust at her chest.

This would never work. She would never get past all these people, find the right magistrate in the melee.

Her robe stuck to her back, soaked through with sweat as the front had been soaked with blood. Heat flared through her body, a desperate white heat that precluded rational thought.

There was Paul, being held back by the others. She slowed, her eyes on his.

"I can't get in!" she yelled across the crowd. "I must get inside!"

Paul glanced at the letter in her hand, seemed to understand that it held importance.

"The weapons of this war are not forged with metal, Daria! Fight your battle with the armor of God, pulling down the strongholds of the enemy!"

She inhaled, backed away, and spun toward the theater once more.

She had been called to fight a battle, Paul had said. A battle in the unseen realm of the spirit. This was her time.

She could not push through to reach the entrance. And the two-storied scenery facade formed a wall that blocked all access to the theater except through the single arch.

But behind the skene, here along the street, the incline was broken into a half-dozen levels of stone, like a massive staircase to the top of the facade.

Daria ran for the wall that banked the street, jumped to the first level, secured the scroll inside the braided belt at her waist, and placed flat palms on the rock level above.

It was a very narrow ledge, two dizzying stories above the stage. Much like an aqueduct. What she would do once she stood there, she had no idea.

But the time for ideas had ended.

42

HOW LONG COULD THIS GO ON?

Lucas watched the crowd, fists and voices raised in unceasing tribute. Did they not tire of their refrain?

"Great is Artemis of the Ephesians!"

Some shouting to his right drew his attention, though it was half-drowned by the chant.

Heads tilted backward, eyes focused upward.

Lucas followed the attention of those nearest the stage to the top of the skene.

Was it a huge white bird? Wings outstretched—

Oh, God, no.

His legs nearly gave out.

Daria, what are you doing?

She braced herself in a wide stance on the top of the skene, her hair loosed and blowing behind her. Was that blood?

His breath came hot in his chest. What foolish madness had brought her to that height? Their afternoon at the aqueduct flashed before his memory. Her fear. Her trust in him.

She was yelling, calling down to the magistrates on the stage. He strained to hear but could not.

"She is speaking!" He called it out to those around him, gaping at the bizarre sight. "Listen, she is speaking!"

They quieted enough for him to catch the edges of her speech.

"Another murder . . . Under the theater . . . Seal the exits!"

Daria fished a scroll from her belt and lofted it high. "I have proof of the killer, proof that you will execute the wrong man!"

On the stage the magistrates glanced at each other, as if debating whether to act upon the word of a woman mad enough to climb to the lip of the skene.

"The murderer is under the theater!" Lucas called it out, left and right, heard it ripple outward across the packed crowd.

As one, people began backing away from the entrance.

Given the space, the magistrates saw the wisdom in caution and dispatched soldiers to the exits of the theater's underground rooms.

She would do this for him? This rash and dangerous thing, so unlike the Daria he knew, to prove his innocence? He kept his eyes on her, though she did not see him there. But he would not take his eyes from her again.

Another murder. The words were carried on the lips of everyone nearby, and across the crowd, Lucas saw Demetrius, his face drained of color, the face of a man certain he is about to receive tragic news.

From her insane perch above the stage, at a level with the top lip of the amphitheater, impossibly far away, Daria could see the Christians and the sorcerers faced off in the square. Her head swam and her breath came heavy and panting, from the climb and from the terror and from her frantic shrieking of the truth. She would not look down. Would not even think.

"The weapons of our warfare," Paul had said. They fought with those invisible weapons even now, and had fought for her when she was in the bowels of the theater. This she knew.

They were sealing the exits.

Had Hektor remained? Was Apphia's broken body still lying among the masks?

But if she was to descend, she must look down. She gave a glance over the far end to the door where she had escaped the tunnels. Two soldiers guarded it.

And there, just beyond the soldiers, among all the upturned faces, one person whose eyes spoke to her even from this distance.

Lucas.

She smiled at him. A brief smile only. There was still work to be done.

She began her treacherous descent down the back side of the facade.

Back on the street, she had gathered an audience while climbing down, and as she ran toward the theater door, the crowd parted to let her through as though she were a visiting dignitary.

At this level, Lucas was lost in the crowd, but the soldiers guarding the door raised their pilum and let her through.

Another dozen soldiers, along with various city magistrates, clogged the tunnel.

"Down the steps! In the room of masks." She called it over

their heads while lifting a prayer that something would be there for them to find.

Others reached the room first. Soldiers stood at the door but stepped aside to let her pass into the room.

There, on the floor, was Apphia's body. And stretched over it, facedown, was Hektor.

She drew up short. Had he killed himself?

A soldier leaned forward, grasped Hektor's shoulder as if to roll him.

The sorcerer's body twitched, his head jerked upright. He turned unholy eyes on the group in the room.

The Hektor she had feared was gone.

In his place was something even more fearsome. Something she had seen in her husband the night he died. Seen in the demoniac in the street when she had first come to this idol-ridden city.

His lips drew back over his teeth. Wispy white hair fell across his eyes.

He was like a rabid dog, hunched over his kill.

Soldiers and city officials alike drew back from the inhuman sight.

Daria stepped toward him, close enough to smell the evil, near enough to touch it.

"We wrestle not against flesh and blood, but against principalities, against powers, against the rulers of the darkness of this world, against spiritual wickedness in high places."

And in the wrestling, in the battle, she was fully armed. She did not understand it, for it did not come from the powers of her mind but from the power that had invaded her spirit, that had somehow taken up residence within her and banished fear.

She held out the scroll to the praetor Zagreus without taking her eyes from the seething, hissing thing at her feet.

"This is a letter from Apphia, wife of Lucas Christopoulos, naming Hektor as responsible for the killings in the city these last ten months. It was penned last night."

"Impossible! The woman has been dead—"

"The woman"—Daria pointed to Apphia's body—"lies even now still warm at your feet."

A beat of silence, then Zagreus grabbed the pilum of a nearby soldier and poked at the thing that was once Hektor until he rolled off the body.

Zagreus glanced at Apphia's face but without recognition. Had he known her in life?

"Who is this dead woman, Hektor?"

Hektor sat back on his haunches, panting. "Not dead. She is not dead."

He scanned the contents of the letter, then turned to Daria. "You expect me to believe—?"

"Do not let your vendetta against Lucas blind you to the truth, Praetor!"

He exhaled, then nodded to a soldier at the door. "Bring the prisoner. Let him tell us if this woman is his wife."

———

Something was happening within. Had they found Demetrius's daughter, murdered as the others had been? Despite the man's failings, Lucas did not wish that upon him. He knew the pain of that loss.

"Lucas Christopoulos!"

He leaned left to see who called his name.

"Bring the prisoner." A soldier at the door waved him toward the opening.

Lucas glanced at his captors, at the quizzical faces of Gaius and Aristarchus. His guards pushed him forward.

It must be something to do with Daria inside. With whomever had been killed. His heart pounded. Would another murder while he was in chains prove his innocence?

He was prodded along the tunnel, then downward into the depths of the theater's back rooms. Ahead, torches in the hands of other soldiers led the way, and he ducked under a low doorway to enter a crowded room.

Daria, with wide eyes and covered in blood. He took in her face, her arms, her body. She appeared uninjured.

Zagreus, frowning, a rolled papyrus in his hand. Soldiers, all watching him.

There, against the wall, well-guarded and crouching, Hektor.

Zagreus nodded to him. "Identify the woman on the floor, Lucas."

He followed Zagreus's indicating finger to a prostrate form he had not noticed. A woman, her head at an odd angle, throat and chest blood-soaked, hair covering half her face. A bloody knife lying near her cheek.

A strange sensation swept him, as though time and space traveled backward, carrying him along, to another place, the edge of the harbor at night. Apphia's body washed up along the rocks, her face so disfigured, but her hair and clothing familiar, the pearl ring he had given her still lodged on her right index finger.

But this woman also, she was familiar.

How could this be?

He rocked back on his heels, away, away from the body.

Someone braced him from behind. The room, the torchlight, the faces swam before his eyes.

"Who is this woman, Lucas?"

He opened his mouth to speak and the word came muted and disbelieving, choked and guttural.

"Apphia. It is my wife, Apphia."

He raised his eyes to Daria and she nodded, her eyes intense and steady, as though she would give her strength to him.

"I—I do not understand."

"And were you not under the impression that your wife has been dead for many months?"

"Yes. Yes—I—she was buried—this is not possible."

"It appears it is possible." Zagreus held up the scroll. "From this letter, apparently written in her hand in the last few hours, it would seem she fled Ephesus some time ago, leaving word for you that was somehow intercepted by Hektor. Apparently Hektor then provided a body resembling your wife, with her possessions, in an attempt to incriminate you for her murder."

"And the others." Daria stepped from the shadows. "All the murders, blamed on Lucas. All of them, committed by Hektor."

"Yes. Well." Zagreus glanced at Hektor, panting at the wall. "Let's secure him before something else happens, shall we?"

Lucas could not take his eyes from Apphia. "All this time? All this time she has been alive? But now—" He searched the faces in the room. "Who has killed her?"

A rope was looped around Hektor's wrists, even as the one binding Lucas was cut. The sorcerer screeched in protest, then spit at Lucas. "No one will have her now."

The pain of the loss hit Lucas afresh, all the accumulated

anger that had driven him mad over the months, all of it focused into a sharpened point of hate, a surging tide of vengeance that once again would control his heart and mind and body.

Two steps and he was beside her body. One reach and the knife was in his hand.

A single lunge and he would bury it in Hektor's chest.

Hot, pulsing anger blurred his vision, like the battle frenzy soldiers spoke of when they returned from war.

"Lucas, no."

The calm, controlled voice of Daria pierced the haze, flowed over his thoughts like cool water.

Hektor cowered before him, small and pitiful. Defeated by Apphia and the demons he thought he directed.

Would this be Hektor's last victory, Lucas's step away from trust in the One God, in the Messiah's atonement, in the promise that both judgment and mercy rested in His hands? Like Hektor, Lucas had raged against the divine, had refused to bow his knee. But to be at the mercy of the One God—was it not a glorious thing because the One God was merciful?

Behind them all, out in the theater, the crowd still chanted their devotion. He heard the words, heard the emptiness of them.

Somehow, impossibly, he would not die today at their feet.

For Daria's sake, to give her the life she deserved, and for the One God, he would choose to trust.

He let the knife clatter to the floor, raised his eyes to Hektor's.

"Great is Artemis of the Ephesians" echoed once more in the tiny room, but Lucas spoke the truth that had set him free.

"And greater still is the Lord, God of all the nations."

Daria clung to Lucas's arm and kept her head down as the two were escorted from the tunnels under Roman guard. Soldiers cleared a path beyond the open doorway, then through the gathered masses at the theater entrance, leading the way out to the square.

Lucas's hand covered her own on his arm, clasped tight around her fingers. She focused on that connection, would not let it go for all the jostling of the crowd.

Inside the theater, the mob was finally quieting. Zagreus had gotten their attention at last and spoke in reasoned tones, his voice carrying over the entire theater.

"Fellow Ephesians, all the world knows that the city of Ephesus is the guardian of the temple of the great Artemis and of her image, given to us from the heavens. No one threatens the great Artemis here today. We must calm ourselves, before rash actions condemn us."

A cool breeze blew through the square, and their guards slowed to hear Zagreus's speech.

"These men have been accused, but they have not been found guilty by the courts—not of robbing the temple, nor blaspheming our goddess. If Demetrius and his fellow guildsmen have a grievance against them, the courts are open and the proconsul will hear them. They can press charges."

At this there were murmurings of dissent, but Zagreus lifted his voice louder, his tone chiding.

"If there is anything further you wish to bring up, it must be settled in a legal assembly. Roman soldiers surround this theater and more stand a stone's throw away. We are in danger of being charged with rioting here today, and we have no justifiable cause for it. For the sake of the women and children, settle yourselves!"

A moment later guards dragged Hektor into the square, cursing and screaming.

The group of his sorcerers, still facing the Christians, dispersed at the sight of their crazed leader and fled in all directions.

At this the crowd of Christians, larger than Daria would have thought possible, sent up a cheer. The sound of it ran a chill of relief and emotion across her skin.

But where was Paul? The guards were hurrying her and Lucas along, as though anxious to clear the square before more violence erupted. Daria searched the group for Paul but did not see him.

She did see Gaius and Aristarchus, though. Unbound and embracing their friends. Her eyes welled at the freedom gained today.

Moments later, when they reached the all-but-empty middle of Agora Street, their guards pivoted back toward the theater where they would be of more use and abandoned them in the street.

Left alone with him so abruptly, Daria turned to Lucas and lifted her face to his, tears flowing. She did not know what to say first.

As it happened, words were not necessary.

Lucas's embrace, his kiss, his tight hold on her waist, and his hand cradling the back of her head said all she needed to hear, were all she needed to know.

She returned his kiss with promises of her own.

When at last they pulled apart, hands still clinging to each other, Daria smiled through tears.

"Come home, Lucas. There is someone I want you to meet."

43

THEY CLIMBED THE HILLSIDE STEPS SLOWLY, BOTH exhausted. Daria held Lucas's trembling hand. Smiled on his tearful face.

In the crushing perplexity of all that had happened under the theater, there had been no time for him to realize the implications of his wife's shockingly recent death.

But there in Agora Street, Daria held him in her arms and whispered his son's name.

There was much to explain, still. Why Apphia had fled Ephesus. Why Hektor had killed her. But none of that mattered. Not today.

Lucas was a man going home to his family. At last.

Frona and Clovis met them at the door, Frona frantic for news but unwilling to enter the city with Kallon.

She looked to Daria for reassurance, and Daria shook her head sadly.

Frona's jaw tightened, but she bore it well. Even she seemed to sense that a more important moment had come. Perhaps there was still some loyalty to her employer left in her heart.

Lucas opened his mouth but could not speak. The words were choked off by emotion.

Daria leaned her head against his shoulder. "Bring the babe, Frona. Bring the babe to his father."

She returned a moment later, and the softness in her arms seemed to have spread to her heart, so tenderly did she hold him, so gentle her touch.

Lucas received the child into his arms with the joyful tears of a man witnessing a miracle, the dead raised to life.

"Kallon." He turned a tear-streaked face to Daria. "Kallon."

She laughed through her own tears. "Yes, Lucas."

Frona touched her lips with shaky fingers, and Clovis wrapped an arm around her shoulders and led her away, leaving the three in the courtyard.

Lucas ran a gentle finger over the baby's forehead, down his tiny nose to his lips, and was rewarded with a smile.

"The boy needs a mother, Daria." He glanced at her, his eyes questioning. "And I need you too."

She smiled. "Yes, we never did finish our language lessons, did we?"

Holding his son with one arm, Lucas pulled her into his embrace with the other and whispered things to her that had nothing to do with lessons.

The others came, later.

They came and filled the courtyard with its newborn garden,

the stricken limbs of the orange tree cleared by Clovis and burned, the fountain repaired and gurgling with life.

Aquila and his wife. Iris and Joseph. Paul, with Gaius and Aristarchus at his side once more. The two friends, Trophimus and Tychicus, and Europa and Seneca with their precious baby, and so many others. They came to rejoice over what was won and what was found, and even to grieve over what was lost.

Demetrius's daughter, Selene, came with them, strange irony. Iris had been teaching her, sheltering her from the sorcerers and even her father, who perhaps would never understand. But Lucas had sent word to the silversmith, to reassure him. And to Zagreus about a secret hall under Hektor's shop and the women who languished there.

As the courtyard filled and the sun went down, the visit became the releasing of Shabbat, no doubt the strangest Shabbat the Jews among them had ever known.

It became, also, a good-bye.

Paul sat close to Daria in the courtyard. "I am leaving in the morning."

She clutched his arm. "Not yet."

He patted her hand. "I had planned to stay until Pentecost next week, it is true. But the others have convinced me that after today, it is best that I leave sooner. Timothy and Erastus are preparing for me even now. The Macedonians will be glad for my safe arrival."

She looked over the gathered crowd. "Will they remember all you have taught them?"

"Perhaps. And I promise to write, to remind you all of the truth of God's immense love, of the battle we fight and the armor we must take up."

Lucas looked up from his son, still in his arms. "The believers will miss you."

"And I am grieved to leave each one of them." He smiled on Lucas. "Including you, my friend, who taught me something I needed to hear."

Daria looked between the two men, amused. Paul in the role of student was a strange thing.

The older man surveyed the crowded courtyard. "For so long I have carried the weight of my own guilt, for the crimes of my past against the people of the Name. I had thought to bear the burden of suffering in my own body alone, to protect them from it, to keep them safe. But you showed me, Lucas, that security is not the same thing as safety." He pointed to Gaius and Aristarchus. "They would keep me safe, those two. But only my physical life. My true *security*, all of ours, this lies in the hands of the One God and can never be wrested from Him. This love God has for us—it has involved risk and rejection, suffering and sacrifice. Our love for Him should be no less."

This was truth that Paul spoke, Daria knew. In some ways, Hektor had proven her right. To try to control power was a dangerous thing. Even Demetrius had taught her something. It mattered little, as he said, whether one performed to please the gods, for man's actions could never be enough. Demetrius had fallen into hopelessness at this truth. Daria chose to fall into grace. She had searched for safety, and found something else instead. Something better.

Paul's attention rested on Aquila, and his voice grew thoughtful. "I am leaving the church under the leadership of a good man. But you will all perhaps be called to suffer, to give up what is safe in exchange for what is life." He straightened and smiled on them. "And I will pass this way again, on my way to Jerusalem."

He reached across Daria to give Kallon a finger to grasp. "By that time, this little one will be running in circles here in the courtyard, disrupting the prayers and teaching when the church comes here to worship."

Daria looked to Lucas, whose eyes registered slight surprise, then smiling agreement.

Paul stood and leaned to kiss her farewell. "And perhaps by that time, there will be another little one born to our warrior here."

She laughed. "I am no warrior, Paul—"

He patted her cheek. "Oh, but you are. And the battle has just begun. You will be called to arm yourself with truth and righteousness and faith, and then to teach others."

To teach? Neither Lucas nor Paul had succeeded in convincing Tyrannus of her qualifications.

But at her look of surprise, he laughed. "Yes, to teach at last." He nodded toward Iris, where she stood with her little group of younger women. "Here, with these precious ones. Iris will help you. You will tell your story, as we all must."

Before he left, Paul embraced her, with one last whispered encouragement. "Your search for knowledge is good and admirable, Daria. But you need not set the world right. Someone else will do that. Find your joy in surrender to His love."

Daria clung to him, but he squeezed her shoulders and moved on to say more good-byes.

They trickled away slowly, Paul and the believers, as if they wished to extend this night, this celebration of the power of the One God.

But when they had all gone at last and Kallon slept in his basket, Daria and Lucas sat in the cool of the courtyard and spoke of the future.

She had unanswered questions about much of it—about the powers that ruled the air and sky, about this One God's supremacy over everything. About the grace He offered, against human logic. But there would be time. The others would teach them.

For now, held in Lucas's arms, she was content in what had been given and in what had been promised.

She need not have all the answers.

Not tonight.

EPILOGUE

AND SO THAT IS THE STORY, DEAR ONES.

Well, it is *one* of the stories. As they all are. Including mine. Including yours.

We are all part of the One True Story that is happening still.

It was nearly forty years after the end of this tale, when my years on Patmos left me starved for the fulfillment of all things, that my aged feet first trod the harbor street of Ephesus, my failing eyes first gazed upon the theater where so many had shouted praise to the goddess. When I first met the new generation of those who suffered for the Name.

So much had happened by then. The emperor Nero had gone mad, and with him all of Rome, it seemed. The city burned and Nero unleashed horrors on a ready scapegoat, the believers in his midst. Such atrocities I will not speak of. Our beautiful Jerusalem and its temple, destroyed. So much blood. But the church itself ignited and spread, a holy fire that could not be contained.

Paul's death grieved us all, but he had trained so many in the faith, and they rose up to take his place across the empire. Why, even here in Ephesus, our own Timothy returned to shepherd the flock and does so even now, a father and grandfather to many. He walks faithfully alongside the church as they flee wickedness and protect the truth. But the work is not without its discouragements, as the flock in many ways has lost its first love.

Perhaps it should have been Timothy who told this tale, but he says that I am the storyteller, and he is the preacher. So be it.

You will wonder about the others, I suppose. Ah, that is a tale for another day. But I will tell you that this battle to which Paul called them all, this they understood, and fought well. They persevered and endured many hardships.

I do my small part here in the city of Ephesus. I tell the Story, for the Story is life. I remind them of my Brother's many promises, of the revelation I have been given of that glorious new day and that New Jerusalem, even as we battle on in the midst of darkness. It was Paul who reminded us that we would shine among them like stars as we held firmly to the word of life.

The days remain dark yet, but we will overcome. By the blood of the Lamb. And by the word of our testimony. By the word of our *story*, yours and mine.

I am an old man, and I am longing for my home.

It is time for your story now.

So shines the night.

THE STORY BEHIND THE STORY . . . AND BEYOND

THE SEVEN WONDERS OF THE ANCIENT WORLD continue to inspire my creative imagination and my passion for historical research. In *So Shines the Night* I wanted to give readers an experience of the Temple of Artemis in a real and tangible way.

By the opening of *So Shines the Night*, this temple had been built, destroyed by a flood's deposit of silt and sand, rebuilt, destroyed by arson, and rebuilt yet again, larger and more magnificent than ever. The tenaciousness of the Ephesian people in their devotion to Artemis is undeniable.

The province of Asia Minor during the reign of the Roman Empire was an eclectic mix of Romans, Greeks, Jews, and others, though the culture was mainly Greek. But the Ephesian Artemis was distinct from the usual Artemis worshipped elsewhere through the Greek world. The "virgin huntress" of the larger

Greek world was, here in Ephesus, changed to focus more on fertility, and from the comment made in Acts 19, the Ephesians seemed to believe that she had fallen to them from the sky—it's believed that perhaps some kind of meteoric rock actually fell and was preserved inside the temple.

Ephesus itself was an important harbor city of the ancient world, though it had been ravaged the century prior by the Mithridatic Wars which had left the city heavily in debt. When Augustus came to power in 27 BC, he made Ephesus the capital of his new province of Asia and began a widespread rebuilding of the city, which brought affluence and luxury. At the point of our story, in 57 AD, there is still more extravagant building to come—for nearly another hundred years—including that iconic image of Ephesus, the Library of Celsus. Readers who have visited the ancient ruins of Ephesus may have wondered at that structure's absence from the story. In fact, it was not built until 135 AD.

All that Greek and Roman history is fascinating, but for me, the most enjoyable part of this book was getting to include some familiar characters from the pages of the Bible—Paul and Timothy, Priscilla and Aquila, and a few other miscellaneous folks we know very little about. One of the challenges for me was pinning down an exact timeframe for the story, and in the end I made a decision based on widely-accepted historical research.

If you have one of those maps in the back of your Bible featuring "Paul's missionary journeys," you'll find Ephesus along the route of Paul's third journey. For those interested in a brief timeline, when Paul came to Ephesus he had already visited many of the well-known cities such as Thessaloniki, Phillipi, Athens, and Corinth. He had worked alongside Barnabus and Silas and picked up Timothy in Lystra. While in Corinth (probably around 53) he met Priscilla and Aquila who had moved there when the Roman emperor Claudius forced all Jews to leave Rome in 49. Paul stayed about eighteen months in Corinth, where he wrote two letters to the Thessalonians. Leaving Corinth, he took Priscilla and Aquila with him and stopped in Ephesus, leaving them there to begin missionary work while he continued on to Syria. Back in Ephesus, the tent-making couple encountered and discipled Apollos, who soon left them to join the church back in Corinth. Paul then returned to Ephesus, probably around 54, and stayed nearly three years, building the beginning of the Ephesian church. I would really encourage you to read through Acts 18 and 19. It's my hope that after reading *So Shines the Night*, Acts 19 especially will leap off the page! Look for some familiar characters you may never have noticed before.

Beyond the scope of this story, Paul left Ephesus and traveled inland through Macedonia (northern Greece), then down to the southern part of Greece, then looped back around and returned to Jerusalem, probably by about 58. It was then that he was taken before Governor Felix (Acts 24) and Festus about two years later (Acts 25). The voyage to Rome then began, including storms, a shipwreck, a poisonous snake bite, and then house arrest in Rome for two years, where he penned the letters to the Ephesians, Colossians, Philippians, and Philemon. He apparently did more traveling after his release from arrest in 63, though we do not have many details. Paul was probably martyred sometime around 67, by the emperor Nero.

Such an adventurous life the man led in his quest to spread the gospel! The events of Acts 19 alone were enough to fill a story for me, and when it was time to write about the "ancient wonder" of the Temple of Artemis, I found this time in its history infinitely compelling.

Choosing John as my narrator in the Prologue and Epilogue

might strike some of you as a strange choice, but I couldn't pass over the fascinating possibility that he may have lived out his last years in Ephesus after his exile on Patmos. Mary, the mother of Jesus, may have lived there as well, perhaps taken care of by John years earlier, before his exile. We also know that Timothy eventually returned to pastor the church in Ephesus.

Besides grafting in the ancient pagan and the familiar biblical history, my desire was to create a sort of old-fashioned gothic romance set in an ancient period, and readers of that genre will no doubt recognize the subtle influences of some of my favorites— traces of Jane Eyre and her Mr. Rochester, and of Maxim de Winter, whose dead wife Rebecca haunts him and his timid new bride. Or perhaps hints of *Jekyll and Hyde*, or even a touch of my favorite age-old motif, that of "Beauty and the Beast." It was great fun crafting a story out of all these disparate elements, and it's my sincere hope that you've enjoyed the adventure.

I have been privileged to explore the city of Ephesus twice, and I invite you to visit my website, www.TracyHigley.com, to browse my travel photo journals. You'll experience the sights and sounds of this great ancient city, see photos of the hillside estates, the agoras and temples and streets, and the vast amphitheater where Daria fought the powers of darkness for the man she loved and the God she was beginning to discover.

You'll also have a chance to connect with me. I love to hear from readers about the adventure of their own lives. Where are you in your own battle to stand strong and to trust? Please visit my site and share your heart with me!

And I hope you'll join me on my next adventure! Check out the "Work-in-Progress" page on my website to see where we'll be headed next!

READING GROUP GUIDE

1. At the start of the story, Daria believes that she must ensure her own safety and survival by her wits alone. How common is it for us to feel we are in control of our own story?

2. In what ways is Daria's desire to redeem herself with a second chance challenged by Paul? Do you think that one person can save another person from himself?

3. With what character did you most identify? Why?

4. How familiar were you with this portion of Paul's life? Did the characters of Paul and Timothy, Priscilla and Aquila come alive for you in a new way?

5. Even Paul learns something in this story—the difference between physical *safety* and ultimate *security*. Did this idea speak to you?

6. What did you learn about the city of Ephesus?

7. How did you feel about the author's portrayal of the spiritual warfare and demonic oppression in the city? Was the

story too dark for you, or did you feel it helped you understand the time and place in an authentic way?

8. Does the passage in chapter 6 of Paul's letter to Ephesus, regarding the "full armor of God," have more meaning after reading this story?

9. Daria learns that she does not need to have all the answers, nor is she truly in control of all the events of her life. How difficult is this truth in your own life?

10. Did you enjoy the relationship between Daria and Lucas? The author included elements of a traditional "gothic romance," as in classics like *Jane Eyre* and *Rebecca*. Did you pick up on these elements?

11. In what ways do you feel the author's travels through Ephesus and other ancient lands have informed her writing? What Bible locations would you most enjoy visiting?

12. The believers in Ephesus are just beginning to come together in the time of this story, and much persecution is ahead. Do you think they are equipped for it? How ready are we for persecution if it should come?

ACKNOWLEDGMENTS

AS I MENTIONED IN THIS BOOK'S DEDICATION, I FEEL a special debt of gratitude to my readers who have interacted with me in various ways through the course of the writing. I asked for input and you gave it. I put questions out to you—what do you think Paul looked like? What was his personality like? What do you believe about demonic oppression and possession? What does it look like to fight evil in one's life?—and you answered. Wow, did you answer! I so appreciate the feedback and the inspiration. You even helped choose the title of the book through participating in a poll. I hope you are pleased with the result. No doubt as you hold this book in your hands, I'm working on the next story, and wanting to hear from readers again, so come and visit me on my website and give me more!

Thanks, also, to the friends in my small groups who helped me visualize Paul and stimulated my thinking as we worked through the book of Acts together.

Speaking of visualizing, my two trips to Ephesus gave me a

wonderful feel for the city, but they would not have been nearly so productive and helpful without my traveling companions—first my dear friend Joan Savoy, and then my dear husband Ron. Thanks, both of you, for taking photos, keeping me grounded, and keeping me safe!

The publishing process is a long one, and so many are involved in bringing a book to completion. Thank you to my agent, Steve Laube, for the years of support and guidance. Ami McConnell and Julee Schwarzburg, both such fabulous editors, thank you for reading so carefully and suggesting changes so graciously. Becky Monds, Katie Bond, Ruthie Dean, and all the rest of the team at Thomas Nelson—you make the process fun!

Thank you to my Street Team, the Caravan, whose names are listed separately. This group of folks has done me the great honor of volunteering to intentionally spread the word about my books, and I am so grateful and delighted to have you working alongside me. As this book goes to print we are only beginning our journey together, but I see great fun ahead!

And as always, a huge thank you to the five fantastic people God has blessed me most with—my husband, Ron, and my four kids, Rachel, Sarah, Jacob, and Noah. Each of you encourages me and allows me to create, and I love all of you very much!

SPECIAL THANKS TO THE CARAVAN!
YOU ALL ARE THE BEST!

As of the printing of this book, the following people are part of my Street Team, the Caravan.

To those who have joined me since the book went to print, I appreciate you too!

If you are interested in joining the Caravan, please see the link on my website, www.TracyHigley.com.

Merisha Abbott
Cherri Abner
Karla Akins
Michelle Aleckson
Glenda Alexander
Amanda Allen
Erin Al-Mehairi
Jean Atwood
Ro Bailey
Diane Baker
Wendi Barker
Janet Barnes
Sheryl Barnes
Lisa Bartelt
Marilyn Baxter
April Beaudion
Jennifer Beierle
Anneke Bennett
Boaz Bett
Lisa Betz
Heather Bireley
Sharon Boland
Richard Bowdel
Amalee Bowen
Linda Brandau
Cynthia Bridge
Sharon Briggman
Thyrsie Cahoon
Kerry Carter
Brenda Casto

Bernice Chapel
Donna Chellis
Jenny Collins
Margaret Cook
Sandi Coughlin
Elise Crook
Toni Cross
Elaine Curd
Rose Curran
Stacey Dale
Betsy Dalstra
Cathy Davis
Megan De Jong
Lora Doncea
Barbara Duncan
Sarai Dunn
Mary Dunn
Deborah Dunson
Debra Edwards
Marsha Elliott
Meghan Emery
Marion Eslinger
Rick Estep
Janet Estridge
Tina Evans
Christine Everhart
Evangheline Farcas
Lisa Marie Fletcher
Sandi Floria
Kim Ford

Jennifer Fowler
Mandy Gagnon
Charity Garner
Jennifer Garver
Carol Gehringer
Anna Getz
Debra Gilbert
Donna Goss
Charleene Greenplate
Nannette Griffith
Christine Grisham
Emma Guenther
Rebekah Gyger
Salyna Gyger
Alan Haarstad
Libby Hall
Beth Hampton
Sue Hardin
Kay Harms
Cheryl Harris
Rachel Harris
Katie Hart
Kara Haschke
Christy Hawkes
Kailey Hedman
Jennifer Heinze
Christine Hindle
Sherry Hofmann
Kathy Hoke
Sarah Holman

Julie Horner
Jenelle Hovde
Sarah Howell
Julie Hughes
Rachel Hughes
Nick Hullett
Eva Nell Hunter
Cheryl Ingersoll
Pam Jeffries
Kathleen Jensen
Sharon Jerop
Lisa Johnson
Vicki Jones
Lisa Jones
Vicki Jones
Susan Julian
Karen Kent
Ladette Kerr
Aline King
Michelle Kinsley
Sharon Klassen
Glenda Knisley
Cheryl Koch
Christine Koehn
Elaine Kraimer
Karen Kukrak
Joy Kutt
Kristin Lail
Jennifer Lambert
Donna Leggate
Bev Lewis
Pam Lewis
Christy Lockstein
Christa Lolley
Kristen Lowery
Megan Lowmaster
Betti Mace
Jennifer Maggard
Lorrie Maggard
Jeannie Mancini
Cortney Mannning
Heather Mannning
Denise Mantei
Wendy Marple

Pam Martin
Melina Mason
Sharon Ann Massa
Kimberly Matthiensen
Rebecca May
Sally Mccombs
Cariann Mccready
Christie Mckee
Amy Mcmillan
Paige Mcqueen
Kaitlyn Mecozzi
Erin Mifflin
Jessica Molle
Kristine Morgan
Missy Morrison
Vanessa Morton
Jennifer Musser
Sherri Myers
Cathy Nason
James Nichols
Erin Nuzzi
Paula Oliver
Jalynn Patterson
Robbie Pink
Cheri Posselt
Mary Preston
Claudia Price
Hannah Pryor
Mary Pursselley
Debi Qualls
Elizabeth Quan
Kathy Rae
Janet Randolph
Heather Reed
Marlaina Reeves
Evelyn Reeves
Liz Riggs
Stephanie Rister
Jacqueline Robertson
Mary Rodriguez
Linda Rorex
Aurora Roth
Annmarie Rozelle
Faith Ruotolo

Marge Schrader
Mary Ann Schreck
Jessica Senn
Craig Shafer
Lauren Sharpe
Cheryl Shipley
Kathleen Smith
Amy Smith
Candy Smith
Jaimee Smith
Rachiel Soliz
Amy Spoede
Jane Squires
Nora St.Laurent
John Stahl
Amber Stokes
Brian Stroka
Kathryn Struchen
Lahoma Stumbaugh
Vickie Taylor
Patricia Tillman
Carol Tims
Madelyn Towe
Debra Trull
Andi Tubbs
Kristin Tyler
Marjorie Vawter
Kim Villalva
Colleen Vukosich
Teresa Walley
Emily Walls
Kathy Warth
Laurie Waters
Alexandria Weaver
Florence Webb
Kaye Whitney
Barbara Williamson
Hananh Wilson
Katie Wilson
Rachel Wilson
Kelley Wolff
Malena Yapel

"A beautifully told tale, lush with details and rich with fascinating history."

—Ginger Garrett,
author of *Desired*

ISLE of SHADOWS

TRACY L. HIGLEY

INTRODUCTORY PRICE
ONLY $9.99

GARDEN of MADNESS

Her father is King Nebuchadnezzar.
Her secret could destroy a nation.

TRACY L. HIGLEY

"An exquisite story of intrigue, elegantly told and rich with all the
flavors of ancient Babylon. Simply magnificent."
—TOSCA LEE, New York Times best-seller, author of Havah: The Story of Eve

AVAILABLE IN PRINT AND E-BOOK

VISIT TRACYHIGLEY.COM

ABOUT THE AUTHOR

Author photo by Mary DeMuth

TRACY L. HIGLEY started her first novel at the age of eight and has been hooked on writing ever since. She has authored nine novels, including *Garden of Madness* and *Isle of Shadows*. Tracy is currently pursuing a graduate degree in ancient history and has traveled through Greece, Turkey, Egypt, Israel, Jordan, and Italy, researching her novels and falling into adventures. See her travel journals and more at TracyHigley.com.